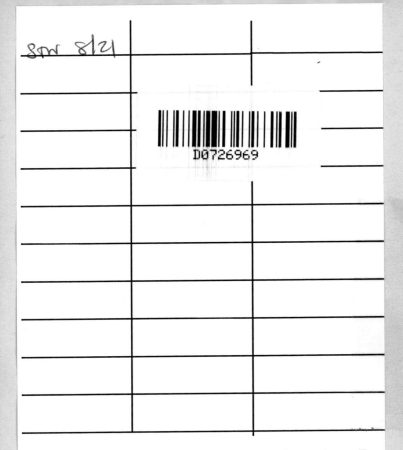

Helen Rolfe writes contemporary women's fiction and enjoys weaving stories about family, friendship, secrets, and community. Characters often face challenges and must fight to overcome them, but above all, Helen's stories always have a happy ending.

You can visit Helen online at www.helenjrolfe.com, on Facebook @helenjrolfewriter and on Twitter @ HJRolfe

The Kindness Club on Mapleberry Lane

Helen Rolfe

ORION

An Orion paperback

First published in Great Britain in eBook serial in 2020 by Orion Fiction
This paperback edition published in 2021 by Orion Fiction,
an imprint of The Orion Publishing Group Ltd
Carmelite House, 50 Victoria Embankment,
London EC4Y 0DZ

An Hachette UK company

1 3 5 7 9 10 8 6 4 2

A CIP catalogue record for this book is
available from the British Library.

ISBN (Mass Market Paperback) 978 1 3987 0024 6
ISBN (eBook) 978 1 3987 0025 3

Typeset by Input Data Services Ltd, Somerset

Printed in Great Britain by Clays Ltd, Elcograf S.p.A.

MIX
Paper from
responsible sources
FSC® C104740
www.fsc.org

www.orionbooks.co.uk

To all the key workers who played their part, and continue to do so, in providing vital services to each and every one of us during the pandemic. May your days be filled with happiness and kindness. A special mention goes to Jo Sparrow, nurse, mum and wonderful friend who had a tougher year than many. With lots of love, Helen xxx

PART ONE

A Summer Surprise

Chapter One

Veronica

A knock on the door would once have had the power to turn her legs to jelly, make her palms clammy and root her feet to the spot. But not anymore. And that, Veronica Bentley guessed, was what you called 'progress'.

She put down the knife she was using to butter her sandwich and went to see who it was. As always, she peeked through the sitting-room shutters – the tilt of the wooden slats was a great invention, letting you spy without being seen – but when she saw it was little Layla from number twenty-five, she rushed to answer the dove-white front door to her home.

Through the open door came a burst of summer – freshly cut lawns, floral scent from the flowerbeds, birdsong – and the chirpy voice of Layla, an eight-year-old filled with more confidence than Veronica had been able to muster for years.

'It's me!' said Layla from behind an enormous box.

'I'm only seventy-one – my eyesight isn't failing me just yet, thank you.' Veronica ushered her inside. 'And what do we have here?'

'I've brought you carrots, onions, a lettuce and tomatoes. All grown at home,' Layla added proudly. She rarely waited before she launched into colourful conversation.

Veronica took the wooden vegetable crate with VEG stamped onto the side. 'It's heavy – how did you carry this all the way?' She went through to the kitchen and set it onto the round table.

'I'm stronger than I look.'

She was so serious, Veronica had to stifle a laugh. If there was one thing this girl brought to Veronica's life, it was her effervescent personality.

'What's your dad up to today?' Veronica knew Charlie would have stood at his front door, watching his daughter walk all the way along the pavement to the garden gate of number nine Mapleberry Lane, and waited for her to go inside to know she was safe. It was the usual arrangement.

'He has to fix my wardrobe door, which came off its hinges again.' She added a theatrical eye roll.

Veronica was already inspecting the produce. 'You should be proud of yourself for growing all these. Veggie patches aren't always easy – I had a terrible time trying to grow lettuces over the years, they'd never work. And when they did, the butterflies got to them before I did.'

'I looked after the carrots mostly, onions too, but Daddy took charge of growing the traffic-light tomatoes in his greenhouse.'

'I don't think I've heard of that variety.'

She pointed to a collection of rich red tomatoes. 'They're the red ones,' she pulled out orangey heirloom tomatoes, 'then we have amber . . . and finally, green.' Beaming, she pulled out a couple of questionable-looking varieties that Veronica thought she'd have to ask Charlie about when she saw him to make sure they were fine to eat.

'I have something else to show you.' Layla grinned, the

bottom of her dark ginger bobbed hair that wasn't fixed in place with an Alice band swinging to and fro as she jumped on the spot in her excitement.

'And what might that be?'

'This!' She proudly held out the curled-up fabric diamond she'd been clutching in her palm. With a purple background and a little pot plant embroidered on the front, along with the words 'Grow Your Own', it was another Brownie badge to add to her collection.

Veronica enveloped Layla in a hug. It felt like the right thing to do, even though until now she'd never held the little girl close. The feeling it gave her took Veronica quite by surprise. She hadn't had affection like this in a long while. But Layla seemed to simply go with the flow.

Pulling herself together, she told Layla, 'You worked hard, well done you.' It was moments like this she should have cherished more with her own family before it was too late, before she pushed everyone away. Having Layla in her life felt like a blessing, the second chance she wasn't sure she deserved. She'd become a surrogate granny without even realising, but that was fine by her. It somehow lessened the pain of not seeing much of her own daughter and granddaughter.

'Brown Owl was impressed with the different things we've grown,' Layla carried on. 'She said she still hasn't managed to grow carrots successfully. She called them her ne-me-sis.'

'Is that right?' She swore the little girl's maturity and vocabulary came from all those books she read. She'd already plucked anything remotely suitable from Veronica's bookshelves and devoured them at home before returning them to the shelves lining one wall of the lounge and another at the end of the kitchen-diner. She'd raced through classics like *Alice's Adventures in Wonderland*, *Charlie and the Chocolate Factory* and, one of Veronica's favourites, *The Secret Garden*. For Christmas last year, after Veronica had seen *The Chronicles of Narnia* collection advertised on the internet, she'd phoned to place an order that same day, knowing it was the perfect gift for Layla. And she'd been right. Layla had started with *The Lion, the Witch and the Wardrobe* on Christmas Day and made her way through all seven books, devouring each one.

'I had to show Brown Owl photographs of me planting carrot seeds and onion seeds, and of me watering the patch after school each day. Daddy took a picture of me picking tomatoes in the greenhouse too. He did most of the work but I watered them every single day. He has cucumbers growing too but they're not quite ready.'

'Well, I'll look forward to trying those. And your dad sent me all the photographs on email, so I haven't missed out.' She wished she'd been able to go over there and see it for herself, but email pictures were the next best thing; they kept her a part of it all.

'Everyone clapped when I was given my badge.' Layla's chest puffed with pride and she couldn't stop smiling.

'I can sew it on like the last badge, if you like?'

'Would you?'

'Of course, I'd be honoured. And I'm very proud of you. I will think of you when I eat my carrots, my lettuce, my onions and tomatoes.'

'Even the green ones . . . Dad says just because things are green, it doesn't make them evil.'

'I think he's only talking about your green vegetables.' Veronica smiled. This kid was too cheeky and clever for

6

her own good. Those emerald eyes were full of intellect and mischief; a perfect combination, and one Veronica was thankful for every day. Layla popped around whenever she could and the pair had formed a tight bond as though they really were gran and granddaughter, even though there was nothing tying them together other than the simple geography of living on Mapleberry Lane.

Layla shrugged off her backpack and shuffled onto one of the wooden chairs at the small round table next to the kitchen area, making herself at home. 'Me and Daddy had scrambled eggs on toast for our lunch. What are you having?' She'd spotted the bread.

'Nothing adventurous. Ham and cheese sandwich for me.' Same as most days. Lunch tended to be basic, but Veronica loved to cook for other people if she got the chance. She carried on buttering her bread.

Layla plucked a tomato – luckily in traffic-light red, as Veronica still wasn't sure about those green ones and she didn't want to get sick and need a doctor's appointment – and passed it over to her. 'Put this in, it'll make it nice.' Next, she leaned over to pull out the lettuce. 'And some of this.'

'I tell you what, I'll deal with the tomato if you could wash some of those lettuce leaves for me. In fact, wash them all and I'll have a salad for my tea tonight.' She had cajun chicken marinating in the fridge and it would go perfectly sliced on top, perhaps with some homemade croutons scattered through.

'Can I use the funny spinny thing?'

'The salad spinner is in the cupboard to the side of the sink.' Layla had seen her use it a week or so back and was fascinated by how the lettuce could be soaking wet and after a few turns with the plastic contraption it came out dry. But she had to remind Layla not to get too carried away with the spinner and yank it so hard that the cord came off the disc inside and had to be wound on again.

When the lettuce was washed and spun, the tomatoes sliced and the sandwich made, Veronica sat down to eat with Layla for company. Yesterday she'd read in the newspaper that lack of social connections and living alone could be as bad for you as smoking, and that loneliness was worse for you than obesity. Smoking and being overweight weren't worries for Veronica; she'd never lit up a cigarette and she was as slim as the day she got married – not that she liked to walk down that particular memory lane very often, given the way things had turned out – and thanks to Layla and Charlie, she wasn't as isolated as some of the people she'd read about in the article. One woman said the only voices she heard were cold callers or the television, so Veronica knew in some ways she was rather lucky to have the company she did, especially when her own family were nowhere to be seen.

'Are you looking forward to the summer holidays?' she asked Layla, who was busying herself emptying the surplus water from the plastic bowl of the spinner as Veronica ate.

'I can't wait. Daddy always lets me stay up later than on school nights.'

'But you'll miss school.' She knew, because Layla was a kid who thrived in a learning environment where she could devour the information at her fingertips.

'I'll miss it, but not maths. Maths is hard, I can't do it.'

'Now I doubt that, a clever girl like you?'

'Daddy says we can't all be good at everything. He says I'm very good at English, but as long as I try my best in

8

all my lessons, then that's OK. I really like art too. We did weather fenomins yesterday.'

'Fenomins?'

'Yes, you know, weird things that happen with the weather.'

'Ah, phenomena.' She pulled over the notepad and pen that were neatly sitting beside the telephone and she wrote out the word in big letters. 'There, another one to add to your vocabulary.'

'I'll learn it.'

'And I'll test you in a few days, when you least expect it.' She finished the last of her sandwich and brushed a stray crumb that had escaped onto the table top back onto the plate. 'Tell me, what does art have to do with weather?'

Layla explained how they'd learned about different climates and weather changes and then they'd been charged in art class to work on a mural for the wall.

'I really wanted to paint the rainbow. Did you know, rainbows are made when light is reflected through raindrops and that sunlight is made up of lots of colours?'

'I did know that.' Veronica might not get out much, but you could learn a lot from reading; books took you to different worlds, gave you a sneaky peek into others' lives. The television did that too and both mediums had been her saviour. She would've been lost without them. 'So did you get to paint the beautiful colours of the rainbow?'

With a sad shake of the head, Layla told her, 'Kelsie got to do that. She sits next to me most days, I like her, so I didn't mind and I said I'd do something else. She broke her leg last term and missed out on our trip to the science museum, so I told Mrs Haines that Kelsie should do the rainbow.'

'That was very kind of you.'

'It got my name on the kindness calendar too.' She beamed.

'What's a kindness calendar?'

'We're doing it at school. I'll show you.' From her backpack she pulled out a folded-in-half piece of paper and opened it out on the table. It was for the current month, July, and on every day it had something written already.

'Mrs Haines had written for next Thursday that someone in the class had to give someone else something that meant a lot to them. She said it meant a lot to Kelsie to do the rainbow and because I'd wanted to do it so much too, I'd fulfilled the task. It means my name goes first on the calendar for that one.'

'Does the whole class take it in turns?'

'Some tasks have one child's name on there, others have a few names because they're easier.' She pointed to a square for 1st July, which had 'Smile at a stranger' written on it.

'I didn't think children were supposed to talk to strangers.'

'We're not supposed to talk or go with them, but Mrs Haines said that shouldn't stop us being friendly. I smiled at the bin man when he took our rubbish away; I made Daddy do it too. Archie in my class stood at the school gate and smiled at every parent who dropped off at the gate. Mr Barnaby, who teaches the other class, had to go and tell him to stop in the end.'

Veronica chuckled. 'I bet a few parents wondered what was going on.'

'He's odd anyway.'

'Archie?'

'He never talks to anyone.'

'It doesn't mean he's odd. Maybe he's shy? So it was extra brave to stand at the gate smiling at people.' Veronica's mouth went dry at the thought of being surrounded by all those parents and children, part of a crowd she couldn't get away from quickly. 'How does your teacher fit all your names on the calendar?' The squares were so small she'd have a job fitting five names on, let alone an entire class.

'The calendar on the wall of our classroom is much bigger than this one. We all have our own copy because we have to think about different tasks and we talk about them in class. And then we have to make sure we do the weekend acts of kindness.' Once Layla got going, she could hold an audience captive for hours. She pointed to Saturday and Sunday. 'We all have to do both of those things at home. See, Saturday, today, is to visit a neighbour.' She delved into her backpack again and took out a fluffy green pencil case from which she pulled a red felt-tip and neatly put a line through today's date square from corner to corner. 'I'm seeing you, so I get to cross it off. Easy peasy. Then when I show this to the teacher, my name will go up on her calendar.'

Veronica read Sunday's instruction. 'Tomorrow you have to give someone a compliment. Any idea what you'll do?'

Layla shrugged. 'Daddy's having his hair cut later; I could not mention it today and then say something nice about it tomorrow.'

'Or say it today and cross it off tomorrow's.' She nudged Layla. 'I won't tell anyone if you don't.' She giggled, enjoying the conspiracy. 'But if you didn't get to do the rainbow, what weather phenomenon did you do?'

'I got snow. I did a big snowflake. Thank goodness I didn't get fog. Fog's boring.'

'Layla, you have more words in your brain than that. Boring is a boring word. Come on, I want at least three adjectives to describe fog: go.'

With a deep breath she thought hard. 'Grey . . . thick . . .'

'One more,' Veronica prompted. 'Think about how it makes you feel.'

'A bit trapped.'

'Yes, I suppose it does.' *Trapped*. It wasn't a nice word but it fitted some of Veronica's experiences perfectly. Still, not here, not in this house.

'Will you come and see the finished mural at school?' Layla asked. 'It's really good! There's the rainbow, snow, fog, heatwave, hurricane, a tornado that Jimmy Jones did and which looks a bit of a mess, but he told Mrs Haines that was the point.'

Veronica looked at the calendar again and wished they were still talking about the details instead. 'I'm afraid I can't, Layla.'

'For the same reason you couldn't see my veggie patch?' She nodded sadly. 'I understand.'

'I knew you would.' She reached out and put a hand to Layla's beautifully soft hair. Her own at that age had been blonde but styled much the same way. Like everything else, her hair had changed over the years; it had been grey for the last fifteen and was long. Too long. It reached down between her shoulder blades when she took it out of the bun she wound it into every day until bedtime. She never went to the hairdresser's – that was something else she'd given up.

'Why don't you ask Daddy to take a photograph of

the mural for me? Then I'm not missing out.' Veronica poured them both a glass of orange juice. 'What time is he coming here to get you?' It was always the arrangement. Layla could walk here from their house but he'd come to meet her at the end of her visit. As a single dad he didn't get a lot of time to himself, but Veronica was only too happy to help him out.

'He said two o'clock.' It was a sure thing Veronica would not only be in but that she wouldn't have to nip out on errands or for an appointment. That simply didn't happen. 'Can we play a game until then?'

'A game sounds like a lovely idea.'

They decided Monopoly would take too long, Layla didn't want to play Ludo or Scrabble, no way was Veronica risking her life playing Twister, and so they settled on Uno. They managed almost ten games, both taking it as seriously as each other, before Charlie knocked on the door.

'I think you have something of mine,' he said, the little scar above his top lip visible after he'd had a shave. He didn't always shave, favouring a bit of stubble, which suited him. Rich brown eyes suggested a man you could depend upon and trust, and his smile had a way of putting you at ease.

'I do, come in.' To an onlooker who didn't know any better, Veronica was like any regular granny, if there was such a thing, but sometimes people gave her little house a strange look when they passed by, and she knew what they were thinking. There's that weird lady from number nine. She'd had similar insults yelled through her letterbox one day. 'You're a freak!' the first voice had taunted; 'Weirdo!' followed a different voice laced with laughter. She had no idea of the culprits – kids who'd heard rumours on the grapevine, probably, and had decided to terrorise her in whatever way they could. But the insults had stuck in Veronica's mind because some days they felt like appropriate labels. She was only glad Charlie didn't think so. He'd always been kind to her and she'd valued his friendship right from the start.

'Who's winning?' Charlie looked at Layla's cards.

'Five games to four in my favour,' Veronica told him, although it quickly became a tie when Layla laid down her last card after saying Uno. 'Looks like it's a draw.' Veronica smiled, shaking Layla's hand. As usual Layla was in no rush to leave, which suited Veronica, as there were too many hours she was on her own as it was. She tidied the pile of cards and wrapped them in an elastic band once, twice, a third time to keep them all together.

Layla frowned at Charlie. 'Didn't you bring it?'

'Of course I did,' he answered with a grin. And off he went. Veronica heard the front door open and close, and after a couple of minutes, during which Layla looked like she had ants in her pants, she was fidgeting so much, Charlie returned with a cake on a board, one of his hands shielding the burning candles as he came towards them.

Layla's face lit up and she launched into singing 'Happy Birthday', along with her dad.

'For me?' Veronica's eyes fell to the chocolate cake decorated with white and dark chocolate curls, a few candles in the centre, still flickering away.

'Seeing as we didn't get to celebrate last week because you had your cold, we thought we'd do it this week.' Charlie set the cake down on the table.

'You didn't have to do this.' Although choked at the gesture, Veronica was thrilled to bits. Last week on her birthday she'd had a terrible sore throat and a runny nose. She'd been thoroughly miserable, but in no way selfish enough to have either of them visit, even though Charlie had insisted on checking up on her, delivering some cold remedies from the local chemist and a pot of hearty chicken soup. With only a brief visit compared to usual, it had been a lonely few days for Veronica and she hadn't liked it one bit.

'Make a wish!' Layla ordered. 'You have to.'

It wasn't hard to know what to wish for, but she didn't tell anyone. It wouldn't come true then, would it?

At Layla's insistence Veronica blew out her candles. 'What happened, couldn't fit seventy-one on?' she teased Charlie.

'Didn't sell that many in the shop.'

'Cheeky thing.' She laughed as she dug out plates and forks and a cake slice she used to cut generous portions.

Another year, another celebration. Lots to be thankful for, lots she wanted to forget.

Charlie smiled at his daughter, who had chocolate smeared below her lip and another streak down the side of her hand. 'You're a messy thing, you need a tissue.'

Layla ran her tongue all the way around the outside of her mouth to get the most she could and went so cross-eyed she had Charlie and Veronica laughing.

'How have I done?' Veronica asked. 'Any on my face?'

Charlie pretended to inspect closely as he handed Layla a tissue to wipe her hand. 'You're a professional, I'd never even know you'd had chocolate.'

'See, Layla, I could teach you a thing or two, one being how to eat chocolate without anyone realising. It's a life skill.'

'Hey, no teaching her naughty things.'

'Would I do that?' Veronica asked innocently, sharing a conspiratorial look with Layla.

'Yes, I believe you would.' Charlie's rakish grin, where his mouth turned up at one side ever so slightly more than the other, somehow kept him looking younger than his forty years. He'd celebrated his birthday a couple of months ago and, in much the same style as now, they'd gathered here at the same table to eat the lamingtons – his favourite – that Layla and Veronica had baked together. Layla had given him three lamingtons in all, telling him he worked too hard and deserved it. And she was right. As well as looking after Layla on his own, he had a challenging career as a paramedic, where he was often the first on the scene, having to make life-saving decisions. Occasionally he talked about making a change, no longer working shifts, fitting in with Layla more, but he loved his job and was good at it, and Veronica knew exactly what that was like. Or at least she had.

Veronica thanked them both again for the cake. 'With that and the veggies, you've made an old lady very happy.'

'Less of the old,' Charlie instructed before he turned to his daughter. 'Are you ready to go, sweetheart?' He took charge of the plates and cleaning the cake slice before Veronica stopped him. Clearing up would give her something to do when they left; it wasn't always easy to fill the days. Sometimes they stretched out endlessly in front of her, and not in a good way.

'Do I have to come with you while you get your hair cut?' Layla whined.

'Yes, because you're getting yours cut too. Now put

your shoes on – you can come again later, if it's all right with Veronica.'

It was always all right with Veronica. And Charlie knew it, but he was so polite he always asked first.

'I'll look forward to it, and if the sun stays out and the heavens open and it rains, then who knows, we might see a rainbow.'

When Layla picked up her pen and ran her finger across the date squares of the kindness calendar rather than putting everything into her backpack, Charlie warned, 'Stop stalling.'

Layla found what she was looking for. '"Bake something for a neighbour",' she read out loud before striking a line right through it. 'We baked you a cake.' She smiled at Veronica. 'And I can tell Mrs Haines on Monday so I'll get my name on the big calendar in class. Anyone who does more than twenty acts of kindness in a month gets a special prize at the end. Last month Elliot Bainbridge got Golden Time – ten minutes extra of play time while the rest of us had to clear up after art class.'

'Sounds like the top prize.' Charlie winked at Veronica. Kids at this age were easily impressed. Unfortunately this stage didn't last anywhere near long enough. Perhaps Charlie realised that and had already decided to make the most of it. And he was never going to be a bad parent – he didn't have it in him to fail. Not like Veronica.

'And don't forget, Daddy,' Layla went on, 'I have to get someone else involved with the calendar – it's a way of spreading the kindness.'

'We'll see, I've got a job, remember, a busy one at that.' With a sigh and a wave, he led his daughter out of the door and in the direction of home.

Veronica watched them go from behind the shutters until Layla's bright pink backpack was out of sight.

When Layla had mentioned needing another person to help with the kindness calendar, Veronica had almost leapt in to volunteer. Helping other people was one of the things she missed, but she supposed it made more sense for Layla to ask for Charlie's help rather than an old lady who might end up letting her down.

Alone again, she went over to the Welsh dresser next to the bookshelves in the kitchen-diner. She took out the framed photograph that had once stood on the mantelpiece with others: a family, the people she'd once had around her. But not anymore. Apart from the occasional Christmas and birthday card or the odd terse phone call, her family had more or less given up on her.

But Layla and Charlie hadn't.

She bit back the tears that threatened to come, jammed the photograph back in the drawer, and began the count-down to when her favourite visitors, the neighbours who felt more like her family than her own, would come back later this afternoon.

Chapter Two

Sam

Someone had once told Sam that if she wanted to make God laugh, then she should tell him her plans.

Well, he must be rolling around the floor right now, because just when she thought life couldn't get any harder, she'd been thrown another curveball.

Over the last decade she'd gone from a stay-at-home married mum to a divorced parent of one, and fought her way from being a customer service assistant to a customer services manager. Today she'd tumbled right back down the career ladder to unemployment after being made redundant. For years Sam had thrown all her efforts into her job, given that her personal life and family life were, for want of a better phrase, absolute shit, and she'd been thrilled to finally land the managerial position. But unfortunately the retail giant wasn't a big enough company to hold onto its eight hundred employees when it merged with a competitor.

She edged her way out of the revolving door of the office, carrying a cardboard box filled with her things. Inside lay a photograph of her and her daughter Audrey standing in front of the Eiffel Tower, smiling away as though things between them were perfect; a plant that looked so sorry for itself Sam suspected she'd throw it out when she got home; her favourite floral mug that held enough coffee to get her through a morning; a spare jumper she kept in her drawer in case the office air-conditioning was overzealous; and the nine packets of Post-its she'd taken from the supply cupboard not because she needed them, but because she could. Nobody in the office had really spoken as those dealt the raw deal had packed up and left. Anyone in the same boat was too angry or upset, and those who got to stay probably felt guilty about their colleagues and an enormous sense of relief that it hadn't happened to them.

The only silver lining that Sam could see to this was that the ones on the receiving end got to leave work straight away – company policy – and wouldn't be penalised for doing so. And her redundancy payout wasn't bad, she supposed. It would keep her going for a while, but for how long was anyone's guess; she had a fifteen-year-old daughter, a mortgage to pay, and an ex-husband who had put them both out of sight and out of mind by fleeing to New Zealand with his new wife who was, as he'd so tactfully put it once, the love of his life.

Shame he hadn't realised that person wasn't Sam when they'd married almost seventeen years ago.

Sam climbed into the driver's seat of her car, ignoring her phone when it rang the second she pulled out of her parking space. Whoever it was would have to wait; she had plenty to deal with right now. She wished she had someone to run to, a boyfriend who could console her for the crappy day she was having. But all her efforts at injecting romance into her life since her marriage broke down had fallen flat on their face. Not that there had been many opportunities over the years, and even when there were, Sam tended to put Audrey first and soon lost focus on anyone else coming into their lives, and she had a certain reluctance to risk getting close to a man who might simply change his mind the way her ex-husband had. Nobody deserved that kind of hurt, and certainly not twice in a lifetime.

She drove the thirty-five-minute commute for the last time, taking her from the office to the smart detached residence she shared with Audrey in a small village in Cheshire, an area of the country far enough away from her home childhood home in Mapleberry that she'd felt like she was starting over when she first moved up here and got married at the age of twenty-two. Mapleberry hadn't held too many good memories in the end, and Sam had been almost as desperate to get out of the village she grew up in as she had her family home.

She pulled up on the drive, struggled up to the porch with the box in her arms and fumbled her attempt to put her keys in the front door to open up. 'Damn it!' she yelled when she dropped the entire lot as Audrey pulled the door open from the other side.

'Not my fault, I was trying to help. You shouldn't be so clumsy.' Audrey's voice was as harsh as the pixie cut she'd had done recently. The haircut had no doubt been an act of rebellion but it rather suited her, with her dark eyes, high cheekbones and button nose, traits she'd got from her father rather than Sam, who was blue-eyed with blonde hair touched up with subtle copper high-lights. Audrey's hair had once had the same big waves that Sam's had now, sitting on her collar bones – but not anymore. Sam had complimented her daughter after she returned home from the hairdresser that day, but even if she hated the new look, she would've still said the same, because Sam was pretty sure Audrey had only had it done to get under her skin. Maybe Sam wouldn't mention how much she hated those slug-like eyebrows the girls all seemed to paint on nowadays. If she did, that would be the next thing Audrey altered about her appearance.

Sam wondered whether it was a teenage thing, the rebellion against anything your mum approved of or liked? Or was it just a sign that her and Audrey's relationship wasn't far from breaking point?

When she'd had a little girl, Sam had been overjoyed. She didn't mind what sex the baby was when she was pregnant, she would've been happy with either, but as soon as she knew, she began to plan for their future. Her imagination had gone into fast-forward, picturing dressing Audrey in the cutest outfits – OshKosh B'gosh, Gymboree, Baby Gap – then when she was a little older, playing tea sets and dolls houses, teaching her how to ride a bike, one of those with the streamers flying out from the handlebars in the wind. She'd pictured the cosy chats they could have as Audrey got older, confiding with her about boys. She'd be the best friend Audrey had, the relationship being one that Sam had never been able to form with her own mother.

What had happened to those dreams? she wondered as she gathered the detritus to put it back into the single box that was all that was left of her job.

'You been stealing Post-its?' Audrey, leaning against the doorframe of the kitchen with a bowl of cereal balancing on one palm, her other hand operating the spoon, noticed the packets scattered over the floor – one near the bottom stair, the other by the radiator, one further down the shiny wooden floorboards of the hallway, some at her feet.

Sam ignored the jibe. 'What are you doing home?'

She'd been so preoccupied with doing household maths all the way home, fathoming how to pay bills when her redundancy money dried up, she hadn't thought about what time it was. But now she could see the kitchen clock and it was well before four o'clock, the usual time Audrey got home from school – five o'clock if she dawdled and hung out with her friends – and the way Audrey was acting so casual, as though it was a Saturday rather than a Monday.

Audrey tilted her bowl to get the last of the milk, turned her back and went out to the kitchen, ignoring Sam.

'Audrey, I asked what you're doing home.' Sam stepped over the box. She'd deal with it later. She flapped the front of her silk blouse; the house was always stifling from early summer until autumn, and then freezing in the winter. 'Are you sick?'

'Nope.' Audrey put her bowl in the dishwasher and flipped the door shut before she turned around and leaned on it. 'Here's the thing, Mum. A friend and I, well, we played a bit of a joke.'

'On who?'

'The school.'

'That narrows it down.' Sam filled a glass of water and downed it in one. Packing up her desk and trying to take in the fact she'd gone into the office with a job and was leaving without one, had already caused a knot of anxiety to lodge itself in her chest. 'Audrey, spit it out, I need details.'

Audrey inspected her nails rather than meet Sam's gaze.

'Me and Sid sent a hoax letter from the Head – to all nine hundred and seventy-one parents.'

Oh dear God, don't let them have created a bomb hoax. She had visions of Audrey being led away in handcuffs. Then again, if that was what it took to separate her daughter from troublemaker Sid, perhaps it wasn't such a bad thing.

Trying to stay level-headed, she asked, 'What was in this letter?'

'It was just a joke. We said that the school was closed until further notice because there'd been an outbreak of infectious diarrhoea caused by a fungus found in the classrooms.' Her voice wobbled with amusement, but clocking her mum's hard stare, she soon stopped smiling. 'How were we supposed to know people would take it seriously?'

'How seriously are we talking?'

The corners of her mouth twitched. 'Over half the school didn't turn up.'

'Audrey.' Sam covered her face with her hands. 'I don't need this.'

'Of course,' she snapped, 'I forgot it's all about you. It's always about you.'

Sam grabbed her daughter's arm before she could stalk away. 'I just lost my job and come home to find my daughter, what, at home for the rest of the day or longer?'

'Suspended,' she said, yanking her arm back. 'You'll get an email to tell you officially.'

'Hang on a minute . . . Surely they didn't send you home – they should wait until a parent collects you or at least gives permission.' She felt her hackles rise; she wasn't sure who she was more annoyed at – Audrey or the school.

'I walked out.'

'You did what?'

'I left, and you know something? I'm glad I don't have to go to that hellhole for two weeks. Which means I'm free from it until September. Thank God!'

'Audrey, come back here.' But this time she made no effort to stop her daughter stomping up the stairs. *Slam*, went her door. If Sam tried to talk to her now she'd have no chance, and she had a headache brewing, right behind her eyes, creeping up to her entire head. All she wanted to do was lie down in a dark room, fall asleep and wake up as though today had never happened.

She took a couple of headache tablets, but going for a lie-down wasn't an option, not with her mind doing overtime. She checked her phone and sure enough the call she'd ignored was from the school. She fired up her laptop in the study, unsurprised to find their email waiting. Reading through it, the suspension would stand for two weeks, and judging by the tone, Audrey should think herself lucky it wasn't more severe after she walked out of school today. The school suggested both she and Audrey go in for a meeting early next week to discuss a way forward. Sam knew that there wouldn't be much point appealing the decision to exclude her either; the last time Audrey had messed up, shouting at a teacher when she was told off for not handing in her homework on time, she'd had a warning that anything else would be dealt with more harshly. Sam guessed this was the 'anything else'.

Despite the hopelessness she felt, Sam couldn't sit there and do nothing until a meeting next week. Audrey was supposed to be sitting her GCSEs next June so this year was important. She didn't throw herself into her school-work as it was, and this latest development would only give her the go-ahead to slack off even more.

She tried to call Audrey's form tutor but he was in a meeting; she attempted to speak to the head of year but she wasn't available, so she resorted to an email asking whether there was any way the school would reconsider the punishment given the importance of Year Ten. Even if they lessened it to one week, perhaps.

She doubted her correspondence would make any dent in their decision. She thought of all those kids and parents inconvenienced by the hoax letter and knew there would be outrage if Audrey wasn't punished for her part in the debacle. Last term a girl had kicked another student at the top of a flight of stairs and when confronted by staff, the girl cried and was let off the looming punishment. The parent of the child who was kicked was furious; she took to social media to vent and it all got very nasty. Sam would do anything to support Audrey, but she didn't want Audrey's business plastered everywhere; she didn't want her daughter judged by those who didn't know her. Sam wanted, somehow, to find the girl she suspected was in there somewhere, the daughter who had once smiled and laughed and loved hot buttered crumpets by the fire on a winter's evening, the six-year-old girl who'd cried when Sam told her that she'd probably want to move out of home one day and into her own house. Back then Audrey had never wanted to be apart from Sam.

Times had changed.

Audrey had never accepted her dad leaving them behind and starting a new life on the other side of the world. She blamed Sam for everything, made comments and had digs whenever she could that told Sam exactly who she thought was at fault. Simon could do no wrong in Audrey's eyes, and because he wasn't in his daughter's life in a big way, Sam had let the blame settle on her shoulders. She held back criticisms of Simon because she wanted Audrey to have a relationship with her dad. She never wanted to be the person who came between them because if she was, she had a funny feeling it would be her who was seen to be in the wrong and would end up losing out.

Audrey didn't appear until well after seven o'clock that evening, lured by the smell of chilli con carne drifting up from the pot on the stove. Sam's headache had gone, her practical coping attitude had come into play and she'd made the dinner as usual. She had a plan – eat, try to talk to Audrey without one of them shouting at the other, then sit down and do her finances.

It was always Audrey's job to set the table. She did so without prompting this evening, but threatened to bring back Sam's headache every time she plonked something down on the table – the cutlery, the bowls, the side plates for the garlic bread.

Damn, the garlic bread. She'd forgotten all about it. And when Audrey noticed her oversight, she uttered her first words in three hours, swear words Sam was pretty sure her own father never would've stood for under his roof.

'Watch your language, Audrey,' Sam bristled, all plans not to clash with her daughter impossible to execute when Sam found herself the only disciplinarian. At least if someone else set the rules sometimes, it wouldn't all be her fault. 'I've been at work, come home and cooked a meal – don't you dare swear at me for forgetting one simple thing.'

'Yeah, well, you won't be able to say that tomorrow, will you?'

So she had heard her say she lost her job. But it hadn't exactly elicited sympathy. 'No, I won't. And have you thought about what me having no job will mean to you?' She was met with a shrug. 'No, you haven't.' She cursed when she knocked the wooden spoon onto the floor and tomatoey liquid splashed across the tiles. She swiped a piece of kitchen towel across the spill.

'It means you'll be home all day,' Audrey said, as though that would be the biggest obstacle. Mind you, she kind of had a point.

'It does mean that. But it also means I have to watch finances. Which means no more allowance.' She shoved the soiled kitchen towel into the bin and slammed the lid shut.

'You can't do that.'

'Call it punishment for getting suspended.' Allowance was due tomorrow and Sam hadn't intended to withdraw it quite so soon, at least not until Audrey had caused her even more stress to add to her day.

'Seriously!'

'We'll need to tighten our belts until I find something else.' And stopping the allowance would mean Audrey wouldn't flit off so much at the weekends or in the evenings when Sam had no idea what she got up to. 'It's not up for discussion, Audrey.'

Her announcement was met with a steely gaze before

Audrey put the oven on and found the garlic bread from the freezer. She must be extra hungry or a revelation like No Allowance would've sent her storming out again.

Sam washed the spoon, dried it and gave the chilli another stir.

'You'll get another job, though, right?'

Sometimes it was like living with two people when it came to Audrey: the one who yelled at her that everything was unfair and everything was Sam's fault, then the Audrey who took a step back and looked at a situation with a different eye. Sam had to admit the latter didn't happen all that often, but when it did, she grabbed onto it with both hands.

'I could leave school early, get a job myself,' Audrey suggested.

'I don't think so.'

'Why not?' The sympathetic Audrey moved over and bolshie teen took her place.

'Because you're fifteen!' She almost added that she shouldn't be so stupid, but insulting Audrey when she was in this mood was like pouring brandy onto a Christmas pudding and setting it alight.

'I could get a part-time job.'

'We've talked about this.'

'No, we haven't.'

'Audrey, we have.'

'No, you talked, you didn't let me have a turn.' Her voice softened. 'Loads of kids my age have a part-time job.'

'And as I said before, when your schoolwork improves, go for it. Until then, your focus has to be on that.'

Audrey toyed with the pieces of frozen garlic bread as she waited for the oven to preheat.

Sam turned the gas off beneath the pot of chilli. She'd learnt to read her daughter's moods through looks, words, tone and body language, and she sensed Audrey was at least willing to enter a discussion now rather than closing her off.

'Are you worried about your schoolwork?' Probably not the smartest thing to be involved in a prank if she was.

'Not really. But I have thought about my future, much as you think I don't give a—' She stopped when Sam gave her a look that suggested foul language wouldn't be tolerated a second time. 'I do care about my life. And I still want to be a make-up artist.'

And there it was. The career choice Sam tried to gloss over whenever Audrey brought it up because it wasn't what Sam thought of as a reliable career path. She wanted Audrey to have job security, a future.

'You still need qualifications. In the long run you won't regret it.'

'I've looked into it. I could get a college diploma – there's no need for me to go on to do A levels.'

'I want you to have options, that's all,' Sam insisted, doing her best to remain calm.

No response. Her sweet, kind, loving daughter was in there somewhere, hidden beneath this firm shell, this exterior that gave off warning signals if she tried to get too close. But Sam was rarely sure how to crack open the surface unless it was on Audrey's terms. Some of it was the usual mix of teen emotions, the egocentric perspective on life that was par for the course at this age, but her father leaving had stolen a part of Audrey's childhood, which seemed to have manifested itself in her defensive attitude when it came to anything Sam might have the audacity to suggest or approve of. Sam felt on tenterhooks with her daughter the whole time. She never knew what to expect from day to day, and without realising it, Sam had slowly become more and more stressed. Her best friend Jilly had suggested she go to a doctor but Sam didn't want to go down that road. They'd likely write a prescription for anti-depressants just to get rid of her and move on to the next patient, and Sam didn't want to admit she was at that point yet. Some days Sam wondered what had happened to her. Even when she was going through her divorce, grappling with the legalities and the practicalities, she'd handled one day at a time and managed to miraculously keep a clear head, telling herself it would all work out in the end. She didn't seem to be able to do that anymore. With Audrey it was a whole new ball game and one she wasn't sure if she could win, or even be a front runner in, for that matter.

She watched Audrey slide the garlic bread into the oven and poured herself a glass of crisp sauvignon blanc. She may not have a job but she had wine and tonight she needed it. She felt the welcome effect of the alcohol make her shoulders relax instantly.

'There are a lot of options in make-up artistry, you know,' Audrey announced. 'I could work with a theatre company or on a television drama. I wouldn't mind working on something like *Poldark*.'

Whether it was the wine or the relief at having a conversation, Sam didn't know, but she was going with it for now. 'Hey, get in line,' she laughed. 'We'd all like more of Poldark.'

Between them they served up the dinner and avoided

talk of Sam's work – past and future – or any discussion of Audrey's suspension. Perhaps she was being irresponsible by doing so, by not issuing her punishment or lecture right now, but just for this evening Sam wanted a moment of calm.

'We could make a deal, you know,' Audrey suggested as she shook her head at the offer of the last piece of garlic bread. 'I could finish school, study hard to get good GCSE grades, but you let me skip A levels as long as I have a place at a college.'

Leaving school at sixteen had never been an option for Sam; she'd never had a choice about following anything other than an academic path.

'We can think about it,' she told Audrey. 'But you would have to knuckle down and get your GCSEs. That's the first thing. And before you tell me you don't necessarily need qualifications to be a make-up artist, I want you to get some so that you have a back-up plan. You never know if you'll change your mind and I'd hate for you to find you were limited.' Her words came out as a diatribe, without Audrey interrupting. She braced herself for fallout, topped up her wine and slotted the bottle back into the fridge. She never drank during the week but seeing as she no longer had a job to get up for in the morning, she let up with her own rules for once.

'OK.' When Sam looked at her in disbelief, she repeated herself: 'I said OK, let's do it your way, Mum.'

'To do what I'm asking, you'd need to be in school, Audrey.'

'Which I will be in September.'

'And how much will you have missed?'

'Not a lot happens in the last two weeks of term, believe

me.' Her nonchalance didn't last when she saw Sam's expression. 'I'll make sure I've caught up with everything by the time we go back after the summer holidays.'

She was saying all the right things, but Sam knew from experience that talk and the follow-through were two very different things to Audrey. Last month she'd gone on and on about how she'd cook the dinner every night for a week after she'd been given a detention for not handing in her homework. That had lasted all of one evening until she looked so stressed with her studies that Sam had given in.

Sam began to load the dishwasher as Audrey handed her scraped plates one by one before she emptied the left-over chilli into a plastic container.

'I know I'm a disappointment.'

Her words took Sam by surprise. 'Is that what you really think?'

'I can see it when you look at me. You're disappointed I'm not more like you, that I don't work hard enough.'

'Audrey, I don't need you to be like me, and I'm not disappointed in you.' How could she explain how disappointed she was in herself? Disappointed she couldn't keep her marriage together enough for her child, ashamed she never had best worked out the way to manage solo parenting and keeping your teen on side when they blamed you for everything. Sam sometimes wondered if she wasn't hard enough on her daughter, if overcompensating for Simon's absence was half the problem.

'I'm disappointed you got suspended,' Sam braved saying. Talking to Audrey was like doing a tentative dance where if you put your foot down too hard then you threatened to shake the entire floor. 'I didn't expect it and you've got to admit that what you did was wrong.'

'I didn't think anyone would take it seriously – I honest-ly didn't.'

'How did you get the email to everyone anyway? You wouldn't know their email addresses.'

'Sid hacked into the school's computer system.'

Sid. The boy Sam had never met face-to-face but who she suspected was a bad influence.

'How on earth did he manage that?'

'He's clever.'

'Not so clever he didn't get suspended. I'm assuming he did too.'

'He did, and his dad went ballistic.'

'Then you got off lightly with me,' Sam barked.

'I'm sorry, Mum. I really am.'

With the food, the apology, the tablets and the wine, her head and her stress levels had at least begun to simmer and she pulled Audrey into a hug and kissed the top of her head. 'It'll all be fine, I promise. We'll be OK.' It's what she'd wanted to say to her daughter, to herself, for years, as though the repetition inside her head would be a way to make it come true. 'I'm going for a bubble bath. Could I leave you to wipe the table for me?'

'Sure.'

Sam trudged up the stairs and ten minutes later sank down into warm water laced with her favourite Diptyque bath oil. She didn't care that it was summer and already warm inside; she needed this, and she soon shut her eyes to let the aroma of the oil take away her heavy thoughts. The hardest thing about being a single parent had to be this: having the whole weight of responsibility resting on your shoulders and nobody else's. Simon was off on the other side of the world doing whatever he was doing, he had brief flurries of contact with his daughter, and when he did, his stories were full of excitement; tantalising tales of a foreign land Audrey had never been to, a lifestyle she wasn't a part of. Whereas Sam . . . Well, she got the day-to-day grind, the pushing her daughter to get out of bed on a school morning, the nagging over homework, the snippy attitude and mood swings, the constant attempt to find a window into her child's life.

Sam lay in the bath so long she'd begun to drift off when she heard the front door bang. She hoped it wasn't anyone to see her; not only wasn't she dressed, she didn't want to have to talk to anyone. She understood why some people didn't let it slip about losing their job. There were people who continued to put on a suit every day and look as though they were driving to the office when really they were hiding out in a coffee shop until they could return home as usual. She got it. Admitting to failure wasn't something she liked to do and it definitely wasn't something she wanted to share.

She hurried to get out of the bath, wrapping herself in a towel while she waited for Audrey's holler up the stairs to tell her who was waiting. She hoped it wasn't Sharon, her neighbour; she'd been over three times last week trying to get Sam to sign up for the bloody park run. The whole street was in on it, going en masse down to the local park in their Lycra and brightly coloured trainers. Sharon saw it as a good way to get to know your neighbours. Sam saw it as her idea of hell. She wasn't a runner and she definitely wasn't one to mingle with the neighbours. She had her friends and at home she liked a bit of anonymity. She wanted to be able to come and go and have an escape in her own space without interruptions.

Maybe she wasn't all that different to her mother.

'Audrey,' she called out from the bathroom door. If it was Sharon, she'd go down in her towel and pretend she was rushing to get ready to go out.

When there was no answer, she went downstairs and called her daughter's name a second time, went into the lounge, the dining room, back up to Audrey's bedroom and then downstairs again. And when she realised the bang of the door had been Audrey leaving, she picked up her phone from the kitchen bench and bashed out a message to her daughter demanding to know where she was.

When she got no response, she lost her temper and typed an angry: *You're grounded!* The get-home-now implication was in those words without even trying.

She slammed her phone down again and when she saw her bag open on the floor by the stairs where she'd left it, her heart sank. She pulled out her purse and sure enough the twenty-pound note from the back section had gone.

Sam called Audrey this time and left an irate message. Audrey didn't call back but Sam's phone pinged with a text message moments later: *Gone to the cinema with Sid. Won't be late.*

Just like that, as though she hadn't stolen money, as if their earlier conversation hadn't even taken place, as if she hadn't been suspended from school. And never mind the rule that Audrey didn't go out after seven on a school night. She spent most of her evenings on her damn phone scrolling through Instagram posts so it wasn't a real hardship, but it was a rule that had been broken tonight on top of everything else.

Sam had been the complete opposite of Audrey at the

same age. Holed up in her bedroom every night, partly because her father was always drumming it into her that she needed an education if she wanted a good life, Sam had studied hard to make him proud. Even after he died, his approval followed her everywhere she went. When she passed her driving test only months after he passed away, she pictured his smile; when she graduated, she imagined him in the audience watching her dressed in her robes and being presented with her degree certificate. When she got her job as a customer services manager, she could hear his congratulations and pride; when she got divorced, she felt his disapproval. But as well as wanting to please her father, Sam had realised very quickly that the harder she worked and the more secure job she landed, the better chance she had to escape the prison of the home her mother had made unbearable to live in. And after she met Simon it became even easier. They got together, married in a whirlwind and moved to a different part of the country to start over.

Thinking of how her relationship was with Audrey, Sam knew she'd messed up just as much as her own mother had. Maybe for different reasons, but the end result was the same. They'd both ended up with a daughter who didn't want to spend time with them, a daughter who wanted to get away. The Veronica Bentley Sam knew from her late teens, and for every year since, wasn't the mum Sam remembered from when she was little. Something had changed along the way, and Sam had no idea what. All she knew was the mum who had once been there for her, laughed with her, shown a sense of pride in everything Sam did, had all but disappeared. And now, history was repeating itself with Sam and Audrey.

Tears streamed down her cheeks. She didn't often cry but with everything she'd had to contend with today, she couldn't stop it. Still wrapped in her towel, she called her best friend Jilly, who lived a five-minute walk away. The pair had been friends since they met when Jilly's son and Audrey had been in the same playgroup. Jilly had been there to pick up the pieces when Simon left, she'd babysat enough times so Sam could meet with her lawyer, she'd listened to Sam bitch and moan when Simon emigrated to New Zealand with someone else. Tonight Jilly let Sam vent over the phone, she listened, spoke in all the right places and was able to calm Sam down. Good friends, but their lives were very different. Jilly had two sisters and two brothers who all lived within a twenty-mile radius, as well as hands-on parents who regularly visited the grand-kids and interacted with them in a way Sam could only dream of. And she had a husband who worked hard but never neglected his family. A husband who was by her side every step of the way. What Sam would give for that kind of simplicity.

Sam went upstairs and got dressed. She sat on the end of the bed, the silence in the house almost too much to bear. When Simon left, one of the big things Sam had wanted was to keep her home, the bricks and mortar that gave her and Audrey stability. Audrey had had enough upset without having to shift schools, move into a new home, leaving behind the bedroom that had transitioned with her from the days of pale blue walls and fluffy white clouds to the black and white phase she'd gone through aged eleven and now, the metallic silver-dotted wallpaper she'd chosen for one feature wall along with three others in white with a hint of grey. Sam hadn't wanted to take anything else away from Audrey and with hard work at her job, it was possible to stay in the house until Audrey finished her education. Then, when the dust settled, when Audrey was a grown-up and perhaps able to see and understand that it took two people to make a marriage work, Sam was planning to look for somewhere smaller and ease the financial pressure on herself. But now, redundancy had thrown everything up into the air.

Thoughts of her finances niggled Sam enough that in the end, she knew that if she didn't look at them right now she'd go crazy waiting for Audrey, and so with a pen and pad, and her laptop open so she could bring up her bank account, she wrote out calculations on how long the redundancy money was going to tide her over.

As she suspected, it wouldn't last long.

It was blindingly obvious she'd have to sell the house. Even if she landed a job in the next few months, the risk of keeping hold of this place was too high. Instead, she'd have to rent somewhere far smaller and in a different area for a while, to at least get rid of this one noose around her neck. She should've done it back when Simon left and Audrey's life had fallen to pieces anyway, then they'd be settled somewhere else already.

Sam moved from her calculations to looking at estate agent websites and rentals. Three bedrooms would be ideal and a garden, preferably detached with a driveway, but after half an hour of finding prices were astronomical, she'd narrowed her criteria to two bedrooms, semi-detached or terraced, anywhere within a five-mile radius of Audrey's school. There was one, perhaps two, options and she sent off queries to both if only to have a look around while she organised the sale of this place. She couldn't afford to be sentimental any longer; she had to be realistic. So before she could change her mind, she fired off two requests to estate agents to come and value her house, the home she loved.

Her head aching from so much time staring at the screen, she made a hot chocolate and moved back to the lounge, where she stayed in the same chair until she heard the front door click open and shut quietly, and footsteps creep along the hallway. Audrey was halfway up the stairs before she turned and saw her mum sitting in silence.

'I haven't got school. I figured being late wouldn't matter.' She shrugged as though it was any other ordinary day, their conversation earlier hadn't happened, and she and Sid hadn't done something so stupid Sam wanted to wring both of their necks.

Finally Sam reached the end of her tether. 'You're grounded, for two weeks!' she yelled. 'You will not leave this house in that time, do you hear me, Audrey?'

Audrey was shocked but stood her ground and soon went back to acting like she didn't care. 'I figured you'd do that.' She turned and took another step up towards the solace of her bedroom.

'And no phone either,' Sam hollered after her. That had her attention.

'You can't do that!'

'I can and I will. And where have you been?'

'I told you, the cinema.'

'Do you want to tell me why you stole money from my purse?'

'It's my allowance.' Audrey's voice wobbled.

'I told you, without my job, that has to stop for a while. And do you really think you deserve it this month? And who is Sid? I've no idea who this boy is and you go out with him until this time of night.'

'He's my friend.' She pulled out her phone and showed Sam a photo of him, a selfie with the both of them, sitting on a slide in the local park eating ice-creams. 'There, that's him, a bit taller than me, blue eyes, Yorkshire accent, not much more you need to know.'

'Sid's a bad influence – you never used to get into this much trouble.'

With a hard stare, Audrey retaliated. 'Yeah, well, we used to be a family – things change.'

'I'm still your mother – you don't get to be rude to me.'

'I'm not surprised Dad left you!' she shrieked, her voice shaky.

Sam shook her head in despair. 'I can't even look at you right now.'

'Fine by me, I don't want to look at you either!'

And that was how the night ended, door slamming, swearing, but Sam couldn't face any of it. She crawled into bed hoping that by the next morning she could somehow wake and find it had all been a terrible nightmare.

Sam woke the next morning and for one blissful moment forgot the night before. But it all came flooding back to her when she looked at the time and realised her body clock hadn't got the memo about her redundancy. It was six o'clock and she was wide awake.

In the kitchen Sam boiled the kettle for tea. Jilly had texted her to ask whether Audrey had got home safely, ask how Sam was coping, but even her best friend's constant support didn't work to lift Sam out of her mood this morning. She stood looking out of the kitchen window, the morning rain shrouding the garden in a dismal cloak of misery.

Sam's desperation over what to do about Audrey had been mounting up for a while, particularly since yesterday. She thought about how other people coped with family life's ups and downs. The time Jilly had a stomach bug and her husband was away on business, Jilly had called her mum to come and look after the kids for an entire week, letting Jilly rest up and get back to normal. Sam's colleague Marcus had struggled with his kids – he'd sent his wayward son off to stay with his granddad, who had been so strict when Marcus was growing up that he credited him with teaching him how to live in the real world. Sam had never really been sure what that meant – or whether it was entirely a good thing – but it seemed to have worked. Marcus's son had come back with an entirely different attitude and all Sam knew was that now he was a lawyer, working in London and on his way to making partner. So something must have gone right.

When Sam tipped away the cold dregs of tea, the warm liquid not working any of its usual morning magic, her desperation about Audrey gave way to practicality, and before she knew what she was doing, she found herself making a decision even she couldn't have foreseen.

Sam had never asked anything from her own mother, certainly not since she moved away from the family home in Mapleberry, but what alternatives did she have?

All Sam knew was that if she didn't do something, she wasn't sure her relationship with Audrey would survive.

Chapter Three

Veronica

Veronica opened up the shutters in the sitting room so the sunshine as well as the floral scents from the garden could spill in through the windows. She wiped the windowsill, a favourite place for the dust to gather. She didn't mind cleaning at all. Some people moaned about it; on television this morning had been a feature about cleaning your home in only fifteen minutes each day, but to Veronica that seemed pointless. Cleaning and keeping things ship-shape was a way to fill her time when it was school term and Layla couldn't visit whenever she liked, or when Charlie was on shifts and times for him to visit didn't line up either.

Once she'd mopped the kitchen floor, Veronica made the gardener, Trevor, a tea, which she left on the front doorstep along with a couple of Bourbon biscuits for when he was ready. Trevor had been coming to the house – modest in size like most homes on the street, apart from a couple of bigger residences at the end – for almost eleven years now. He kept everything looking marvellous, weeding the beds below the sitting-room window where passionate red geraniums flourished at the end of their cycle, mowing the lawn and trimming its edges, pruning bushes that overhung windows or the path, keeping the privet hedge on either side of the front gate a neat welcome for those who ever came to number nine Mapleberry Lane. A quiet chap not much younger than her, Trevor was very polite and if Veronica wasn't in the mood to talk he'd simply tip his cap in greeting or farewell. She'd made an effort to chat with him this morning, though, and he respected some days she could manage more conversation than others. Layla told her she was unique and quirky, although Veronica thought those adjectives were perhaps a bit generous as she really wasn't all that interesting.

With her own cuppa on the table beside her in the sitting room, Veronica took out her needle and thread to sew on Layla's Grow Your Own badge to the sash she wore for Brownies. While she stitched, she thought about her next knitting project. She hadn't picked up her needles in a few days, but it was halfway through the year already and she knew it was time to put in a phone order with the wool supplier and make a start on another cardigan for winter. She didn't get to shop on the high street for new things so this was her way of treating herself. Perhaps she'd even go for something luxurious this time: a chunky wool in winterberry or a crocus-blue cashmere, or a rich plum colour she'd seen last time she looked on the website.

Just after four o'clock, after Trevor had packed up and gone home, Layla went past with her childminder, Bea, and as usual held up both hands so Veronica could see as she looked out of the window. She held up ten fingers, clenched them into fists, then flashed another ten, scrunched them again and did it a third time. That meant she'd be over in thirty minutes. Veronica put up a thumb and went into the kitchen. She'd got some chocolate milk delivered as a treat for Layla, as well as the Bourbon biscuits that were her all-time favourite. Her late husband Herman had disapproved of treats, so Veronica used to prepare vegetable sticks with homemade dips for after-school snacks, but when Herman was away she would make pancakes sprinkled with sugar and drizzled with lemon juice. She knew the importance of healthy eating – she'd been a nurse once upon a time before she'd been forced to leave the career she loved – but Herman had always thought he knew best and Veronica had done her best to keep the peace as much as possible. Now she was free to do as she liked, so she set out a few chocolate biscuits on a plate in readiness for Layla. Everything in moderation, she thought.

'How was your day?' she asked when Layla finally joined her.

'Fun.' The little girl smiled, skipping inside with the usual pink backpack on. 'And Bea says I can stay for an hour before we have to go to my swimming lesson.'

'Then you'd better eat quickly so you can digest them and not have your tummy too full. You'll sink otherwise.' Veronica ushered her towards the table and the awaiting plate of biscuits.

Veronica approved of Bea, at least from everything Layla and Charlie had told her. She was living at home with her parents while she studied through the Open University and so she was flexible when it came to Charlie's shifts, an essential job requirement for whoever he hired. He'd been caught out once and it was the reason Veronica had met the pair of them. Charlie and Layla hadn't been living in Mapleberry for long when Charlie came to the front door. Veronica had peeked through the shutters in the lounge and seen a stranger, and so she ignored the knocks at first, hoping he'd go away. But when she looked again and saw how frantic the man was and that he had a small child in tow who was sobbing by that point, she unlocked the door and opened it with the chain on. Charlie's account of the problem had come out garbled in his panic. His phone line still hadn't been sorted, he was late for his shift at work and he was desperate to get hold of the childminding agency to tell them that his regular childminder was sick and couldn't make it today. Charlie had asked to use Veronica's telephone and she'd let them in to do so. Layla had been so upset, clutching at her daddy's leg as he made the call, but it was easy to see that this was a man managing the best he could. He made his frantic call, Layla begged him not to leave her, and he briefly explained to Veronica that their lives had been chaotic for a while, that his wife had died when Layla was a baby and so now it was just him, and Layla sometimes took a while to trust anyone new.

They hadn't stayed long, but the following day Layla knocked on Veronica's door clutching a plate of home-made chocolate chip cookies to say thank you. Charlie was with her and had noticed Veronica's front gate still didn't shut properly. He'd offered to fix it there and then, they'd had a cup of tea, and rather than counting down the minutes until they'd leave her alone, Veronica had found herself warming to the pair. Ever since that day, the three of them had formed a friendship that felt like family, and now, when Charlie had childcare problems, Layla came to Veronica's. She even stayed for the odd sleepover if Charlie was working a night and Veronica thrived on the company.

Layla slurped her chocolate milk sitting at Veronica's

table, her legs swinging from the chair as she drank. 'My teacher showed us how to smash up a plate today.' Layla beamed, wiping away her chocolate moustache.

'You smashed up a plate?'

'Yes, it's for the community flower wall.'

'Ah, that makes sense now. I read about the flower wall on the local news website this morning.' The community centre past the big field in Mapleberry had a wall separating it from the road and the council had given their approval for a community project to add flower mosaics as though it was an upright garden. To do this, they'd need lots of coloured china smashed into pieces.

How Veronica wished she could be a part of something so significant in Mapleberry. Once upon a time she might have been.

'It's on the kindness calendar.' Layla smiled. 'We can do it as part of the class in a group or with family or friends outside school. Our teacher says it will make people who don't normally talk to each other more friendly.'

'I can see how that would work.'

'The class is having an after-school club to come up with a flower design for those who want to.' She shrugged as though unsure.

'And you don't want to do it?'

'The club is on a day I have Brownies.' Her spirits fell. 'I can't be a part of it.'

Veronica almost blurted out that she'd do it, she'd form a club with Layla instead. But how could she?

'Daddy said he'll go to some second-hand shops and see if he can find some colourful old plates or china for me to break up, but he doesn't know when he'll have enough time to work on the wall with me. He says he doesn't have a creative bone in his body. Is it true? Do we have a creative bone? And where is it?'

Veronica grinned. 'We don't have a creative bone, no. It's a figure of speech.' Poor Charlie. He did his best, juggling work with parenting. And while she wouldn't be able to help with the wall, she could take part in a different way, perhaps. 'I have some crockery you could smash into pieces if you liked.' She went into the kitchen and foraged in the back of the corner cupboard where an old teapot and a couple of mismatched cups and saucers sat. She'd kept them as spares, never had got around to getting rid of them. She pulled them out and handed them to Layla. 'You can have these.' The teapot was duck-egg blue, the cups an off-white, perfect for making mosaic pieces. 'And if you reach even further back in the cupboard, there are a few cups that'll be perfect.'

Layla's tiny body almost disappeared into the cupboard as she got the items Veronica couldn't reach. She pulled out three white cups with a gold rim – perfect to add a bit of shine in a mosaic pattern.

Layla, satisfied with her new collection, began to talk about the teddy bear drive, another item on the kindness calendar. 'We all had to bring in teddy bears that we don't want or need anymore.' She looked down at the floor. 'I took in Boris.'

'The bear I knitted you for Christmas?'

Layla nodded.

'Now you look sad. What's wrong?'

'It was a special present – I shouldn't have given it away.'

Veronica had knitted the bear with green trousers and red braces, and the December Layla and Charlie were first in Mapleberry, she'd given it as a gift to Layla when she invited her and Charlie over for supper one evening. She knew Layla hated her dad leaving her and working nights, and Veronica wanted her to have the bear for a bit of extra security, something to remind her that she was loved and thought of.

'When you gave me the bear you told me whenever I'm sad that Daddy has to go to work, I'm to hug the bear tight and remember all the people he's helping.'

'I remember,' said Veronica. 'And I also remember your daddy telling me that Boris the bear helped you a lot.'

'He really did.' Happier now, Layla told her, 'I slept with him every night and I didn't cry once. Boris is special . . . but I think it's time he helped somebody else now.'

'Well then, that's incredibly kind, Layla.'

'You knitted me another two bears, so I have enough.'

She had too. And those bears had been over to Veronica's house for several tea parties, all three of them perched on the floor, bent at the waist, with Layla serving them pretend food on plastic plates, pouring imaginary cups of tea for them.

'We used to get teddy bear donations to the hospital when I worked as a nurse. And it was never the bears that looked brand new or expensive that produced the most smiles, it was the well-loved bears a child had clutched for years and parted with because they were thinking about someone else. It really made a difference to some of those children.'

'Daddy told me that sometimes if a child has to go on an ambulance ride, they might be a bit scared and a toy could help.'

Veronica smiled. 'You know, the more I hear about this kindness calendar, the more I love it.'

'I want to do everything on it.' Layla's broad smile faded after the next biscuit was demolished. 'But I can't.'

'Why not? The things you showed me the other day looked simple enough.'

Layla took out the calendar from her backpack. She pointed to one of the squares on the calendar and Veronica grabbed her reading glasses to look more closely at the text. '"Learn a musical instrument". How is that kind? You know, it might be kinder not to learn one. I played recorder when I was your age and my neighbours weren't very happy about it, let me tell you.'

'Mrs Haines says that as well as being kind to others, we need to remember to be kind to ourselves.'

'Your teacher sounds wise to me.'

'She is,' Layla responded, as though it were obvious. 'She says she's starting recorder lessons for the whole class next week.'

'Well, there you go, mission accomplished. I don't see what the problem is, Layla. You can easily cross off the item on the calendar and I'm sure I can order you a recorder online.'

'I wanted to learn something new. I don't like the recorder.'

'Neither did my neighbours,' Veronica sighed. 'What instrument do you have in mind?'

'I've always wanted to learn piano.' She looked down into her lap. 'Mummy used to play. She played Christmas carols every December at my grandparents' house in Wales, on their grand piano. I've seen her on Daddy's old video camera tape.'

'Then that's a special memory for you to treasure always.'

'She had the same hair as me.' Layla smiled. 'Daddy says hers was more the colour of Tizer. I don't even know what that is.'

'A funny fizzy drink.' She pulled a face that should ensure Layla didn't try it any time soon. If they even sold it anymore. Veronica wouldn't have any idea; it was a long while since she'd set foot in a shop to find out.

'Do you think my fingers are long enough to play the piano?' Layla wondered. 'My mummy's were and she always had nice nails.'

'I'm sure your hands are perfectly suited to the piano. Would you really like to learn like she did?'

'We can't afford lessons and we don't have a piano at home and school doesn't have any either.' Something occurred to her and her face brightened. 'They have them at the high school, though.'

'High school is a long time to wait.'

'Three years and three months.'

It had been a while since she'd heard the sounds of the piano within these walls, but Veronica knew what she said next would be an incredible surprise for Layla. 'If you follow me, I may be able to help you.'

Excited to share in a bit of mystery, Layla followed Veronica towards the study, the room where the door was always shut. No matter how comfortable they were with one another, Layla knew boundaries and she didn't go into rooms without Veronica's permission, the study included. It was only a small room and full of files and things that could probably be cleared out, but it was the only room Veronica didn't spend a lot of time cleaning. In fact, she avoided it. Because sitting inside was the piano she'd had as a little girl, handed down to her from her parents who'd loved the instrument and taught her to play when she was younger than Layla. She'd loved to run her fingers over those keys, and as soon as Sam was old enough, she'd taught her how to play too, until Herman had convinced Sam that her studies were far more important than messing around playing a musical instrument. No matter how many times Veronica argued that learning an instrument was good for brain development, hand–eye coordination, the memory, he refused to have any of it. And eventually Veronica stopped playing too because he'd complain it gave him a headache when he tried to work, or it disturbed him. He'd battered all of the enjoyment away for Veronica with his complaining, but now, with Layla, was she really ready to find the magic again? If anyone could help her do it, it was this bubbly little girl.

When Layla saw what was waiting on the other side of the door to the study, her eyes widened. She stepped forward at Veronica's approval and lifted the polished wooden lid of the mahogany instrument. The brass pedals matched the shiny brand name on the underside of the lid now that it was open; the keys had lost their brightness in colour but the piano was as intact as Veronica remembered.

Layla tentatively touched a key and giggled when a sound rang out. She hit another and another. 'Can you play?' she asked.

'I used to play, a long time ago.'

Veronica watched a lot of television for company, and a recent documentary had looked into children who played musical instruments and how it benefited them. They'd moved on to discussing adults who kept up with learning and playing, and Veronica had found her jealousy mounting. She'd gone and stood by the piano, eventually sitting down on the stool, but still she hadn't played anything. What she did do was slam her hands down on the keys and swear out loud, something she never did, berating Herman for the control he'd had over her and the way she'd never fought to be her own person. Everyone deserved that, surely. And as his wife, she'd deserved his support. For better or for worse, they'd said those vows, but Herman hadn't supported her when she was at her worst; he'd tried to pretend it wasn't happening and his way of doing that was to make her feel small and worthless.

'You have a play,' she told Layla, 'I'll be back in a jiffy.'

Layla didn't need telling twice and sat down on the piano stool, which was still filled with all the old music Veronica had once used.

Veronica stopped before she passed through the doorway. 'I forgot to ask. How do you spell phenomenon?'

Layla grinned, eyes upwards as she thought, teeth biting down lightly on the skin beneath her lower lip until she said, 'P-h-e-n-o . . .' She hesitated. 'm-e-n-o-n.'

Veronica gave her a round of applause. 'I knew you could learn it.'

'Do you think I'll be able to learn how to play the piano as quickly?' Layla's voice followed after her as Veronica went to the downstairs bathroom for a breather. It wasn't often Layla gave her cause to do it, but unveiling the piano and knowing there was no going back – Layla would be persistent after today – it took her a few moments to accept the change. But she didn't mind the din already coming from the study, it filled the quiet and she'd get used to it. Maybe she could grow to love it.

*

Back in the dining room, she had Layla shuffle over so she could sit on the stool too. It was a long time since she'd taught Sam to play and she'd forgotten how to instruct someone on the basics. Already she could feel her fingers twitching; she knew she'd be able to remember the notes. A bit like riding a bike, except this could be done in the comfort of her own home.

'There are so many keys.' Layla looked daunted as her eyes drifted from one end of the piano to the other. 'I'll never remember them.'

'How many do you think there are?' Layla's mind ticked over, counting, until Veronica said, 'All you need to remember for now is that while there are a lot of keys, there are only seven names of notes for you to learn.'

'There are way more than seven.'

Veronica explained exactly what she meant before getting a piece of paper and a pen to draw the keys and write the notes on each of them in a group of seven. 'You can take this home so you can learn them.'

'What do the black keys do?'

And as Veronica explained about sharps and flats, octaves and where to position your hands, letting Layla have a play around each time, she found herself enjoying this in the same way she'd been rewarded in her job as a nurse. Looking out for others, nurturing, helping, being kind was what she missed the most now. Sometimes she got so angry that she'd given it all up. All that time she could've still been working at the hospital, whether full- or part-time as she got older, the daily interactions and busyness the very things she loved.

With Layla here now still enthusiastically hammering out the worst din in history, it kickstarted her spiritedness.

She went online and ordered a beginner's book for learning to play the piano, with exercises Layla could make her way through each time she came, which could be as little or as much as she liked.

'You've stopped,' Veronica said, putting the iPad away. Charlie had helped her order an iPad last year and she'd never looked back. She had a laptop too and used it often, but after some basic lessons from Charlie, she now found the iPad an absolute gem to get things done quickly, especially when she couldn't get out to the shops – you could buy anything online these days, everything from electronic items to loo rolls.

Layla shifted from the piano stool. 'Play something else, Veronica, please.'

'I'm not really sure what to play.'

Layla lifted up the lid to the piano stool and began rifling through the music in there. 'These two are Christmas tunes,' she said, discarding the top two music books. 'What about this? Who are The Beatles?'

Veronica let out a chuckle. 'In my opinion, the best band in the whole world.'

'I've never heard them on the radio.'

'Before your time, dear, but you will as you get older, I'm sure.' She nodded for Layla to go ahead and open up the well-thumbed Beatles Collection that Veronica had had since she was first married.

The music book evoked an avalanche of memories. Back in those Beatle-loving days, everything between her and Herman had been perfect, they were giddy and head-over-heels in love. Back then he'd enjoyed listening to her play music or sing. They hadn't been able to afford to go to a Beatles concert but he'd had a record player at his house, and on lazy summer evenings in the garden, with the windows to his upstairs bedroom open, they'd listened to track after track, singing along. Herman wasn't musical at all. When he sang in the shower, it was as though two cats were outside being tortured in the alleyway, but she'd loved listening to it anyway. And he loved how she had perfect pitch if she sang and could rattle out tune after tune on the piano.

Veronica opened the music book up to one of her favourites, 'Hey Jude', and with a deep breath she began. She had a false start and started again, then it began to flow from her fingertips as though she hadn't neglected the beautiful instrument for years on end as it stood feeling sorry for itself and gathering dust. Her life had changed incredibly since she last enjoyed playing the piano. She'd gone from being sociable and happy to a woman who shrank away from nearly everything. And now she had a sad measure of daily interactions with only a handful of people – Charlie, Layla, Trevor the gardener, and Ian the mailman, who sometimes hung around for a bit of conversation on the doorstep if Veronica was in the mood.

Veronica had a problem but she was too scared to do anything about it. Her existence had become sad, contained, like nothing she'd ever imagined.

She was still playing, her fingers moving deftly along the keys. The piano was well and truly out of tune, but not enough that the song didn't shine through, and the longer Veronica played, the more the sound washed over her like a balm she couldn't explain. And the more she played, the more she wanted to. Layla was swaying in time with the music, a smile on her face that Veronica returned again and again.

'Another,' Layla demanded when the tune came to an end.

She'd have to look up a piano tuner; it would give her something to do when Layla left. But for now, in tune or not, she was on a roll with the piano. It was on to 'I Want to Hold Your Hand', which brought some more lively moves from Layla, followed by 'Yellow Submarine', which Layla joined in with. One of the teachers at her school had taught them the song and she remembered most of the words. Veronica was so enthused by the end of the rendition and playing the piano with such vigour that she almost didn't hear the phone ringing.

'One day I want to learn to play like you,' Layla announced as Veronica vacated the seat and she jumped right in her place.

'You will,' Veronica called back over her shoulder, shutting the door behind her or she'd never be able to hear who was calling.

In the kitchen she picked up the wall-mounted phone. 'Mapleberry 459.' She'd always answered in the same way: the village and the last three digits of her number, never her name. You got so many nuisance calls these days and if they didn't know her name already, it was a red flag. There were a few of those – requests for bank details, telling you you'd been in a car crash, for goodness' sake. Funnily enough they hung up when she told them she hadn't left the house in years, let alone run amok on Britain's roads.

'Mapleberry 459,' she repeated when she got no response. She'd been tempted by these nuisance calls to have a whistle handy and blow it down the phone. She would've done as well if part of her didn't know she'd then lay awake for weeks stressing that she'd ruined the eardrums of the scam artist. Probably no less than they deserved but she didn't have it in her.

'Mum . . .' came a voice from the other end.

Her heart thumped. 'Sam? Is that you?' It wasn't Veronica's birthday, or Easter, or Christmas, and Sam rarely called unless it was one of those dates. They weren't close, not by a long shot, but something in the timid way her daughter had said 'Mum' had Veronica worrying.

There was a pause at the other end of the line, and then it all poured out: the loss of Sam's job, the teenage daughter she didn't seem able to reach. Veronica knew first-hand about that particular dilemma. She listened as her daughter's voice wobbled. Veronica wondered: was she crying? As a child Sam had never fallen apart or ended up in tears unless she'd really hurt herself. She'd always had a strong character and rarely let her weaknesses show through, but there was a hint of vulnerability in her voice now, and if Veronica wasn't mistaken, she was doing her best to hold back a sob.

'Sam, I can't come up there and help. You know that.' Her meek reply sounded weak even to her own ears. Her daughter was in crisis and, as usual, she couldn't save the day. By the sound of it, Audrey, the granddaughter she'd not been allowed to get to know apart from a quick hello on their brief visits, had got into trouble and been excluded from school, and according to Sam, that was the tip of the iceberg.

'I don't expect you to come here,' said Sam, as though it were obvious. Silence hovered between them until Sam spoke up again. 'I need you to do something for me.'

Veronica almost spoke but any words dried up before she could say them.

'I don't ask for much . . .' Sam went on.

She never asked for anything. And Veronica had never been able to help her before. Sam had never once asked her to babysit Audrey or even to step in when one of them was unwell, which must have happened somewhere down the line. Even when Sam got divorced from Simon, she hadn't reached out to Veronica. The divorce had been revealed on a rare visit by Sam and Audrey when they came to Mapleberry for Auntie Dotty's funeral, a farewell Veronica had no intention of participating in herself. But it was different for Sam. She'd got close to Auntie Dotty over the years. Dotty, Herman's sister, had always looked down at Veronica, never approved of her brother's new wife, and when Veronica showed weakness and could no longer hide her problems, Dotty always had one of those told-you-she-was-crazy looks on her face whenever she stopped by. She'd stepped in to help with Sam, though, and taken her to after-school clubs, to the shops so she could buy something before she went out with her friends. Veronica had never been able to begrudge their relationship.

'Mum, are you there?' Sam was getting impatient now, adopting the same frustrated tone she often used with Veronica when she couldn't be the mother she wanted her to be.

Veronica, leaning against the kitchen bench, cleared her throat. 'I'm here.'

Sam's voice juddered again, irritation replaced by worry. 'I don't know what to do with Audrey. I'm worried, about me, about her . . . If I don't make a change, I'm scared I'll lose her for good.'

Veronica held her breath, hoping her daughter had a

plan, that she wouldn't make the same mistakes as she had and drive a permanent wedge between herself and her daughter.

'What are you going to do?'

'I want to send her to you,' said Sam all of a sudden.

Veronica heard a big exhale down the phone. She knew how hard those words would've been for Sam to say, to admit she needed help from the one person she never thought she'd ever have to ask.

'Mum, say something . . .'

Unsure of the reaction she'd get, she braved speaking up. 'Surely you can't think sending her here would be better than having her with you?' They never spoke about it but Sam's childhood hadn't been a happy one and Veronica had played the starring role. 'I barely know Audrey.'

'Then maybe it's about time you got to know her.' Sam's anger must have been brewing beneath the surface of all the other emotions she was feeling and now it was unleashed in a voice that said: *You owe me, you can't let me down again.* 'I'm begging you, Mum, I don't know which way to turn.' She garbled on about all the turmoil over the years since Simon had left. Veronica had never much liked him but now wasn't the time to share her opinions.

By the time Veronica had finished on the phone with Sam, Layla's inquisitiveness had seen her abandon the piano and come into the kitchen to find Veronica looking out of the kitchen window, wringing her hands in the tea towel she'd left lying on the draining board.

'Can we keep this a secret from my daddy?'

Veronica turned and smiled, trying to get back to the

girl who was here right now. 'Keep what a secret?'

'The piano-playing. I want to come here and learn and then surprise him.'

'I'm not sure I like keeping secrets, but I think on this occasion I can make an exception. Any special reason you want to surprise him?'

'I just think it will make him happy. Like Mummy did when she played.'

When Bea knocked on the door, Layla winked at her and put a finger to her lips. Veronica repeated the action and sent Layla on her way.

In the quiet of her house and her own space, Veronica wondered how she was going to cope with having her teenage granddaughter come to stay with her. If she messed it up in any way, she'd fail Sam yet again and push her even further away.

But if she got it right, maybe – just maybe – she could put their fragile relationship back together again.

Chapter Four

Audrey

Audrey stomped down the stairs to ask her mother where the bigger suitcase was hiding. She still needed to pack before being sent to her gran's in the middle of nowhere, like an evacuee being sent away for safety. Ridiculous. Sid was one of the few friends she had, and just because he knew how to have a laugh and joke, her mum thought they needed to be separated by more than one hundred and fifty miles. She'd at least had the decency to let Audrey send him a text message to tell him she was leaving.

Sid was a friend, nothing more. In fact, Sid was gay, the whole school knew. But her mum didn't, so Audrey wasn't going to be the one to enlighten her. Where was the fun in that?

'Where were you anyway?' Audrey called when her mum finally came back inside with a whole load of cardboard from the car. 'What are they for?'

'Packing. I'll help you make up the boxes. I got four, that should do for now.'

'Mum, I only need a suitcase, that's way over the top.' In the kitchen she opened the fridge and pulled out the bottle of orange juice.

'A suitcase isn't enough.' With a huff of frustration, she added, 'You need to spend some time away from here.'

Audrey set down the bottle of juice and reached for a glass. Maybe this was about more than Sid. 'You said that already and I've agreed. I'm going to Gran's for a couple of weeks, I get it.' Her mum had dragged her up to the school for a meeting and they refused to budge on the suspension, saying she'd had enough warnings about her behaviour and the punishment fit the crime. Mr Burgess's eyes had twinkled when he'd said that word, as though he loved nothing more than to set an example by dishing out punishments. But whatever, it didn't bother Audrey all that much; she could use the online portal to keep up with her schoolwork for the next two weeks and she didn't plan to spend that many hours cooped up with her gran anyway. She planned to get out and about, find the nearest town, hopefully somewhere with a bit of life.

'Audrey, it's not only for the rest of this term.'

'Then how long is it for?' She supposed she was getting off lightly going to a village to hang around instead of here. Sid was being hauled into his dad's office every day, doing boring things like photocopying and making cups of tea for people, although he said it was marginally better than school, apart from the fact nobody in the office really spoke. He said one day he did an experiment: he held a pin up high above his dad's desk and asked the lady sitting at the desk next to him if she heard anything. When she said she did and he announced it was a pin dropping, she failed to see the funny side. All that happened was that he got told by his dad to stop clowning around.

And her mum wondered why she didn't want an office job?

'It's for the two weeks and the summer holidays,' her mum announced.

'Please tell me you're kidding.' What was she supposed to do in a village all summer? Sit around and watch the flowers grow and the sun set later in the day?

Her mum was busy trying to make the folded-down boxes lean against the wall without slipping down, until she gave up and shoved them out in the hall. 'Audrey, I've thought long and hard about this. It's a temporary solution I think might help us both. We need some time away from each other.'

She'd been right to think Sid was only part of the problem. 'You want to get rid of me, more like.'

'I never said that.'

'You didn't have to.'

'Audrey, I love you, you're my daughter. But let's use this time to turn things around. You'll have the summer holidays in Mapleberry and then you can come back ready to knuckle down in Year Eleven. And we'll talk about what happens after that at a later date.'

Audrey pulled a hand through her hair, tugging the wisps of fringe, usually artfully separated on her forehead, out of the way. She didn't have many friends, but she had Sid. And one friend, a single ally, was better than none. She'd have nobody in Mapleberry except for her gran, and the murmurings she'd heard about her over the years, not to mention the awkward couple of visits she'd been subjected to, hadn't exacted filled her with warmth and love. She wasn't surprised Mum didn't talk about her that often, and now here she was, going to stay with her.

'Audrey, do you understand what I'm saying?' Her mum pulled one of the boxes into the kitchen and began to fold it along the creases already made until the bottom was formed. She flipped it up the right way and frowned Audrey's way.

'Of course I do, I'm not stupid.' And actually, not having to go to school for a fortnight was already a blessing. At least she wouldn't have to face the Wotsits – the gang who went around lording it over everyone else, including Audrey, and made her daily life a misery. They'd earned their name because of their overuse of fake tan, which made them look orange. And they all wore tons of make-up too, and one day one of them fell on the trampoline in P.E., wiping off one of the eyebrows she'd carefully coloured in, leaving a big black smudge above one eye. Sid and Audrey had laughed so much they'd both been crying. But usually Audrey wasn't laughing; she was facing the spite and the daggers and the nasty online messages or posts that came her way. The picking on Audrey was never physical, it was hidden, they did it all from behind their phones. Part of Audrey wanted to tell the teachers, but she did that once and, after that, worse came her way because she'd told tales.

Audrey had never shared how miserable school was; her mum was always so stressed and busy trying to make their lives perfect, setting ground rules, refusing to listen when Audrey told her she didn't want a desk job, not ever. But there was nothing her mum could say or do to bring back her dad, who had left when he couldn't stand it anymore. Perhaps she'd done the same to him, fussed around him, always worried about what he was thinking and doing until he couldn't take it anymore and walked away. There was nothing her mum could do to make up for the fact that her dad wasn't in her life much anymore, that he now had children with his new wife and they had all become his focus. Well, one day, before too long, that would change. Audrey was his first child and he'd never turn his back on her.

Her mum had stopped folding the next box to gauge her daughter's reaction. 'I thought you'd be furious I was making you leave here.' She looked suspicious, her default look.

'I don't exactly have a choice – no point getting annoyed.' She was only happy that sending her away meant she got her phone back, because Mum couldn't stand the thought of her daughter being so far away yet not able to communicate with her. She liked to stay in control, and without a phone, Audrey would be free to float around wherever the wind took her.

'I think this will do us both good,' said her mum.

'Whatever.'

'See, this is what I mean.' She wrestled with the last box, the flaps refusing to bend the way she wanted. 'One minute you talk to me, the next you're rude. I don't know where I stand half the time.'

'Welcome to parenting.' If the doorway wasn't blocked with these cardboard boxes, she'd go shut herself in her room. It was bad enough she was going to have to sit in a car for more than three hours with her mum this afternoon. 'When am I coming back here then?' Audrey asked. 'At the end of the summer break? Mum?' She knew that look; there was something she wasn't telling her.

'I've got no choice but to sell this house, Audrey. The mortgage is crippling, which was one thing when I had a job but totally another when I don't.'

'But you'll buy another one, right?' She wasn't sure she

could handle living with an old lady she didn't even know indefinitely.

'I might rent for a while.'

'Rent?'

'Yes, Audrey. Plenty of people do it,' she snapped.

Audrey dragged the boxes upstairs, refusing any help from her mum. She'd go away for the summer, then come back up here to whatever pit her mum found for them to stay in, but deep down she couldn't wait to put her own plans into action as soon as she could, then she'd be free from this; she'd do things on her own terms.

'Mum, please, you have to go back,' Audrey insisted. They'd only gone ten minutes down the road.

'Why? What did you forget?'

'One of my books; I'm in the middle of reading it.'

'We're already late – I told your gran when we'd be there and I still have to get petrol. I'll send it on to you, I really don't mind, or read something else and you can come back to it when you're home again.'

'No, I want to go back and get it.'

'For goodness' sake, Audrey. Tell me where it is, I'll post it.'

'Don't worry about it,' she grumped. There was no way she was going to tell her mum what the book was.

The journey took a little over three hours and Audrey swung between being annoyed they hadn't gone back as she'd asked, talking about Mapleberry to pass the time – it didn't sound all that exciting a place but at least it had a café and a few shops – and shutting her eyes to be with her own thoughts. She wondered what Sid was up to now. She hoped he would lie low over the summer and not run into the mean girls from school who liked to go to the local bowling alley as much as Audrey and Sid did. The Wotsits sounded tame, but they were nasty. She hoped they wouldn't up the ante with Sid; they laughed at him with his dyslexia and taunted him when he got extra time in school tests, and the last time they'd gone bowling and Sid slipped on the shiny floor and banged his head, that had made their day.

As they got closer and followed the signs into Mapleberry, Audrey sat up and took interest. Mapleberry was pretty, she supposed, albeit in a dull sort of way. As you drove in at one end of the village, there were rolling fields on either side of the road that narrowed and went into a single lane over a bridge with walls low enough to see a winding stream below. A thatched-roofed house with enormous gates came next, then a pub, then shops on either side of a street with black iron lampposts dotted at intervals, each with a garden bed at the base, full of colourful flowers.

They drove past a playground, two kids on a seesaw, and then the road bent back around and passed it in the opposite direction before they pulled up outside Gran's house.

The house was well kept with its cute front garden and prim flowerbeds. Audrey had a vague memory of the inside being clean too, not a thing out of place. At least her gran wasn't living in squalor or was one of those hoarders you saw on the news – imagine trying to add in those big boxes on the back seat and in the boot if she was – although from what her mum had mentioned, Audrey deduced she was somewhat of a recluse. Loosely translated, that meant she didn't like people and didn't have any friends. What a fun summer *this* was going to be.

'Come on, Mum,' Audrey urged, but her mum couldn't seem to bring herself to get out of the car.

Audrey got fed up waiting and went to ring the doorbell herself. If she waited for her mum to get herself together, she could be standing there until the summer was over.

The front door opened slowly and her gran smiled, although it looked a little forced. 'Audrey, so lovely to see you again, come in.' Very formal. Her eyes darted to the car and then down the street and again in the opposite direction as though she suspected someone was lurking, waiting to pounce.

Audrey couldn't remember her gran being much of a hugger so she didn't even try. 'Mum's coming, she must be on the phone or something.' She wasn't, but it felt rude to imply that perhaps Mum simply didn't want to see her own mum, or that it was taking a lot of courage to do so.

'No doubt your mum will follow when she's ready.' Gran walked away towards the kitchen. 'Cup of tea?'

'I'm not a tea drinker. Do you have anything cold? Anything fizzy?'

'I'm afraid not – all those bubbles don't agree with me. But I can get some in,' she added as an afterthought, as though it might be enough for Audrey to want to stay here.

'I'll just have a water then, please.' Audrey hoped they'd get into their groove soon, that they wouldn't have to be quite this polite for the entire duration of her stay, or it was going to be the least fun summer ever.

Audrey took the glass of water as the front door opened and her mum finally came in.

'Sam, lovely to see you,' said Gran, although Audrey picked up on the undercurrent of tension, the same feeling she got the last time she'd seen them both within the same four walls. They didn't hug either and Audrey wondered what it took to drive such a wedge between the pair. Although maybe she didn't need to wonder – it was the way things were heading between her and her mum too; perhaps it was a family trait.

Mum accepted the cup of tea, Audrey busied herself bringing in all of the boxes, although by the time they'd all been taken up to the room that was to be hers until the end of August, the atmosphere was still just as stilted as before. Anyone would think they didn't know each other at all. Her mum was rambling on about the storm last week, Gran told her about a magnificent rainbow she'd shown to one of the neighbours, and then talk moved to the vegetable curry Gran was making for dinner. Audrey was impressed; curry didn't sound like a gran thing. Perhaps it wouldn't be so bad staying here after all.

Audrey grabbed a chocolate biscuit from the tin in the kitchen and headed back to her bedroom. She wanted to make it as homely as possible to survive this exile.

'Audrey,' came Gran's voice, intercepting her. 'Please eat that in the kitchen, it's the place for food, nowhere else.'

Jeez, even her mum wasn't this strict.

Audrey returned down the three stairs she'd progressed up, scoffed the biscuit and then charged up the stairs before anyone could stop her again. She opened up her boxes: onto the white table along one wall went a stack of books, all thrillers. She plugged her phone charger in and got that going, she put out her Hollywood make-up mirror with its lights up each side, she put her make-up bags beside it and her hair accessories on one of the shelves beneath. There was a second table in the room and onto that she dumped her schoolwork. She positioned her laptop there, too, in front of the little window that looked out over the playground opposite.

The bedding was at least a nice purple rather than the swirly browns or greens you'd expect in an old person's house, and the bed was a double rather than the single she had at home. And so Audrey put in her earphones, lay back on her bed and blasted out her Billie Eilish album.

She could get used to this. Away from school, not sharing space with her mum – this was going to be like a holiday in comparison to being at home. Apart from not being allowed to even enjoy a biscuit in her bedroom, that was.

The next day Audrey had a completely different perspective. It seemed Mum had briefed Gran before she left to travel home, and so rather than Audrey schlepping off to a local shopping centre with the paltry allowance her mum had finally caved in to giving her so she wasn't a burden to her gran, Audrey was to be at her desk by nine o'clock every morning. Gran checked on her too, so she daren't not abide by the rules. This was Gran's home, after all, and she was doing her a favour by having her here. It was a pretty sad state of affairs, though, that Gran had so much time on her hands that she could spend so long obsessing about where her granddaughter was at any given moment of the day. Didn't she have her own life to deal with? Mind you, the saving grace in all of this was that Gran could cook and she kept Audrey topped up with delicious meals, cakes and treats. You name it, she made it.

Her mum rarely cooked unless it was a necessary meal, so it was a novelty that Audrey was pretty sure wouldn't wear off.

On day four of her stay, Audrey was faced with a new rule. Keeping her door open while she did her schoolwork. This came when Gran caught her sitting opposite her mirror experimenting with make-up when she was supposed to be studying. And it hadn't gone down well.

'You look like you've got war paint on,' her gran told her.

'I haven't finished yet. I've got to blend it all in.' Even her mum never came into her room without knocking. She picked up her beauty blender sponge to go over the concealer she'd dotted on areas she wanted to contour.

'Whatever are you trying to do?'

At least Gran was taking an interest, that was a positive.

'I'm enhancing the structure of my face. I want to highlight the tops of my cheekbones; I want to shadow my jawline to give a better shape.'

Gran shook her head. 'Nothing wrong with the shape of your face – wait till you get to my age and then you'll know all about losing shape.'

Audrey smiled, but her grin faded when Gran told her that from now on, she'd have to work with the door open. She didn't come up here often, but when she did, she expected Audrey to be beavering away with schoolwork, not doing her make-up.

Audrey wondered how many of these rules had been set by her mum, or whether these were exactly the types of rules and regulations that had driven her mum away from Mapleberry. As far as Audrey understood it, Mum had got on better with her auntie than her own mother – that's why they'd come down for her funeral. But Audrey had long since given up trying to work out what was going on in this family, certainly on her mum's side. Her dad's side was totally different. It was only him, for a start. He was an only child, his parents were long gone and now he was in New Zealand. And his life looked amazing. When he'd written to Audrey a couple of weeks ago, he'd sent photographs of a holiday to somewhere called the Bay of Islands. He'd been scuba diving and sailing, and shared stunning pictures of the landscape that Audrey yearned to see for herself.

Two weeks of this. Two weeks and the rules would have to relax when term finished.

'What do you think about this colour?' Gran turned around the iPad to show her granddaughter the wool website she was browsing.

Audrey shrugged and instead went into the kitchen to cut a piece of the lemon drizzle covered by a plastic cloche.

'Not that,' her gran called out, the sound of the cloche lifting enough to alert her. The woman didn't suffer from hearing problems, that was for sure.

Audrey went over to where Gran had taken out her sewing kit. 'Why not?'

'There's not much left.'

'There's quite a bit.' Audrey had seen three generous slices. 'Expecting company?'

'As a matter of fact, I am.'

Finally. 'Who's coming?' Since she and her mum had arrived, and Mum had subsequently left, not a soul – unless you counted the gardener who knocked on the door or the mailman who came this morning – had stepped over the threshold of the Bentley residence. Audrey was beginning to wonder whether her gran actually had any friends – or wasn't it a thing when you got to her age?

'My friend, Layla.'

'Then there's one piece each.' With less of a defensive attitude, she got her way when Gran told her to help herself. 'Thanks, Gran. All the studying makes me hungry.'

'How much more is there to do?' she called through to the kitchen where Audrey was lifting a slice onto a plate. 'It must be wrapping up with the end of the school year.'

'It's starting to, thank goodness. After next week I'll be free as a bird.'

When there was a knock at the door, Audrey headed off to answer it. She left her cake in the kitchen, of course; she knew better than to run the risk of dropping crumbs. And now she was craving company and she wanted to meet this Layla, see what she was like; perhaps she'd inject a bit of life into the house. There certainly wasn't much atmosphere here since she'd arrived.

But when she opened the door, it wasn't anyone with grey hair or wrinkles, it was a little girl with a bright pink backpack. 'Can I help you?'

'I'm Layla.' She held out her hand to shake.

'Audrey.' Stunned, she shook her hand and stood back to let her inside. Gran's only friend wasn't what Audrey had expected at all.

Audrey went back to her cake and listened to Gran give Layla a warm welcome, nattering on about a funny calendar of sorts.

'Audrey, bring in the other two slices, would you.' Gran's demeanour had lifted a notch, as though she wasn't the same woman who'd done housework for the last few days, watched television, cooked and pottered about as though she had no place to be in the near future and was solely responsible for making sure Audrey didn't get up to no good.

Audrey delivered a slice of lemon drizzle to Layla and one to Gran. So they ate at the table or in the kitchen – unless Layla was involved. Favouritism ruled. Audrey would've found it funny if she didn't see her favourite jeans on her gran's lap.

She put down her plate. 'What the hell are you doing?' she boomed.

'Excuse me?'

'What are you doing to my jeans?' She snatched them back before Gran could push a needle into the fabric. She'd saved up to buy these, a trendy pair with rips at the knees, a pair she liked to wear with an off-the-shoulder black top that showed off her collar bones.

'I'm fixing them for you. You won't want those holes in them come winter.'

'The holes are supposed to be there!' Audrey yelled, shocking both Gran and Layla into silence. 'It's called fashion!'

'You need to go to your room and calm down, young lady.' Gran's stern expression had Layla looking to Audrey and Veronica in turn, her mouth open as she pushed in another piece of cake, almost forgetting to chew with the drama that was unfolding.

Audrey stropped upstairs and pushed in her earphones, drowning out her thoughts with music, and she stayed there a good hour until her tummy grumbled that it needed to be fed the rest of the slice of cake she'd abandoned.

She crept downstairs and into the kitchen. Gran and Layla were talking about something called a kindness calendar. Layla was prattling on about boys and girls in her class and whose name was written down first. Audrey finished her cake quietly and took the opportunity to escape. Now Gran had her friend, she might not launch into the usual questioning every time Audrey moved, particularly in the direction of the front door – but Audrey wasn't quick enough this time.

'Audrey, could you come here, please?'

Audrey stood in the doorway, looking at Gran.

'I'm sorry I nearly ruined your jeans, Audrey, but this is my house – I won't have you yelling at me.'

Audrey almost walked off and out the door, but something stopped her – either a desire to set the right example for Layla or the hope her mum wouldn't hear about this.

'I apologise.'

'Fine, then let's move on.' Gran pulled a five-pound note from her purse. 'Now, could you please go over to the shops and pick up some more toilet rolls? We're almost out, but the little corner shop is open until late.'

Audrey took the fiver. 'Sure.' At least it was a reprieve – time off for good behaviour.

Last night Audrey had gone out for a walk at nine o'clock and Gran had all but blocked the front door until Audrey told her to go with her if she didn't believe her. She'd backed off then and Audrey had made her way to the small high street, where there was nothing open but an off-licence. All she wanted was a wander, a bit of space, and after a lap she went back towards Gran's and sat on the swing in the playground opposite the house. She stayed there until the sun began to fade. She'd seen Gran's shutters move a few times when she was over there too – Gran seemed to think because the wooden slats gave her a lot of privacy, nobody could detect when they moved from their tilted position to more horizontal, enabling her to see out – but if she had a curfew and was supposed to be home, Audrey decided her gran should stop being lazy and come over to get her. Honestly, it was the height of summer and Gran hadn't so much as walked to the end of the path and down the road. She'd get sores from sitting too long if she wasn't careful.

Audrey pocketed the fiver and decided she'd call Sid before she went to the shop. Over in the playground she sat on the swing the second a young boy vacated it. She messaged Sid to see if he could talk, and when he called, it was a relief to hear a familiar voice.

'You're so far away,' he told her.

'Miles,' she said. 'How's work?'

'Last day today. I think Dad sees me as more of a hindrance than a help. I talk too much, apparently.' It was something he was forever being told off for at school. Sid wanted to be an actor, a choice his parents didn't wholly approve of, and a reason why he and Audrey understood one another so well. 'What's it like living with your gran?'

'She's pretty strict and she watches me, like, *all* the time.'

'Is she watching you now?'

'Well, no, but . . .'

'She must have her own life.'

'Not really. I wish she did. Then she'd have some hobbies so there'd be less focus on me. But she does have a visitor right now, so I took the chance to escape.'

'When are you coming home?'

Home . . . Interesting word, given that the house she'd grown up in and that she loved probably wouldn't be theirs for much longer. Sid's parents were at least still together and they were a family. They might not understand him but he still had a solid foundation. Audrey felt as though her world was too messy to make sense of; she didn't feel like she had a solid place in it. She knew her mum cared about her but she didn't see her, not really, not beneath the surface, anyway. All she saw was what she wanted to see: the rebellious teen, the girl getting in trouble. She said she supported Audrey's dreams and aspirations, but Audrey wouldn't mind betting the pressure to go on to A levels after GCSEs and not enrol in a make-up artist course would soon be back.

Audrey and Sid chatted until Audrey's phone battery died, but she still didn't go back to the house yet. She wanted to taste a bit more freedom, so she walked around the block, past the bigger houses with their grand gates, a couple of cute thatched cottages, another playground where she went on the roundabout before she got bored. She went back to the playground in front of Gran's house and went on the swing again. She could do this for hours, soaring higher and higher towards the clouds, the different colours above that took the sky from day to night as the sun set.

When she eventually went back to the house, she had one foot on the stairs to go and put her phone on charge before she made some toast when Gran appeared.

'I thought you'd be in bed.' She smiled, but it soon faded when she got a glare in return.

'What time do you call this?'

She looked at her watch. 'Ten fifteen.'

'You know what I mean. Didn't we say no staying out late on a school night?'

'Er, I don't go to school.'

'Same rules, though, Audrey, and your mother did ask me to keep them in place until summer.'

There was no way she wanted to completely take the piss and have her phone confiscated. She didn't even want to be sent home, much as she missed Sid.

'I'm sorry, it won't happen again.'

'Thank you. Now, have you had enough to eat?'

'I'm going to make toast after I put my phone on charge.' She held up the device as though to justify her trip up the stairs.

Gran let her get on with what she was doing. Her phone plugged in, Audrey went to make toast, cutting off thick pieces of bread, which she slathered in butter and jam. She'd just put her plate in the sink and mumbled a good-night when Gran called her back.

'Audrey, you've left crumbs everywhere, the side of the jam jar is smeared with raspberry jam, and the plate should go in the dishwasher.'

Eyes sent heavenward and cheeks puffed out, she sorted the mess, wiping the sticky jar and slotting the plate in the bottom rack of the dishwasher. 'There, happy?'

'There's no need to be rude.'

'I'm going to my room.'

Gran's voice followed her. 'Audrey, where are the toilet rolls?'

She pulled the fiver from her jeans pocket and left it on the shelf in the hallway. 'I forgot.'

'But Audrey, we don't have enough left.'

'Then stop being so lazy and go get them yourself!' She

hadn't meant to be so spiteful but it flew out before she could control it. She was sick of the constant observation, as though she was Layla's age, not fifteen. 'I hate all the obsessing about what I'm doing, how I'm behaving, what I'm saying. It's no different to living with Mum!'

Gran looked too shocked at her outburst to do or say anything else, so Audrey ran upstairs and threw herself onto her bed. She shouldn't have yelled, she knew it wasn't fair, but today was one of those days when her temper flared.

Once her phone had enough charge, she unplugged it and texted Sid, but if she thought she'd get a ton of sympathy she was mistaken. Most of his advice was to go and apologise or she'd feel much worse in the morning. Audrey put it off as long as she could before venturing out onto the landing. She could hear the low murmuring of the television, the odd chuckle from her gran. It was as though this little house was her world and Audrey had come like a meteor to smash everything into pieces. She didn't want that; she was sick of being the person nobody wanted around.

She crept downstairs and hovered at the lounge door until Gran noticed her.

'Come in, don't be shy.' Gran pressed the mute button on the remote but left the picture dancing away in the background.

'I'm sorry I yelled. Again.' Sheepishly she added, 'And I'm sorry about the toilet rolls.'

'We have a couple left, just use it sparingly.' Gran looked more nervous than she was. 'Would you like to sit down, Audrey?'

She nodded and sank down onto the soft sofa. She

spent so much time in her room at home and had already done so here, but it was stifling and it wasn't the way Audrey wanted this to go. As much as her mum probably thought she enjoyed being difficult or arguing, she didn't – she hated it. It was exhausting.

Audrey had wondered if her sitting here meant a big heart-to-heart with her gran; she braced herself for it, but all they talked about was the vegetables Layla had been growing.

'Layla says the cauliflowers are ready to be pulled from the ground,' Gran added. 'She's done a mighty fine job.'

'I've never had a veggie patch.'

'I'm sure Layla would take you to see theirs if you asked,' said Gran. Audrey shrugged. 'Well, anyway, she'll drop the cauliflowers over tomorrow. I'll make us a big cauliflower cheese, if you like.'

Audrey wrinkled her nose. 'I've never tried it.'

'Well, it's about time you did. It was your mum's favourite.'

'Yeah?'

'She never told you?' Her bright expression faded away as quickly as it had come. 'I don't suppose she would. Well, you'll love it, as long as you like cheese.'

'I love cheese.' Audrey began to relax a little as Gran began to talk about how she made it.

'I'll serve it with half a jacket potato cooked in the oven – microwaves leave the skin soggy – fresh salad leaves and tomatoes, also from Layla's garden.'

When Gran had exhausted the details of her speciality cauliflower cheese, Audrey asked, 'Did you decide on a wool colour?'

Puzzled, Gran realised she'd shown her the line-up

earlier when she was investigating online. 'I'm going for plum. Or rich plum, to be exact.'

'Are you going to knit something?'

Gran laughed. 'What else do you think I'm going to do with it? Yes, I want to knit a jumper and I thought Layla might like some gloves and even a bobble hat.'

As long as she didn't knit Audrey anything like that, they'd be safe from another row.

'Do you knit, Audrey?'

She couldn't help but let out a laugh. 'Me, no. I wouldn't be able to sit still for long enough to concentrate.'

'Now why doesn't that surprise me?' Gran grinned.

She looked quite different when she smiled. Her eyes twinkled with amusement, it lifted her cheekbones and added a rosiness to the skin tone. Audrey wished she'd do something with her hair. It was always scraped back from her face and pulled into a harsh bun at the nape of her neck, and she wore zero make-up. With a few little touches, Audrey bet Gran could take at least a decade off her age, and she'd likely feel better for it too. She might even want to leave the house.

Maybe it wasn't so bad in Mapleberry after all.

Chapter Five

Veronica

One minute Veronica thought her granddaughter was the most pleasant, approachable and beautiful creature on this earth, the next she could very well strangle her. She was beginning to understand exactly what Sam meant when she said Audrey could be two very different people.

Veronica pulled the door to the dining room shut behind her. It was only eight o'clock in the morning but Layla was having half an hour on the piano before Bea came to collect her and take her to school. Layla had told her dad that Veronica liked to talk about the kindness calendar so she was getting up half an hour earlier to spend with their neighbour before school. And so far, Charlie was buying it. Unfortunately, the same acceptance couldn't be said for her granddaughter, who stomped down the stairs demanding to know what the racket was and when, approximately, she'd be given a break from it. It was just another thing to upset Audrey, Veronica supposed. So far she'd annoyed her granddaughter by asking her not to eat food in her room, by setting out rules for her study and by trying to mend the jeans that were apparently supposed to have rips in them. Trying to make her granddaughter happy was like walking a tightrope with someone at the other end doing their best to topple her off. Veronica had no idea how she was supposed to get the balance between discipline and love right, and when she panicked that she never would, her throat constricted and her palms got clammy, and unfortunately she found herself snapping at Audrey unnecessarily.

'Please tell me it won't be going all day,' Audrey moaned about the piano before Veronica could get a word in edgeways.

Veronica deliberately slowed her breathing and tried to take this one battle at a time. 'She hasn't played for days because you were settling in here.' Veronica led her away to the kitchen and shut that door too. Perhaps it would be enough to calm the storm that was brewing. 'She'll be off to school soon.'

'Good, then I might be able to study in peace.' Audrey yanked a bowl out from the crockery cupboard and thumped it down onto the counter, but after a review of the cereals decided there was nothing to her taste and exchanged the bowl for a plate, treating the plate to as much brutality as its predecessor. She shoved two pieces of bread into the toaster and pressed the lever.

Veronica daren't even mention she hadn't heard Audrey have her shower yet and that she was pretty sure she hadn't done anything closely resembling study. 'Layla is lovely, Audrey, and she needs to learn properly. At least if she does, we'll all have less of a headache.' She exchanged a look with her granddaughter but her joking wasn't working, and so she went back to the study and left Audrey to have her breakfast.

Now Layla had had a bash – the only way her playing

could be described – it was time to have a quick look at the book that had arrived yesterday afternoon. It was full of exercises but Veronica only intended to teach formally for fifteen minutes a day, or else Layla wouldn't take it in. They could likely get more done over the summer when the holidays arrived, but then again, if Audrey maintained this ghastly mood, Veronica didn't hold out much hope for harmony between them all.

When Sam first asked her to have Audrey for an extended summer break, Veronica had panicked. Then, as she waited for her granddaughter to arrive, she began to have a change of heart. She'd talked with Ian the postman about Audrey – he had a daughter the same age and agreed it was a testing time – and he'd told her it would be a lovely summer surprise to have family staying with her. He knew her life was limited, he knew there weren't many comings and goings at number nine, and after Veronica shut the door to him that day, she'd tried to think about it differently. It was a surprise, he was right, and she'd tried to look forward to it rather than dread it. She'd even had Trevor make up extra vases of fresh peonies to put around the house, not that Audrey had noticed.

Since Audrey's arrival, Veronica swung between being more than happy with her summer surprise and wishing she could give it back like a gift that came with a receipt and you were able to return. She'd never tell Audrey that, or Sam either; she'd never admit she dreaded failing all over again.

Back to focusing on Layla, Veronica took her through the hand and finger positioning at the piano again, and with a very simple exercise using only the right hand and three notes, Layla did her best to follow it. It helped that she'd learned to read music with the recorder; it was treble clef so they'd deal with that first, and when they finally moved on to more complicated tunes, Veronica could play the bass clef with her left hand.

Veronica didn't miss the slam of Audrey's bedroom door above and the footsteps before she must have thrown herself down on the bed and likely shoved those earphones of hers in. The girl would have ear problems before long if she kept insisting on doing that.

'I think it's time we got you organised for school,' Veronica prompted Layla, checking her watch. 'I don't want to make you late.'

Layla picked up her things, finished the glass of water on the side table and went through to the lounge, where she knelt on the armchair closest to the window and flipped the shutters to horizontal so she'd be able to see Bea. And when Bea walked along the pavement and waved, Layla hugged Veronica and called a goodbye to Audrey up the stairs.

'She's probably got her earphones in,' Veronica told her, when there was no reply. Layla's hugs were starting to become a feature of her life, but each one still made Veronica take pause. She'd spent so many years alone in this house, convincing herself that she didn't need those moments of affection – and now they'd become a highlight of her days, and one she looked forward to more and more.

Layla happily ran out of the front door, down the path and turned back with a wave before she went off with Bea.

Audrey didn't grace Veronica with her presence until halfway through the morning when she came to get a snack, which timed with Charlie's arrival. He'd just come off nights and looked exhausted.

Veronica introduced him to Audrey before she disappeared into the kitchen.

'I'm not interrupting, am I?' Unsure after meeting the infamous granddaughter, he wiped his feet on the mat before stepping into the hallway.

'Not at all.'

He handed her a punnet of raspberries. 'It's not many, I'm afraid, but they're good.'

Veronica inhaled their summer aroma. 'Nothing like home-grown, you're too good to me. Come through, I'll make some tea.'

'I'll pass today, I need to get home to bed. But I wanted to give you these – Layla was supposed to bring them over with the cauliflowers. And, I confess, I have another motive.'

'Oh?'

'I wanted to make sure you're happy with Layla coming over so early in the mornings. She says you like to hear about the calendar.'

'I'm very happy with the arrangement – I enjoy her company.' No more information needed; the piano would hopefully be a lovely surprise come the end of the year if she could get Layla to practise so she was good enough to play Christmas tunes.

'Pleased to hear it, but make sure you tell me if you change your mind.' A yawn pulled his handsome features into a totally different expression.

'Tough night?' Veronica often loved to sit down and talk shop. She missed working at a hospital with so much to think about and keep you on your toes. It was when you had too much time alone with your thoughts that it became a problem. She managed to fill her time with the few visitors she had, a lot of television, she read a lot and kept up her activities like baking and knitting. But there was nothing like hearing about the rush of dealing with patients, being the saviour in an emergency, interacting with people who needed you the most.

'Very tough, I'll tell you the details another time.'

Veronica put a hand to his arm. 'Sleep well, and let me know if you need me to mind Layla.'

'What would I do without you?'

Veronica smiled before she noticed Audrey watching them from her position leaning against the kitchen door-frame, as she ate a chunk of cheese. Her granddaughter didn't always talk but Veronica had no doubt she was taking everything in as she went along.

'Good to meet you, Audrey,' Charlie said her way.

Charlie had only just left when Veronica saw Trevor coming up the garden path. With a big grin he handed her a bulging carrier bag that was so heavy she had to put it straight down.

'Whatever is all this?' she asked, peering in the top.

'China.'

Audrey had a look for herself. 'You're giving Gran all your rejects?'

Trevor took his cap off to let the breeze run through white hair that was always cut so neatly. Veronica wondered whether his wife made sure he was presentable at all times. Even when he was gardening, the only signs he'd been working with dirt was the odd muddy trouser leg or elbow.

'When we talked the other day, you mentioned the mosaic wall,' he said to Veronica, 'and you seemed en-amoured with the idea. It's not my thing at all, I prefer genuine flowers rather than mosaics, but we've been meaning to get rid of some of this for ages, it just sits in the cupboard taking up space. There are all sorts of colours in there.' He nodded to the bag.

'I'll say,' enthused Audrey, taking out a grape-coloured teapot and a sunflower yellow mug.

'Do with it what you will,' said Trevor before suggesting, 'perhaps your granddaughter here might like to be a part of the community project.' Even though he knew what Veronica was like, he wasn't giving up on her and it was the little acts of kindness like this that kept her going on some days.

Veronica watched Audrey rummage through the bag as though it was filled with little treasures rather than someone's unwanted items. 'Well, thank you, it's much appreciated.' And if Audrey didn't want it, Layla would.

Trevor roared with laughter, and when Veronica looked again at Audrey, she was wearing a pair of plastic goggles held tight against her face with an elastic strap that ran around the back of her head. 'Whatever have you got on?'

Audrey giggled away, her head turning to Trevor, who shared the amusement. Each time she moved, the ends of the elastic strap flapped around the enormous goggles.

'I added in three pairs of those,' Trevor explained. 'If you're going to smash china, you need to protect your eyes.'

'All I need is a hammer!' Audrey announced.

'God help me,' said Veronica with a shake of her head.

'You've got your hands full with that one.' Trevor winked. 'Good luck.'

Trevor went on his way and before Veronica had a chance to shut the door as Audrey took the bag of china inside and admired her own reflection in the hallway mirror, a Tesco delivery truck pulled up outside. Without complaint, Audrey helped her bring everything through to the kitchen once it arrived on the doorstep from the delivery man, who seemed most amused by Audrey's face accessory.

Audrey helped refill the cupboards and the fridge, finally took off the goggles and poured a glass of lemonade.

'You can take that upstairs with you, if you like,' said Veronica. But when Veronica shut the fridge door after putting the lemonade away, Audrey was still standing in the doorway. 'Would you like something else to eat?' she asked her, anxious to do the right thing and make her feel welcome. 'We have raspberries. I was going to make muffins, but I can use an alternative, chocolate chips perhaps.'

'Raspberry muffins sound good.' She still wasn't leaving. 'Gran, I've been wondering . . . the supermarket deliveries, the fresh produce from your neighbours, your visits from people . . .'

'What about them?'

'Don't you ever go out to bowls, or bingo or something?'

'Bowls and bingo?' Veronica chuckled. 'That's stereotyping of the elderly. You'll be suggesting I ride around on a bus next, just because I've got a free bus pass.'

But Veronica's sense of humour didn't deter her granddaughter, who sipped her lemonade and watched her gran closely. 'Seriously, you've not been out since I arrived and I've been here over a week. Did Mum tell you I was so bad you can't leave me alone? I'm not going to burn the house down or have a party, you know.'

'I know.' She washed the fresh raspberries in a colander.

'Then why don't you do something for yourself – go over to the shops?'

'I don't need anything.' Veronica emptied the raspberries onto kitchen towel to rid them of most of the water so they'd be ready for muffin-making.

'That day you asked me to get toilet rolls and I forgot, you lost your temper at me.'

'I apologise, it was unnecessary.'

'I deserved telling off – you'd asked me to do it. But why didn't you go to the shops? You had all day to yourself.'

'Audrey, really, why all the questions? I hope you're this inquisitive at school; it's good to have an inquiring mind.' She hoped her rambling might deter Audrey but her wish fell flat at Audrey's direct question that came her way.

'Gran, why don't you ever leave the house?'

And there it was, the question she'd been waiting for, the question Sam obviously hadn't answered for her daughter. Instead she'd sent her here to Mapleberry to discover for herself, when Veronica could hide her secret no longer. Her granddaughter was about to find out what kind of misfit her gran really was, how she'd failed her entire family so badly she was surprised they wanted anything to do with her at all.

And she had to live with her mistakes for the rest of her life.

Chapter Six

Sam

E ver since she dropped Audrey off in Mapleberry, Sam had been frantically trying to find work and sell the house that had always been too big for just the two of them. She'd found a buyer for her property quickly and the sale had progressed rapidly, but as the months marched on through July and now well into August, the search for a new place to live was getting even more desperate.

Her first impressions of the rental house she'd come to view today weren't bad at all. The gate was still on its hinges, for a start, and although on a busy main road, the terrace was close to shops and just about walkable for Audrey to get to school come September.

The last four rentals Sam had looked at had been a far cry from what she wanted – the first had been next to a pub and the noise even during the day was intolerable; the second had a brown bathroom suite that looked like it belonged in the 1940s, and a kitchen in similar disrepair; and the third property was so far from the bus route she would have had to drive Audrey to school and back every day.

Surely somewhere along the line, Sam was going to

strike it lucky in the rental lottery. She had a good feeling about this one.

A smart navy-blue door opened up into a long hallway with vintage oak flooring, rooms off to the right-hand side. First was a beautiful sitting room with a fireplace surrounded by turquoise tiles. The curtains, thick and luxurious, were cream like the carpet and there were floor-to-ceiling bookcases that Sam could see housing not only books but photo frames and perhaps an indoor plant. She nodded her approval and it was on to the next. OK, so not quite as nice: a sparse dining room with nothing in it apart from a dusty light fitting. But she could work with that. Perhaps she'd turn it into a study.

She followed the estate agent into the kitchen, which hadn't been put together at all well. The cooker was a slot-in style with gaps either side just waiting for food to fall down. And on closer inspection, it seemed whoever was in this place before had had that very problem. Sam didn't want to look too carefully and find out exactly what the remnants were, so she moved on to the downstairs toilet, which wasn't bad, although it had no window and the door didn't shut fully.

'I assume there's a bit of wiggle room with the month-ly rent,' she said. 'Given the state of disrepair this place is in, the price tag is rather high.'

He shrugged. 'No wiggle room at all, I'm afraid, and it's a fixed-term rental for a year.'

The year wasn't a problem, but the price was, not to mention the downsides of what she'd seen so far. The rent was top of her budget, which was already looking too generous unless Sam found a job in the next couple of months. She had a third interview right after this, hence why she was wearing a skirt and heels and a silk blouse, which she was careful not to get dirty when she walked past the built-in fridge that looked like it hadn't seen a cloth in the whole time it had been there.

Upstairs, Sam approved of the biggest bedroom; when it came to the bathroom, she'd seen far worse, but the other bedroom could more accurately be described as a cupboard.

'Is this really the second bedroom?' She peered into the room with the salmon pink carpet that she knew Audrey would hate, possibly more than the restrictive space that barely seemed big enough for a single bed, let alone a teen's paraphernalia.

'The previous tenants used the dining room as a bedroom instead,' the estate agent told her as they went downstairs, the grand tour over. There was just enough time for Sam to look out at what the agent described as a bijou garden. A patch of lawn feeling very sorry for itself was punctuated with paving slabs making a path down to a dilapidated shed', while' a washing line gathering cobwebs hung limp outside the kitchen window. It made her realise how much she was going to miss her own garden with its planter boxes filled with pink crocuses, the daisy-like hot yellow flowers of the heleniums planted in among taller grasses, the rose beds filled with deep reds and creams. There was a patch at one side where snowdrops grew every winter too and the bed she'd planned to plant tulip bulbs in ready to bloom next year. But soon, all of that would belong to someone else.

'I'll think about it,' she told the estate agent.

She tried to leave with an air of positivity and went to possibly her worst interview so far. The first few jobs she'd gone for had been the same as what she was doing before, but then she'd begun to apply for anything in that realm, even if it meant demotion and a fraction of the salary. This position wasn't even customer service, it was telemarketing. She had no interest in the work itself; it was antisocial hours answering the phone, working towards daily targets in an environment with shouty twenty-year-olds.

As she drove home Sam wondered how different her life might have been if she'd followed a different path or if her home life hadn't panned out the way it had. She'd chosen to study psychology at university, intrigued by the way other people's minds worked or why they behaved the way they did. During the degree course she'd found her niche too – educational psychology, something for which she devoured the subject matter, and aced all of her essay assignments. But she'd never really got the chance to follow through with her dream career helping children with special educational needs. Life had had other plans for her by then.

Home after her disastrous morning, Sam called Audrey in Mapleberry. Since they'd got a bit of distance between them, Audrey at least managed the odd conversation on the phone. She never offered much, but it was better than the battlefield they'd so often found themselves on before. She always politely asked how the job-hunting and house-hunting was going, but little else. Sam had a feeling she was happy enough getting out and about in Mapleberry and having time away, although she was surprised Audrey didn't moan about her gran more. She wasn't sure whether to be offended Audrey appeared to prefer her gran's company to Sam's, or pleased the plan hadn't gone belly up when it very easily could've done.

Sam spoke to Veronica briefly – she was never one to have a long telephone conversation – and these days it was all about Audrey and whether she was helping in the house, respecting rules, not getting into trouble. She thanked her yet again for stepping in to help, but it was a relief to put the phone down. And she'd made sure she'd got the call out of the way before she poured a glass of wine so she could enjoy the relaxation without any stress to take her by surprise.

She stood at the kitchen window looking out to the garden, the patio, the outside space where she and Simon had once hosted gatherings with friends. After the split, friendships were strained and only the strongest had come through. Jilly was one of those friends who had always been there and always would be, she'd stuck around, and it was only after Simon left that Sam realised so many of the people they'd spent time with had merely been to add to their group to make up the numbers. These days she preferred to put quality over quantity when it came to her friendships.

A knock at the front door was a welcome diversion from feeling so down. Sam opened it to see a smiling Jilly on the other side.

'You beat me to it.' Jilly pulled out a bottle of wine from behind her back as she eyed Sam's glass already in her hand.

'What are you doing here?' But she was beaming, she needed a friend. As much as she and Audrey weren't getting on, the house was way too quiet without her.

'I've come for a sleepover.'

'No way.'

'Yes way, and it was my husband's suggestion before

you put up a fight – he even handed me the wine. You're moving out soon – we need to get very drunk and commiserate.'

The evening was exactly what Sam needed. They got through all the wine, they talked long into the night and the next morning Sam still didn't have a house or a job on the horizon, but she felt as though she was still in control. She'd just needed to hear it from someone else. And this morning she decided she'd make a start at packing up the house. It would have to be done eventually and putting off the inevitable was only making her worry more.

Sam assembled the flat-packed cardboard boxes she'd picked up a few days ago in anticipation of her move. She started with Audrey's room, which was a task in itself. The amount of clothes one teenager needed was baffling – multiple colours, fabrics, shoes in all colours and styles. She tackled the desk drawers, one littered with old pens with dried-out tips, another with scraps of paper that resembled schoolwork, although clearly not the to-be-handed-in version. She piled everything together for Audrey to deal with later, and as for the overflowing rubbish bin beneath, it looked as though Audrey hadn't emptied it in weeks.

Sam grabbed the bin, about to take it outside, when something caught her eye. And when she saw what it was, she felt nausea surge through her body. It was a book about New Zealand, and tucked between the first couple of pages was a printout of instructions for how to apply for a visa. And not just any visa – there was no mention of a tourist or a temporary stay, this was permanent.

Sam slumped down on the end of Audrey's bed. Her daughter intended to move to the other side of the world to be with her dad.

How much research had Audrey already done? Had she made official enquiries, looked up requirements? And when was she going to tell her? When she bought her ticket? When she got to the airport?

Sam found her way downstairs, dazed at the discovery. A cup of coffee hit the mark, but still she was lost. The equilibrium she'd found with Jilly's help last night had all but disappeared as she called Audrey's phone – she needed answers.

But Audrey didn't pick up. Sam tried her mum's land-line instead, and when Veronica answered and explained Audrey was doing her schoolwork and probably had her earphones in, it all poured out. The woman who had never been Sam's confidante suddenly became the one person she felt she could tell. The one person she prayed could help her from spiralling into the abyss and losing her daughter.

'I bet Simon put her up to this,' Sam said. 'Just like him to do something like that.'

'Let's not jump to conclusions,' was all Veronica said.

Sam persuaded her mum not to mention it – Audrey would only accuse her of snooping and then it would be back to the battlefield with her daughter – and she ended the call after a mumbled goodbye.

She turned her attention to her computer and bashed out an email to her ex-husband, demanding to know how far this thing had gone, what progress had been made.

Sam could feel the walls closing in around her; she felt as though her relationship with Audrey was hanging on by a gossamer thread and it wouldn't take much to sever the attachment.

Out of character for Simon, he replied to her email

pretty much straight away. Was it nighttime there, evening, morning? Sam didn't care – all she wanted was answers.

She seems pretty insistent, he told her in his message. *She's looking into visas and wants me to somehow get her over here.*

Audrey had always worshipped her dad and now Sam had the proof jeering at her from that book and the email from Simon.

Until now Sam had held onto the hope that she was overreacting, but this was real. It was no overnight dream – Audrey had been mulling this over for a long while.

For the next two days Sam's determination overtook anything else. The completion date for the sale was threateningly close, and so with Jilly's help, they packed up Sam's entire house between them. Her furniture and most of her belongings went to a storage facility, keeping back the bare essentials, then they cleaned the place top to bottom ready for the new owners. Sam hadn't heard anything about her latest job applications and right now she couldn't care less because there were more important things in life. And with nowhere suitable to rent around here, it made sense to Sam to try to save her family in whatever way she could. Which meant there was only one option left now.

Sam barely glanced at the house when she reversed off the driveway after a tearful farewell with Jilly, she was too focused on the next step. She had to do this for Audrey, but her mother was part of the equation too. She'd ignored their estrangement for too long as it was, burying her head in the sand, hoping it would all go away if she kept calm and carried on. She only hoped this choice now would be the right one for all of them.

The drive went smoothly, as though the traffic had cleared a path for Sam, and when she pulled up outside number nine Mapleberry Lane, she sat for a moment. It was the same when she'd brought Audrey here. She needed time to settle her mind, to remember that this wasn't a return to her teenage years, this was different. She had to do this. She was an adult, in control, and it was time for her to step up.

She pulled two suitcases from the boot, passed through the little gate at the front, not a blade of the immaculate lawn daring to blow in the light summer breeze as she made her way up to the front door.

Sam hadn't slept under this roof in almost two decades; she barely managed a civil conversation with her own mother, let alone came to stay. But all of that had to change if she wanted to put a stop to history repeating itself. And so now, three generations under one roof was the way it would have to be. She hadn't forewarned her mum of her arrival either; she hadn't wanted her or Audrey to argue a case against it because now she was here, they all had no choice but to go through with it. She was moving in.

Sam raised a hand to knock but she might have known her arrival had already been witnessed by the slight tilt of the shutters in the sitting-room window, the immediate sound of the door being unlocked the other side.

She was here. This was real. And there was no going back.

Not if she wanted to put her family back together again.

PART TWO

An Autumn Promise

Chapter Seven

Veronica

Veronica's daughter had only moved in with her a week ago and already number nine Mapleberry Lane was fit to bursting with tension.

Seeing Layla coming down the front path now, pink backpack bobbing up and down, waving farewell to Bea, Veronica felt a sense of relief – the little girl's infectious enthusiasm was just what she needed after another day with her own family. To think that she'd been feeling so lonely a few months ago – but as the saying went, be careful what you wish for!

Veronica had the door open before Layla could knock, and the little girl ran straight into her arms.

'I missed you!' she squealed.

Veronica hugged her tight. 'I missed you too.' Layla had no idea how special these hugs were. She was the only person Veronica got them from – Sam and Audrey might be here now, but they were all a long way off being able to show affection to one another. Sam had descended on Mapleberry and Audrey had gone from amicable to biting Veronica's head off for no reason, schlepping around the place, leaving laundry on the bedroom floor, crumbs on the kitchen bench and unrinsed crockery in the sink.

Some people might wonder how it was possible for so much tension to come between a parent and child, but Veronica knew more than anyone how easily it could happen. Sam and Audrey had been pleasant enough to each other on day one, but by day two they were less tolerant, day three they'd stopped talking, and now they could barely be in the same room. The only way Veronica was coping with the shift in the dynamics was to dig her heels in and stick with it because this might be her last chance to claw back some semblance of a relationship with her daughter. She longed to be the person who helped rather than the one who ruined everything.

Veronica had gone from living on her own and barely hearing from family, let alone seeing them, to having three generations all living under one roof, and to say it wasn't easy was an understatement. But at least Sam had timed her arrival well, coinciding with young Layla being away on holidays with her dad. It meant Veronica could focus on the changing dynamics, not that she hadn't yearned for a distraction now and again when tensions mounted with her daughter and granddaughter. She'd missed Layla's company. She'd been teaching her to play the piano and Layla was improving all the time, keeping the secret from her dad. The little girl wanted to be good enough to play Christmas songs, as her mum once had before she died. Seeing her determination to succeed brought a tear to Veronica's eye at the loss Layla had been through, as well as the memories she was trying to honour.

Before Sam turned up Veronica felt she'd begun to make some headway with Audrey, despite her granddaughter's changing moods. Lord knows she'd had to work hard at it, tolerating rudeness and setting ground rules without seeming to be a total ogre, and all while hiding her own insecurities. When Audrey had come right out with it and asked Veronica why she never left the house, Veronica had finally admitted her fears. But it had felt like a blessing rather than anything shameful, not that Veronica had given her problems a label in front of Audrey – she hadn't needed to. Audrey got it, she understood Veronica had agoraphobia, and that day had marked a change in her granddaughter's attitude. Audrey had become more pleasant to be around, more polite, and although she had her moments – she was fifteen, after all – they were making progress. Veronica had even been starting to think she'd be able to send Audrey back to Sam a happier person; she'd have won at something and maybe it would be a path back into her daughter's life too.

But now, with Sam around, Audrey was back to taking offence at the simplest of things. Yesterday it had been when Sam dared to ask whether she'd tested the walk to her new school around the corner to see how long it took. The way Audrey reacted was as though Sam had asked her whether she was going to do the walk naked. Although given Audrey's reaction to changing schools when Sam had told her they were staying on in Mapleberry for the time being, and the way she'd frozen Sam out after she told her, Veronica supposed the filthy looks and huffs and puffs were a step up from the silent treatment. Mind you, this morning Audrey had slammed the front door so hard on her way out for a walk that Veronica thought she'd have to call a glazier to reinforce the glass ready for next time.

Layla's visits brought a bit of normality for Veronica.

She might be the weird lady from number nine, but she had a friend in Layla, and Charlie too.

'What's that tucked under your arm?'

'The kindness calendar, of course.'

'How could I forget something so important?' Veronica smiled. The kindness calendar was something Layla had started at school well before the long summer holidays set in and the children were all tasked with carrying on with the allotted tasks during their break. 'Now, how does chocolate milk and a slice of carrot cake sound?'

Layla followed her into the kitchen and sat herself down at the little wooden table as Veronica cut the cake. 'Did you use the carrots from our veggie patch?'

'Of course I did, you gave me enough before you went away!' Veronica poured the chocolate milk and handed it to Layla. 'I want to hear all about your holiday – how was Wales?'

'I loved camping.' Layla's dark ginger bobbed hair swung as she animatedly told Veronica all about the muddy field they'd stayed in, the trek to the toilets in the middle of the night, the cows at the farm nearby who'd woken them with their mooing every morning. 'They were so loud, worse than my alarm clock when it's time to get up for school.'

'It sounds as though you got plenty of fresh country air.' She looked at the rolled-up kindness calendar Layla had set down on one of the chairs. She was a part of it now that she was teaching Layla to play the piano, and being involved had lifted something in Veronica, it made her feel as though, despite her limitations, the big wide world out there hadn't been completely taken away from her. 'Did you manage to do any of the calendar while you were away?'

'I ticked off "Be a Good Samaritan". That was easy. You could do *anything*.' She didn't leave a crumb behind from the cake. 'We helped two people who couldn't put their tent up. The wind made it really hard and they needed more pairs of hands. I got to hammer in the tent pegs with the big wooden mallet – I like doing that.'

'That was very kind of you.'

'The people let me take photos with daddy's phone too, because then I can show the class when we go back to school.'

'Let's look what else there is for this month.' Veronica unrolled the calendar to look at the squares. The children hadn't been inundated with items; you could probably do them all in a week if you put your mind to it, Veronica thought, but she approved of how the children were having to come up with ways to help people with simple things. She pointed to a square. 'Now this one is easy: "Pick up litter".'

'I picked up some litter in Wales; one man was very naughty and left behind empty tins and a box from his tea bags.'

'Very naughty,' Veronica agreed.

'I put it all in the right bins – rubbish and recycling.'

'Why haven't you ticked the item off yet?' Usually Layla put a big coloured line through the square the second she'd completed another task.

'It was only one bag; I'd like to do more first. Daddy said I can go over the road to the playground and pick up any rubbish there.'

Veronica zoned in on another item on the calendar.

'What will you do for this one?' The square had the words 'Help a local'. Talk about ambiguous.

'My teacher says that's the good thing about the calendar: it makes us think. I want to come up with something really good.'

'Then we'd better put our thinking caps on, hadn't we?'

Veronica was always happy to listen to Layla natter away. She rabbited on at ten to the dozen and the sound filled the lonely walls of Veronica's home. It wasn't exactly quiet with Sam and Audrey both living here, but they both spent a lot of time in their rooms, avoiding her and steering clear of each other. It was amazing how three people could live under the same roof and yet Veronica still felt lonely. At least she had until Layla had come. It was the highlight of her day, not just today, but every day she showed up.

Layla talked about how the community mosaic wall was coming on, how she and Charlie had been down there already and played a part sticking pieces of broken china to the wall that separated the community centre from the road. Veronica longed to be a part of it. Even Audrey had been smashing up china and gone down there to join in, although Veronica wondered whether Audrey's favourite part was the destruction of bowls, cups, and any old crockery. It was a good way to vent her frustration, if watching her from the window was anything to go by.

Veronica told Layla all about her latest visitor to the house. She'd already met Audrey, of course, but Sam was new.

Layla's eyebrows knitted together. 'It's nice you have company,' she said after a considered pause.

'Yes, I suppose it is. And I was thinking we should

give the piano-playing a rest this week, let Sam settle in a bit more.' If Veronica was honest, it would also give her eardrums a break. Layla did love to use the loud pedal whenever she thought she could get away with it. As for Sam settling in, she wasn't sure that would ever happen.

Layla groaned but reluctantly agreed. 'I missed it when I was away. Daddy asked me one day why my fingers kept twitching.' She giggled. 'I keep trying to remember the tunes and I can't help it but my fingers move when I don't mean them to.'

Veronica laughed. 'It's our secret, but he'll be glad of the surprise in the end. How about we make a deal? Instead of practising every morning, I could phone your house when my daughter and granddaughter go out – let you know when the coast's clear.'

Layla's smile returned. 'Is your daughter like you?'

'Does she look like me? Not really, she doesn't have grey hair or so many wrinkles, for a start.'

'Does she like to stay inside like you do?' Children definitely had a way with questions. Veronica thought about the looks that passers-by sometimes gave her if she was at the front door taking a delivery or talking to the gardener, the looks that told her she was an anomaly, she wasn't like them, she was the odd one out. 'It's OK if she is,' Layla went on, 'because I like you just the way you are.'

'I'm pleased you do. But no, Sam isn't like me in that way.' Veronica smiled, basking in the affection that had been so absent from her life in recent years. 'Speak of the devil.' Sam had come downstairs and into the kitchen, Veronica assumed in search of coffee, although she had her handbag over her shoulder.

'Hello.' Sam beamed a smile at Layla. 'Who do we have

here?' You wouldn't think she'd been wandering miserably around the house for the last couple of days, lost in her own world.

Veronica introduced Sam and Layla, who instantly launched into a getting-to-know-you conversation covering where they both lived, the long summer holidays, camping and a fondness for Veronica's delicious carrot cake.

'Do you know Veronica used the carrots that *I* grew?' Layla asked.

'I'll be sure to remember when I have a slice later – it'll make me appreciate it more.' Sam turned to Veronica, managing to stop a frosty exterior taking over. 'Do you have a spare key I could use?'

Veronica fished in the top kitchen drawer and found one at the back to give to Sam. 'Are you going anywhere nice?'

'I've got an interview.'

'A job interview?'

'What else would it be, Mum?' So the defensive attitude was back. 'I'll see you later.'

Veronica cut herself and Layla another slice of cake to take the edge off what should've been a conversation with her daughter, not a confrontation. But it seemed the latter was all they could manage at the moment. Baking was at least a distraction neither Sam nor Audrey resented her for, so she was happy to carry on making cakes, biscuits and delicious meals. She'd do anything if it meant another chance with her family.

When Audrey clattered into the kitchen in search of something for lunch, Veronica suggested Layla do the litter run now. 'I can watch you from the front window.'

Audrey muttered, 'Litter run . . . eww,' under her breath and didn't even look over.

'Audrey, could you please see Layla across the road?' Veronica seized the opportunity to involve Audrey, although she couldn't deny her hands were clenching at the thought of Audrey turning around and telling her she would do no such thing.

Veronica's tension abated when Audrey grunted but didn't protest. 'Come on then, but be quick, I'm hungry.'

'Take a bag,' Veronica called after them, snatching a carrier bag from the cupboard in the hallway, but Layla was out of the door, Audrey close behind.

Veronica watched Audrey hover at the front gate while Layla crossed the road carefully. She tried to get Audrey's attention, waving the plastic bag, but Audrey's gaze was firmly fixed on the other side of the road. Either she was doing it to be responsible with Layla or she was deliberately avoiding her gran. Veronica had no idea which. Her role seemed interchangeable, from ally to enemy, with only the slightest nudge; giving Sam the last remaining room upstairs and forcing Audrey to live with her mum in close quarters again hadn't gone down well. Veronica had never been to Sam's house in Cheshire but she had looked up the address on the internet and seen it on Google Earth, so she knew they'd both had a lot more breathing room when they were still living there. Sam had bought the house with her ex-husband Simon – typical of him, doing anything he could to impress those around him. Well, he'd never impressed Veronica. The fact he reminded her so much of her own husband Herman, when he was alive, made her wish her daughter had had more sense than to marry a man just like her father.

Veronica pushed the front door so it was only open a crack and retreated more inside the house when a couple she recognised from the neighbourhood looked her way. She'd kept a low profile for years and couldn't see any way for that to change. She tried to remember the last time she'd walked over to the shops on Mapleberry's main street, or bought an ice-cream on a hot summer's day. She couldn't remember when she'd last taken the bus to the nearby National Trust stately home where she could walk the grounds in autumn and have the leaves crunch beneath her feet, or when she'd visited the local café to enjoy a hot chocolate with a side order of whatever cake they had on special that day. It had all become too hard, and as for being a part of a team of nurses at the hospital where she'd once worked, those memories almost felt as though they belonged to someone else.

With tears in her eyes, she sniffed and left the girls to what they were doing. She cheered up when she saw the kindness calendar on the table, thinking of all the items Layla had managed to tick off so far: baking for a neighbour, being a Good Samaritan, being kind to yourself. The list was endless and hearing about it always brought a brightness to Veronica's day. She wondered what she and Layla could come up with for 'Help a local'.

Veronica had only just finished rinsing the plates from the cake and wiping the ring of chocolate milk from the table when she heard giggling and commotion from the front of the house. Audrey and Layla came barrelling through the door together. A far cry from the way Audrey usually acted around Layla, detached yet polite; now they were thick as thieves and Veronica saw a warmer side to her granddaughter that she wished Audrey would show more. Although she was one to talk: she'd found smiling difficult when Audrey first came to stay, not knowing whether it was welcome or not, and her first attempts at talking to a teenager had been as tentative as if Audrey had come from another planet, Veronica feeling unsure of the best way to communicate with her. But now, watching the animation on Audrey's face, it seemed like the barriers were lowering enough from each of them to make a difference. Veronica only wished those barriers wouldn't spring back up every time Sam was around.

'Put everything in here.' Veronica opened up the plastic carrier bag and held it out for them. 'What's so funny?'

Audrey was laughing so hard she even had tears forming as she shoved the dirty crisp packets, chocolate wrappers and a piece of discarded foil into the bag. 'Her . . . She's hilarious.'

'Layla?' She did her best not to stare at Audrey. It was good to see her laugh.

Audrey wiped her eyes with the back of her hand. 'I went over to help her because she was taking ages, and when some kid left the swings, he dropped his crisp packet. Layla, hands on hips, demanded he pick it up. Bossy little thing.'

'But he was naughty,' Layla insisted as she too pushed everything she'd collected into the bag.

'It was the way you said it,' laughed Audrey. 'You sounded *eighty*, not eight.'

Veronica could well imagine. Layla definitely wasn't shy, especially if telling someone they were doing the wrong thing. 'You be careful, you never know who you're picking on,' she warned.

'I had her back.' Audrey pushed a dirty plaster and a

cigarette butt into the bag. 'I'm taking gloves if we do that again.' She pulled a face but Veronica noticed she wasn't entirely displeased at being involved. Maybe everyone needed other people, no matter how much they acted like they didn't.

'Go wash your hands, both of you,' Veronica urged. 'Revolting what some people leave behind. Do not touch anything until you're clean.' She binned the refuse after tying the bag up tight.

Audrey squirted a generous amount of soap onto her own hand and then some onto Layla's. Audrey and Layla, who stood on tiptoes, battled for the tap like two young siblings eager to be first every time. Watching them reminded Veronica of what she'd once had but had lost, through nobody's fault but her own.

'Gran . . . Gran . . .' Audrey's voice pierced into her thoughts. 'You should wash your hands too. I saw you pushing the rubbish into the bag before you tied it up. Here . . .' She held out the soap dispenser and, when Veronica put her hands out, squirted a generous blob.

Veronica worked up a good lather and even used the nail brush kept in reserve she'd been tending the pot plants lined up on the windowsill. 'That was an awful lot of rubbish,' she remarked, if only to distract the pair from the emotional pull she'd just felt. 'Did you really pick it all up in the playground across the road?'

'It was in bushes,' Layla reported. 'Some of it might have been there years. I found bits beside a tree, a few other items under the roundabout.'

'You be careful fossicking around in these places.' You never knew whether there might be glass or worse, a needle, although in this little village she never saw much out of the ordinary. At least she hadn't the last time she ventured beyond the garden gate.

Herman had never understood Veronica's condition and he'd never tried to either. His way of coping was to deny there was a problem, carry on as normal and yell at her or ridicule her when she behaved in a way he couldn't fathom. She'd kept her nursing job as long as she could until the mayhem and the people became too much for her to handle. Veronica often wondered, if she'd had Herman's support, whether she'd have been able to get on top of her problem before it was too late, before Sam had pulled away and Veronica did something she'd never ever forgive herself for. You were supposed to be there for your children no matter what, and she hadn't been, had she?

But there was no use living on what-ifs. Not now. Perhaps being trapped inside these walls was her comeuppance for what she'd done.

Veronica watched Layla take out her pencil case from her backpack, find a felt-tip and cross out 'Litter-picking' from the kindness calendar. 'You're done with that now, are you?'

'I'll pick up more but I can still cross this off. Mrs Haines says that even after we've crossed off an item, we can keep doing it; our kindness doesn't have to have a start and an end.'

'Your Mrs Haines is instilling some good life lessons with her students.' Veronica wholly approved. Kindness didn't have to be measured with a start line or an end goal, it was something to carry with you throughout life. Charlie should congratulate himself at having a daughter who really got it despite her young years. He'd done a far better job at parenting than Veronica ever had.

Veronica and Layla talked about the other items on the calendar, including how next week Layla was going to make chocolate chip cookies and take them to the school crossing lady.

'We always thank her for stopping the traffic but I want to say an extra thank you,' Layla declared. 'I wonder who will have crossed off the most over summer,' she went on as Audrey sat next to them to eat the beans on toast she'd made for her lunch.

'I think you'll be up there at the top of the class.' Veronica smiled. She looked closely and recited from one of the days: "Do a sibling's chores". Looking at Layla, she suggested, 'You'll have to think outside the square for that one.'

'You could do my chore, if you like,' Audrey put in, without even looking up from the piece of toast she was scraping through bean juice. When she did look up at Veronica, she told her, 'I'm not saying it to be lazy, I'm helping her fill in the calendar. And I did help with the litter-collecting, kind of.'

'What are your chores?' Layla wanted to know.

'Gran doesn't make me do too much; she keeps the house clean anyway and probably thinks I'd never do it as well, but I do have to take the bins out on bin day . . . although they are heavy some days, so maybe not that.' She thought again. 'I'm supposed to cook dinner a couple of times a week, although I'm not a very good cook.'

'The shepherd's pie you made was perfectly fine,' said Veronica.

'The potato on top had lumps,' Audrey confided in Layla. 'And I'd made it so thin the juice from the mince seeped through and kind of ruined the effect. It was a pile of slop by the time we got it to the table.'

'I can help with dinner, and I'm good at mashing potatoes.' Layla looked between them. 'Daddy lets me do it all the time.'

'See, good idea of mine, wasn't it?' Audrey looked to Veronica. 'And it means Layla gets to tick off the item on the calendar. I can be your surrogate sibling,' she told the little girl.

'I'd like that.'

'Well, that's settled.' Veronica managed to hide her pleasure that these two were getting on after weeks of Audrey moaning about the piano-playing. 'How does tonight sound? You could make my one-pot chicken. And you should of course eat with us and invite your dad. Unless he already has something planned.' She was getting carried away now and wondered whether it was Audrey or Layla's presence in the house that had made her grasp at any opportunity to socialise. Perhaps it was a bit of both.

'He's planned a Chinese takeaway. He's been working and said he wouldn't get a chance to shop.'

'Then that's settled. We'll all eat together.' She got a look from Audrey, who seemed to think she'd gone doolally. But it was Layla's company, her and Audrey not butting heads, the infusion of youth, not to mention the kindness calendar, which all had Veronica's spirits soaring. And these days she was learning to go with it, enjoy the moments as they happened. She had a flutter of panic that she wouldn't cope with guests, but Charlie had a way of diffusing any tension, and she felt sure he'd bring his A game tonight. At least she hoped he would. Or there'd be more fireworks than she saw sparks in the distance every November the fifth.

'Audrey will be your kitchen assistant,' Veronica told Layla, with a look in Audrey's direction, 'on hand to help with anything you need.'

After a pause Audrey agreed. 'As long as I'm not the only cook, I'm happy.'

Veronica clapped her hands together. 'You'll be able to cross another item off that calendar. Oh Layla, you're doing really well with this. Do you have September's yet?'

'Mrs Haines is going to give us that one on the first day of school.'

Audrey, one hand using her fork to scoop beans into her mouth, looked closely at the calendar. Veronica watched the two of them discuss what it was like at Layla's school, which children had done things properly, those who weren't managing so well, like the boy in her class who'd washed his dad's car but managed to collect a pebble in the sponge and left an enormous scratch on the boot.

'I can't wait to see what's on next month's calendar,' Veronica told Audrey, reeling her into their plans, making her a part of it too. 'I'm already involved by helping Layla learn the piano.'

'We have to be kind to ourselves,' Layla elaborated, 'and one item was to learn a musical instrument. I chose piano.'

'I didn't hear you today – I thought you'd be straight on it after a week's holiday.'

'Veronica said we needed to give your mum and you a break.'

'I don't mind, kid, go for it while Mum's out.'

Veronica couldn't have been more shocked. In fact, if

she hadn't been sitting down, she may well have slumped into her chair.

'She's right, make the most of it, Layla. You go and warm up and I'll join you.' She knew so little about her daughter that she had no idea whether Layla's piano-bashing – they couldn't call it playing just yet – would irritate her. Veronica worried that it might bring back memories of when she used to play herself. That was something else Herman put a stop to, as he did with anything out of the ordinary or that he couldn't see a straightforward use for. Academia came first and it was as though anything else was considered a waste of time.

'Does a piano really need warming up?' Audrey wanted to know as she rinsed her plate beneath the tap and they were left in no doubt that Layla had already found the instrument.

Veronica raised her voice above the noise. 'The piano might not, but you should make sure your fingers are warm, and your wrists. You need to build up strength, and you don't want to strain anything.'

'Maybe if you're a concert pianist.' Audrey winced at the same time as Veronica when strains of something very non-professional came from the study. 'She's not quite there yet, and it's a shame she's not shorter.'

'Shorter?'

'So her legs can't reach the pedals.'

Veronica burst out laughing. 'I try to encourage her not to use the loud pedal – she must think she's entertaining us. I'm sure she'll get better,' she added, enjoying the togetherness. 'Do you play an instrument?' There was still so much she didn't know about her granddaughter, so much she wanted to learn.

'I tried the cello once. Hated it, too big and bulky, and I was always jealous of the other girls at school who had flutes or clarinets, or a guy who got to learn saxophone. That would be cool.'

'It's never too late to learn.'

'It's never too late to make any change, Gran.'

Having others try to help and show they understood was nice, but Veronica's avoidance of going out of the house had gone on for so long it had become normal to her. Audrey was young, it was never too late for her to do anything, but Veronica wasn't so sure it was the same for a person of her age.

Veronica left Audrey popping ice cubes into her glass of lemonade and with a teen magazine at the table. In the study she took Layla through a few of the exercises, her young face tight with concentration, her little fingers splayed on the keys as they stretched between the notes. Half an hour later, Layla packed up her things and met Bea out front, ready for their trip to town to buy another pair of shoes for the new school term.

Veronica wondered whether Audrey had organised her uniform for her new school yet, but she wasn't going to mention it in case it ignited any kind of fury that she'd bear the brunt of. Shortly after her arrival, Sam had made her announcement that they would be living in Mapleberry for the foreseeable future once she found a home and a job, which Veronica suspected had to be largely due to the trouble Audrey had been in at her previous school. Sam had managed to get Audrey a place at the local high school and Veronica only hoped the transition would go well and they wouldn't have World War Three on their hands.

After Layla left, Audrey was still browsing through the

same magazine, and Veronica explained to her the importance of keeping quiet about the piano lessons.

'Fair enough, I won't breathe a word.' Audrey turned back to the magazine, but as soon as Sam waltzed in through the front door, she flipped it shut and made a sharp exit, stomping up to her room, claiming she'd promised to call her friend Sid.

Sam dumped her bag on the sofa, and in the kitchen filled a glass of cold water from the tap. 'She's pleased I'm here, then.'

'How did you get on?' Best to ignore the dramas between mother and daughter for now. Nobody would thank her for interfering.

'I got myself a job.' She beamed.

'You did? That's wonderful. And quick. Where?' Sam had been living under a shadow since she showed up in Mapleberry, and for the first time Veronica saw how being happy could transform a person. Sam's face lit up, which added a shine to her blue eyes, the same as her own; it dazzled her already beautiful features, with colour flooding to her cheeks.

'It's at the Mapleberry Mug. It's not a career position,' she added before Veronica could even congratulate her, 'it's a stop-gap.'

She could see that Sam was still conditioned to think the way her father had: that she had to be in a career that would impress, a formal career in an office with a desk rather than a local café. Veronica had always thought Sam would pursue her interest in psychology and wondered how much of her career path had been mapped out with her father in mind and how much of it had been down to Sam herself.

'I think they recognised desperation when they saw it,' Sam went on. 'It'll be money coming in, at least. It should tide me over and I can give you some housekeeping while I look out for a flat to rent.'

'I'm happy to have you here.' She didn't add that it had been so long since she'd been able to spoil her daughter and her granddaughter that she feared this may be her one and only chance to do so. 'I can loan you money if you need, Sam, I have—'

'We've talked about this.'

'The offer is there if you change your mind.'

Sam was nothing if not independent. Veronica supposed Herman may have had his faults but he'd instilled strengths in their daughter. Veronica only wished she got to see the other side of Sam more often, the side she knew was in there, the softer side that was warm and caring.

Neither of them looked at the other. Conversation was difficult at the best of times, let alone when they were acknowledging Sam's predicament.

'I'm looking forward to something totally different,' said Sam, surprising Veronica with her willingness to carry on a conversation when she'd expected her daughter to sneak off to her room again to call best friend Jilly and likely moan about what it was like living with her mother after all these years. 'It'll keep me on my toes. Learning to make coffee is one thing but I'm really nervous about carrying plates to customers and not being able to balance them like the professionals do.'

'It's the Mapleberry Mug, not a Michelin-star restaurant.'

Sam managed a laugh but turned serious quickly enough. 'And this means I can look for our own place,

Mum. I know it can't be easy having me and Audrey here.'

'It can't be easy for you to live here either.' Veronica, nervous, fiddled with the watch on her wrist. They both knew how caged in Sam had felt when Veronica's problems started all those years ago, how desperate she'd been to break away. And Veronica did wonder whether Sam, back under the same roof, would find her condition as stifling as before.

Veronica finally left her watch alone. 'I hope you don't mind but I've invited Layla and her dad over for dinner tonight.'

'Really?'

'Don't look so shocked – I do have some social skills, you know,' she bristled. It was the first time she'd done anything other than reply politely and dance on tenterhooks around her daughter.

'That wasn't what I meant.'

'Layla will be here early, she's making dinner with Audrey's help, then Charlie will be over at 6.30 p.m. Do your best to be nice.'

'Mum . . .'

Veronica waved her hand and disappeared off to the downstairs bathroom. She didn't need to use the loo – she needed breathing space. One minute she'd been happily hearing about Sam's new job, the next, she realised, looking in Sam's eyes, that she'd probably always be the mum everyone had talked about in the playground, the mum who hadn't been there in the way she should've been.

She looked in the mirror above the vanity and adjusted the bun at the nape of her neck. Her hairstyle tended to get more and more straggly as the day went on, and today was no exception. It was now totally grey, and she wondered when the strands would transition to all white, when the wrinkles on her face and around her eyes would deepen even more, when she'd go from not wanting to leave the house to not being able to because she was so old she could no longer manage it.

She thumped the edge of the basin. She got so angry with herself sometimes, furious she'd wasted all this time she could've been getting out and about, meeting new people, having a life. Instead, she was here, feeling sorry for herself. And she'd been doing it for so long she didn't know how else to live.

She flushed the loo, even though she hadn't used it, and went back to the kitchen. She may hide out from her neighbours but she couldn't do the same inside her own home.

'Whatever are you looking for?' She found Sam peering at the shelves, inside cupboards.

'Where's all your wine?'

'I don't drink,' she said, earning herself a look of absolute horror from Sam, so much so that she began to laugh, and even Sam may have smirked somewhere beneath her shocked exterior.

'What about for dinner tonight? Does Charlie drink?'

'I've no idea.'

'Might be nice to offer him something.'

It had never been an issue before.

'There's an off-licence on the high street – grab something if you like.'

'I might do, and if Charlie doesn't drink, I won't open it.'

'And you're sure you don't mind people coming?' Veronica swung between wanting to be the boss in her own house and bending over backwards not to upset anyone.

'Of course not.'

Maybe Sam was hoping it would be more enjoyable than the staid dinnertimes so far, with a lack of conversation, each of them eating as quickly as they could to avoid prolonging the agony.

Sam took out a mug and found the tea bags. She paused. 'Tea?'

'Yes, please,' Veronica stammered. 'That would be lovely.' It was the first time the gesture had been extended; she wasn't going to push it away now.

Who knew, maybe over time they'd be able to sit at the table and chat over a cup of tea, like any normal family.

Chapter Eight

Audrey

Why did her mum have to turn up and ruin everything?

Audrey lay on her back on her bed, staring up at the ceiling, earphones pushed in and Ariana Grande smashing out her music to drown everything else out. She'd already called Sid, her best friend and partner-in-crime when it came to their suspension from school, to moan to him about the unfairness of it all and, despite him being in the hairdresser's at the time, he'd let her whinge away. He was good like that; they were each other's sounding board when it came to hassles with their parents, something they had in common.

Since coming here, not only was she beginning to enjoy Gran's company, but, with distance between them, all the arguments with her mum had fizzled into the odd phone call rather than the millions of questions her mum fired her way, all day, every day: What are you doing? Where are you going? What time will you be back? Now her mum was here at Gran's house too, Mum had ramped up the questioning again and was constantly nagging Audrey about being prepared for the new school year and quizzing her about whether she'd apply herself better than she did last time. Well, she hadn't come out and said exactly that, but it was sort of implied.

Audrey had almost lost it when Mum first announced being in Mapleberry was permanent. But her fury hadn't lasted. After all, she'd be moving a lot further away than a car trip one day, and as she wouldn't have to go back to school with those horrible bitchy girls, she soon saw the change as a blessing in disguise. Now she was enrolled in a local school here for her second year of GCSEs and already she was feeling positive about having a fresh start. Sid was originally gutted she was staying in Mapleberry, but he was the kind of person who always looked on the bright side, and had told her she might surprise herself and enjoy it so much she never wanted to leave. She'd laughed at that.

Over the last week Audrey had channelled her frustrations into investigating make-up artist courses near here, and she'd found one at a college a short bus ride away. It meant that if her mum finally let up and didn't make her do A levels, she could make a start on the career path she dreamed of. Then, if her application to move overseas took time, which she'd found from several online queries that it might well do, at least she could train in what she wanted to do, ready for when she moved to New Zealand to be with her dad. Audrey missed her dad incredibly; she hated that it went so long between visits. She'd begged her mother to take her over there on holiday but she'd always insisted it was too expensive and so Audrey had had to wait for her dad to visit, and because he had a job and a family, it wasn't easy for him.

Audrey couldn't wait to move on with her life. Mapleberry was a necessary and, now thanks to Mum, painful stop-gap, but she'd get to be with her dad in the end.

Audrey stayed in her bedroom for as long as possible after her mum came home from wherever she'd been, and didn't emerge until she really had to, when Layla turned up and they were in charge of Gran's one-pot chicken. Thankfully Sam was hiding away in her own room by then and it would give Audrey a chance to calm herself down and make this a pleasant experience. Since she'd realised Gran was going through something nobody seemed to understand, least of all her own daughter, Audrey had tried not to be such a pain. Gran didn't deserve the drama, especially when she was stuck inside. Audrey wasn't sure how she did it, she didn't fully understand why either, but the thought of never going outside was unimaginable.

'Right, Layla, apron on.' Gran was already bossing the little girl around the kitchen. She fixed on an apron for her, doubling it over at the waist a couple of times so it didn't drag on the floor. 'There's another in the drawer,' she instructed Audrey.

'Remember I'm the assistant,' Audrey told Layla. 'I only do what you tell me.'

Layla did a little click of her fingers. 'Get me a knife!'

Audrey laughed but looked at Gran as though to ask whether she was allowed to hand over a weapon to an overexcited eight-year-old. When she nodded, Audrey did a salute and got the knife from the block at the end of the bench.

Between them, with Layla bossing Audrey around as much as she could, they soon had the one-pot chicken slotted into the oven and Layla insisted they set the table. She folded serviettes into triangles, positioned cutlery the way they did in restaurants, upturned wine glasses in each position, even if the person at that place setting would only be having water, lemonade or juice. And by the time Charlie knocked on the front door, the smell of the dinner and the accompanying bubble from the pan of potatoes showed that everything was in hand.

'I brought dessert,' he announced, taking something in a foil tray from the carrier bag he had with him. 'I'm afraid it's shop-bought, not homemade, but I'm assured by a work colleague that it's the finest shop-bought apple crumble you can find.'

Gran smiled. 'It sounds good to me, and I've got plenty of ice-cream to go with it.'

Layla's dad wasn't bad to look at for a man who had to be at least forty, and he seemed all right as far as parents went. He'd come around a few times since Audrey had started living there and he seemed good company for Gran.

'I've had a hard week,' he told Gran when asked how work had been. 'We were all set for takeaway tonight but this is far nicer.'

'I'll bet it's more nutritious too.'

'Don't tell her we had takeaway three times last week,' he whispered to Audrey as he came to investigate the antics in the kitchen and ruffled Layla's hair.

Already he was earning himself brownie points from Audrey. She couldn't stand it when adults talked down to her because they were separated by a generation; she much preferred being treated as an equal, a friend. She'd always imagined that's what it would be like with her mum when she was older, they'd go on spa days together or out for lunch, but the way things were going it would be a miracle if they even managed to talk on the phone when she finally left home.

Layla took her dad through the entire process of what they'd made for dinner, how she'd wished she had her swimming goggles when she chopped the onion because it hurt her eyes so much, how the garlic had left a smell on her fingers, the variety of vegetables they'd added and how she would be in charge of mashing the potatoes because 'it's something Audrey struggles with'.

Audrey had laughed at the comment, but watching dad and daughter together made her miss her own father even more. Charlie and Layla seemed so close. Charlie had dark hair that looked on the verge of fading, but he was a cool dad, just like hers, wearing jeans that fit him well and a T-shirt that showed he wasn't a layabout like some dads she knew. Charlie was a paramedic, which must keep him active. Her own dad was a businessman but he was into sports too – running, kayaking and hiking. She'd seen all the photographs to prove it. He got to see the most amazing places; his life was a big adventure. That was what she wanted hers to be like, too.

As she watched her gran laughing away with Charlie about Layla, Audrey thought of all the things she took for granted and that her gran was missing out on by never setting foot beyond this house. Gran never got to view the sky from a different vantage point, she never saw flowers other than those in her own garden. Gran never got to say hello to people in the street or exchange a simple thank you with a stranger if they held a door open for her or she for them. And most of all, she didn't get to help anyone, and if there was one thing Audrey was slowly learning, it was that helping was second nature to her gran. Last week

Audrey had overheard Charlie talking about a patient he'd assisted that day, and Gran had been full of talk about her experiences as a nurse. The way her eyes had lit up when she spoke of it was the same way her face changed when she talked to Layla about the kindness calendar. She had a passion, a yearning, and it wasn't being fulfilled. It was a shame too that Gran didn't see how important it was for her to help herself as well as striving to help others.

Audrey saw something in the corner of her eye. It was her mum beckoning to her from the doorway so nobody else saw.

'What?' she said at the foot of the stairs where they couldn't be seen from the kitchen table.

'For tonight, for your gran, can we please make an effort? I know you're not happy I came down here but I had little choice. I did what I thought was best.' The story of Audrey's life, probably of her dad's too, and it had driven him away in the end. 'I want us to get along. It's hard living in such close quarters, but you'll try?'

'Of course I will; I do know how to behave,' she answered with an eyeroll.

Her mum had looked exhausted when she first arrived in Mapleberry: no make-up on, her glasses not her contacts, scruffy clothes she rarely wore given her regular attire was usually business suits with perfectly ironed shirts, or jeans and a T-shirt on the weekend. But now she'd made an effort. Freshly washed blonde hair fell in natural waves and settled around her shoulders, she'd done her make-up in a way Audrey approved of with subtle pink lipstick and mascara to widen pale blue eyes, and she had on dark jeans with a purple micro pleat top that fell just above her hips and showed off a slender waist.

'Thank you, Audrey. Did you hear I found a job?'

'That was quick.' When her mum told her she'd be working in a café, Audrey couldn't have been more surprised. It wasn't very corporate, was it?

'I know it's not ideal,' said Mum, picking up on what Audrey might be thinking. 'It'll do for now while I look for somewhere else for us to live, and in the meantime, if a different position turns up, I can always apply.'

'Whatever – it's your life.' And she wouldn't mind staying here with Gran, if she was honest, although maybe now with dinner imminent, it wasn't the time to discuss that little gem.

When they went into the kitchen, Gran jumped up. 'Charlie, I'd like to introduce you to my daughter, Sam.'

Charlie extended his hand and met hers. 'It's lovely to meet you at last. Veronica has told me all about you.'

Mum didn't look too sure what to make of that. 'It's a pleasure to meet you too.' She beamed, doing that flick of her hair away from her face and shoulder.

Audrey might only be fifteen but she'd seen enough soaps and romantic movies to pick up on an undercurrent. And Charlie already looked more interested in her mum than in anyone else, as though her stepping in made him lose all focus. Typical. Divorcee and widower united. It was a match made in heaven, and unfortunately neither Gran nor Layla seemed at all bothered by the obvious spark.

'Can I interest you in a glass of wine, Charlie?'

Audrey didn't miss Mum's cheeks take on almost the same tinge as her pink lipstick. She wanted to stick her fingers down her throat, so she looked away from her mum, who was going to embarrass herself in a minute. OK, so

Charlie seemed like a nice guy, but still. There should be an age limit on romantic hook-ups, at least when other people were around.

'Sure,' he answered, handing her a couple of glasses from the table so she could do the honours.

Mum poured, but as she handed him a glass, she was still gawping at him, and not in a subtle way. 'You look really familiar. I'm not sure why.' Any minute now she was going to ask: *Do you come here often?* or something equally cheesy. 'Have you always lived here in Mapleberry?'

Charlie leaned against the kitchen bench. 'Not right here in the village, no. I lived about ten miles down the road when I was younger, before we moved down to the south coast. I finally headed back this way. I always liked Mapleberry.'

Mum's mind was ticking over in the way it did when Audrey tried to pull the wool over her eyes. Audrey rarely got away with it because her mum hardly ever gave up. 'Where did you go to school?'

'I was at Halverston Primary, then—'

Mum gasped. 'That's it!'

'I'm missing something.' His killer smile was firmly directed at her mum. Not even Layla could get his attention now. Maybe if Audrey got her to wave a big knife around they'd have a hope of getting in on the conversation.

'I went to Halverston Primary too,' her mum gushed.

Gran managed to get a word in. 'We couldn't get her into Mapleberry Primary – oversubscribed, even back then – so we drove her to Halverston every day. Thankfully we got her a place at Mapleberry Middle after that.'

Mum wasn't really listening to Gran. Wine glass cupped in her palm, she asked Charlie, 'Do you remember one summer sports day in the worst storms to hit the UK in decades?'

'If you're referring to the indoor sports day, then I have to say, I remember it very well. Were you there?' His mega-watt smile was sickening from where Audrey was standing. She'd liked him up until now, but she sensed she'd soon change her mind if he and her mum got any closer.

'You don't remember me,' Mum chuckled.

'She had white-blonde hair back then,' Gran put in, more talkative with Charlie around, 'and big round glasses.' But Charlie still shook his head.

'I'll mention one event,' her mum tried, 'and I bet you'll remember.' The flirting was cringeworthy, Audrey thought. 'Indoor swimming in the hall.' Mum grinned.

When Charlie roared with laughter, the lines at the edges of his eyes crinkled even more and he was still an-noyingly handsome. 'I remember!'

Mum was laughing hard now, and Layla was begging for everyone else to be let in on the joke. 'How can you even do indoor swimming without a pool?' she asked. 'You can't float.'

'It was as bad as it sounds,' Mum told her.

'Terrible!' Charlie agreed.

'We had to lie on the floor on our tummies and move our arms and legs and get from one end of the hall to the other. I thought I'd won gold, your dad thought he had, and when we went to stand on the podiums on stage – upturned crates, as I recall – we couldn't agree who had come first.'

'They told us it was a draw,' said Charlie. 'We didn't think it was and carried on arguing until your mum pushed me off the stage.'

'You didn't,' Audrey gasped. 'Mum!'

'She did,' said Charlie. 'It was a big shove too. How do you think I got this?' He pointed to his top lip and went up closer to each of them so they could see the little scar Audrey had noticed the other day when he was laughing at something Gran said. 'I fell face first onto one of the upturned crates – there was a bit of plastic jutting out, and my mouth caught it.'

Mum shook her head after Charlie showed her the lasting damage. 'I really am very, very sorry. There was so much blood,' she told the others. 'You told the teacher you tripped.' Eyes back on Charlie.

'Of course I did; no way was I admitting being beaten up by a girl.' He pulled an awkward face, stretching his scar in another direction.

'You saved me from the wrath of Miss Dickenson.'

'Now she was evil.'

'I will be forever in your debt, Charlie. She would've made my final days at that school a living hell if she'd known what I did. I'm really sorry.'

Audrey rolled her eyes and did her best to focus on the dinner preparations rather than her mum making eyes at the neighbour and giggling in a way that suggested she wasn't a fully grown adult.

The one-pot chicken was a success. Layla had pulled it off with Audrey's help, and Audrey even went back for seconds, congratulating Layla on the smooth potatoes.

'You can tick off the item on the calendar now,' she prompted. 'After dinner, I meant,' she added when Layla got up. Funny how little kids took things quite literally.

After some animated discussion of the calendar, the

veggie patch Layla had with her dad and Mum's new job at the café, it was Audrey's turn in the spotlight.

Charlie turned his attentions to her. 'Your mum says you're doing your second year of GCSEs soon.'

'That's right.'

'What's the plan after that?'

'I don't know yet.' Although Mum had her own plans, Audrey had had them drummed into her often enough. A levels, university, then you'd have more doors open to you. Apparently. But Audrey didn't buy it.

'No career aspirations? Good to keep your options open, I guess,' he said.

'I do have aspirations, but none my mum approves of.'

'Audrey . . .' Mum's voice warned.

'I'm not trying to start an argument. I've been asked a question and I'd like to answer it.'

Mum couldn't argue with that and waved her assent in a way that suggested she might give up fighting it tonight and instead sit back and enjoy her food and wine.

'I'd love to be a make-up artist,' Audrey announced.

Layla was enthralled. Talk about how to impress an eight-year-old easily. Eyes still wide, she speculated, 'You could work with movie stars, people on television.'

'That would be the dream, yes.' Grateful someone at least was enthusiastic, she added, 'But it takes a while to get that far. I'd have to work my way up.'

'What sort of thing would you learn?' asked Layla.

'If I did a make-up artist course at college . . .' She shot a look her mum's way but wanted to answer Layla's question honestly. 'I'd learn about skincare, corrective make-up, colour therapy, editorial make-up – when people are on set on TV or stage – special effects, trends, and I'd get to learn from tutors who already do it.' Audrey didn't miss the flinch from her mum, the surprise that Audrey didn't just want to mess around after her exams and do something that was a waste of time; she'd looked into it already, she knew details. Would she be so impressed if she knew she'd investigated other things? Guilt gnawed at her, but it was her life and she'd never forgiven her mum for giving up on her marriage. Marriage took work; even a teenager who'd never been in a relationship knew that basic element.

'Could Audrey do my make-up?' Layla asked her dad.

'You're eight years old,' said Charlie, picking up his wine glass.

She clasped hands together in a little prayer. 'Please?'

'It's probably better than letting her loose to do it herself,' said Gran, who was surprisingly undaunted by the number of people at the table. Over the last two months Audrey had come to realise how close Gran had become to Charlie and Layla. Maybe it was time for her mum to see it too. Perhaps she would if she stopped ogling Charlie for long enough.

Audrey looked Charlie's way. 'I promise to do it tastefully.'

'Are you sure you don't mind?'

'Of course not.' Charlie would've picked up on the negative vibes when Audrey first arrived in Mapleberry and the fact that she resented anyone in her space. But she'd grown to enjoy having Layla here; even the piano-playing was improving so much that Audrey didn't always push in her earphones the second it started up. 'Come over after school one day,' she told Layla. 'I'll try to work my magic.'

'She's welcome any time,' said Gran. 'You know that, Charlie.'

Audrey realised then how little family support her gran must have had. On the rare occasions that Mum had talked about her mother, she'd always said she had 'problems'. Audrey had never really understood what that meant, but since realising Gran had something called agoraphobia, Audrey had become a little resentful of her mum. She'd never been given a chance to get to know Gran. In fact, before coming here this summer she could've passed Gran in the street – if she went out, that was – and wouldn't have recognised her. Was Mum embarrassed by her own mother? Audrey couldn't help thinking Mum was as bad as the neighbours around here, who she'd spotted staring at the front door.

'Well, it sounds as though you have a direction,' Charlie told Audrey, completely oblivious to the way Mum kept her eyes on her plate, staying out of the conversation. 'Sometimes it takes more guts to follow a completely different path than the one everyone expects of you.'

Immediately, Charlie was back in Audrey's good books. Why couldn't her mum see something he'd just summed up perfectly with one considered sentence?

'Audrey and I have talked about it,' Mum began, most likely on a path to spoiling everything, as usual. 'We'll see how she goes with her GCSEs first. And at least she'll have some focus here at a different school.'

'What was so bad with the last one?' Charlie wondered.

'There were a few distractions.'

'She's talking about Sid, my best friend,' Audrey announced to everyone sitting at the table at such close quarters. The round wooden kitchen table was fine for just her and Gran, a little uncomfortable now her mum was living here, and tonight for five of them it was a real squeeze.

'Audrey,' Mum warned.

The tension in the room mounted but Audrey had to have her say; she so rarely felt her side was heard. 'That's what you mean, isn't it?'

Charlie was trying to carry on eating, Gran looked at her plate and even Layla, despite her young years, picked up on something going on and kept her gaze focused on her dinner.

'If you must know, yes, I think Sid is a bad influence. He got you suspended from school.'

'We both got suspended because we both did something we thought was funny. And yes, I know it was stupid, we deserved what we got, but when are you going to see that I'm my own person – I'm not led along by some-one else?' When she noticed Gran beginning to look even more uneasy, she backed off. 'There were some horrible kids there, bullies, and Sid and I, well, we stuck together.'

'It's good to have a friend,' said Layla with the same positivity she always brought to the house. 'That's what my teacher always tells us. She says we need someone our own age to talk to and tell our problems to. Is that what Sid does for you?'

'It is.' Audrey smiled. Layla and Charlie between them saw more in Audrey than her own mother did these days. 'I tell Sid things and he tells me his troubles too. Sid wants to be an actor, but his parents are digging their heels in about him wanting to go on to study performing arts at university.'

'Sid's going to university?' Mum asked.

'Don't look so surprised, Mum, he's clever. He helps me with my maths homework all the time; he's even agreed to tutor me online while I'm here if I get stuck. But he also has talents for singing and dancing and acting. In his spare time he goes to a stage school to study all three disciplines.' She was enjoying the gobsmacked look on her mum's face. Mum had never liked Sid, but she'd never *asked* about Sid either, and Audrey hadn't volunteered information to a person so adamant that he was a bad influence on her.

'He sounds like a lovely lad,' Gran said, while Charlie nodded an approval as he sipped more wine, and Mum looked like she didn't quite know what to do with herself.

Audrey nudged Layla with her elbow, which wasn't hard given they were practically sandwiched together in the confined space. 'Mum's worried I'm going to fall in love with Sid, run off and get married.' She got a giggle for her jokey efforts. 'What Mum doesn't realise is that we are just friends. And besides,' she added, scooping up another piece of broccoli with her fork, 'Sid's gay.'

'He's gay?' a shocked Mum asked. 'Why didn't you tell me?'

'Why would I need to? Doesn't make any difference to being his friend.'

'Well, of course not, but—'

'That's what I meant by Sid has had some problems,' she clarified. 'He inevitably got stick from people at school, he's had some nasty comments, things scribbled in the school toilets about him and other people, all pretty nasty. When he was going through that, I wasn't having a very nice time with some of the girls in my year, and we just bonded, I guess.'

'Then hang onto him,' said Gran. 'You're friends for life, I'd say.'

Mum twiddled with the stem of her wine glass. 'You never told me about the girls in your year giving you a hard time.'

Audrey shrugged. 'Nothing I couldn't handle.' Although she'd skived off school twice, forging a letter in her mum's signature both times, when the girls were at their worst. Once she befriended Sid and they stuck together, it was as though they managed to repel the worst of the trouble, and whatever did come their way they tackled together. Audrey knew, even if she went to New Zealand – a decision Sid thought crazy, although he had promised to visit the minute he had a job and enough money – they'd be friends for ever. Some friends passed through your life and left a small mark, others left a dinosaur-sized footprint that meant you'd never forget them. Sid was one of those people.

Charlie topped up his wine and Mum's. 'There's a bully in every school year, that's what my dad used to say.'

'Were you picked on, Daddy?'

He put his hand out and stroked Layla's hair. 'I wasn't – I was lucky.'

Audrey went back for seconds as Mum and Charlie started reminiscing about teachers they'd shared, those they'd loved, those they didn't like and couldn't get away from. Glad the focus had shifted away from her, Audrey watched Gran talking contentedly to Layla, Charlie talking happily to Mum, and she wondered what it was between her mum and Gran that stopped them having a normal relationship. Gran had a life before, Audrey knew that much hearing her shared anecdotes about nursing when she chatted away to Charlie, but how had that life evolved into this one and what had driven the wedge between mother and daughter?

With the main course over, Audrey preheated the oven ready to put the dessert in. They'd already agreed to have a break first so they could appreciate the crumble and ice-cream when they weren't so full. Layla was marking off the square on the kindness calendar that said: 'Do a sibling's chores', and she had Mum looking at it now as she recapped everything she'd done so far. Monday last week she'd taken a box of vegetables to another neighbour, Tuesday she'd taken a bag of clothes that no longer fitted to the charity shop, Wednesday she'd played at the park with Archie from school, a kid she thought weird because he was so quiet, which meant she could cross off the day that asked the kids to: 'Befriend someone you know but have never spoken to'. Poor Archie had been bossed around, according to Charlie, who told the story when Layla ran off to use the bathroom mid re-cap. He'd been ordered to go on the roundabout then do a circuit via the swings, onto the slide and over to the café for a milkshake.

'School sounds a lot of fun,' said Audrey when Layla came back to the kitchen. 'Make the most of it at primary, kid – high school is different.'

Layla moved the calendar in Gran's direction so they could look at it together.

'I can't wait to see what's in store for next month,' said Gran, before regaling the story about the teddy bear drive.

'I gave them Boris,' Layla explained. 'He's the bear Veronica knitted me. I thought other kids might need

142

him more than I did and I have so many teddy bears.'

'I can vouch for that,' Charlie called over from where he was rinsing the plates before Mum loaded them into the dishwasher. 'It's a wonder she can even get into bed some nights.'

'You knitted a teddy bear, Gran?' Audrey asked.

'I've knitted quite a few in my time.'

Audrey looked over at her mum. 'Wait . . . Mum, is that where the bear in your bedroom came from?' Sitting on the shelf in Mum's wardrobe, alongside a collection of perfumes, was a pale brown knitted bear with a simply sewn face, navy trousers and a sky-blue jumper. Audrey could remember Mum putting it on that shelf out of reach when she was little because it wasn't for playing with; it didn't take part in the teddy bear picnics Audrey had done as a kid with her friends when they came over.

'It is,' Mum confessed, visibly thrown by the question, as was Gran, who stared at her daughter as though begging to know the answer to a question neither of them really understood.

It took Layla a while to bring Gran back to the conversation, but when she did, all Gran wanted to talk about was the kindness calendar. 'You make sure you bring the new calendar month to show me after school as soon as you can, Layla.'

'Of course. I have swimming lessons the first day back but I'll come the morning after, nice and early.' Luckily Charlie was too busy helping Mum to see the wink the pair shared over the secret piano lessons Gran was giving. 'I think Mrs Haines was pleased with the last teddy bear drive so there'll be another one before Christmas.'

Gran beamed. 'Then I'll start knitting. I've got enough

odds and ends of wool around to make at least one or two bears. It'll keep me busy.'

'He'll be a multi-coloured bear if you use odds and ends.' Layla smiled. 'And if he's too nice, I might not want to give him away.'

'I know you will, you've got a good heart,' said Gran.

Watching them together, Audrey felt her anger rise again at missing out on forming this kind of special relationship with her gran. Her mum had seen to that by keeping them apart, and looking at Gran now, Audrey couldn't work out why.

When they finally sat down for dessert, Audrey watched her gran closely. She joined in bits of conversation, she never ignored her or Layla, but Audrey knew the mention of Mum's teddy bear still being in existence had left an effect. It was as though Gran's mind wasn't sure what to do with that titbit of information and she kept trying to bat it away so she didn't have to deal with it.

Audrey helped clear up after dessert but soon excused herself to go to bed, even before Layla and Charlie left. She used her laptop under the duvet and feigned sleep whenever she heard footsteps on the stairs that inevitably paused outside her room. Only when she was sure she wouldn't be interrupted did she open the laptop, the screen providing plenty of light, and used the search engine to find what she wanted.

Thinking of moving to New Zealand? the title screamed out to her. She was immediately sucked into the website's promises of a great outdoor lifestyle, unique culture and scenic beauty, and the gorgeous photograph only confirmed what she already knew: that on the other side of the world was her dad, waiting for her, ready to help her start a new life and leave all her troubles behind.

'I'll be there as soon as I can, Dad,' she promised to the screen, to herself, the way she'd promised in her last email to him, the one before that, and the one before that. 'Let's wait and see what happens,' he'd said when she asked if he'd looked into it more or applied to get the ball rolling with visas. 'I'm not going anywhere,' he'd said the last time she moaned it was taking for ever. And that was when she'd told him she promised to be with him again very soon. She hadn't got a say in who she lived with last time, but the older she got and the more she clashed with her mum, the more she wanted to make a change.

And despite growing to love and appreciate her gran at last, this time nothing was going to stop her.

Chapter Nine

Sam

Sam had forgotten how beautiful Mapleberry could be in autumn. She'd been here since August, when the sun had set late in the evening and the days and nights were layered with warmth and fresh breezes. But this morning she observed, as she walked from the house to the Mapleberry Mug, where she'd been working for exactly a month today, the leaves were starting to turn and the weather no longer let her venture out without at least a cardigan over her jeans and shirt. The sun took almost as long as she did to wake up now, and by the time she started work, the high street was groaning its way into operation. Shop doorways were unlocked and ready for custom, parking spaces on either side of the road began to fill and voices rang out along the street. In another hour schoolchildren would pass by to get to their own daily grind, a handful popping into the café for a trendy take-away coffee they'd most likely have to finish before they were allowed in the school gates.

The morning in the café got off to a brisk start, but the rush didn't send her into a blind panic as it had done on her first couple of shifts. She'd been lost here on day one, not knowing where anything was, let alone how to make a cappuccino, flat white or a long black. But she was getting the hang of it now, working five days a week rather than four, and although not her dream job, it was money coming in and it was time away from the house that was beginning to suffocate her as much now as it had when she was a teenager. Last night she'd needed to escape so badly she'd got in touch with her boss Clare on the off-chance she was interested in meeting up, and at Clare's suggestion they'd taken themselves off to the tiny local independent cinema Sam was surprised hadn't closed down years ago, but there it was, a welcome respite from the tensions at home. With a bucket of popcorn, they'd lost themselves in a movie and followed it up with a glass of wine over at the pub, and although Sam missed her best friend Jilly, Clare was becoming a close confidante already.

Her mother had started to change when Sam was around eleven years old, and Sam remembered some of it all too vividly. There'd been the time Veronica didn't show up to watch her represent the school in the cross-country championships. Sam had come tenth overall, run her little heart out and crossed the finish line with a smile on her face. She'd looked over to see her dad applauding, so proud. But there'd been no sign of her mum, and Sam had felt the absence more than she'd let on. Her mum was still working and managed to get out of the house for that, but couldn't seem to turn up for her own daughter. Sam had heard her parents rowing about it the second they got home, ripping even more of her glory away with every word slung at each other. But she hadn't blamed her dad – he was livid on her behalf.

The next time it happened was when her mum refused to leave the house to attend parents' evening one year.

Sam was to choose her options and it was an important time, discussing subjects, what she struggled with, what she particularly excelled in. Her dad had hauled her mum to the car and ordered her to get out at the school, and Sam knew more than one other parent had witnessed the embarrassing display. She'd been mortified, but at least her mum didn't say much during the talks with the teachers; Sam and her dad had led the conversation. There'd been stony silence all the way home and then another almighty row. Sam had always appreciated how much her dad stood up for her; he was in control, he wasn't going to let this affect his daughter. Sam would never forget the way he looked out for her. And after he died and the more her mum retreated, the more Sam felt trapped in the house. It was as though she had the opposite of what her mum had; not agoraphobia but the need to not be within the four walls of the house, at least not when heer mum was there, which was all the time. She still went to work, but came straight home, and on her days off she never socialised. Sam learnt quickly to make sure she checked her mum's schedule and be out when she was in, in when she was out.

Now, even if she didn't feel the same level of desperation, this job was still her solace.

She busied herself serving drinks and snacks as the schoolkids rushed in. When they finally had a lull, her boss asked, 'How's Audrey doing at school? She settling in?'

'She seems to be, at least as far as I know. She doesn't talk to me much.'

Clare, the kind of boss who didn't shy away from mucking in with other staff, stacked fresh cups on top of the coffee machine. Flame-red hair tied back, she yelled into the kitchen to let Monty know that the wholesaler's van had pulled up outside.

'Honey, join the club,' she said, switching back to her conversation with Sam. 'I've got three young adults living at home and they've gone from barely speaking to me in their teens to being out so much it's as though they're figments of my imagination rather than people who eat me out of house and home.'

'I'm pleased Audrey doesn't hate the new school; I was worried she would. I've spoken with her form tutor and apparently she's making friends, getting her work done on time and her expected GCSE grades are good.'

'All we can ask is for them to be happy,' Clare smiled as she excused herself to take over the coffee to table two, calling over her shoulder, 'although I wouldn't mind their help around this place to give it a bit of a facelift, get the walls around the counter painted.'

Sam laughed, imagining how that suggestion had gone down with Clare's kids. She'd tried to get Audrey to help her paint the study once and she'd made every excuse under the sun not to do it until Sam had given up trying.

Sam served another customer, thinking how much she wanted Audrey to be happy. It was why she was making an effort to listen to her daughter more whenever she mentioned make-up artistry. She'd even faked needing advice from Audrey last week when she woke up with a spot on her chin. She was thirty-nine, well past the spotty stage, but it seemed just when you thought you had everything under control, life liked to remind you who was boss. Audrey had talked about the importance of blending, removing the cover-up at the end of the day to let your skin recover. It had been one of those moments where, watching them, you'd never know they had problems. And with a wedding to attend in December, Sam had been able to ask for more advice, about make-up subtle enough for an afternoon event but that would last into the evening.

Sam wiped down a few of the tables, threw away discarded napkins and took a plate and cup to the kitchen. When she came back through to the café, she looked up to see Charlie coming in through the door, still in his paramedic uniform.

'You just finished or just starting?' she quizzed. 'And where's your coat, it's chilly today?'

'I finished a night shift a couple of hours ago. My coat's in the car.' He grinned. 'And I don't feel the cold. Well, perhaps I do, but I've been traumatised. I've come from Layla's school, where I was required to take part in emergency services week and talk to sixty kids about the work we do as paramedics.'

'Layla must've been proud.'

'She was – she loves it when I show up at school in my uniform.'

Layla wasn't the only one to appreciate the uniform. Dark cargo trousers showed off a taut rear and biceps stretched the T-shirt sleeves as far as they could go. Although Sam sensed Layla's appreciation would be summed up a little differently to her own.

When Clare called over a greeting to Charlie and winked at Sam, Sam wondered whether she'd let something slip out loud. Clare now seemed to have made it her personal project to ensure nobody but Sam served Charlie whenever he stopped in, which so far was frequent enough for Sam to wonder whether he had a bagel and coffee addiction or perhaps was interested in her as more than a friend.

Sam hadn't been out with a man since the time she went to the movies with a guy from work who'd kissed her goodbye at her front door. Audrey had seen them and lost her temper, screaming at her that she was an embarrassment and should know better. Sam would never understand why it was OK for Simon to have someone else in his life but not her, and she'd grown tired of trying to figure out the teenage psyche. All she knew was that she had to put Audrey first, and since that date she'd avoided having another one. She'd thought it best to do so for as long as it took for Audrey to see that her mother wasn't the enemy; she was on her side and always would be.

But all those feelings had been before Charlie came on the scene. Since the first time he'd come for dinner at her mum's, when Sam had expected a polite but likely dull guest, and he'd turned out to be someone she'd known a long time ago and who was now jaw-droppingly handsome with his dark hair and slightly crooked smile, she'd thought about Charlie a lot. Her tummy did a little jolt whenever he came into the café, she listened carefully whenever his name was mentioned at home, she always checked her hair in the mirror before she answered the door at home in case it was him, and every time they crossed paths she found herself wondering when they'd next bump into each other. But Sam still wasn't sure about dating anyone right now, especially a man who had a little girl of his own. She couldn't help sometimes getting ahead of herself and wondering what would happen if she and Charlie got serious. Audrey would end up with a little sister, she'd have a stepdaughter, and the thought sent a chill creeping up her spine because she knew she was doing a pretty bad job of being a mother to Audrey, let alone having responsibility for Layla.

'What was so traumatic about talking to a bunch of kids?' Sam asked Charlie now, preferring to focus on his predicament than her own.

'One kid put his hand up in front of everyone and asked me if I'd ever used a vibrator on anyone.'

Sam's laughter had Clare turning around with an approving look her way. 'You can't be serious!'

'I am. Turned out he meant a defibrillator.'

'I'm a little relieved, I have to say.'

When Charlie laughed and he got those crinkles beside his eyes, it hinted at how genuine and kind he was. When he smiled, the right side of his lip turned up ever so slightly more than the left, and since they'd talked about how he got the little scar, she found herself focusing on it every time he was near enough. He was incredibly sexy and Sam felt increasingly out of her depth around him. She wasn't used to flirting or getting attention from a man, and she definitely hadn't had much practice at hiding her feelings.

'Earth to Sam,' Clare's voice trilled as she tried to get past with a tray piled high of empties. 'Excuse me.'

'Sorry, Clare.' Sam had been lost in thought as Charlie read over the menu blackboard behind the counter. Clare had probably been trying to get past for a while. 'So, what'll it be?' she asked Charlie.

He went for a coffee – black, the easiest one to make, thankfully; she wouldn't mess that up. Honestly, it was as though she was Audrey's age whenever Charlie was around, not a together woman who'd made her own way in the world.

'I'll take a smoked salmon bagel too,' he added.

Using the tongs, she pulled out the bagel of choice and added it to a plate with a napkin. 'I'll bring the coffee over to you.' She needed a moment to pull herself together while she turned the various bits of the complex machine. It might only be a black coffee but given how nervous he made her feel, there was always room for error.

By the time she took Charlie his order, she was back to being in-control-Sam, not pathetic, teenage-hormone-Sam. She asked him how his shift had been; he didn't recall the more horrific details of an accident on the motorway this morning but instead told her about the little old lady he'd helped last week after a fall on the stairs in her block of flats.

'She brought me a box of chocolates to the hospital.' He smiled. 'A big box of Thorntons; I'm surprised she could manage it with her bruised wrist. But the team is always appreciative when people do things like that.'

'It must be a difficult job. Does it ever get to you?'

He shrugged. 'Occasionally, but the good outweighs the bad most days. Veronica loves hearing my stories, even the gory ones.'

'They're probably nothing she hasn't heard or seen before.' Sam thought back to the days when her mum had come home from work smiling and regaling them with tales of her day – never too disturbing, but more box-of-chocolate stories like Charlie had shared. And then those days had gradually faded away. Her mum had begun to withdraw from the people around her, including Sam, and suddenly it had been too late to get through to her. Sam had tried on more than one occasion to imagine her mum having ever left the house for a job, working with a team of people whose daily routine was chaotic and, at times, out of control, because the image Sam had been left with when she moved out of Mapleberry all those years ago hadn't involved even a glimpse of positivity. Even now, living under the same roof again, they didn't talk like other mothers and daughters did, but the close confines of the house meant Sam had begun to know a little more about her mother's life. She knew without having to ask that her mum still didn't go outside most days, and if she did, she never got beyond halfway down the front path or as far as the back garden gate. Veronica still hated courgettes but loved roasted carrots and whenever the meal allowed would use a pile of them big enough to feed a family of eight. And Sam knew her mum missed being a nurse because she'd heard those conversations with Charlie. Her mum reacted the same way with him as she did with Layla talking about the kindness calendar. It was as though both of those subjects held a magic key that turned in a lock Sam didn't know how to access.

'Audrey seems happier now than when she first arrived,' said Charlie after a sip of his coffee.

'She seems to be finding her way at last and school gives her some structure. She's made a good friend called Vicky, who sounds nice – sensible and a hard worker too – and they've hung out outside of school at the cinema or here for hot chocolates. They've even done a bit of the community mosaic together.' Sam was getting used to people being interested in her and her family, and was even beginning to appreciate it. She'd avoided all things Mapleberry for years, but coming back to the village hadn't been anywhere near as bad as she'd anticipated. 'But despite finding her feet,' she added, 'she's no happier with me.'

'I had noticed.'

Sam had Jilly up in Cheshire to talk to whenever she needed, and they'd had some long drawn-out conversations on the phone about her relationship with Audrey. Now she had Clare to talk to as well, but Charlie brought another perspective and she found herself blurting out what it had been like over the years for her, everything since the divorce, the way her daughter idolised her father.

'Is he in contact much?' Charlie wanted to know.

'Not as much as I'd like when it comes to Audrey. I don't particularly like getting in touch with him, but I do on occasion, for her sake. He lives in a bit of a bubble, really – the Simon-bubble, I call it. He's almost ethereal, at least for Audrey. He stays in touch via email and phone calls, and most of what he shares are details of him living the life I know she wishes she had. He sends photographs of the most beautiful places you've ever seen, landscapes that are impressive to a teenage girl who has the monotony of school, dreary weather a lot of the year, as well as a strained relationship with her own mum.'

'Surely Audrey knows it's not all real life. It's like social media, only showing the good parts.' His velvety brown eyes were full of understanding. 'Veronica said your ex has remarried.'

She wasn't sure whether knowing that her mum talked about her and Simon to Charlie was a good thing or not.

'He married the woman he left me for.'

'I'm sorry.'

'Don't be. I'm not. I rushed into getting married when I shouldn't have, but I won't ever regret it: I got Audrey.'

'True.' And there was that reassuring smile again, the one she could look at a thousand times or more and still not have had enough. 'He has two more kids now,' Sam added.

'How does Audrey feel about her half-siblings?'

'She doesn't know them.' Yet. But she'd be a part of their family if she went through with the idea of moving to the other side of the world. And although Sam hadn't meant it to happen, her bottom lip trembled; she bit down on it but all it did was allow a tear to snake its way down, and when Charlie covered her hand with his, she bolted across the café, Clare staring after her, and she hid in the kitchen.

Monty, short and with a shaved head that made him look more of a brute than he was, didn't say much apart from 'Excuse me' when he needed to get out to the floor and give a plate of scrambled eggs on toast to a customer at table five.

'Stop hiding,' he told her when he came back. He hooked an arm around her shoulders and gave her a reassuring squeeze. 'Clare needs help out there.'

Pulling herself together, she went out to find a next-to-empty café apart from the customer with scrambled eggs and, of course, Charlie, waiting patiently. She noticed he had another cup of coffee in front of him.

'There's an extra cup over there for you,' Clare whispered as she floated by.

Sam should've known she'd never get away with walking off without explanation, so she went over to join Charlie and nodded when he asked whether she was OK. The table they were sitting at was by the window, looking out at crisp brown leaves skittering past, the tree that had shed them destined to be bare in a few short weeks.

'Kids are hard,' he began, 'whatever age they are. I

remember shutting myself in the utility room when Layla was two and acting up. I covered my ears and everything. I may have even hummed a tune so I really couldn't hear her.'

Sam's smile didn't last. 'I don't know what to do anymore.'

'I don't have many pearls of wisdom apart from telling you to hang in there.'

'I wish I had a magic wand to wave and make everything all right.'

'May I suggest we don't talk about Audrey for a moment,' said Charlie. 'What about you?'

'What do you mean what about me?'

'As parents we are often guilty of focusing on our kids and forgetting everything else, but we need to be happy too.'

'My happiness seems way, way down on the agenda.'

'Well, it shouldn't be. You've moved to Mapleberry, you're working in a café, which, judging by what I know, isn't your first choice of career. Management, am I right?'

'Sort of.' Sam smiled. She toyed with the handle of the coffee cup and recapped where her career had taken her over the years. 'Management was where I ended up, at the top of the ladder I'd tried to climb for a while. I had some control, prospects, more money, security. It's what I was always told to work for.'

'By your mum?'

'Actually no, more my dad. Mum never said much. She'd kind of gone by then . . . not in a physical sense.' She shrugged, awkward saying this out loud. 'But emotionally she was out of reach, so it was Dad's advice I got, his support.'

'And he approved of the path you took?'

'My dad died when I was seventeen.'

He ran a hand through hair that was long enough on top that it didn't settle exactly the same as before, and if it were possible, looked even more handsome in the low autumn light filtering in through the window. 'I'm sorry, it's rough, I know. I was older when I lost my parents, but whatever age you are, it sucks.'

'It does suck.' They exchanged a grin at their youthful phrasing. 'Layla seems to cope remarkably well without her mum around. Sorry, tell me to be quiet if you don't want to talk about it.'

'No, fair's fair, you're telling me all your secrets.' He grinned. 'It hasn't all been plain sailing; sometimes Layla misses her incredibly and I don't know what to do. It's why Veronica has been such a blessing, and Audrey turning up too. Layla has had very few female figures in her life and I know she needs them.'

'Tell me about your wife.'

And so he did. Charlie talked about how they'd met at the hospital where she was a nurse, how they'd dated for a couple of years before he plucked up the courage to ask her to marry him, about their wedding reception that hadn't had a band but a pianist.

Layla wanting to learn to play and coming over to practise so often made perfect sense to Sam now.

'Amanda loved the piano,' he said wistfully. 'Other music was never an option.'

'Did she play?'

He smiled. 'She did, and she was pretty good. She had a go on the wedding day as well, everyone cheering her on as she sat there in a white gown at the ebony grand piano in the corner of the room.' Sam didn't miss the tear in his eye. 'I have some of her music recorded. Layla listens to it often – it's a way of keeping her memory alive, I suppose.'

'You're an amazing dad.'

'And you're a good mum – you're just having a hard time.'

'Single parenting is tough.' When he nodded, she told him, 'My dad was always the strong one; he seemed to keep us all together.'

'You must take after him. Tell me about him.'

'We didn't always get on,' she explained. 'He pushed me to do well at school, to aspire to a career that would offer me a future. I'd told him I wanted to study psychology at university and he hated the idea. He said I had a real flair for maths and sciences and I should be studying those. He died before we ever got to finish that argument. I did do psychology, got my degree and thought I knew which direction I was headed in. But then things got so bad at home, I couldn't focus on the career I really wanted.' It didn't help that as well as losing her father, she'd lost touch with her brother, Eddie, too. But they didn't talk about him. Not ever. 'I got a job in a customer services department answering the phones, I made friends there, and I found myself enjoying life at long last. I met Simon, saw my escape route from Mapleberry, moved to Cheshire with him when we married, and we had Audrey. After that I wanted part-time work and my experience was in customer services. I'd fallen into the role initially but I kept working hard at it, Dad's voice constantly in my head, and a series of promotions finally led me into management.'

'Tell me, what would you have done if you hadn't fallen into that job?'

Surprised by the question and more so by the fact she knew the answer straight away, she told him, 'I always wanted to be an educational psychologist.'

'You'll have to help me out. What's one of those?'

'It's applying psychology to help children who have special educational needs, such as autism, anxiety, dyslexia. It would mean working with children and families; I wanted to make a difference to them and make their lives easier. I wanted a career with people, not a desk job like I ended up with. I'm being really honest here sorry.' She frowned.

'Never apologise for that.' He held her gaze for a while, before she looked away and he told her, 'You know, I think you take after Veronica as well as your dad.'

She gulped because he was right. And she rarely gave it much thought.

A minibus from the Women's Institute pulled up outside the café and it was all hands on deck, but not before Sam thanked Charlie for the talk. 'I really appreciate it,' she told him. 'You're a good listener.'

'So I've been told.' He finished the dregs of his coffee. 'Now, I'd better get home or my legs won't be able to take me there. It was a twelve-hour shift, then the trauma of the school visit, and I need my bed.'

She tried not to think how good it would be to climb in beside Charlie, lie in his arms and be comforted by a man who she knew could take all her worries away. And as she was plunged into café mayhem with a group of women who settled in for the duration after they'd pulled four tables together, Sam realised that as well as Audrey settling in, she was finding her place in Mapleberry too. Was that even possible?

Sam felt like she was floating on a cloud – until she had a call to say the flat she was viewing at five o'clock today had already gone to someone else and that the other place she was due to view lunchtime tomorrow had been taken off the availability list when the owner decided to sell. On top of that bad news, she overheard the WI ladies talking about a planned trip to New Zealand, of all places!

Sam left the café that afternoon and sat down on the bench outside, took out her phone, hooked the strand of hair that had blown from her ponytail behind her ear, and went into her email. As she'd listened to the women in the café extolling the virtues of New Zealand, she'd been going over and over what she had to do. And now, she knew she had to email Simon. Enough was enough. If he was concocting a plan with her daughter to get her over there to join him in his exciting new life, she'd rather know more details sooner rather than later.

At least once she knew, Sam could do whatever it took to not lose her daughter entirely, the way her mum had done with her.

Chapter Ten

Audrey

Audrey ran down the stairs to answer the door on Saturday morning, knowing it would be Layla. She'd been pestering her for days to do her make-up, but with schoolwork, Audrey hadn't had a chance until now. Amazingly enough, the incentive of choosing to go on to make-up college if she worked hard at her GCSEs was spurring her on. She'd never worked this hard at school, but without the distractions from the nasty girls back in her previous school, as well as the novelty of a new environment, she'd got into a new routine.

She ushered Layla inside from the blustery autumn day. 'Do you have the "you know what"?'

Layla nodded and attempted a wink, although the movement was less than discreet. Luckily Gran was baking this morning, so they wouldn't be interrupted – they had something else to do other than the make-up and it was something Audrey had gradually begun to think about as her gran became all the more special in her life.

'I thought I heard voices.' Gran came along the hallway, all smiles, dusting her hands on her apron. Not that Layla minded – she ran in for a hug anyway.

'What are you making?' Layla took off her shoes so she didn't bring in the dirt from outside.

'Bakewell tart this morning. You two go and have fun with the make-up – I'm in the middle of making pastry and I don't want it to spoil. I'll take a look at the kindness calendar later, if you don't mind.'

'That was close,' Layla giggled when Gran returned to her pastry and Layla followed Audrey upstairs. The last thing they wanted was to let Gran see the calendar before they swapped it with the one Audrey had been working on and kept under her bed.

Once they were in her bedroom, the door open so they could hear Gran pottering around downstairs, Audrey took it out. 'This covers October and I'm working on another for November.'

Ever since Audrey had realised Gran's mood lifted when they discussed the kindness calendar and how Layla could fulfil her tasks, Audrey had begun to look for ways to help her gran out of the rut she was in. Perhaps rut wasn't the right word, she had an anxiety disorder that couldn't be fixed with a simple click of the fingers, but Audrey wanted in some way to remind Gran of the woman she once was and still could be. The way her gran spoke to Charlie about her time as a nurse conveyed how much she missed that side of her life, and what Audrey and Layla had talked about doing was getting Gran involved in anything that would mean she was helping again, whether it be big or small tasks.

Between them they'd concocted a plan. Layla had been stopping by ten minutes earlier for her piano lessons when she knew Veronica would be in the bathroom – a schedule had had to be drawn up as Sam and Audrey both needed to get out of the door at particular times. Audrey had started to get up earlier than usual to smuggle Layla inside and have their powwow before Gran was any the wiser.

Now, Layla, finger outstretched, ran her way through all the items on the calendar, some coming straight from Mrs Haines but others she and Audrey had put in themselves.

'Now, what did we agree you'd tell Gran?' Audrey prompted. She didn't want Layla to get it wrong and for Gran to realise what they were doing. She'd think they felt sorry for her and they definitely didn't want that.

Layla thought hard and, as though she'd learnt her lines for an important part in a play, said, 'Mrs Haines wanted us to include someone else in the calendar. Daddy is too busy with work so I thought you would be perfect for the job.'

Audrey high-fived her. 'Spot-on. Sounds genuine enough.'

'"Water plants for a neighbour",' said Layla, running through the tasks they'd been given. That one came from the teacher. 'Easy: I'll do Veronica's for her. And here, "Bake cookies for your neighbour": that's easy as I can do some at home and Veronica can do some for me and Daddy.' She moved to the next square and gasped. '"Get a makeover"! That's what we're doing today!'

'Sure is – hair and make-up for you today, and that's one of our items I added so Gran has to have one too.'

'Veronica doesn't wear make-up, and she never gets her hair done.'

Audrey tapped the side of her nose. 'I'm sorting it, don't you worry.' She pulled out a collection of magazines from the top drawer in her bedside cabinet and inside one were the pictures she'd cut out of women in their sixties and seventies with styles she knew would suit her gran. Most of the styles were short, but Audrey had a feeling it would suit Gran. 'The hairdresser I go to recently left her permanent job to set up on her own, so I need her to come to the house and do mine anyway. She's coming tomorrow and I've briefed her. While she's here I'll hopefully persuade Gran, using the power of the kindness calendar and you, of course. She'd do anything for you, you know that.'

'I'd do anything for her too; she's kind to me.' She looked down at the carpet and ran her toes through the pile. 'I don't have any grandparents or a mummy or any brothers and sisters.'

Audrey didn't have a sibling, not unless you included her half-brother and half-sister on the other side of the world, but she liked to think that they'd get on like her and Layla.

She took Layla's hand. 'You've got me, remember.'

'Yeah.' She smiled before her attention went to the calendar again. 'What am I going to do for "Join a group"? That one wasn't for school, was it?'

'No.' Audrey smiled. 'That's for Gran, like we discussed. It will get Gran to realise there's a big wide world out there and people might judge but they can also be a friend, be there for you. I was thinking you already have that square marked off with the brownies, and I have something in mind for Gran.' She leaned out of the bedroom and sure enough Gran was still humming away in the kitchen. 'We'll do everything on the calendar, I promise you, and the more challenging requests will always have a solution. It's part of the fun. Now come on, we'd better do your make-up or Gran will get suspicious. Your chair, madam,' she said with a flourish, pointing to the director's chair with a fresh towel looped on the back.

Layla took her seat in front of the long desk that had more than half of its space dedicated to make-up kits, lotions and potions.

'I've always wanted one of these,' Layla said of the Hollywood make-up mirror with the lights up each side. 'It's so glamorous.' She was already preening, pulling at the strands of her hair to ensure they looked neat and tidy, readjusting the Alice band so it was perfectly straight.

Audrey found her make-up toolbelt that fitted around the waist. Multiple pockets held the brushes she washed with soap and water between uses, and she also had a new wedge-shaped blending sponge.

'Wow, you have so many brushes,' Layla marvelled, letting Audrey wrap a clean towel around her shoulders. She secured it with a clip to keep it in place. 'What do they all do?'

Audrey ran through some of them. 'They all do slightly different things. This one,' she pulled out the chunkiest brush, 'is for loose powder. Then you have this flatter brush, which works well for foundation,' she said, taking out another, 'and then these,' she pointed at the tips of another few, 'are for eyes, depending on whether you're using an eyeshadow, shaping brows or doing liner.' She took out the fan brush and tickled the tip of Layla's nose with it. 'This is for brushing away mistakes.' She grinned. 'I'm hoping I don't need that one.'

Half an hour later, Audrey was proud of what she'd achieved. Layla's dark ginger wavy hair had glamorous big waves, her make-up was tasteful and Layla couldn't stop gawping into the mirror. Audrey picked up her phone and got Layla to stand next to her before they crouched down, both pouted and she took a selfie.

'You mustn't post that anywhere without my permission,' Layla warned.

'I wasn't even thinking about it. I was going to print it out – one for me, one for you, a souvenir.'

'You're the best big sister ever.' Layla threw her arms around Audrey.

'Go show Gran.' Audrey's voice shook as Layla trotted down the stairs – because she was starting to matter to other people; it wasn't just her mum anymore, there was Gran, Layla, and the new friends she was making at school. All of a sudden it started to mean something that one day she'd be leaving it all behind.

Downstairs Gran was flabbergasted at Layla's transformation and Layla was still twirling around, preening her hair, alternating between showing Gran and looking in the hallway mirror by the time Audrey joined them.

When eventually she stood still, Audrey asked, 'Layla, do you know the most important thing when it comes to wearing make-up?'

'What's that?'

'To take it all off properly at the end of the day before you go to sleep.' She handed her a packet of make-up remover tissues. 'Take these, there are a few left, they'll work on eyes and skin.'

'I can't wait till I'm allowed to wear my own make-up every day.'

'That's another important thing.' Audrey bent down with her hands on her knees so she was eye-level with Layla. She touched a finger to her nose with a light flick. 'Don't wear it before you need to – learn to see the beauty you already have, the beauty everyone has.'

'Daddy always says beauty is on the inside as well as outside.'

'And he's exactly right.' She turned to her gran. 'Maybe we could give you a makeover, Gran. What do you think?'

But Gran laughed at the idea and instead cut slices of Bakewell tart before Layla showed her the latest kindness calendar. And if she suspected they were tampering with it, she never let on. All she remarked upon was how full it was and she seemed to be excited more than anything else.

'Mrs Haines wants us to include someone else in the calendar this time, to be a team.' Layla pointed to the sentence written across the top in small letters to squish it all in. Audrey had tried to make her writing as much like a teacher's as she could – neat and uniform and clear. She just hoped Layla wouldn't do one of her winks right now or it would be startlingly obvious.

Gran peered more closely and read out: '"Find a friend this month and join forces for double the fun". You mentioned that before – is Dad helping you out?'

'He's too busy with work.' She managed to look glum despite the makeover.

'That's a shame.'

'Would you help me, Veronica?'

'You want me, really? To help with this?' Although excited at first, she looked a little doubtful. 'I don't want to mess it up if I can't do some of the items.'

Audrey hadn't thought this might make her feel bad in any way. 'Gran, I'm sure there's plenty required that won't involve doing anything you don't want to do.'

'I don't know.' Gran shook her head, already looking overwhelmed.

Audrey had to think fast. 'How about I help out too? You're Layla's main helper, of course, but if there's something you can't do, then I can step in.' She looked at the calendar and pointed out a square. 'This one, for example: "Rake leaves off the path for a neighbour" – I can help Layla with that, but some of the others we can do together. Look at this one, Gran.'

Gran read out loud: '"Join a group".' Her eyes pleaded with her granddaughter, and Audrey could tell she was beginning to panic.

To quell the rising anxiety, Audrey put a hand firmly on her gran's. 'We'll do it together, us three. I'll help with as much as I need to, I promise you that.'

'You promise? I don't want to let anybody down.'

'I promise, Gran.' When her gran nodded, she added, 'We'll be in a club. And I do believe that's an item on the calendar.'

'The Kindness Club!' Layla called out.

Gran jumped, a hand at her chest. 'That's an outside voice if ever I heard one.' But she hugged Layla. 'I like the idea and I really do want to help.'

'Then it's decided,' said Audrey. 'All three of us will work on this, all three of us will do as many tasks as we can, but some will only be for two.'

'We need to make a promise, a bit like I had to do when I joined the Brownies,' Layla announced.

Audrey stood and held her right hand to her temple in a salute sign. 'I, Audrey, do solemnly swear to offer random acts of kindness using the kindness calendar. I promise to help Layla and Gran fulfil all the tasks on the calendar, leaving nothing out.'

Gran and Layla stood and adopted the same pose.

'I've forgotten it already,' Gran admitted.

'Repeat after me,' said Audrey, and took each of them through the promise stage by stage. And at the end their hands met in the middle of their circle and launched into the air as they declared the Kindness Club officially open.

Gran was rummaging in a kitchen drawer and took out a pen. She found 'Join a club' on the calendar and crossed a line right through it. 'First item done! Let this be the first meeting of The Kindness Club on Mapleberry Lane.'

And over another slice of Bakewell tart, Audrey and Layla shared a mischievous look. Everything was falling into place.

Chapter Eleven

Veronica

It was midday on Sunday and Veronica had made roast beef with all the trimmings. It had been years since Veronica embraced a weekly Sunday lunch; it was hardly worth it on her own, but with three of them under the same roof, she'd been glad to bring the tradition back. Cooking for others as well as herself brought a certain kind of comfort, one she missed and that had faded away along with so many other things in her life. She set down the bowl of golden crispy potatoes next to another filled with an embarrassing amount of Aunt Bessie's Yorkshires and one almost spilling over with glazed carrots. She watched her daughter and granddaughter: Sam tiptoeing around, afraid to say much at all, Audrey on the defensive with her mother and only relaxed when her mother wasn't in the house.

Audrey brought the gravy boat over, walking gingerly she'd filled it up so high. 'I like my gravy,' she justified when Sam gave her a look.

Veronica knew she was changing since these two had come back into her life, and although she was a wimp outside of her house, each day she felt mounting confidence that she wasn't that way within its walls. Layla had brought some of that confidence with her kindness calendar; Veronica had sailed through the days, excited to do something to help, whether it was a simple task of thanking someone for a job well done – Sam had been on the receiving end of that when she cleaned the cooktop to a brilliant shine – or making dinner for someone you love, which Veronica had done with this Sunday lunch.

'How's the schoolwork going?' Veronica asked Audrey in an effort to lead the atmosphere inside the house in the right direction.

'It's fine.' Audrey added a third Yorkshire to her plate.

'And how was work this morning?' she asked Sam, who didn't usually work Sundays but was covering for another member of staff.

'Busy,' was all her daughter said before she, like Audrey, drizzled enough gravy over her roast to sink the *Titanic*. Veronica smiled at how alike mother and daughter could be, though they'd never admit it.

Veronica savoured the sweet taste of the carrots, some from Charlie and Layla's garden after Charlie had dropped a bag over this morning, the others from the supermarket to make up the numbers.

'Did you see the latest teddy bear I knitted for Layla?' she asked.

They both looked obediently over to the sofa, where three bears were sitting all in a row.

Audrey smiled. 'They're cool, Gran. Are they all going to the teddy bear drive for Layla's kindness calendar?'

'They most certainly are, and I've got another halfway finished.' At least Layla and her kindness calendar gave them all some common ground, something to talk about that didn't involve discussing or even hinting at their own faulty dynamics. Even Sam seemed to take a bit of an interest. 'I could teach you to knit, if you'd like, Audrey,' offered Veronica.

'I'm not sure if it's my thing.'

'Nonsense.'

'It was never mine.' Sam's eyes were on her dinner, but when she looked up she must've realised how off she had sounded. 'Sorry, but it wasn't. Remember you tried to teach me on pencils?'

'That's right,' Veronica chuckled. 'I think that was my downfall. You saw it as a joke and never wanted to carry on after that.'

When there was a knock at the door, Audrey leapt up. She'd got through her lunch quickly enough in anticipation of her appointment. 'That'll be Tanya . . . the hairdresser,' she said by way of explanation to Sam. 'I'll get her settled then come back and help clear up.'

'I thought Audrey used the salon in the high street,' Sam wondered when Audrey left them to it to show Tanya upstairs. The girl was doing door-to-door service for a haircut so the bathroom was the best place.

Veronica relayed what Audrey had told her about Tanya setting up on her own. 'It'll save Audrey money, for a start – some of these places charge a fortune.'

'Now there's something I can get on board with.' Sam smiled.

Veronica offered more glazed carrots to Sam, who hadn't eaten anywhere near as much dinner as she should, but she declined. 'You seem tired.' Was she allowed to make a comment like that? It had come out before she could think too much about it.

To Veronica's relief, Sam smiled tentatively. 'It's the

extra shifts I'm doing, but I need the money right now and I'll be off for a couple of days next week.'

'That's good.' She knew better than to offer financial help again. She didn't want to give Sam any further cause to avoid conversation, and denting her pride would definitely do that.

'I'm enjoying being there far more than I ever thought I would.'

'Really?' This was progress, Sam offering titbits of information voluntarily, and Veronica knew it was a promising sign. She suspected Charlie's presence had a lot to do with it. Not just because there was an obvious attraction between the pair but that it showed Sam her mother wasn't all bad – some people actually liked her.

'It's different,' Sam went on, 'and I think "different" is what I needed. Perhaps it's what everyone needs now and then; it seems to have worked for Audrey with her schooling, and I think once I find a place to live I'll feel even more settled.'

'How's the house-hunting going?'

'It's proving quite difficult.'

'I blame the schools in this area – they draw families here.' Veronica finished her last piece of cabbage she'd added to the meal, thinking Audrey wouldn't touch it, but she'd eaten the entire lot. She had the appetite of a teen, the figure of a model, just like Sam had been at that age – hollow legs, they used to say.

'I got my hopes up earlier when the agent called to say he had a brand new flat available. I wanted to yell at him when he told me it was one bedroom. It's down near the river, lovely views, would've been perfect.'

'You know you could always let Audrey stay here.' She

would never have thought when the sullen teen turned up on her doorstep in the summer that she'd end up enjoying her company, let alone want more of it. It seemed every time she got a little injection of companionship into her life, whether it be Charlie, Layla, Audrey or now Sam, she wanted it to flood her body, stay with her always, an antidote for the loneliness she hadn't realised she'd been feeling for so many years because she'd simply got used to it. The four walls of her home had become enough, they'd embraced her in a comforting safety blanket. The television, the odd caller, a handful of telephone conversations and her bookshelves and house plants had kept her going, but lately Veronica had begun to feel as though perhaps she needed more. Quite how she was going to get more when she wouldn't leave her home and garden, she wasn't sure.

'I'd rather have her with me,' Sam admitted.

She was probably worried Veronica would ruin Audrey's life like she'd ruined Sam's. 'Well, the offer's there.'

Veronica busied herself clearing the plates, swishing away Sam's offer to do it for her. She didn't like to say that perhaps both Sam and Audrey needed their space; it had worked doing that in the summer and now they were in closer proximity, the tension was back. But she couldn't give her opinion. She'd be the last person Sam would take parenting advice from given the monumental mess she'd made of bringing up both her children.

'I appreciate the offer, Mum,' Sam said softly at her shoulder as she stood at the sink rinsing the plates. Sam took them from her one at a time and slotted them into the bottom rack of the dishwasher, and for a moment it felt as if they were working together, putting everything to rights.

They heard Audrey's laughter coming from upstairs, and Sam glanced at the ceiling. 'She seems happier here.'

'I'm glad I could help. I know you must want to get out as soon as you can, but don't feel you have to.'

'I'm thirty-nine, I need to have a place of my own.'

'I know you do. But . . . well, we're getting into our groove, aren't we?'

Sam's laughter broke the tension. 'Yes, I suppose we are.'

Sam had gone out for a long walk before meeting Clare to go to the pub, and Veronica had almost forgotten Tanya was even in the house until Audrey came downstairs to show off her new haircut.

'Beautiful,' Veronica complimented. The short pixie cut with a fringe trimmed but styled to sit right above her eyebrows suited her and drew attention to defined cheekbones that Veronica would've loved to have had at her age.

'I'm going to add a bit of colour next time,' Audrey declared, admiring herself in the hallway mirror.

'Dear God, not pink or blue or anything like that, please.'

'No chance. Something tasteful that enhances my natural colour. You should add a bit of colour to yours.'

Veronica didn't disguise her amusement. 'What a waste of time. Nobody's going to see it apart from me – well, and you, your mum, Layla and Charlie.'

'Gran, never mind anybody else, do it for you.' Audrey perched on the arm of the chair and Veronica noticed some magazine clippings in her hand. 'Here, Tanya is touting for business and gave me these taken from a magazine I flipped through while she was doing my hair. These women, all a similar age to you, they look really good.'

'They're all beautiful, I agree.'

'And so are you. Come on, Tanya's desperate to build up her client base, and think about it: if you get a haircut tonight and let me do your make-up too, you'll be able to cross off the item on Layla's kindness calendar.'

Veronica's interest piqued. She so wanted to be involved with as much of the kindness calendar as she could. She swore something seemingly insignificant had brought a sense of joy to this house she could never have predicted. It sounded silly, she'd never say so out loud, but every time they dealt with another item on the calendar, it gave her an uplifting feeling she thought she'd lost for good. And calling it The Kindness Club on Mapleberry Lane made it feel real, like she was part of something important. They'd even taken to having their own colour to cross off tasks – a red pen for Layla, blue for Veronica and green for Audrey.

'It's years since I've had it cut,' said Veronica. 'Tanya won't want to work on an old maid like me.'

'Rubbish, she does or she wouldn't have suggested it. And if you do this, we'll get Layla over to see the results, she'll be amazed.'

'I don't know.' She touched a hand to her hair. Grey, wiry, lacking anything resembling oomph, it had simply become easier to pin it all back into a bun and ignore it.

Tanya chose that moment to appear. 'Hey, Mrs Bentley.'

'It's Veronica,' she told her. 'Come in, I don't bite. Audrey has told me this idea of yours but I'm a bit old for primping and all that business.'

'You're not at all.' Tanya smiled, the gap between her front teeth endearing. 'I hope Audrey isn't pressuring you; she's trying to support me and get others on board because the more clients I have, the better reputation I'll build. I've got an eighteen-month-old at home – I'm doing this for him, really, so I can be with him more often rather than tied to shop-opening hours.'

Veronica asked a bit about her little boy. She didn't look much older than Audrey, blonde hair wound up into a chignon with a few arty strands at either side, mascara precision-applied to open up trusting eyes. But it was the nervousness that made her appear younger, and Veronica was reminded of the times she'd panicked when she was in situations she couldn't read. This was nothing like that, of course, but she felt for the girl who was doing her best for her young family, and it was Tanya's next remark that clinched it.

'It really would be a very kind thing to do if you could help me out, Veronica.' Tanya took the mug of tea Audrey had made for her. It seemed she wasn't in a hurry to get going.

'Well, maybe just a trim,' Veronica relented.

'No chance,' said Audrey the second Veronica stood up. With one hand on her back, she guided her out of the room towards the stairs. 'This is a makeover, let's go for it.'

Halfway through the transformation, Veronica had looked down and seen the amount of hair pooling on the floor. She'd closed her eyes then, letting Audrey's warm voice wash over her, keeping her calm. Tanya even had some colour in her kit and added something called lowlights in an ash blonde that blended beautifully with the silvery grey already there. By that point Veronica had given up asking questions; she'd let the girls make the decisions, putting her faith in them. Tanya had mixed peculiar colours that Veronica tried not to worry about, she moved deftly with her comb, painted strands of her hair before wrapping them up in foil that looked like what she'd used to cover the beef earlier. But all the while Veronica had uttered the mantra in her head that she should just go with it. She should trust Audrey and Tanya, and think of what Layla was going to say when she'd proven she could be a part of the Kindness Club as much as anyone else could. Imagine how she'd feel crossing the item off the calendar with her blue pen.

The girls hadn't let Veronica see her hair until after it was finished. Instead, Audrey had taken her to her bedroom for make-up and removed the mirror so she was still in the dark. In the meantime, Tanya had been in charge of more cups of tea, hanging around to see the final results, and by mid-afternoon it was time for the big reveal.

Standing in the downstairs hallway with her hands over her gran's eyes, Audrey asked, 'Are you ready?'

'I don't know.'

'Gran, this is a good thing.'

'Is it?' With her eyes squeezed shut, she wasn't so sure.

'Gran . . .' Audrey had a hold of her hand. 'This is the start of you thinking a little bit about yourself.'

'That all sounds far too self-indulgent.'

'It's not, it's something you need to do. For yourself, for me, promise you'll start thinking about what you need and what you want. I mean it, Gran.'

Veronica, eyes still closed, took a deep breath. 'I promise.'

'I'm going to need that in writing,' Audrey giggled. 'Now, are you ready?' She made a theatrical noise like a drum roll.

She could do this, she could think about a way forward. Even if it was within these walls, things could still change, couldn't they? And now she'd promised Audrey, maybe she'd have to put in extra effort to ensure they did.

'Come on, Gran, would you open your eyes already!'

Veronica knew the hallway mirror was there in front of her and that when she opened her eyes she was going to look different to earlier in the day when the usual image had sailed past the glass, not giving her cause to pause. Since then her hair had been done and Audrey had fixed her make-up, going for a natural but thickening lashline, brightening her eyes – whatever that meant – and curling her lashes. Veronica hadn't used make-up in years. She only hoped they hadn't made her look like a clown. She didn't want to scare Layla half to death.

'Too late to back out now,' Audrey said, doing the drum roll again.

'Yes, I suppose it is.' She could hear Tanya getting excited too and, caught up with the moment, Veronica opened her eyes.

'Gran, what do you think?' Audrey, smiling, peered in the mirror alongside her, but her smile faded.

Veronica couldn't speak. Audrey had even made her put on her favourite top – a soft teal wool with a high neck. And the woman looking back at her now wasn't a woman she knew anymore. She hadn't known this woman for years. Her hair cut short at the back but with wispy layers on top and at the sides looked more elegant than her bun ever did, and the colour in it warmed her skin rather than leaving it washed out like it usually felt. It was quite the transformation.

'You hate it.' Audrey panicked because she'd seen the tears forming.

'What you've done . . . it's . . . it's . . .'

'I'm so sorry, Mrs Bentley.' Tanya was at her side, her hand touching her arm.

'Gran, I just wanted to help.'

Veronica shook her head as a lone tear trickled down her cheek. Audrey came to her other side and touched her arm as they all stood there looking in the mirror.

Veronica finally said, 'What you've done is . . . well, it's nothing short of amazing. I love it. I don't know quite how to thank you.'

Layla and Charlie couldn't believe it when they turned up later that afternoon. Charlie was obviously looking for Sam, who was out and about, but Veronica supposed the sight of her standing here in the kitchen was enough of a distraction.

'You look beautiful!' Layla enthused.

'You really do, Veronica.' Charlie kissed her on the cheek. 'Who did this to you?'

'Guilty,' said Audrey. 'And the other person was Tanya, but she's gone home now, so you'll have to blame me.'

Veronica hugged her granddaughter again, already disappointed that come tonight she'd have to take the make-up off and go to bed.

But so many people she cared about were around her now. And when Layla unrolled the kindness calendar, which had taken to being kept here at the 'club head-quarters', she, Veronica and Audrey looked at the square in question and watched as Veronica used her blue pen to put a line through it. A cheer erupted in the kitchen before Charlie whisked Layla away to a friend's birthday party at a local soft play centre.

Veronica made mugs of tea for herself and Audrey. 'I feel like a different person.'

'You've always been the same person underneath.' Audrey blew across the top of her tea. 'You were hiding away, that's all, and now you look amazing, Gran.'

'I do, don't I?' She grinned. 'My neck feels bare with this hairdo, though.'

'I know that feeling from when I chopped off my hair, but it suits you. So does the make-up. You have cheek-bones, Gran.'

'I thought they were long gone!' She noticed her reflection in the wall oven when she passed by to sit at the table with Audrey.

'Not gone, always there, just needed a little encouragement to show themselves, that's all.'

They spent the next half hour chatting away. Audrey had a new friend called Vicky and, not only that, she was interested in a boy. His name was Alex and, according to Audrey, he was popular, handsome and he'd even smiled at her a few times.

'You're really settling in here, aren't you?' Veronica only dared to hope this was a sign of things to come. If only she and Sam had been able to have such frank conversations.

Audrey smiled. 'I feel like I am.'

'Hopefully one day you'll get to put make-up on models or TV stars rather than a little old lady like me,' Gran concluded, collecting the mugs and leaving them in the sink.

'I don't mind who it is, as long as I get to do it.'

'I feel bad you worked so hard, and Tanya did.'

'We didn't mind, and you paid Tanya; she was only too

happy to do it and build her business. No need to feel guilty.'

But she did. 'You worked hard and nobody will get to see the results, not apart from those who come here, and that list is hardly long.'

Audrey ignored the remark and instead looked again at the calendar. 'There's so much on here that you can do, Gran. This one, for example.'

'"Get to know the local community"? That's not a good one for me, Audrey.' Her heart sank. She'd never be able to tick off many items from the calendar at this rate, and she'd already heard Layla going on about having all three coloured lines on all of the allotted squares if she possibly could. But how could Veronica make that happen?

'Nonsense,' Audrey batted back. 'Come with me.' She beckoned Veronica to follow her upstairs.

Veronica sneaked another glance in the mirror at this woman whose life was changing with every passing day. In Audrey's bedroom she sat on the bed and waited for Audrey to clear a space at her desk that more often than not resembled a make-up station. Audrey ran downstairs and brought up another chair, positioned her laptop on the desk and flipped it open.

'What are we doing?'

'When I was walking past the newsagents a few days ago, I saw a sign in the window advertising the Mapleberry Village Residents' Group on Facebook.'

'I don't use things like Facebook. I can do emails, that's about it.'

Audrey pointed to one of the chairs. 'Sit, you're about to get a crash course.'

Veronica found her granddaughter most persuasive and

within minutes she had a Facebook profile – no photograph as yet – and Audrey had given her a rundown of how to navigate the social media site. It was complicated, Veronica knew she wouldn't remember half of it, but Audrey said any time she had questions, fire away, and she even left a bit of a cheat sheet with simple tips, such as her password – kind of essential – and what the symbols at the top of the screen were for, for her to look at if Audrey wasn't around.

'So I can find anybody on here, anyone I like?' Veronica wanted to know.

'Sure. I mean, a lot of people have privacy settings that won't allow you to view much about them, but you can find out enough. Here, let's search for Mum.'

'Your mum is on this?'

'Of course. Go on, type in mum's name and surname.'

Veronica did as she suggested and grinned when not only did a few unknown faces appear, but also her daughter's. 'Now what do I do?'

'You can ask her to be friends with you, if you like.' When Veronica hesitated at doing anything, Audrey went on. 'Gran, you don't have to be one of those people who shares photos and details all the time like some of the people I've shown you. Why don't you lurk for a while as you get used to it?'

'Lurk? You make me sound like a criminal. And I don't understand how this will help me to fulfil the "Get to know your local community" item on the calendar.'

With a few more taps on the keyboard, Audrey had navigated her way to the Mapleberry Village Residents' Group and clicked on Join.

'Did you just . . .'

'I joined you up, yes. You live here. I joined too but so far I haven't posted anything. This will let you explore a bit, find out who your neighbours are, discover a bit about Mapleberry and things that go on. Here, let's sign you out and me in.' She changed over to her own account and went into the group under her own name. 'You can scroll through and have a look for yourself.'

Audrey left her to have a tinker around, and scrolling down the group didn't seem all that bad. It had over a thousand members who belonged, and so many names had posted that Veronica thought she'd never remember them all. Some people were selling old toys, one was advertising his plumbing business, another asked for recommendations for a painter and decorator, which had got more than sixty responses!

She kept on scrolling; it went on for ever and ever.

'You having fun, Gran?' Audrey delivered her another cup of tea.

Veronica was smiling. She'd stopped all the way down the group feed at a post from December last year.

'Whoa, you must've had to go through hundreds of posts to get that far back,' said Audrey.

'This is the Christmas tree last year. There's always one on the field, or some call it the green, out past the end of Mapleberry Lane, the end past the high street. I'd forgotten how beautiful it was.' The autumn winds rattled the window pane, as though to remind them both that Christmas wasn't all that far away and the seasons were gearing up for a change.

'I'm looking forward to seeing it.' Audrey smiled.

Veronica tried to focus on the video below, on the tree

and the green space, and the faint sounds of carols in the background. The sounds of a season she'd loved right up until her own world fell apart. Then it had only reminded her of what she'd lost, and even Layla begging her to have a tree last year hadn't worked.

'Let's go back into your Facebook, Gran, see if they've approved your joining request.' With a few taps on the keyboard, they were back there as Veronica kept her brain in gear remembering her password. She scrubbed it off the cheat sheet. 'It'll keep my mind active, having to remember it, and besides, you should never write passwords down.'

'You're right,' Audrey replied as Veronica typed in her details, and once she was into her account, the notification was already there to say her request had been accepted.

'I'm not sure I want to write anything just yet.'

'It's all totally up to you.'

But Veronica wasn't daft. She knew, like most things, the more you put into it, the more you got out of it.

'Look at this post,' she said, peering closer at the screen, 'it's from Carole, who works in the bakery, to let everyone know she's taking maternity leave. I remember her, she was always nice to me.' Veronica could also remember the panic attack one morning out front and Carole taking her home on her arm, shutting up shop to do so, thinking not of herself but of someone else. She'd been kind that day and Veronica had never forgotten it. 'I'm going to send my best wishes.'

'Go for it!'

Veronica typed a short message into the comments, wishing Carole well, saying she hoped to hear news of the addition to her family soon.

Audrey beamed. 'See, you're getting to know your local community already. And you met Tanya today too, she's local, so that's someone else. Gran, I do believe you're really doing this.'

Veronica supposed that in a weird way, she actually was.

Veronica woke before midnight needing the loo. It must have been all the tea she and Audrey got through yesterday evening as they chatted and then had another play with Facebook. Sam was out at the pub with Clare, Layla would've been in bed hours ago, and she and Audrey had sat in the study and looked at the various social media – some odd, some useful. There were even book groups she could join and talk about current reads. Veronica saw she could be a part of something more without having to think about leaving the house. She wasn't sure she would ever be ready for that, but Veronica knew that's what Audrey was trying for and she wasn't about to disappoint her granddaughter by telling her it might never happen.

Veronica was heading back to her room when she noticed a light coming from downstairs. She realised Sam must be home and when she reached the kitchen, her daughter was standing at the sink facing the window. And if Veronica wasn't mistaken, she was crying.

'Sam?' she said softly so as not to wake Audrey. 'Sam, what's happened?'

Sam had her back to her, her blonde hair pinned up with wet strands dangling down, the bunched collar of her snuggly dressing gown wrapped around her neck. 'I'm losing her, Mum.'

'Whatever are you talking about? Losing who?' She

wanted to hug her close, comfort her, but they had never been physically affectionate, not since Sam was six or seven and she'd needed her mother's loving arms around her. Then her father's arms had taken their place and that was that.

'I'm losing Audrey.'

Sam turned and, after wiping away her tears, noticed the change. 'Mum, your hair . . . it's gone.'

Veronica smiled. 'It has. What do you think?'

'About time,' was all Sam said, and managed a little laugh through tears.

'Audrey did my make-up too. I'll get her to do it again sometime so you can see the finished results for yourself.'

'I'd really like that.'

'Come, sit down over here.' She led them over to the table, hoping Sam would open up to her. Her daughter didn't take much prompting.

'Audrey wants to go to New Zealand.'

'To see her dad?'

'To *live* with her dad.'

A familiar feeling of panic rose within Veronica. She couldn't let that happen, not now. She was inside, in her house, she was safe. She had to keep that in her head for Sam.

'She's never mentioned a thing to me.'

'Nor to me either. She's thrown it at me a few times in anger over the years, but I figured all kids do that, so I never took it seriously, until I found some leaflets and books in her room.' She shook her head and swore loudly. 'I've emailed Simon to ask him exactly what's going on. I need to know what plans have been made, how far they are along, what formal applications with regards to visas have been lodged.' The anger turned to tears again. 'This is all such a mess.'

Veronica handed her a tissue and waited for her to calm down. There wasn't much she could say; she knew what it felt like to lose a child, to have a distance between you that was so vast you couldn't possibly reach the other side. And when Sam's tears showed no signs of drying up, Veronica did the only thing she could think of.

She pulled Sam into a hug for the first time in years. And for once, Sam let her.

Chapter Twelve

Veronica

After breakfast the next day, the hug with Sam still at the forefront of Veronica's mind, she felt as though a warmth had wrapped comfortingly around her shoulders for the first time in years. And despite the worry over what Audrey was going to do – or, more to the point, what Simon was up to – Veronica felt as though these walls were finally filled once again with family. A real family. She'd woken this morning thinking it might have all been a dream until Sam smiled at her and said 'Good morning' in a cheery tone that suggested she'd also felt something shift the night before as she'd poured her heart out.

It was as they cleared the breakfast dishes that Sam came up with an idea that very nearly floored Veronica. Layla had just finished her piano practice, Audrey was packing her school bag and Veronica was washing up when Sam confided that the Mapleberry Mug was looking tired these days and in need of a bit of attention.

'The paint around the menu board is peeling, same with the door leading out to the kitchen, the sofas and tables all look dull and in need of a lift.'

Up until now Veronica had hardly dared to hope her daughter was becoming a part of Mapleberry, but this surely showed she was. Sam's boss had given her a lot more than a job, she'd given her friendship, another person Sam's own age, another mum to hang out with and a way to escape the four walls of the house.

'Perhaps Clare will give it a makeover in the new year,' Veronica suggested.

'Like our makeovers,' Layla chimed. She'd done her piano practice already, filling the house with tunes that these days had Audrey humming away rather than complaining.

Veronica winked at Layla. 'Yes, I suppose it is a bit.'

Sam found a plastic container to put in a couple of freshly baked chocolate chip cookies for Layla to take to school and handed a couple to Audrey to slot into her packed lunch.

'That's the thing – she wants to do a makeover, but doesn't have the money. I was thinking after I saw some of the items on the kindness calendar – helping a local, make something for someone, help with housework – that perhaps we could work together and tick off a few of those tasks.'

Layla was all ears, of course, even distracted from the heavenly scent of cookies. Veronica, never much of an actor, did her best to hide her surprise at Sam's reference to the calendar, her hands still immersed in the warm soapy water she'd used to wash one of the mugs that couldn't go in the dishwasher.

'That's a really kind idea, Mum.' Audrey was no actor either and surprise was written all over her face. If only this girl knew what her plans with her dad were doing to her mum. Would it change her mind at all?

Layla was already getting excited about the items they

could tick off the calendar, and with a promise they'd make some plans straight after school, Veronica persuaded her it was time to go. Audrey was walking her there today and the little girl couldn't be more excited, and if Veronica wasn't mistaken, Audrey seemed to enjoy being in charge of a surrogate sibling.

That evening they all sat around the table and made their plans, Sam clearly mindful of involving Audrey but trying not to boss her about. In fact, she'd let Audrey lead some of the planning. Veronica was to be in charge of knitting some new cushion covers, some in purple and others in yellow, to inject a little colour to the worn sofas at the café. Sam would go and buy the actual cushions as well as the honeysuckle paint Audrey had suggested would work with the other décor already at the café. Audrey and Layla were all set to help with the painting, so they planned to get all their homework done in good time, and Sam had somehow persuaded Clare's children to muck in after-hours the day after tomorrow.

Veronica wished she could have been at the Mapleberry Mug to help out and see the changes come to fruition, as well as to witness the look on Clare's face when she opened up the café. Well before school hours, Audrey, Sam and Layla had bundled over there together to see her reaction for themselves, and at least they'd taken plenty of photographs for Veronica.

'She was thrilled,' Sam reported the minute she returned from the café after her shift. They were having a cup of tea and Sam was putting her feet up before going back to meet Clare for a celebratory glass of wine at the pub. 'And she loved the cushion covers.'

'I'm pleased.' Veronica had knitted faster than she'd ever done before to get them all finished, but seeing the photographs of the transformation now, her handiwork on the sofas as well as the new paint on the walls around the counter, she felt a part of it all.

Sam, mug of tea clasped between her palms, smiled. 'Audrey has changed so much since she came here. That's a good thing,' she added. 'I was really proud of her last night; she was bossing Clare's kids around, even though they're a lot older, making sure it all got done and nobody cut any corners. She had one of them polishing the coffee machine until you could see your reflection in it.'

'I can well imagine she had you all organised. You should be very proud of her.'

'I am.' A look passed between them both before Sam finished her tea. 'Now, do you mind if I take over the bathroom? I want to relax before I go back out again to meet Clare.'

'Help yourself. You and Clare get on well.'

'We do – I couldn't ask for a better boss, and even though Jilly and I go way back, Clare and I seem to have really hit it off.'

'I'm pleased for you.'

Veronica sat and finished her tea as Sam went upstairs. And when Audrey finally barrelled through the door after doing homework at her friend Vicky's, she put the kettle on again and this time Veronica enjoyed the company of her granddaughter, who seemed to be blossoming right before their very eyes. And, it seemed, so was her mum.

Charlie had stopped by the house a lot before Sam came to Mapleberry, but he was around even more often these days. They were all in the hallway as he and Layla waved goodbye, Charlie talking about the café and how he'd like his regular table by the window at eleven o'clock today if Sam could possibly arrange it.

Veronica grinned as she filled the little watering can to feed the remaining houseplants in the lounge. Layla had done a few of them already after they'd finished their secret piano lesson and before her dad came over nice and early to walk her to school. Nice and early to see Sam, more like, and Veronica loved to see the pair of them getting close. He and Sam were alike in more ways than one: solo parenting, both doing right by their children and putting their own happiness second, at best. And Charlie was a far better man that Simon had ever been. Not that Simon was a bad man: he was easy on the eye, friendly enough, held down a good job, and provided for wife and daughter. Until he'd left them to run off with someone else.

When Veronica found Sam in the kitchen, her daughter had a smile that could've taken the place of the sunshine outside if it had bothered to put in an appearance today. It was one of those grim autumn mornings where the only leaves on the pavement would be damp, the wind blew sideways and any beauty of autumn colours from the vantage point in her house tended to get overlooked by miserable black clouds passing overhead.

'I'm off to work now,' Sam told her, scooping up her keys and phone.

'Enjoy your day,' Veronica said, wishing she could be a fly on the wall to see how Charlie and Sam got on at their pre-arranged rendezvous. Maybe she shouldn't call it that, but there was always hope.

Sam grinned. 'I keep forgetting you've changed your hair and then I catch sight of you and it takes me by surprise.'

'You're not the only one,' said Veronica.

'I'm pleased you did it.'

'And I'm pleased that you're pleased. And I emailed you Tanya's contact details.'

'Thanks, I'm desperate for an appointment – I'll book her in now before I go to work and hopefully get a spot before the end of the week.'

Veronica mopped up the water around the base of her spider plant on the mantelpiece and then emptied out the remains of the watering can in the kitchen. She started to flip through her recipe book to see what to cook tonight. Audrey was supposed to be helping her, so it couldn't be anything that took too much time. For once Audrey was knuckling down. This new school had clearly been a bit of a magic ingredient, that and the discussions that had seen Sam suggesting that if she did well with her GCSEs then a college course of her choice would be a lot more likely.

When she looked up as Sam came back into the room, she knew something was wrong.

'Bloody Simon,' Sam cursed.

Veronica's heart sank. 'He's got the visa, hasn't he? He's taking her away from us.' Somewhere in the mess of all of this, Audrey had become a shared entity, a part of both their lives, and Veronica would be heartbroken if she left.

Sam looked as though her mind was racing at a million miles an hour and couldn't quite let anything else into her head right now. 'What? No, no he's not.'

'Then what's the matter?'

'He hasn't put any of the wheels in motion.'

'Well, that's good, isn't it? You don't want her to go – perhaps between them they've decided it's not the best decision.'

'No, it's not that. Audrey is still looking into it, still pestering him to help her do it.' She swore again, very unladylike, but this was no time for manners. 'He wrote back to me and said he loves Audrey, but he doesn't want her to go and live with him. He says he's started a new life, he's married to someone else now and they have two kids. He says this won't work.'

'The selfish—'

'What am I going to do? I've moved heaven and earth to make sure Audrey never hated him for leaving us, never knew he'd been unfaithful, that his selfishness broke up our marriage and he never looked back. I wanted her to have a relationship with him; I didn't want to poison her mind against him. And now, now I have to tell her that her own father doesn't want her enough. This will totally crush her.'

'Why did he make her believe he did want her to join him over there? I don't understand.'

'Because that's what he does!' Sam's voice rose, taking Veronica by surprise. 'He's always the one to come out on top, I'm always the bad guy; he's been stalling all this time and now *I* have to tell her!'

Veronica's throat went dry. It was like history repeating itself, because what Sam didn't realise was that the way she'd described Simon – how he was the father who could do no wrong, the man her daughter worshipped – was a stark reminder of Veronica's own marriage. Sam had worshipped Herman till the day he died in just the same way

– but Sam had never been able to see it.

Veronica watched Sam snatch up her phone and her bag ready to bundle out the door to work before she was late. She thought again about the way she'd comforted Sam, her daughter's emotions being pulled from pillar to post at the thought of losing Audrey. She thought of how proud Sam had been of Audrey for taking charge of the Mapleberry Mug makeover, as it had been aptly named on Layla's calendar as they crossed off several tasks at once.

'Sam, listen to me.' Her voice stopped her daughter from leaving. When Sam first came back to Mapleberry, Veronica never would've dreamed of taking this tone with her, speaking up, giving advice. 'You are going to have to tell Audrey, but what we really need to do is make sure she knows how much she's loved, how much she's wanted *here*. And who knows, maybe it'll be enough to give her a reason to stay.'

And just like that, they were a team. This family might have been torn apart, but they were slowly finding a way to glue themselves back together again.

PART THREE

A Winter Wish

Chapter Thirteen

Sam

S am made herself a cup of tea and cradled it against her chest, the heat warming her through her dressing gown; her mum's old house didn't have quite the same level of insulation as she'd been used to in her previous home. It was early December, the weather had well and truly turned, and already Sam had no doubt they'd be enjoying the open fire in the lounge today. The good thing, if there was one, about her mum never leaving the house was that it was never a waste of time lighting a fire; it would be appreciated and watched over the entire day.

Winter frost set the scene in the back garden of number nine Mapleberry Lane as Sam stood looking out of the kitchen window. A dusting of white glistened on trees and shrubs when the sun shone down, and already Sam suspected it was going to be one of those beautiful crisp days you could watch for ever. A robin redbreast came to perch on the bird table, disrupting the frost, which scattered to the ground.

'Always makes me think of Christmas.' Her mum had crept downstairs so softly Sam hadn't heard her. Or maybe she'd just been in a world of her own.

'What does?'

'The robin.'

'That's right, your Christmas card every year has a robin as part of the design.' Sam watched the bird as its little head kept flicking left to right, beady eyes taking everything in and spindly legs ready to take flight whenever it liked. Her mum's cards weren't exactly the same every year, there was always some variation. Perhaps it was a robin with its breast as vibrant as the pillar box it stood on top of, or the bird was perched on a log covered in snow, or maybe it was nestled among holly and big red berries.

Her mum's celebrations of Christmas included sending cards, to whom Sam had no idea, but very little else. Or at least that's how Sam remembered it. Sam had been the one to put up the tree when her mum retreated into herself all those years ago, it had been Sam who organised presents to be around the tree so it was some semblance of normality for everyone. She had no idea what her mum did now to mark the occasion.

Her mum made a cup of tea for herself. 'Audrey won't be up for ages yet. Teenagers sleep for hours – I remember those days.'

Soon it wouldn't affect Sam quite as much because yesterday she'd finally signed on the dotted line for a one-bedroom flat. Audrey was to stay with her gran for the time being while she finished school, and although Sam had been resistant at first, she'd wondered whether a little distance between them could end up bringing them closer in the long run. Audrey had certainly seemed very happy with the idea.

'You need to tell her, Sam.'

Sam didn't need to ask what her mum was referring to.

She knew, and she'd put it off for a long while now, ever since the autumn. Her ex-husband, Simon seemed to be leaving it up to her to tell their fifteen-year-old daughter that although he had this wonderful new life in New Zealand, he didn't want her to go over there to join him. No doubt Simon was worried about what this would do to his relationship with his new wife and children, but Sam liked to think he was also concerned about Audrey. And so he should be; it was his fault she'd been so wrapped up in the idea in the first place, whether it was intentional or not. If he'd said from the start that she was better off in the UK, at least until she was much older, if he hadn't filled her head with all these images of a life that seemed out of reach, then Sam wouldn't be having this dilemma now.

'She's only just started talking to me more,' said Sam. The robin had hopped off somewhere else while she'd been distracted.

'None of this is your fault – it's Simon's.'

'You really think she'll see it that way?' Sam tipped the dregs of her tea into the sink and rinsed her cup, looking out again to see the robin this time perched on the highest point of the frosty rockery at the end of the garden. 'It's beautiful out there today.'

'It's what you might call a perfect winter's day,' said her mum. 'I can't wait for it to snow, that muffled effect I can feel even inside the house.'

Sam didn't often mention her mum's agoraphobia. She'd always known what it was; she'd covered similar topics in her degree course, as well as picking up enough from literature she'd read when she tried in vain to cope with it, at a time when all she wanted was her mother back, but understanding and sympathising was different when applying it to your own family, especially when its effect on you had been so powerful.

'How about we walk to the end of the garden together later?' Sam suggested.

Her mum hesitated. 'I'll see. Maybe.'

Sam sighed. 'I wish you'd get some help.'

'Leave it, Sam. I'm happy as I am. Content. Old.'

'You're not fooling me or anyone else.' Sam could see plenty, apart from the new hairdo – fear, worry, all etched into her expression, even when she was smiling. Sam had noticed Audrey trying to coax her gran into doing more, becoming a part of the bigger world hovering outside the doors of her home. Or were they trying to fix something that couldn't be fixed? 'I'm going to go for a long walk around to the fields today to see the big Christmas tree. I walked the other way to the community centre last night so I didn't get to see it.' There'd been no talk as yet of having a tree in the house and Sam didn't like to mention it too often.

'You'll enjoy it. I'm hoping the Facebook residents' group has lots of photos on there.'

'How are you enjoying the new group?' Audrey had got her gran involved in the online Mapleberry Village Residents Group and Veronica seemed to have got into the swing of it. 'Did you see the photos of the community mosaic wall?'

'They're impressive. I did my best to spot my crockery in pieces but . . .'

Sam smiled at her mum's little joke. The community mosaic wall now had flowers, leaves, grass, a couple of butterflies and even a gnome decorating it, making the most glorious colourful garden scene against what had once been a rather dull wall. Last night had been the grand unveiling, and although Sam hadn't got to go with Audrey, she'd seen her face through the crowds, looking on and glad to have been involved in the destruction of china, as well as adding her creative flair to some of the tallest flowers.

'The photos don't do it justice,' said Sam. 'It's wonderful, really colourful. A little bit of summer even though we're now into winter.' She almost wished she'd been in the right head space to help with it along the way, but seeing the finished results would have to be enough.

'I could easily waste a lot of time looking at everyone's posts and photos if I'm not careful,' said her mum, before Sam took her turn in the bathroom while it was free.

Sam left the house less than an hour later, bundled up in a midnight blue wool coat with a grape-coloured bobble hat and matching scarf, as well as ankle boots lined with so much fur it made her feel as though she had a pair of slippers on. The high street across the way was ready for the season. Although not lit up now, even at a distance Sam could see the lights that had been strung from lampposts; as the day went on and the sunlight faded, the darkness would give the illuminations their full effect. Shopfronts had twinkly lights around their windows and the pub in the distance had enough lights around the entrance, it would be like a beacon come nightfall. The café was kitted out for the festive season too, and along with the winter-themed menu, they had fairy lights strung along the walls, a tree in one corner with multi-coloured twinkle lights, and Christmas music played softly in the background, lulling customers into a relaxed, cosy environment they didn't want to leave. Clare had even added a deep grey sofa to one corner as well as an armchair that was a customer favourite, and Veronica had knitted some lovely charcoal cushions to go on them both. Charlie, however, always stuck to his favoured table by the window each time he came in.

The wind lay low and as Sam turned the corner towards the field – the same green where she and local kids had played rounders every summer – a big smile spread across her face. She hadn't seen the Mapleberry village tree in years. Not visible from the café when she finished work, this was her first chance to see it in all its glory since the big switch-on a few days ago. She'd heard plenty about it from those coming into the Mapleberry Mug, but seeing it for herself was something else entirely. She crossed the grass, frost crunching beneath her feet, and she put out a hand to touch the branches, just like she had when her parents, and later just her dad, had brought her here. The spiky pine needles left their scent on her gloves and put a smile on her face.

Footsteps behind her made her turn and a big smile greeted her. 'Feels like Christmas, doesn't it?' Charlie, wrapped up with his collar grazing his jaw, reached out to touch the tree himself. 'Not long until the big day.' He pushed his hands back into the pockets of his navy jacket.

'What brings you here this morning?' She watched his breath come out white against the cold air.

'I've worked overtime for a few days – this was my first chance to see the tree. And I couldn't coop myself up at home when it's such a lovely day. Look at that sky.'

'I know, that's exactly why I couldn't stay in the house any longer.' It was little moments like this that made her heart clench to know her mum only ever got to experience the changes in weather, the hopping from one season to the next, from behind glass or, at best, up to the perimeter of her house. Coming here had been a real family affair, once upon a time. 'I'm hoping for snow this year. I don't normally wish for it, when it creates havoc on the roads and getting to and from work becomes a nightmare. But this year . . .' She tilted her head back in the direction of the high street.

'You've got such a terrible commute – I don't know how you do it. I mean, the café must be all of a few hundred metres from home,' he teased.

When he stood beside her, the sleeve of his coat brushed against her arm, and even though there was too much material between them to feel much of a difference, she felt a jolt at how close he was. Charlie had certainly been a pleasant bonus when it came to starting over in Mapleberry, although for a long time Sam had been reluctant to let her feelings towards him show when she felt sure Audrey wouldn't like it. Then there was the fact she'd likely leave the area soon enough. True, she had a flat lined up now, but Audrey's feelings had to come first . . . Still, it didn't stop her enjoying his company whenever she could, appreciating the moments as they came along: the warmth of his smile, the kindness in his voice that had the power to settle her.

'I'm all for snow this year too,' he announced. 'I've got a fortnight off over Christmas. But I'm hoping for the kind of snow that keeps people indoors with their families and not on the roads, then whoever is out in the ambulance won't be as busy.'

'It must be hard when you work over Christmas. How does Layla cope?'

'She gets it, she's understanding for an eight-year-old. I try to have every other Christmas off if I can manage it, and if I'm working and we're quiet, sometimes I sneak in to say hello. I managed to pop in on her and Veronica last year.'

'She went to Mum's for Christmas?'

'I thought Veronica might have mentioned it?'

Sam shook her head. 'We've started to talk a lot more, but not about Christmas.' Her attention was drawn back to the big tree, wondering what it would look like tonight, bedecked in all its glory, lights showing off the chosen ice-pink and silver baubles, the soft pink ribbons tied to branches. 'Mum stopped celebrating Christmas properly a long time ago. Unless that's all changed.'

'I don't think it has,' Charlie confided. 'But I was stuck last year and you know Veronica, she stepped in.'

Actually Sam didn't know Veronica as a person who had ever been able to save the day, at least until now, until she and Audrey had landed themselves on her. Sam often wondered why she'd really done it. She probably could've managed with Audrey up in Cheshire, but maybe subconsciously she'd thought it time to test whether her mum could ever be a part of their lives again.

'Do you mind your mum being so close to Layla?' He must've misread her reaction, the surprise that Veronica had been able to step up and help out.

'Not at all – it's nice she has her, and you too.'

'Last Christmas Veronica did the big Christmas day dinner with pigs in blankets – I provided the food, so didn't leave her much choice – as well as a chocolate yule log Layla got to help with, so she stepped up to save the day with my daughter by letting her be as festive as she wanted to be. They watched three movies that day and Layla was as happy as ever when I collected her. I'm not sure what I would've done if your mum hadn't helped – paid through the nose for a babysitter, no doubt, and it wouldn't have been the same. Layla felt like she had family and wasn't deserted.'

'That's nice. I'm glad for Layla and for Mum.' She was beginning to see that as much as she thought she knew her mum and her ways, there was so much she still didn't understand.

'I wasn't sure what kind of neighbours I'd end up with when I moved to Mapleberry, but Veronica was a complete surprise. I hope you know that we watch out for her as though she's a part of our family.'

'I'm beginning to see that.'

'Layla hugs her all the time now.' He smiled. 'I think she was wary at first, but it was always going to happen sooner or later.' They moved away from the tree when others came to admire it and they wanted their conversation to remain private. 'May I ask why your mum doesn't celebrate Christmas? She sends cards but other than that, I don't think she does anything.'

'It's kind of a long story.'

'Layla is at a friend's house for lunch so I'm free all day. How about we head to the café and get ourselves warm?' He was smiling at her in the way he always did, the way that somehow told Sam he wouldn't judge, he'd listen, he'd understand.

Clare would love that; she was forever teasing Sam about how often Charlie came to the café, most likely so he could see her. But Clare wasn't working today.

'You're on. We've just started serving festive treats that are ridiculously bad for the waistline.'

'In that case, show me the way!'

Inside the Mapleberry Mug, they sat at Charlie's usual table. While Sam hung her coat on the back of the chair, he went up to the counter to order two hazelnut hot chocolates.

'I had them put the whipped cream in a dish on the side,' he said when he came back with the tray. 'Might be a bit sickly otherwise.' He took off his layers and they settled in by the window, the low hum of conversation blanketing the café so they could talk discreetly.

It was time for Sam to make an admission. 'I'm pleased you and Layla are so close to Mum,' she began. 'We rarely talked before I sent Audrey down here, and when I realised she wasn't as alone as I'd first thought, it made me feel less of a terrible daughter. What?' She met his gaze. 'Surely you're not going to claim otherwise. You knew I existed, right? You must have had an opinion.'

'I tried to not think anything,' he replied, diplomatic as ever. 'Veronica never said a word against you. But she did mention you from time to time. She never went into detail but I've been around enough to know that what we see on the surface isn't necessarily what we should believe.'

'Well, Layla is very good for her,' said Sam.

'And so is Audrey.'

'I don't think that was the case when Audrey first hurtled her way into Mapleberry. Off my hands, but into Mum's, and it sounds as though sparks really did fly.' She added a dollop of the cream and stirred it through her hot chocolate, making it a little richer but not too sickly.

'It was hard for them both at the start, I believe – Layla filled me in on a few confrontations. But Audrey soon began to slot in. And over time Layla and I came to think of Veronica's home as having two people living in it rather than just one.'

'Does Layla ask about Mum's problems?'

'The agoraphobia? Layla and I talked about it from the start. You know what kids are like, she just asked me outright: "Why doesn't Veronica ever leave her house?" We talked about anxiety, the feeling Layla gets when she has to stand up in front of the class and talk out loud. She's always a little afraid of that. I told her it was like that except on a much bigger scale and it makes Veronica scared to even leave her own house. Layla got upset at the thought of Veronica being frightened, but I think she's made it her mission to look after her.'

'You must think I'm ten times worse, if an eight-year-old gets it and sticks around.'

When he reached out and his fingers rested on top of hers, she wanted to savour his touch, something she hadn't felt in a very long time.

'Sam, I don't think it's that simple. You and your mum have a history; Layla and I don't have anything other than what we have now. We all went into this friendship knowing the boundaries from the start. Believe me when I say: nobody is judging you.'

Sam wished he hadn't taken his hand away. She wondered, did her body language give the game away and show she was fast developing feelings for him?

She stirred her hazelnut hot chocolate and added in more cream she wasn't sure she even wanted. 'Seeing the village tree today . . . Well, it makes me even more sad that

Mum never sees it. She used to love it. The Mapleberry Village Big Switch-On was the title on the leaflet that sailed through the door every winter around this time of year. We'd wrap up warm, take our torches to find our way across the field and wait for the crowds to applaud as the lights reached all the way up into the sky.'

'When did she stop going?'

'I'm not completely sure what year it was, but I remember her refusing to put on her coat, let alone go outside. She sat in her favourite chair, the one she sits in now with the worn upholstery, and she wouldn't budge. I cried all the way to the field. I was devastated. I didn't understand how she couldn't, just for one night, put her worries aside and do it for me. I don't think she ever went again.' And although Charlie was easy to talk to, Sam wasn't about to tell him the unforgiveable turning point that her mum reached.

'Remember I'm here whenever you need to talk, Sam.' There was a softness to his voice that made her relax in his company. It was all she needed to hear in that moment.

'After the year Mum didn't come to see the tree, Christmas was different. There was a sadness hanging over us, which always started with her absence at the village tree-lighting ceremony. Sometimes I'd look at her and I'd feel so angry. I wanted answers, I wanted to know why she stopped coming with us to an event she looked forward to all year, why she couldn't bring herself to be a part of the audience at my school performances, what her reasons were for leaving her job as a nurse that she loved. She was a shadow of the woman I knew she could be.' Sam's eyes filled with tears as it all poured out. Most of all she'd wanted to yell at her mum for letting her blow their family apart. 'I'm sorry to lay all this on you. Not that I've been able to tell you much.'

'Sam, did you ever talk to anyone the way you're talking now? To Audrey?' She shook her head. 'How about with your ex-husband?'

She harrumphed. 'Definitely not. Simon met Mum a few times but he joined the many people who thought Mum was an oddball. He never said so, he held his tongue, but I could tell he wanted distance between us all. I think if he'd been on board then I might have made more effort when Audrey was little. I don't blame him for it, I'm a big girl and should've made the decision for myself, but I suppose he gave me an out. I had a new life and it was a hell of a lot easier than the one I'd had with Mum.'

'What made you ask for Veronica's help with Audrey?'

'I had no idea what else to do, no clue how to stop Audrey and I becoming as estranged as Mum and I. I needed to get Audrey away from that school; she was getting into trouble and I knew a different place could be the answer, even if it was only temporary. And part of me needed to see whether Mum and I could salvage our relationship.'

'And have you?'

She smiled gently. 'I think we're starting to make tracks, but it's a long road. I'd always felt that she was more of a burden than anything else. Maybe deep down I wanted to give Mum one last chance to prove that she could be the parent I'd always needed. That sounds cruel, doesn't it?'

He took her hand again, and her stomach did a little flip.

'Not at all. And for what it's worth, I think you did the right thing. I've noticed a change in Veronica since

Audrey came along, and even more so since you arrived. Maybe Veronica also saw it as a chance to reconnect with you.'

'I feel like I'm getting to know Mum all over again. Does that make sense?'

'Totally, and you're lucky, you get a second chance. I never got on with my dad and not making peace with him before he died still haunts me.'

'I'm sorry.'

He shrugged. 'It is what it is, but I'm glad when I see people like you doing their best to work through it before it's too late.'

Too late. Two little words that meant so much. Sam didn't want to be too late to make things right with her mum and she didn't want to be too late to sort out her relationship with her daughter either. Because being here in Mapleberry, she knew family was the most important thing on her agenda right now.

Charlie lightened the conversation by asking about Sam's new flat, her moving plans for the New Year. And when they made their way back towards Mapleberry Lane, Sam wasn't sure but she thought she felt Charlie's fingertips brush against her own as they walked, as though they both had their hands out of their pockets on purpose.

'Mum,' a voice called from across the road. Audrey had been sitting on the swings and came across as they arrived back at the house. 'Where've you been?'

'I went to see the tree, bumped into Charlie, and we went for a coffee.' It was like the roles had been reversed: daughter quizzing, mother supplying answers.

Disappointed, Audrey told her, 'I was going to see the tree but thought I'd wait until dark.'

I haven't seen December's yet – Layla's bringing it later.' Her mum frowned. 'I feel we'll be leaving Layla out if it's something us three do together.'

'Then we'll buy four gifts,' said Sam simply. 'Audrey and I will get two each, then you and Layla can be in charge of wrapping. She'll love it. I'll get some of that gorgeous green velvety ribbon and silver paper you used to love. Layla will enjoy making the bows and dressing the gifts up.'

'You remember my colours?' Her mum smiled.

'Of course I do.' Years ago, when she still loved Christmas, Her mum had insisted that all gifts came in silver paper and green velvet bows. It didn't matter whether you were getting a train set, a Barbie doll or a football, it would be wrapped the same way.

Sam left Audrey and her mum looking at some of the shopping websites for ideas, making a list of possible gifts, and when Sam went into the kitchen to get a start on making some sandwiches for lunch before she was tempted to cut a big chunk of tea loaf, she thought about her chat with Charlie. He'd been right when he said her mum was changing as people came into her life. All of them in their own way were giving her life more meaning, enriching her limited world. And whether it was always set to be this way or whether they could make a difference, as long as they were helping in some way, Sam knew that was what really mattered.

Chapter Fourteen

Veronica

Veronica was always eager to be a part of the Kindness Club, but nothing was quite as exciting as when Layla brought around a new calendar to show her, unveiling the new month's tasks. When Layla had informed her that a friend would have to complete tasks alongside her and that she wanted that friend to be Veronica, it had sent Veronica into a mini-panic. She understood the purpose – it would spread more kindness that way – but when she couldn't leave the house it made things difficult. At least it had until she, Layla and Audrey had come up with the solution of The Kindness Club on Mapleberry Lane. Not only would it solve the problem of her not leaving the house, but it also fulfilled one of the tasks: 'Join a club'. And when she'd marked off that item, Veronica had felt a shift. And she knew what that shift was now – it was something verging on happiness.

What Veronica hadn't realised that afternoon as they unrolled December's calendar was quite how many Christmas-themed tasks it would include. Layla's teacher's enthusiasm seemed to mount every time the months flipped, but Veronica should've known. December always made people overexcited; it was the time to be over the top, the season of joy, goodwill, magic and all of the other feelings it evoked. She'd had Christmases like that once, but ever since she failed to bring the simple traditions to her own family, she'd shied away from the whole debacle, keeping only the habitual sending of cards. Christmas had never, and would never, be the same, and celebrating always felt like a bit of a betrayal. Why should she feel so happy when she'd made others' lives a misery? Not only did she not want to celebrate Christmas, Veronica didn't think she deserved to. Last year had been hard enough, having Christmas lunch with Layla while she minded her for her dad. But she loved the little girl's company, and although Veronica hadn't had a tree or decorations, Layla had brought Christmas into this house simply with her personality and enthusiasm. There was also Audrey to think of now, a teen who perhaps didn't have the excitement of Father Christmas anymore, but a girl who deserved Christmas done right. Veronica only hoped it wouldn't all get too much. The last thing she ever wanted was for Audrey or Layla, or Charlie for that matter, to see her have a panic attack, to see her at her worst. She never wanted to frighten away the friends who'd come to mean so much.

Layla sat on the lounge carpet at Veronica's and rushed through reading the calendar tasks, gabbling on at a rate of knots as she went off at tangents talking about how all three of them could accomplish what was required of them. Veronica hadn't read many of the words on the calendar yet, she was still looking at tomorrow's square. The words 'Put up your tree' stared back at her. It was years since she'd had one inside her house, the smell drifting up the stairs in the cold morning air as she woke.

'You don't have to go out to get one,' said Layla, following Veronica's eyeline and knowing what she was staring at.

'No, I don't.'

'Come on, Gran,' Audrey pleaded. 'I get why you never had one when you lived on your own, but now we're here it's different, right?'

So Sam really had never told her why it was that Veronica gave up on Christmas as well as so many other things. She supposed for that she should be grateful. She sneaked a look at Sam, who gave a tentative smile in return.

'I don't like needles in the carpet, they hang around for ever,' she told them all. 'And they smell.'

'How can you not like the smell, Veronica?' Layla looked so disappointed, and for a moment Veronica wanted to curse that calendar for putting her in an impossible position. She'd a good mind to give this Mrs Haines a call and ask her why she was insisting on putting others through this rigmarole, making them alter their lives for a blessed calendar.

'Mum, why don't you get a tree?' Sam came to her side. 'I'd like to see one in the lounge again.' A look passed between them, a shared hope that they could come out the other side after all that had happened since Sam was little.

Maybe it was time to step up, do this for everyone else, not herself. 'I suppose I could get a small one.'

Sam put a hand on her shoulder. 'The scouts have a lot outside the village hall – how about I go down there, take a look and see what I can get?'

'Would you?'

Sam looked at Audrey and Layla. 'You know, I'm only doing this if you let me into your club.'

Audrey began to laugh and suddenly stopped. 'Oh, you're serious.'

'Of course I'm serious.'

Veronica had a sneaky suspicion Sam was doing it to be as much of a part of Audrey's life as she could. After all, this was the last month of them living under the same roof and it would bring them together without being overwhelming. She had to hand it to her daughter for never giving up. She wished she'd had the same strength when she'd needed it the most.

'We'll have to take a vote, Sam,' she said. 'All those in favour, raise your hand.'

Layla's shot up. Audrey lifted hers, though she still seemed surprised her mum wanted to be a part of this, and Veronica was, of course, in favour.

'Well, Sam, I'm happy to declare you a formal member of The Kindness Club on Mapleberry Lane.'

'And I'm honoured to be a part of it.'

Layla jumped up from her seated position. 'You need to do the promise,' she insisted, gathering all four of them into a circle and making them position their right hand at their temple, thumb and little fingers meeting to make a salute sign. Veronica didn't miss the wobble of amusement in Sam's voice as she was required to take the same pledge all three of them had taken back in the autumn, promising her allegiance to the Kindness Club.

'You can help me walk Penny Croft's dog next time, if you like,' said Layla the second Sam had been sworn in. 'At the end of November my task was to offer to walk a neighbour's dog and hers is huge.' She winked at Sam. 'You know what they say . . . big dog . . .' To Sam's questioning glance, she finished: ' . . . big poo.'

'Well, as appealing as that sounds, Layla, I'm hoping my club duties avoid anything poo-related. I'll head off now and choose us a tree.'

'Thanks, love.' The words were out before Veronica thought about them. It was many years since she'd used that phrase.

Sam froze in the doorway of the lounge until she remembered the mission she was on, bundled herself up again and ventured out.

She was back less than an hour later. 'Sorted,' she said, once she'd taken her boots off. 'One Christmas tree ordered, to be delivered tomorrow around four o'clock.'

Audrey clapped her hands together. 'Now it's feeling like it's almost Christmas. And Mum, Layla has something for you.'

Layla held out a round disc covered in plastic. 'I made these with my badge maker. If you're in our club, you have to wear it to every meeting.' All three of them already had their badges on, although Layla had made the rule only moments ago.

Sam pinned the badge to her top and Layla took charge of the meeting by handing Sam a purple pen. 'This is your colour. We all have one so that when we cross out items we know who has done them.'

Veronica didn't miss the amused edge to Sam's serious expression as she asked Layla to explain the colour scheme. She was humouring the little girl, involving her in their family, and although Veronica knew she'd done a lot of things wrong over the years, she also knew she must have done something right with Sam because she was a beautiful person inside and out. Sometimes she just didn't realise.

Layla held one end of the kindness calendar and, with it unrolled, Audrey held the other as they went through the tasks. One day had 'Make a gift for someone in need', so they'd covered that with the wishing tree idea they'd discussed earlier, and Layla was already happy she'd get to wrap the presents.

'"Bake a treat for the postman",' Sam read out. 'That's easy. Mum, you're the best baker in Mapleberry.'

'I don't know about that, and remember, you all have to help.'

'We'll bake together,' said Sam, surprising everyone, even herself by the looks of things.

It was many, many years since Sam had stood at her side in the kitchen and helped her mix a batter, ice a cake or weigh out ingredients to come up with something delicious. But if she was willing to give it a go, so was Veronica.

Veronica took a deep breath. She wondered if she closed her eyes for too long, would this all disappear? It had been such a quiet house before, with loneliness soaking into the walls until Layla, Audrey and Sam had come along.

Veronica needed a focus and turned her attention back to the calendar. 'I was looking at that same square earlier and I have a better idea. I was on the Mapleberry Village Facebook group this morning and someone was moaning away about the bin men, how they don't always come on the right day, having a good old go at them, he was.'

'You're thinking we bake him poisonous muffins?' Audrey suggested.

Veronica loved that her granddaughter had developed a sense of humour in her time here. 'Of course not. But I was thinking, postmen always get thanks, I've left biscuits for mine before now, but the bin men get nothing but grief and garbage. Let's bake something for them too. And you can add it on the calendar in one of the free squares, although there aren't many this month.'

'Your teacher is very enthusiastic,' Sam remarked. She took a pen and wrote it into one of the free squares.

Veronica noticed a look between Layla and Audrey, but then they both agreed it was a fine suggestion. They'd make Veronica's legendary brownies with the white chocolate chips and box up a few batches as there were a number of men who came each week on the various bin trucks.

'You might have to get up a bit earlier,' she teased Audrey, 'they usually come before noon.'

'Very funny. I'll set my alarm on bin day, don't you worry.'

'I'll get all the ingredients for the brownies, Mum, if you could leave me a list,' said Sam.

'I'll be at school when they come,' Layla complained.

'Doesn't matter,' said Veronica, 'you'll be making them and boxing them up so you've played your part.' She patted the little girl's hand. 'Now, how about we have your piano lesson before your dad turns up to get you? You need to practise for those carols, remember.'

Sam stayed in the lounge to read her book and Audrey headed out to see friends, meeting an approving look from her mum. Veronica knew what it was like. When your child was happy, part of you couldn't help but be content. Despite any other problems, that one simple thing always had the power to ground you and make you realise things weren't so bad.

Veronica went into the study. 'Remember your posture,' she prompted Layla, who was sitting on the piano stool. Layla immediately sat up a little straighter. 'Let your arms relax and have freedom, put all the weight into your fingers.' She wasn't sure Layla really got what she meant but Veronica could feel in her mind what it was like to play the piano. She sneaked in here sometimes when Sam and Audrey were out; it was an escape right here in her house that she hadn't realised she needed until Layla got her playing again.

Layla had four Christmas carols in her repertoire and was improving each time she practised. One of the items on the calendar this month, Veronica had been delighted to see, was a simple: 'Do something special for someone' – and the carol concert for Charlie would mean they could all play a part. Veronica was coaching, Layla was the performer ready to put a smile on her dad's face, Audrey would make refreshments for the evening and Sam would be taking photographs that Layla could show off to all her classmates.

Charlie collected Layla an hour later and Veronica started preparations for dinner. She loved cooking for people, but over the last month they'd drawn up a bit of a rota so Audrey and Sam could help out, but the kitchen was still Veronica's domain and where she felt comfortable.

Sam appeared beside her, book still in her hand. She stretched languorously after sitting in the same position so long to read. 'What's on the menu tonight?' Her reading glasses suited her: chunky dark frames that contrasted with her thick blonde hair.

Veronica tore off leaves from a cauliflower and discarded them in a pile for the compost. 'Cauliflower cheese. Don't tell me you've gone off it,' she said when she caught Sam's look.

'I love it. The look is because in all these years I've never been able to make it quite like yours, no matter how hard I tried.'

'What cheese did you use?'

'Vintage cheddar. I swore that was what we'd had here too.'

'Full-fat cheddar?'

'Low fat,' Sam confessed. 'Is that where I went wrong?'

Veronica had seen Sam's lean stomach when she stretched a moment ago, her pale pink shirt riding up to show her skin.

'This is a good cauliflower cheese recipe, but it's not exactly healthy,' she confessed. 'Well, apart from the high vegetable content, of course. My recipe uses full-fat cheddar, double cream and whole milk.'

Sam whistled through her teeth. 'I won't fit into any of my clothes if I eat too much of that.'

'Should I do something else? Maybe cauliflower curry?'

'No! Not a chance.'

Veronica glowed inwardly. This had been Sam's go-to dinner when she was in primary school. 'I've got some ciabatta to cut up to go with it too.'

'Careful, Mum, or I may end up coming back for dinner even when I move out.'

Veronica daren't look at her daughter because she hoped for nothing less.

Dinner lived up to expectations just as Veronica had hoped it would. The cauliflower cheese was creamy, golden-topped and oozing with cheesy goodness. And Audrey informed her that they would be having that again and she'd be buying the cauliflower too. When Veronica told her that Layla and Charlie had grown cauliflowers in their veggie patch and they tasted even better, Audrey's only question had been whether Gran would start her own veggie patch here.

'She's so much happier, don't you think?' Sam asked when Audrey left them to it so she could go upstairs and FaceTime Sid.

Veronica piled her plate on top of Sam's, putting the cutlery on top and doing the same with Audrey's, before taking them all over to the sink. Sam brought the remains of the cauliflower cheese that would keep in the fridge until tomorrow. They could all fight over who got it for lunch.

'The girl who landed on my doorstep in the summer would never have been interested in cultivating vegetables.'

Sam laughed. 'Don't I know it. Coming here has been good for her, Mum. It's more laidback being in a village; she had space she'd never have had at home and that alone has helped her more than I even thought it would.'

'It's partly your doing, you know. This isn't only because Audrey came here.'

'It's a very large part of it,' Sam insisted.

'It's also your doing because you recognised she needed something and you made a decision. You're a good parent, Sam.'

'I'm not sure about that. I haven't told her about Simon and what he said – that's not exactly exemplary parenting.'

'That ex-husband of yours has made his mess and expects someone else – you – to clear it up. That's not on.'

Over time, since Sam had arrived in Mapleberry, she and Veronica were extending their conversations. Veronica was no longer quite as hesitant around her daughter and it worked both ways. There was a time Veronica wouldn't have dared to share her opinion, particularly when it came to Sam's life or anybody in it.

'It's not on, but I do have to be the one to tell her. I just need to find the right time. She's so happy here at the moment, being part of this club you all started. I want to thank this teacher of Layla's – I hope she realises the magic she's worked for us!'

'Hopefully for a lot of other families too.'

'Let's hope so.' Sam filled the sink with soapy water to wash the pans that wouldn't fit in the dishwasher.

'Audrey is so kind and patient with Layla. And that is down to you, Sam, not anybody else. She's been brought up properly. She knows right from wrong.' When Sam didn't look so sure, she added, 'I don't mean all of the time, no child does, they test the boundaries. But Audrey's heart is in the right place and, if you're patient, she'll see the truth in time.'

'The truth about Simon?'

Veronica paused, putting down the cloth she'd used to wipe the cooker. The cauliflower's overzealous boiling had left remnants on the flat surface of the induction hob but they came off easily enough. 'Yes, but not only about him as a person, I'm talking about you and him as a married couple, as her parents. She'll see that there are always two sides.'

Sam seemed to be thinking hard about what she was saying and, as Veronica took out the bin from beneath the sink and twisted the top of the liner into a knot, she said, 'Are you talking about me and Simon, or you and Dad?'

'I was referring to you and Simon,' Veronica explained, 'but also to me and your dad.' She hesitated. It felt wrong to speak ill of the dead. But he was gone and she was here, and there was nobody else who could let Sam know what it had been like for her. 'You worshipped him, he could do no wrong in your eyes.' Veronica looked directly at her daughter. She never would've done when Sam first arrived, she'd avoided eye contact, proper conversation; she was so worried that any confrontation would be the last of it and *poof*, loved ones would be gone from her life for ever. But having her and Audrey here, spending time with Layla, having more of a focus with this calendar business and a life on social media, had started to make Veronica feel brave.

Last night she had even put her first post up in the residents' Facebook group, a yule log recipe that she'd had for years and made tweaks to – instead of having a smooth creamy filling, she added some chocolate chunks to it for texture and surprise, rather than only using a fork to create the log markings. She did this but also added holly and ivy made out of fondant at one end. She'd become absorbed in the conversations on other Facebook posts where people were sharing table-decorating ideas, favourite recipes, techniques for cooking a turkey. She'd leapt right in and used other peoples' posts to model hers on so she knew what to say, what not to. And when she'd pressed enter she'd felt nervous but excited, connecting with people outside of this house for the first time in years. She'd already had thirty-three likes and eight comments – people were talking to each other, and they were talking to her!

'Leave those pans, Sam, I'll wash up.' Veronica's tone was so firm that Sam took the hint and stepped back from the sink.

This enormous upheaval in Veronica's life – Audrey coming, and then Sam – had been the best possible thing, and she'd welcomed it! But right now, so close to sharing all her feelings with her daughter, she needed a moment to gather herself. And the washing up, the wiping down surfaces and putting utensils away was the normality she needed.

Sam left her to it and after Veronica cleared the kitchen, put all the big pots and pans away and set the dishwasher to take care of the rest, she got her knitting bag from where it lived in the corner of the lounge and sat down in her favourite chair. She had a feeling she wouldn't be disturbed for the rest of the evening. She'd already finished knitting a rich plum jumper for herself and in the same wool she was about to make a start on a hat for Layla. Layla loved wearing bright colours; her dark ginger hair suited her for that very reason.

Veronica got out her circular needles, tied a slip knot in the wool at one end and knitted eighty-eight stitches. She made sure they weren't twisted, used a safety pin to mark the beginning of each subsequent round, and then she was off. It was knit one, purl one, and the therapeutic clickety-clack of the needles let her mind drift. Luckily for her, despite her lack of outside life, her body didn't seem too troubled by the experience. So many others her age had arthritis; she'd watched a program about it and it could affect the hands and fingers, but Veronica was thankful hers seemed to be working as deftly as they always had.

As she knitted, Veronica's mind flitted to her new-found group on Facebook. She enjoyed the interaction from behind the screen, it didn't make her feel panicky at all, and there was one member of the group in particular who had caught her interest. Morris Alby was the name he went by and he'd not just 'liked' her post about the yule log, he'd 'loved' her post. He'd written a whole paragraph about his lack of culinary skills, including amusing anecdotes such as the time he left giblets in the chicken, when he misread how much flour to use in pancake batter and ended up with something he could've used to wallpaper his living room, and the time he left some of the film from the packaging on his new frying pan and ruined both his dinner and the vessel. Morris was talkative, but he wasn't one of those moaners. Veronica had sniffed a few of those out fairly quickly, the kind of people who posted a complaint rather than something positive, and then when others joined in, they replied with more and more whinging and whining. It was sometimes entertaining to read, she had to admit, but Morris's comments were much more interesting.

In fact, Morris was part of what Veronica liked to refer to as her spin-off group on Facebook. There were just four members – Veronica, Morris, Bridget and June – all roughly the same age and, as they'd realised from reading each other's posts, all interested in the same topics, like cooking, gardening, quiz shows on the television and the odd film. Slowly Veronica was finding connections outside of her own home. She smiled to herself – this wasn't just something she could mark off on the kindness calendar, it was something she could keep for herself.

'Nice colour, Gran.' It was Audrey, coming downstairs to make some toast, as she often did. Her teenage body seemed to need the fuel at all hours of the day and evening, and Veronica had got used to her appearing just when she thought the house was quiet.

'What are you watching?' Audrey stood in the doorway waiting for the toaster to pop up.

'I'm knitting, waiting for something good to come on.' It sounded better than admitting she enjoyed the television for the noise, the company. On the screen was a documentary about dairy farming, probably quite interesting if she hadn't been daydreaming as she knitted. She'd not needed background noise quite so much lately, what with her newly discovered social media outlet, as well as two others in the house and Layla and Charlie's visits, but it was part of her norm, part of what calmed her, especially after her earlier conversation with Sam when she'd almost laid out all the truths, told Sam exactly how much help her father had been to her over the years when her problems felt insurmountable.

'Mind if I eat this upstairs?' Audrey asked when she'd buttered her toast and slathered it in marmalade.

'Go on.' She smiled. She'd spent too long living by her own rules that even she was tired of them. What was the worst that could happen? A few crumbs dropped or a splodge of butter if Audrey wasn't careful. It didn't really matter, did it?

'Thanks, Gran, you're the best.' And she came right over and kissed her on the cheek, taking Veronica quite by surprise. 'I said I'd FaceTime Sid again – he's got a date and I need to hear how it went.'

Audrey swept out of the room, leaving Veronica wondering what had just happened. Audrey was blossoming before her very eyes, becoming chattier as time went on. Yesterday she'd told Veronica how keen she was on this boy Alex, who had apparently picked up her textbooks for her the other day when she dropped them in the corridor in a rush to get to her next lesson. Veronica had wondered whether soon enough her granddaughter would have her first date with this boy. He certainly put a smile on Audrey's face, and smiling was something Audrey seemed to be doing a lot more of these days.

Veronica laid down her knitting, too distracted to carry on. There was a distant murmur from upstairs in Audrey's bedroom, so she assumed she'd managed to contact Sid. It was good she had a friend. She knew Sam hadn't been keen on the boy but she now suspected, like her, Sam was pleased Audrey had people on her side. And she was often out too, always going for coffee or to the movies with a group of others.

The television still didn't have much to choose from after Veronica flipped through the channels, so she picked up her laptop from the study and brought it in so she could log on to the Facebook group. She started with the residents' main group and replied to comments on her yule log recipe about the strength of chocolate she used, whether she'd tried fresh cream in the centre. Someone else had shared a recipe for rum truffles and Veronica copied it down so she could give it a go. She went from there into the closed group, where Bridget was asking whether anybody knew someone who could fix up her shed come the spring. Veronica recommended her gardener, Trevor, and it led to all four of them sharing photographs of their gardens, which they agreed would be riots of colour in the right season. None of them wanted to rush it, but they were starting to form a real friendship, and Veronica felt her happiest in this little group. Could it be a tiny slice of a new beginning?

Audrey came back downstairs and washed her plate, as the dishwasher was full. When she first arrived in the summer she would've left it for Veronica, as well as the butter out on the side, and a used knife on the benchtop. But she was a pleasure to be around these days.

Veronica was about to reply to June's query in their closed group about making scones when Audrey peered over her shoulder. 'You have a message.'

'Do I?'

Audrey pointed to a symbol at the top of the screen with a funny squiggle in the middle. 'Click on that one.'

Veronica did as she was told.

'It's from Morris.' Audrey grinned, nudging her. 'Is he in the secret group?'

'Closed group, and yes, he's a member. All very above board.'

'You know what you should do?' By Audrey's expression Veronica could sense a suggestion coming her way, but then Audrey had run up the stairs and come back with her phone. 'We should totally load up the photograph of you with your hair and make-up all done, the one I took after the makeover.'

'For what reason?' Veronica saw the photo, it was a good one, but she much preferred the incognito approach.

'Put it on your profile picture so people know who you are.'

'I'm not sure I like that idea.'

'Why not? I bet the others in the group have all got a photograph.'

'That's true.' She wanted to read Morris's message but she'd gone back into the group instead while Audrey was here. 'How would I do it?'

'Would you like me to?' Audrey offered.

When Veronica nodded, Audrey snatched the chance before she changed her mind, connected up a cable, got the photograph and, just like that, there was her photograph next to her name on Facebook. It felt adventurous, new, an exciting part of her life that had been out of bounds until now.

'You reply to Morris.' Audrey winked. 'See you in the morning, Gran.'

Veronica didn't have much of a rebuke to her granddaughter's teasing, so with the television for company, she clicked on the message symbol to see what Morris had to say for himself.

She ended up conversing with him for well over an hour. She'd had her computer on her lap so long it made her hot, and eventually she'd had to move over to the kitchen table. She'd looked at his picture, as she was sure he had seen hers. At her age you couldn't beat around the bush, so she'd asked him outright how old he was. Seventy-four, he'd told her, and she wasn't surprised when her stomach did a little flip, a jolt that told her she might be seventy-one and confined to this house, but she wasn't dead yet.

They talked more about cooking, gardening, grandchildren, and how the reduction in bus services around Mapleberry meant he didn't get to see family as often as he would like. He'd always loved to drive but got rid of his car when it became too expensive to use for only a quick journey to the shops or to see his only son and his family. Instead he'd used the money to install a wonderful summer house at the foot of his garden. When Veronica asked where he lived, it turned out he wasn't all that far away. He was on Applecroft Lane, which ran on past the field with the enormous Christmas tree. He had a hundred-foot garden – he'd accidentally pressed the return button after saying 'I've got a hundred foot' and Veronica had collapsed into fits of laughter. He'd picked up on his mistake and said, 'Bet you wondered what I was going to write then.'

Veronica told Morris all about the kindness calendar Layla had introduced to them. He told her that his grand-kids were older now but they'd once done something similar, although on a smaller scale. Morris loved the sound of the Kindness Club and Veronica was pleased he didn't ridicule it. That could've been make or break time as far as she was concerned. Herman had never laughed at her but he'd been embarrassed by her behaviour, didn't take her seriously, and she didn't think she could form a friendship with another man who thought she was less of a person if she showed weakness.

Veronica had watched programmes about how social media lulled you into a false sense of security, made you share personal details online when you wouldn't in real life, and she saw how easily it could happen. But seeing as she'd already thrown caution to the wind by being on here in the first place and sharing a photograph, and after Morris told her about a family rift he'd had with his son that went on for twelve months, the worst year of his life, she found herself confessing everything. Somehow it was easier than talking to the counsellor who'd come here several times. Perhaps it was the informality, or the shield of a computer screen, or maybe even time that had made the wounds less painful. She told him everything, all about Sam and her devotion to her father, the strain between

Sam and Audrey, and how she was doing her best to help them out. And she told him all about Herman, as well as the thing she never told anyone, the thing she hadn't even spoken to Sam about.

And she realised by the time she stole away to bed like a teenager who had broken curfew, that without leaving this house she'd managed to find a real friend.

Chapter Fifteen

Audrey

Audrey fumbled in her school bag for her key as she walked down the front path of her gran's house. She wasn't sure what had happened between her gran and her mum, but they both seemed a little odd when she came downstairs after talking to Sid yesterday. Her mum even asked how Sid was – now that was peculiar. Still, whatever was going on, Audrey decided it had to be a good thing because they didn't seem as tense around one another. And at breakfast this morning they'd been talking away with a much softer edge, moving around in a shared space as though there was no longer the force field they'd each secured around themselves.

The sweet smell of baking hit her the moment she opened the door and so did the chatter. Gran and her mum were baking brownies in the kitchen as though they were any other normal family who had their problems but put them aside, rather than two women who'd barely had much of a conversation in years.

'Are those the famous brownies?' she asked as Gran cut the moist chocolate mixture into squares. Still in the tray, they smelled rich and decadent, and Audrey's mouth was already watering.

'They are, and I'm making a lot so we can box them up and give them to the bin men, but don't worry, there's plenty for us as well. By the time you get changed these will be ready to eat. I have another four batches in the oven so this house is going to smell glorious.'

'It already does,' Mum declared.

Audrey headed off to get changed. Not only would the brownies be waiting but the Christmas tree would be arriving any second, and before that she had some Kindness Club business to get on with.

'I'll get it,' she yelled when there was a knock at the door. She knew it would be Layla, bang on time.

Layla waved down the street to her dad or Bea, whoever was in charge, to say she'd arrived safely, stepped inside and, although distracted by the sweet smells wafting towards her, handed Audrey December's kindness calendar. 'What are you going to write on it?' she asked.

'Shhh . . . I'll explain later.' Audrey called into the kitchen, 'I'm just showing Layla my new make-up,' and they trotted upstairs, shutting the door behind them.

Audrey took a pen and scribbled another task into one of the squares. 'They won't realise I've added it,' she said. 'There are so many other things squeezed in. They both just think your teacher is working you too hard.'

Layla looked at 'Take care of an animal', the latest task to be added to their kindness calendar, which would look totally different to any other kid's in the class. Good job Layla's dad wasn't overly friendly with any of the other parents. If they discussed it, he'd know something was up, and Audrey and Layla didn't want their interfering to get back to Gran. She might not appreciate it.

'Why are you adding that one? I've done dog-walking so I ticked it off a month ago.'

They sat down on her bed while Audrey explained. 'This one is for Gran. She's never had a pet, but a few times I've noticed her watching television programmes about birds in particular. When she's watching something that isn't what you would call light entertainment, she gets this look on her face.'

'Like when Dad watches Wimbledon?'

Audrey didn't really know how to answer that. 'What happens when he watches Wimbledon?'

Layla did such a frown that Audrey could totally see Charlie doing it too. 'Yeah, a bit like that,' she laughed. The kid was nothing if not perceptive. 'So animals have to be important to her, right? And she always sends Christmas cards with robin redbreasts on them.'

'She always points them out to me when they're in the garden,' said Layla, before admitting, 'she didn't like it once when I found a pretend robin in the kitchen drawer and played with it.'

'I saw her holding that thing the other day. She was looking at it like it was a precious piece of jewellery.'

Layla looked into her lap. 'I have a necklace that once belonged to my mum. If Daddy lets me look at it, I can stare at it for ever.'

'You must miss her.' And it made Audrey feel guilty for all the times she'd moaned about her own mum. As much as they clashed, she'd never want to lose her like Layla had.

'I do.' She brightened. 'When I'm eighteen I can wear the necklace.'

'Then it'll be super special.'

'Are you saying the robin is as special as my necklace?'

'I don't know – maybe.'

Gran's voice called them and the girls conspired to keep their actions with the calendar a secret. 'We'll pretend that item was on the calendar all along,' said Audrey. 'There are so many it could've easily been missed. Perhaps Gran could make a bird feeder to hang from the bird table in her garden, or she could sponsor an animal, you know, via the zoo or something.'

'Like a panda?'

'Whatever she likes,' Audrey whispered as they joined her mum and Gran in the kitchen. Mum handed a brownie on a plate to Layla and another to Audrey. Wearing an apron just like Gran, it really was the picture of domesticity. And Audrey would've loved to have known what happened to start the thaw between these two.

'The tree will be here soon,' said her mum.

'Dad will be too,' Layla added, unaware of the effect the announcement had on Audrey's mum. But Audrey hadn't missed it. She knew those signs. She reacted the same way whenever Alex was near. She got a fluttery sensation in her tummy, her mouth went dry and when he looked at her she became all clumsy. He'd said hello to her as he rocked up late to science class the other day and she'd put down her test tubes without a rack. They would've tumbled to the floor had her friend Vicky not put a hand out to stop them.

Mum put another brownie onto a plate and placed it at the table ready for Charlie. Audrey had a sneaky suspicion her peeking out of the front window now wasn't really because of her excitement to get the tree but more to do with Charlie's imminent arrival. Audrey shook her head and tucked into a second brownie Gran passed her, but not until she'd hugged Gran so tight she couldn't get away. She was glad she'd got to know her after all these years. Gran, despite her obvious problems, was someone Audrey suspected didn't fluctuate much from one day to the next. Too many people of Audrey's age were nice to you and friends with you one minute, then the next it was as though you were their arch enemy. Older people like Gran had probably seen it all before; they didn't have time for such games.

Audrey watched her mum checking her hair in the hall-way mirror. It always looked good, even when she wasn't trying; her mum was beautiful. Sometimes she wondered why her dad had ever left. She always told herself it must have been her mum being so difficult to be with, but per-haps she'd been blaming her all along for no reason at all. She was definitely trying now, and she'd never put a wedge between Audrey and her dad. As Gran and Layla didn't seem to have much problem with this newly blos-soming romance, maybe she shouldn't either. Audrey had never questioned her dad having another partner; he'd met someone else so quickly and so long ago that she'd just gone along with it. And she'd never want to protest because she wanted her dad to be in her life in whatev-er shape that took. If she started to get awkward, it might come between them and push him away. Audrey liked to think she was mature, accepting another woman into her close domain whenever she did see her dad, which wasn't often, but she knew she wasn't that grown up. Audrey had tried to chase away every man Sam had ever been in-terested in since her dad left. She'd dug in her heels, as subtly as she could, and it had worked; she'd kept her mum for herself. Audrey couldn't bear the thought of another parent starting over without her and her having to fight even more for what most kids had without even trying – unconditional love. Sometimes she thought she had it with Mum, other times it felt as though her mum was trying to mould her into someone she wasn't.

'Layla, could you please box up the brownies when they're cool enough?' Gran asked.

Layla was more than happy with her assigned role, and Audrey tried not to laugh because when she agreed, she could see Layla still had much of her brownie stuck between her teeth.

When the door went again and Sam answered it, Gran tutted good-naturedly. 'It's like Piccadilly Circus in here.'

It made Audrey smile – rather than Gran being nervous at the sound of someone coming to her home, the way she'd been the first time she peeked around the door in the summer when Audrey arrived, big suitcase in tow, she was revelling in the company now. They were making progress, Audrey was sure of it, and when she shared a smile with Layla, she wondered whether the eight-year-old had managed to pick up on the change in atmosphere too.

'Tree's here, Gran!' Audrey called when her mum and Charlie navigated the tree through the front door between them. The scouts must've handed the job over straight away.

'Honestly, you don't need to yell,' said Gran, 'but quick, tell the delivery boys to wait up, would you.'

Audrey did so and Layla appeared at the door moments later with a box of brownies only just cool enough to hand over. 'Veronica says thank you very much. Your services are appreciated. Come again next year,' she added cheerily and waved them off down the path. They were already tucking into the brownies by the time they reached the gate, unconcerned by the rain that had just begun to fall.

Audrey shut the front door. 'Gran,' she called into the kitchen, 'there won't be any brownies left for the bin men at this rate.'

'Did someone say brownies?' Charlie put a hand on his stomach.

Mum smiled. 'Don't worry, I saved you one.'

'Let me get the tree into the stand first,' he said. They'd retrieved the stand from Gran's loft last night so it had been ready and waiting all day.

'Gran, where are you?' Everyone else was in the lounge but Audrey could hear the tap running in the kitchen. 'Gran, come on, the tree is almost in position and it smells wonderful.' She went through to find her gran staring out of the back window into the garden, the crisp finish on the leaves this morning replaced by the dreary downpour.

Audrey leapt forward to turn off the taps before they had a downpour inside as well as out.

'Oh dear,' said Gran, 'I was in a world of my own.'

'The tree, Gran.' When Gran didn't move, Audrey took hold of Gran's hand and led her into the lounge, where Charlie was in fits of laughter, head stuck in the tree as he attempted to get it straight. Her mum was making a similar fool of herself until she declared it straight enough for him to fix in place, but watching the pair of them had all three onlookers laughing, even Gran, who'd taken to her favourite chair already.

'You've got some in your hair.' Charlie, out of breath,

stood up, looked down at Mum and plucked an offending portion of tree from her hair.

If Audrey ever got to flirt with Alex, she hoped they'd do it somewhere a little more private. 'Come on, Layla, want to bring the decorations down with me? They're all on the landing ready.'

Layla followed her up the stairs, tried to take one of the biggest boxes, but Audrey persuaded her to go for a smaller one. 'This one has the most delicate things inside.'

'Then I'll be very careful.' She waited for Audrey to pick up a box too. 'Veronica has funny moments,' she said. 'She had one when the tree arrived.'

'What do you mean "funny moments"?'

'Wimbledon moments.'

Audrey grinned. 'I like the way you think, kid. Let's call them Wimbledon moments, it can be our code,' she said, thinking back to their conversation about how Charlie's face changed if he was watching tennis, much like Gran's expression could change when she was watching something on the television or gazing at robins out of the window, or even like a moment ago when the tree's arrival in her house seemed to have shifted something.

'Maybe she just likes to think,' Audrey suggested. 'Perhaps she's already planning what decorations go where on the tree.' It was likely to be a whole lot more than that, she thought, but would she ever find out what it was?

When her mum first arranged for the tree to be delivered, Audrey had wondered whether this tree decorating should be just the three of them, no Charlie and no Layla. But it had been Mum who suggested they join in and Audrey agreed. Charlie and Layla had been more of a family to Gran than they had in recent years, and this was mostly about Gran and what they could do to help her. It seemed to have become an unspoken aim between them all, and one Audrey was happy to go along with.

It wasn't long before the pristine living room was awash with colour, ornaments, tinsel – mess everywhere! But when Audrey looked at Gran, she was getting into it as much as everyone else. She didn't have a lot of choice when Layla had her helping to untangle the lights. Between the pair of them, they lifted the lights over to the tree and started at the top – they needed Charlie's height to reach the very top where the angel would perch – and wound their way down to the bottom. Audrey sorted through Gran's decorations, unwrapping them from tissue paper or taking them out of bubble wrap or, in some cases, newspaper. They'd been preserved for years and most of them had fared well. Nothing was broken apart from one china bell that had a crack in the side. Gran told her to throw it out, it wasn't a particularly special ornament. But that was it when it came to getting rid of anything, despite some shockers in the collection, like a gold and jewelled swirly thing that stood out a mile, a crocheted Santa, a pottery star with a painted-on face that probably suited Halloween more than Christmas. There were plenty of nicer, classic ornaments Audrey loved, including a set of little gingerbread men, delicate silver bells tied with red bows, a couple of felt miniature Christmas stockings and half a dozen baubles, each with a different Victorian Christmas scene, all ready with delicate green wire to fix onto branches.

By the time the tree was trimmed, they were all hungry, so Audrey and her mum set off for the local fish and chip shop. They left Layla at home to box up the brownies ready to pass to the bin men tomorrow. Layla had told her teacher what they were doing and she was very impressed by the sound of the Kindness Club and their apparent 'thinking outside the square' to include bin men as well as postmen.

The scent of fish, hot potato and pie filled the lounge when Audrey and her mum returned and they all opened up their parcels onto trays on their laps. Both Audrey and her mum were astounded that they hadn't been ushered over to the table; Gran never liked food eaten anywhere other than the kitchen or at the table, and although Audrey had got away with snacks in her bedroom, meal-times were totally different.

'Can we turn off the lights?' Layla asked. 'We'll eat by the lights of the tree and nothing else.'

Gran even agreed to that, and as Charlie turned off the main lights in the room, she contentedly sat in her chair, enjoying the piece of fish in its golden batter. Mum perched on the hearth beside Gran's chair and it reminded Audrey of the way she'd liked to sit at her dad's feet on a Sunday morning when she was little. He'd read the paper on his lap while she watched cartoons, and as long as she knew he was there beside her, she was happy.

'I can't see what colour my sauce is,' Layla declared.

'You know it's red,' Charlie told her. 'We can't put the lights on, it'll ruin the atmosphere. And besides, it was your choice, remember.'

As they finished their food parcels, slowing towards the end given the enormous portions, Layla mentioned the Mapleberry village tree again. 'It looks so good all lit up, Veronica. You should see it.'

'Plenty of folks sharing it on the village Facebook group page. One of my new online friends put up a video of it too, although she wasn't too good at holding her hands steady – I think I saw more of people's coats than the tree itself.'

'Can we go tonight, Daddy? Please? Audrey said she was going with her mum.'

Charlie and Mum exchanged a look. 'We don't have to do it tonight.'

Gran picked up on the subtext immediately. 'I'll be right here when you all get back. I'm too full to even get up so I'm going to enjoy some peace and quiet for a while.'

'Are you sure, Gran?' Audrey asked, as twenty minutes later the others were bundling into their coats, gloves and scarves.

'Very sure. You lot go, you'll enjoy it. I've got my knitting to work on.'

Layla started to ask what she was working on and Audrey sensed the next question would likely be whether she could see it, so she encouraged her out of the door after her mum and Charlie.

The rain had eased off by the time they reached the field but the ground squelched beneath their feet where the mud was thicker at the entrance. Beside the impressive tree that had to be at least fifteen metres tall, possibly more, Audrey stood with Layla looking up at the mesmerising twinkling lights. Her mum and Charlie were side-by-side behind them, equally as quiet as they took in the magic.

'So much better than in the daytime,' Mum declared. 'I love the short days in winter.'

'No way – I'm a summer guy, the long days and warm evenings,' said Charlie.

Layla winked at Audrey and leaned in to whisper, 'They like each other.'

Audrey shushed her. 'They'll hear you.' But she didn't hate the idea as much as she once would have, the thought of her mum making a new life for herself. Maybe she needed to and, once she did, she'd see that Audrey could too. Although where that life would be and what shape it would take, Audrey didn't really have any idea. What she did know was that back at number nine Mapleberry Lane was a woman who should be here with them tonight, looking up at the inky sky dotted with a handful of stars. On a clear night here in Mapleberry, they seemed to dazzle in a magical way that made you sigh and revel in the season. Gran had a sadness Audrey couldn't pinpoint, but slowly, bit by bit, she was changing. Because Gran needed a new life too; Audrey just wasn't sure whether she realised it yet.

Audrey took plenty of photos of the tree. She knew Gran had already seen lots, but she'd taken shots from all angles to make sure nothing was missed.

Mum took out her phone and took some pictures too. They all changed positions so they could each be in them, and when a woman walked by and offered to take a photo of the whole family, they happily agreed.

'She thought I was your sister,' Layla announced proudly as they made their way back to the house. She slipped her hand into Audrey's. 'I hope you don't mind.'

'Of course not.' In fact, she quite liked it.

'It's so cold out there,' Audrey declared the second they got home. They'd dropped Layla and Charlie at their house. 'How's the knitting going?' she asked, poking her head around the lounge doorway.

Gran must've shoved it all in the bag, thinking Layla was going to show up again, because she was pulling it all back out again now. 'Not much more to do.'

'Tea?' Mum trilled, although she'd already gone to the kitchen and Audrey heard the kettle flick on.

Gran got out of her chair and came through to the kitchen. 'I'm going to stand up for mine,' she declared as Mum dropped tea bags into cups. 'My joints will cease up if I'm not careful; all this sitting is bad for me.'

Audrey saw the rich plum woolly hat sitting on the arm of Gran's chair. 'Layla's going to love it.'

'I hope so.'

'You could make me one too.'

'You'd wear something I knitted?' Gran didn't seem convinced.

'Sure, why not?'

'Because you're way too fashionable.'

'Don't put yourself down. If you knit it, I'll wear it.'

Gran began to laugh. 'Careful what you say, young lady.'

Audrey set down her cup and showed Gran the pictures she'd taken of the tree. Mum showed her all of the photographs of the four of them: the one where Layla was laughing as Charlie lifted her onto his shoulders and she was the tallest of them all, touching branches way up high; the picture that captured them looking like a family to anyone who didn't know any different. Audrey just wished Gran's smiling face had been a part of that particular shot.

Audrey picked up her tea again, the steam pleasantly warming her face. 'How's the cyber boyfriend, Gran?'

Mum almost slopped her tea. 'The cyber what?'

250

'His name is Morris,' said Gran, 'and I'm seventy-one years old, young lady. "Boy" is not the correct term. I prefer "manfriend".'

'He's been messaging Gran,' Audrey told her mum. 'He's got a photograph too, want to see? As long as you don't mind, Gran.'

'I've got nothing to hide,' her gran dismissed.

On Gran's laptop Audrey opened up Facebook, found Morris and clicked on his photograph so it filled most of the screen. Gran didn't seem at all bothered at their scrutiny; in fact, she seemed rather proud to show him off.

'Mum,' Audrey's mum gasped, 'Morris is a silver fox.'

Audrey laughed. That was such an old phrase, but Gran seemed happy with it. Audrey wondered what phrase could sum up Alex. He was good-looking, tall, on the rowing team, he was funny and seemed to attract a crowd, and he had a slight Irish accent that all the girls went on about. And sure, he'd looked her way more than once, smiled, even, but it didn't mean he was keen on her. Although, according to Vicky, his eyes had followed her in the café the other day when they were all in there – he hadn't looked at any other girl.

When they'd finished stalking poor Morris, Audrey clicked away from his photograph and onto the Facebook residents' group to see if anyone else had posted photographs of the tree. She paused at a post that caught her eye. It had a photograph of an old lady who had to be at least a decade older than Gran, with a beautiful ginger cat curled up on her lap.

Gran took charge and scrolled back down the village page to read the entire post. 'I don't think this lady has posted in the group but her daughter posts quite often.

Usually it's things about shop opening times and home delivery slots, but this one is different.' She put a hand against her chest. 'Oh, how sad. She says this is a photograph of her mum and she'll be moving into a nursing home tomorrow. She says she still doesn't have a home for her cat, Claude. What a great name for a cat. Claude . . . I like it.' It was as though she was trying it on for size.

'Why doesn't the daughter look after it?' Mum wondered.

Gran read some more. 'Her son is allergic so she can't take it. The cat's old, he doesn't go outside much. Sounds a bit like me.'

Audrey shared a smile with Gran and a more conspiratorial look with her mum. 'You do it, Gran.'

'Do what?'

'Give Claude a new home.'

'No, I couldn't possibly. I've never had a cat, or a pet, for that matter. I wouldn't have the first clue how to care for it.'

'But you could learn,' said Audrey, 'and it's not like you don't have time on your hands.'

Before her mum could call Audrey out for being rude, Gran began to laugh. 'You've got a good point there.' She looked from Audrey to her mum and then back again, and it was as though a light had suddenly been flicked on, something inside her simply clicked. 'You know what, I'm going to do it.' She tapped the table decisively with the palm of her hand. 'I'm going to be Claude's new owner and he's going to love me as much as I know I'll love him.' She stood up. 'I'm really going to do it.'

'Where are you going, Mum?'

Gran sat back down. 'I don't know!'

'Reply to the post, Gran,' Audrey urged. 'Before somebody else gets in first.'

Gran leapt into action and left a comment to say she would love to take Claude; she was at home all day so he'd have company. She was about to add her phone number until Audrey told her to send the woman a friend request so they could exchange more details away from the group.

'You have to look out for people who might be up to no good,' Audrey warned.

'Good point, thanks, Audrey.' She sent the request. 'I do hope I got in first.'

So did Audrey. She'd learned to watch Gran's expressions, particularly when she didn't say much, and watching the rising excitement at the thought of adding Claude to her life was like one of those Wimbledon moments she and Layla had discussed. The look on Gran's face said she wanted Claude more than she was prepared to admit.

Audrey put the dishwasher on once their tea cups were inside. 'Hey, Gran, you can tick something else off the kindness calendar if you get to take care of Claude, and if Mum, Layla and I help you with him, we all get to put a line through the square that says: "Take care of an animal".'

Gran frowned. 'I don't remember seeing that on there.'

'There are a lot of items this month,' Audrey agreed. 'I keep forgetting them myself.'

'Must've missed it.' Gran smiled. 'Never mind. Now, don't forget to set your alarm for bright and early tomorrow. Remember we're doling out brownies to the bin men. Layla has already packaged them up.'

Audrey did a mock Brownie salute, the way she remembered Layla doing when she talked about her Brownies and when she'd made them take the Kindness Club pledge in the autumn. 'Operation Bin Men is a-go!'

'Goodnight, Audrey.' Gran smiled.

'Goodnight, see you in the morning. Goodnight, Mum.' She smiled across at her mum, who looked like she was about to fall asleep on the sofa right where she was. She'd never been this relaxed when she first rocked up in Mapleberry.

Audrey headed up to bed feeling like at last they were something resembling a family, disjointed but getting there. It left a strange feeling in the pit of her stomach. It had almost been easier when she hated her home life, when she'd dreamed of being far away from all of this. Her heart sank. New Zealand. The country that had been on her wish list for ever, when 'family' to her consisted of nothing more than her and her mum sniping at each other, getting on edge about every little thing, when Gran wasn't a part of her life, when Mapleberry was simply a place where an old lady lived that they didn't have much to do with.

And now there was Layla too. She thought of Audrey as a sister and a little part of Audrey's heart sang when she thought of her that way too. Was New Zealand still what she really wanted? Could she really go there for good and turn her back on everything and everyone else?

Why did life have to be so hard?

She hadn't heard from her dad in over a week, not since he'd thanked her for the parcels she'd sent. He always gave her money for Christmas, a lot of cash, and she had a great time every year spending it in the sales. It was something she looked forward to but this year she'd planned on saving the money to put towards her travel. Seeing it mount up as she waited for the visa would be motivation enough to know her dream was real.

She sent off a quick email to her dad. She always found it easy to talk to him this way, better than on the phone when he had the distractions of his other kids in the background or concentrating on a road if he had her on hands-free as he drove to work. She told him all about the big tree in Mapleberry and its impressive lights against the night sky, she said they'd put up the tree here at Gran's and she ended her message asking him what he'd done so far for her visa. He hadn't told her anything. She assumed no news was good news, but she was getting tired of waiting, and to know what she really wanted, she needed to know how far along the line she was. Whether she'd stop the process she wasn't sure, but maybe she'd know when he filled her in.

When her phone pinged with a text message, she thought it was her dad already. Sometimes it came up with unknown number if he called from work, but he never normally messaged.

It didn't take long to work out who it was actually from and she held her breath for a second. Her palms clammy, she lay back on her bed with an enormous smile on her face. The phone hovered in the air in her hands as she read the message a few times. It was from Alex, *the* Alex. He said he'd seen her at the tree tonight but he'd been with his brothers so hadn't come over to say hello, and he'd seen her dad there so was worried he wouldn't like it.

Audrey messaged him back, fingers flying over the keys as she explained it wasn't her dad but a neighbour. She told him how impressed she was with the tree; it was far bigger than any she'd seen before. They messaged about science class and the accident he and his friend had when one of them caught their shirt alight on a Bunsen burner; he told her about the time he and the same friend had stripped off in the boat after a race one season and gone skinny dipping. That one hadn't gone down well with the coach but Audrey thought it was pretty funny. Alex was hot, fun, a complete escape. She stared at her phone, willing him to reply, and each time he did, she savoured every word, particularly the last text.

She clutched her phone against her chest. He'd asked her out. Alex Ratcliffe had asked her out!

And although she set her alarm for bright and early, she didn't think she'd get a wink of sleep.

Chapter Sixteen

Audrey

Gran hovered at the window the next morning when the bin trucks rolled along Mapleberry Lane and came to a standstill outside the front of the house, and after she'd counted how many men she could see, Audrey picked up the cardboard box filled with brownies to take out to them. The guy shyly his cap at her in thanks, wished her a Merry Christmas and waved over to Gran hovering in the doorway. The recycling truck came right after the garbage truck, so Audrey ran down the path to grab the second box and handed them over to one of the guys she'd said hello to last week. He told her he'd take them back to eat once they'd finished their shift.

'Thank you!' he bellowed over to Gran with a wave. She was still hovering in the doorway. 'She's always got a smile for us,' he confided to Audrey. 'Most people don't talk to us unless it's to moan we're taking up the whole street with our trucks.'

Audrey suspected it was the most conversation he'd had with a resident on the street and it gave her a little buzz to know she'd helped. 'Enjoy the brownies, they're the best.'

He patted a portly tummy. 'I'm sure I will. And Merry Christmas.'

'Merry Christmas.' Audrey smiled in return before she went back inside to grab her school bag and head off.

Alex had texted her this morning to say he wouldn't be at school today. To be honest she was glad as it would give her the day to settle down after he'd asked her out – not that they'd arranged a date yet, but it was coming, she just knew it. She had a test today and wanted to do well, which she wouldn't do if she was too distracted. It was new to her, this eagerness at school, but life was far easier doing it that way.

After school Audrey let herself into the house.

'I'm getting a cat!' was the first thing to come out of Gran's mouth as she charged towards Audrey.

'The cat from the Facebook post? That's amazing! When?'

'The day after tomorrow. The owner is passing on Claude's scratching post and little bed, and I've ordered the right food, a litter tray and some cat litter.'

'I'm almost as excited as you are.' Audrey beamed. She'd never had a pet either. She'd gone through a phase of wanting a dog, then a cat, then a gerbil and then an iguana, but it had never happened. She suspected she'd been so fickle, her parents and then Mum, when it was just the two of them, worried that if she got one, she'd soon lose interest.

Gran pointed to a Christmas card on the mantelpiece. 'From the bin men,' she told Audrey.

Audrey screwed her nose up. 'Another person's trash is someone else's treasure?'

'I don't think they got it from a bin,' Gran admonished with a roll of her eyes. 'One of them popped it through the door, said we're the first to remember them in the whole of the seven years he's worked this area.'

'Well done to the Kindness Club,' Audrey said proudly. 'Was it the man I was talking to this morning?' Gran nodded. 'He was nice.'

Without even leaving the house, Gran was slowly becoming a part of the community whether she realised it or not.

'Where's Mum?'

'Out Christmas shopping.' Apron on, Gran headed back into the kitchen, calling over her shoulder, 'She worked all day but headed off to find an outfit, something about attending a friend's wedding on Saturday.'

'Talking of Saturday, I'll be out in the evening.' Audrey followed after her to see milk in a pan and proper chocolate melts ready to go. 'Hot chocolate?'

'When your mum gets home.' Gran smiled. 'Where are you off to on Saturday?'

'Friends are going for a movie and pizza – that's OK, right? It's not a school night. It'll be a great way to celebrate the end of term. We're breaking up so close to Christmas this year.'

'I don't know why schools can't give the kids a bit longer at Christmas; they wear you out these days. Who's going on this pizza and film night?' she asked in the next breath.

'Oh, just the usual.' Audrey shrugged. And to avoid being specific, she went off to get changed, which took for ever because it involved stopping every other minute to message Alex. Luckily she didn't have any homework set for tonight so she could let her concentration go, especially after today's science test. For once she thought she might have done well in it, possibly down to the fact she'd actually revised.

Her mum was home by the time Audrey came downstairs. Darkness had descended over Mapleberry, leaving only the streetlamps outside. Audrey put the tree lights on and switched the main light in the lounge off. With the fresh hot chocolates, with extra chocolate curls laid on the frothy tops until they vanished into the hot liquid, all three of them sat around the table comparing their days.

'I found a bit of ketchup on the carpet by the sofa when I was vacuuming up pine needles today,' Gran admitted. 'Must've been Layla from fish and chip night.'

Audrey saw her mum's mouth twitch in amusement. 'Did the mark come out?'

'It didn't, but don't worry, I dragged the sofa over it.'

Mum took a sip of hot chocolate to hide a smile. Back in the summer Gran would never have reacted so flippantly. She moved on to telling them both about the wedding she'd been invited to in Cheshire, near where they'd once lived.

'Funny how Sophie from my primary school ended up living so close and I never realised until I came back down here. She got in touch a couple of months ago on Instagram and we've been messaging ever since.'

'You don't mind going to the wedding alone?' Gran asked.

'Not now she's told me I'll be seated on a table of ten, all of whom are single.'

'Oh no, they're not going to try to pair you up with anyone, are they?'

'I hadn't thought of that. Great, now I'll be nervous. What do you think I should do with my hair – up or down?' She clutched some of it to give the impression of what it could like if she used pins and some styling, and Audrey found herself offering to help.

'I could do your hair and make-up, if you'll let me.'

'She's good, I can vouch for that.' Gran touched her hair, and although Audrey hadn't been the one holding the scissors, Gran liked to remind her that it had been her magic that introduced a bit of style.

'Would you mind, Audrey?' Mum used her spoon to scrape out the last remnants of chocolate from the mug.

'Happy to do it. I've got some big rollers we could put in that would give it some bounce, and I think leave it down, the colour's good already and it's more you.' It was a softer look for her mum too. Sometimes it looked too harsh when she scraped her hair up, and Audrey was all for curating a more relaxed version of her mum, who used to be a giant stress ball before they moved down here.

'I'm leaving just before lunch on Saturday, so if we could do it in the morning, that would be ideal.' Mum smiled.

Gran got on with making a comforting shepherd's pie for dinner while Mum agreed on make-up colours, and Audrey made sure the fire was ready to light after they ate so they could all relax with the lights of the tree, perhaps even a festive movie.

When Audrey's phone pinged she thought it might be Alex, but it was Layla via Charlie's phone. She groaned.

'What's up?' her mum asked.

'Every December Layla writes a letter to Father Christmas and she puts it into the flames of the open fire. When it burns, the wishes travel up to the North Pole, or something like that.'

'I miss the magic of Christmas as a kid,' Mum confessed.

'Don't we all,' Gran agreed, but moved on quickly. 'Has Layla written her letter?'

Audrey turned the phone to show them the photograph. 'You can just about see it in the flames. She wants to know if we've done ours. She's really keen we all do it at the same time so the wishes go to the North Pole together.'

'I'll get the paper and pens,' Gran said. 'We'd better get a move on or she'll be going off to her swimming lesson. They're having some kind of end-of-term party tonight.'

Armed with their equipment, they each had to think of a wish. 'It can be anything,' Audrey prompted, 'but we don't need to share it; we fold them over and put them into the fire. And we'll take a photo for Layla. She's desperate to see it,' she added when Layla hurried them along with another text. The girl was bossy for sure but Audrey kind of liked it. Some nights she'd dreamed of her half-siblings in New Zealand and wondered what life with them would be like. Would they hang out together like she did with Layla? Would they get up to mischief? Would they even like each other?

All of them scribbled away, although Audrey's wish hadn't been as easy to write down as she'd first thought. If you'd asked her a month or two ago, it would be one thing and one thing only – to go to New Zealand to live with her dad. Other than that it could've been to get her mum out of her life, or to go to college and study to be a make-up artist. But now, she had friends, she had family, she might even have a boyfriend. She was building a future without realising it. With all of that came a certain amount of confusion, but what she did know was that all of those things had been about her. And now, there was someone else who needed this wish more.

She scribbled down her wish – to get Gran her life back. A few simple words, but it was what she really wanted. And she folded her note before placing it between two logs right at the back, making it stick out enough that Layla would see it easily in a photograph.

'Mum, put yours in, and you, Gran.'

All three pieces of folded paper stuck out from between chunky logs as another text arrived from an impatient Layla.

'Where are the matches?' Mum rooted around behind the log basket, she looked on the mantelpiece and then on the windowsill.

'Here, got them.' Audrey picked up the box she'd found inside the log basket, but it was empty. And when her phone pinged yet again, she took a photograph of the fireplace as it was. She'd send another when they finally got the thing lit. 'That'll keep her quiet, at least until after swimming, when I'm sure she'll be onto me again if I don't send a better photo.'

When Mum's phone rang upstairs, she went to answer it. Gran was alerted by the oven timer and, as Audrey puzzled over how to light the fire when Gran didn't even have a gas hob to get a flame going, she wondered what the others had written for their wishes. Had they gone for frivolous Christmas presents or meaningful thoughts like hers? Was she included in their wishes at all?

She could hear her mum laughing away on the phone upstairs – probably the bride-to-be; they'd apparently earned the collective nickname of 'the gigglepots' at primary school. Gran was making up some gravy to go with the shepherd's pie, her attention fixed on the stove. And although Audrey knew it was naughty and told herself it wasn't right, she couldn't help but sneak towards the fireplace and very carefully unfold each of the other two notes in turn.

Her mum had wished for Audrey to be her friend, and Audrey just about burst into tears when she read those words. It was easy to forget her mum had a sensitive side, that she was a person who had strengths and needs as well as flaws.

But it was Gran's Christmas wish that had her the most perplexed. As soon as she'd seen the words, when she heard Gran call for her to set the table, she put it back in exactly the same place as it had been before.

Find Eddie and tell him I'm sorry, was all Gran's note had said. And those words went around and around Audrey's head while she found the cutlery from the drawer and positioned it beside the three placemats already at the table.

Who was Eddie? And why did Gran have to apologise to him?

'Found some!' Mum came running down the stairs and Audrey stood up abruptly. She must've looked guilty but her mum didn't pick up on it. Instead she brandished a box of matches. 'I had a box upstairs in the bathroom where I use my candles. Mum, come in here a second – we're lighting the fire so we can get the picture off to Layla.'

Gran joined them, Mum lit the kindling and paper, and they watched as the flames roared into action, their wishes shrivelling up at the corners, and soon their embers took off up the chimney, carried far, far away.

And when Audrey sat down to dinner, not only did she want her wish to come true, she wanted all three of them to get what they wanted.

But most of all she wanted to know who Eddie was.

Chapter Seventeen

Sam

Sam fastened on her badge for another Kindness Club meeting. Both Audrey's and Layla's schools had finished with a half day, which worked out well, because they had wreaths to make for some of the front doors in Mapleberry. It was a last-minute decision from her mum when she saw 'Add some surprise cheer to someone's Christmas' on the kindness calendar. She also wanted to do wreaths for the people who'd sent her a card this year and told her how good it was to see a tree in her window this Christmas.

This morning Sam had worked the early shift at the café and then driven to the florist to collect the mossy wreaths that had already been covered in greenery and were ready to decorate. She'd also picked up a supply of holly and ivy, floristry wire, fresh and colourful berries, pine cones, sparkly twigs and cinnamon sticks.

'He's loving this,' said Audrey, dragging a piece of silver ribbon around the lounge floor for Claude the cat to chase, pounce on and roll over with.

Mum scooped up her cat. Since Claude had been delivered yesterday to his new home, she had been enraptured by the feline. He'd taken to her quickly enough, cautious at first, but her mum was wrong about not knowing a thing about animals. They needed love and attention, and she put no limits on that.

'Now,' said Mum, 'what will we do with you?' She had Claude in her arms, his paws up in the air like a baby, as she took him to the study where she'd put his scratching post. 'I'll feed him, that's the easiest thing to do,' she told the others.

With Claude safely tucked away, Sam watched her mum as they worked with the accessories to make festive wreaths. Her wish in the fireplace had been for Audrey to be her friend, but if she'd been able to wish for anything extra it would've been for her mum to change. Not to change the woman she was, but to evolve into the woman she could be. She wanted her mum to find a peace, a happiness she didn't quite have yet, although the appearance of Claude seemed to elicit a certain kind of joy.

Since she'd talked to her mum about Simon and Audrey, Sam sensed she had been on the verge of divulging more truths than Sam had realised were lurking in the background. Her mum had said Sam worshipped her dad, that he could do no wrong in her eyes, and she couldn't deny this. Had Sam failed her mum in some way by laying all the blame at her feet? Was there more to the story than she'd been led to believe?

'We're good at this.' Audrey smiled as they each took what they needed, winding and pushing extra elements into the greenery.

'That's because you're arty,' Sam complimented her, looking at the way she'd added red berries around a few silver twigs, interwoven holly with pine cones and added the same green velvet ribbon they'd wrapped the gifts in to her wreath so it was all ready to tie to a front door. Audrey had done some reconnaissance of the houses they'd chosen and they were good to go with all of them – some had hooks already there but no wreath yet, the others all had a knocker that would be easy to use to thread the ribbon through.

'All these people who I haven't heard of or who haven't contacted me in years and have sent a card to say how good it is to see my tree,' said Mum, 'they'll all be getting a wreath. Well, apart from Mavis Turner, Niall Bent and the couple from number seventeen, because they all have one already.'

'I think if we'd had to do another three wreaths, my hands would start yelling at me,' declared Sam.

'Veronica has good hand cream in the kitchen,' Layla told her. 'We bought it for her last year – it's proper gardener's hand cream.'

'Is that right?' Sam went and found the hand cream as Audrey tied the last bow onto wreath. Layla's artistic skills had been flamboyant, adding way too much, but Audrey had tactfully shown her how less could indeed be more.

Audrey and Layla pulled on their coats for Operation Add a Wreath as Claude sensed he was missing out on all the fun and came trotting through to the lounge again. Mum scooped him up before he could get up to too much mischief and followed the girls to the door.

'Remember,' said Sam's mum, 'say: "From Veronica at number nine", and then if they say anything else, just add, "Merry Christmas". And make sure the one with the tartan bow goes on Morris's door,' she added before they set off along Mapleberry Lane and beyond. 'And stay together, it's dark.'

They went away giggling.

Sam hadn't missed the way her mum talked about Morris, how her cheeks pinked up a little every time she said his name. Not a bad-looking chap, as it happened, and from reading his comments on Facebook she had no doubt he had a good heart.

Sam put the rest of the wreaths out on the front door-step for the girls to collect and do round two. 'You like this man, don't you?' She ran a finger up and down Claude's cheek as he purred in her mum's arms in the hallway.

'Morris? He's nice.'

Sam shut the front door and followed her mum through to the kitchen. 'I'm happy for you.' She picked up some of the ribbon off-cuts and stray pieces of twig.

'And I for you,' she added, to Sam's surprise. 'Don't pretend you haven't noticed the way Charlie looks at you.'

'He's a lovely guy.' With her mum's arms out of action thanks to Claude, Sam took out a dustpan and brush to rid the table of whatever remnants the wreaths had left behind and reached for a cloth to start wiping it down.

'"Lovely" – that's it?'

Sam tried to hide a smile and let her hair fall around her face to hide any sign she might be giving away about how she felt when it came to Charlie. There was no way she could introduce romance in her life any time soon, she had plenty to deal with for now, so she'd just have to do her best to dampen her feelings when he was around.

'Are you going to do anything about it?'

Sam put the rubbish into the bin, carrying on as normal to throw her mum off the scent. She hadn't talked to her mother about boys even when she was a teenager, let alone now as an adult. 'I'm not going to do anything apart from pour myself a glass of wine and relax.' She held out a glass to her mum. 'Are you sure?' she asked when her mum shook her head.

'I haven't touched a drop in years. Although I was thinking perhaps you could get a bottle of Baileys Irish Cream for Christmas. I always liked that, with lots of ice.'

'Done, consider it on the list.' Sam peered in the freezer, found there were no ice-cubes so filled each of the trays she found in the cupboard. 'Now we're prepared.'

They sat and talked about the food they'd have for the big day, their first family Christmas in a long time, except there would always be certain people missing. But for now, this was enough. Usually Sam and Audrey had Christmas at home on their own, one year they'd been to Jilly's, but mostly Audrey sat through the dinner and scarpered with friends in the afternoon.

Audrey was back less than an hour later after delivering all the wreaths. She'd already taken Layla home. She stroked Claude between the ears. He was comfortably curled up on the arm of Sam's mum's chair, paws tucked beneath him, eyes sleepily opening every now and then to check his surroundings. He'd well and truly made himself at home.

'Did anyone catch you in the act?' Sam wanted to know when her mum went to the bathroom.

'One person. Morris,' she whispered conspiratorially.

'What's he like? I'm desperate to know.'

'He's lovely and, like you said, a total silver fox. When I said who sent the wreath, you should've seen him – it looked like all his Christmas wishes had come true.'

'Whose Christmas wishes?' Sam's mum came back and settled into her chair, and Claude's tail lifted in a sign of approval.

'Morris,' said Audrey smugly. 'I met your man.'

'Oh, be off with you, he's not my man.'

Audrey looped an arm across her gran's shoulders. 'Chill, Gran, he's a cool dude.'

'That means nothing to me.'

'He's really nice. He says to thank you for the wreath, he'll send you a message soon, and I was to tell you he hasn't had a fresh one hanging on his door in years.' She took out her phone from the back pocket of her jeans. 'Here, a photograph of it.' She swiped to the side. 'And another of him with it. I could print it out for you, if you like; you could keep it by your bed.'

'Audrey,' Sam warned. 'That's enough teasing.'

The mood was high in the house that evening. Sam poured a second glass of wine, they watched *Home Alone* together, and when her mum turned in for the night, Audrey helped Sam empty the dishwasher and put everything away.

'Gran seems to really like Morris,' said Audrey as she put the knives into the cutlery drawer.

'I think it's early days.' Sam smiled. 'Let's see what happens.'

Audrey took out the forks one by one from the plastic cutlery section. 'Mum, do you know anyone called Eddie?'

The plate she was holding almost slipped from her grip. 'What makes you ask?'

'I heard Gran mention the name.'

'Really?' Not a chance. Her mum didn't talk about

Eddie to anyone; she hadn't since the day she told Sam he'd 'gone to a better place'. Those were her exact words and Sam had never forgotten them.

'Maybe I misheard.' Audrey used a tea towel to get the drips off the upside-down cups on the top racks before neatly slotting them into the cupboard. She hung the tea towel over the handle of the oven door to dry. 'I'm off to bed, but I'll see you for your wedding makeover tomorrow.'

'Goodnight.' This was a start, a border crossed, perhaps, and the start of them being not only mother and daughter but good friends too. 'I'll see you in the morning.'

Sam looked through the window into the darkness, at the garden that hadn't changed a bit since she was a child. The only differences were the moss growing on the roof of the shed, which seemed to build up each time she came here, the rockery that had sprigs of colour in the right season, and the low wall separating the patio from the lawn, which had been repaired and was now straight enough to sit on comfortably. Even the washing line was the same, one strand broken the way it had been when Sam was a kid.

She looked at the Christmas shopping list she and her mum had drawn up together. She'd be shopping for all of that in the morning with Charlie, and so before the weight of the name Eddie being mentioned in passing by her daughter who knew nothing of him got too much, Sam headed off to bed. She'd do her best not to let thoughts of her little brother creep into her head tonight. Those dreams never ended well, much like reality, she supposed.

*

Charlie took charge of the trolley in the supermarket, which was heaving even though they still had a few shopping days left before Christmas. It was such a long time since Sam had had a man at her side to do a food shop; she was enjoying floating up and down the aisles, choosing exactly what they needed, adding a few extras that weren't on the list. Dampening down her feelings for Charlie was getting more difficult by the day, and every time he smiled her way, she wasn't sure how much longer she could keep up the pretence she was happily single.

'Now those are definitely on the list.' Charlie stopped next to the luxury pigs in blankets, although quite what the difference was from the bulk-standard version at half the price, Sam had no idea, unless it was all down to the fanciness of the packaging.

'You sure we have enough?' she asked.

About to answer, he changed his tune. 'I detect a bit of sarcasm.'

'There are only five of us.'

Three packets clutched in his hand, he said, 'About that – are you sure it's OK to have Layla and I over at Veronica's for Christmas? I know it's a big ask – this is the first year in a while she's had family around her.'

Without thinking, Sam reached out a hand and put it over one of his. 'Charlie, you and Layla are as much family to Mum as Audrey and I are, I can see that. You're coming for Christmas lunch, end of discussion.'

Their gaze held a moment longer until they broke apart when someone asked to get past and Charlie dropped the products into the already sizeable collection of shopping. 'Just in case,' he said, snatching one more tray of pigs in blankets from the shelf before Sam could argue the point any further.

She grinned and they walked on to the next aisle to pick up the turkey. They moved to hams, debating which size to go for, on to cold meats and then the prawns. They made sure they had a selection of sweet treats, plenty of gravy powder, ingredients for the stuffing and a box of the tackiest crackers they could find.

'They're all rubbish anyway,' Charlie declared. 'Might as well see if we can make them as terrible as possible.'

'Agreed.'

'I hear the Christmas wreaths went down a treat,' said Charlie as they hovered near the Christmas puddings, perusing the boxes to select whichever sounded the best.

'The neighbours we chose were incredibly grateful, according to Audrey. Particularly Morris.'

'I've heard about Morris,' he said with a knowing smile.

'Mum seems rather keen on him and Audrey says he's lovely.'

'So why the face?'

She made the final choice for Christmas pudding and added it in; Charlie would get first dibs on ice-cream in the next aisle. 'Because she's my mother. Because she has issues. Because she's seventy-one.'

His laughter bellowed a bit too loudly in the frozen section. 'Good for her, I say. Romance and sex don't die because you reach seventy, or forty, for that matter.'

Sam, watching the scar on his lip as he spoke, moving each time he laughed, side-stepped the reference to their own ages. 'I know it doesn't. But . . .'

'It's your mother.' He opened up a freezer compartment,

shivered at the rush of cold air and pulled out a big tub of mince-pie-flavoured ice-cream.

Sam nodded in agreement before he added it to the already-full trolley. 'It's my mother.'

They grabbed two big bottles of Baileys Irish Cream before they left, and back at his house they unloaded as many items as would fit in his freezer, saving the things for the main meal for her mum's house. And after they'd crammed everything into the fridge at number nine, Sam walked Charlie to the end of the path.

She looked up at the sky, him on one side of the little gate, her on the other. 'That was a snowflake.'

'You're imagining it.'

'I am not! There, another one.' And when one landed on his cheek she reached out for it to prove it to him but it melted on the tip of her finger. 'I promise it was there.'

'I believe you. There's one in your hair.' But he didn't attempt to reach it, instead he was looking down at her and she felt her stomach flip.

'I wish you were coming to this wedding with me.' She should've asked him, told him she needed a plus-one.

'I'm working later, I couldn't have gone with you. You know, had you asked me when you got the invite . . .' he teased.

She gave him a playful nudge at the gate. 'I'll see you again soon, Charlie.'

'You can count on it.'

She stayed at the gate the whole time he walked down the lane, up his own garden path and waved from his front door.

And when she finally went inside she told her mum, 'Not a word.' She hadn't missed the hopeful look on her mum's face; it was the same look that came Sam's way every time Charlie's name was mentioned.

'I'm not saying anything – well, apart from you'd better get your skates on.'

She checked the time. 'I thought we were quicker than that. Is Audrey out of the bathroom?'

'She's gone to do a bit of Christmas shopping in the village. Bathroom is all yours.'

Sam had a long, luxurious shower. Even though she didn't have as much time as she'd planned, she was usually generous in her estimates and she still had plenty to spare for hair and make-up. She used her matching Chanel Coco shower gel and body lotion, then put on jeans and a shirt for travel. She laid out the silk navy and caramel dress with dropped shoulders and a tie belt, which would go perfectly with the Ted Baker heels she hadn't worn since she'd stopped working in an office. Her uniform was now far more casual and although she was looking forward to dressing up this afternoon, she wasn't sure she wanted to go back to doing it full-time. It was oddly liberating not to have to do it.

When she heard the door go she trotted down the stairs, excited to get going with her hair and see what magic Audrey could weave. They'd planned large rollers, sexy waves and subtle make-up colours that brought out her blue eyes. She hadn't fought the make-up artist career choice in a while. Strangely it didn't seem all that important these days, or perhaps she was finally seeing the person her daughter had become.

'I'm all yours.' She smiled at Audrey, but she didn't exactly get the reception she'd expected when her daughter glared back at her, hands firmly planted on her hips.

'Everything all right?' Sam asked.

'You tell me.' Audrey even ignored poor Claude, who weaved between her ankles, desperate for some attention.

'I'm lost,' said Sam. A moment ago she'd been all relaxed, the afterglow of a morning with Charlie lingering enough to light her up inside.

'When were you going to tell me?' Audrey yelled, bringing Sam's mum out from the kitchen.

'Tell you what?'

'That you've known for months that Dad doesn't want me to go to New Zealand. Not now and probably not ever. Thanks to you.'

'Audrey, wait a minute. I—'

'What did you say to him? You must've told him how horrible I've been, the trouble I've got in at school, how I couldn't choose decent friends, how I was throwing away my future playing with make-up. You put him off having me there. You did, didn't you?'

'No, I promise you I didn't.'

'You expect me to believe he just changed his mind?' And with that she stomped up the stairs and slammed the bedroom door so hard both Sam and her mum jumped.

Her mum grabbed Sam's arm before she marched on up there. 'Sam, not now. You've got a wedding to go to and the last thing you need is to rush because you're late. You need to go and do your hair and your make-up, and then drive safely and calmly. Please.'

Sam's heart thudded. Why hadn't she told Audrey the truth, that her dad didn't want her? That he was a selfish prick and expected everyone else to fit their lives around him?

She knew why not. Because Audrey would find a way of blaming her like she had just now.

Sam should know because she had done it to her own mum enough times.

Chapter Eighteen

Audrey

Audrey was a little bit calmer when she came down-stairs ready to go and meet her friends. But the anger was still bubbling away inside after the confrontation with her mum. How could she poison her dad's mind against her and make him not want her to go to New Zealand? It was cruel, that's what it was. And just like that, the close-ness she was beginning to feel had been thrown right back in her face.

'I don't want to talk about it,' she warned her gran the second she saw her.

'Fair enough,' Gran acknowledged. 'Don't you look lovely.'

Audrey managed a smile. She was excited about going out with friends, but nervous too. Alex would be there and he'd already said he'd like to spend some time alone with her after the pizza restaurant. He'd suggested he walk her home and her tummy was doing somersaults every time she thought about it, whenever she recalled the de-tails of their text messages that had flown back and forth while she tried to style her hair, put on some make-up, and chopped and changed her mind about what to wear at least a dozen times. She'd settled on her favourite ripped jeans with an off-the-shoulder jumper as soft as the skin on her delicate collarbones. Alex had asked her once if she was a dancer; she looked so graceful, he'd said. The thought of his compliment made her giddy now but she hadn't let on to her gran that she might be spending time with only Alex later on.

'What's the movie?' Gran asked.

Glad they weren't talking about Mum, Dad or New Zealand, she told Gran what they were seeing at the local cinema. 'There's a showing of *It's a Wonderful Life.*'

'Well, that's something I wholly approve of.' She pulled her granddaughter in for a hug. 'Do you have your house key?'

'Yes, Gran.'

'And you have enough money? You'll be back no later than eleven o'clock?'

'Yes, Gran, I have enough money, and yes, Gran, I'll be back by curfew.' She smiled.

'I'm not sure about you walking in the dark, although Mapleberry is quite safe.'

'Gran, stop worrying.' She kissed her on the cheek. 'And have a lovely evening.'

Gran waved her off and Audrey made her way past the playground and over to the main street in the village. She waved at Clare, who was bustling around inside the Mapleberry Mug serving customers, continued on her way and, with her friends already at the cinema, she did her best not to make it too obvious she was scanning faces for Alex.

'He'll be here,' Vicky whispered so the others couldn't hear.

Audrey almost thought he wasn't going to turn up but

as they stood in line to buy tickets with a crowd who all seemed a lot older than they were, she heard a deep voice at her side, and caught a waft of the aftershave he used at school.

Vicky made sure Alex and Audrey sat next to each other for the movie, and the group of seven chatted away until the lights dimmed and the movie began. It was then his hand drifted to hers, their fingers linked, and she held her breath so long she wondered how she'd make it to the end of the movie with these unfamiliar feelings whooshing around inside of her.

'I'm not really in the mood for pizza,' Alex told her when the credits rolled and they began to file out. 'I've got some beers in my bag,' he whispered, sending her insides into meltdown he got so close. 'We could go somewhere, just the two of us.'

She turned to him but Vicky snatched her away to go to the ladies.

'You should go,' Vicky urged the minute they were behind closed doors.

'You heard what he said?'

'I did, and this is your chance. I knew it!' She clapped her hands together. 'I told you he liked you.'

'He really does, doesn't he? But what about pizza? I don't want to desert you all.'

'Don't even think about it – just promise me you will tell me *everything*.' She hugged Audrey. 'And don't do anything I wouldn't do.'

Back in the foyer the others drifted off, and Alex, who'd been leaning up against the marble pillar near the front desk, came her way.

'So, that was fun,' he said as they met with the night

air, walking side-by-side down the front steps of the classic old building housing the independent cinema. Gran had told her that fifteen years ago there had been plans to demolish it, as well as part of the woods surrounding Mapleberry, and build a big complex with shops, restaurants and a bigger cinema, but locals had put up a fight and it never happened. Audrey was kind of glad. Even though she hadn't known the village before, she liked it just the way it was – more cosy, a bit romantic.

'It was a good movie,' Audrey replied, doing up her top button. Inside she'd been so warm next to him she'd almost forgotten it was winter outside.

'I wasn't talking about the movie.'

Audrey didn't want to put her gloves on in case Alex held her hand. She didn't care about the cold, the threat of frostbite. It would all be worth it for him.

'Where are we going?' They were heading across the road towards the woodland that surrounded Mapleberry, not the same side as the field with the beautiful Christmas tree she'd been to see with her mum, but the dense area she'd never been to.

'You'll see.' He grinned. He took her hand and when their fingers slotted together the same way they had for the entire movie, her tummy fluttered just like before.

Audrey's excitement pushed away the fury caused by her mum. They'd been so close looking at the tree, working on the kindness calendar together, both of them a part of Gran's life as she began to find her way again. And what had it all been for? Nothing, as far as Audrey could see now. Her mum still wanted to pull her strings, as though she was a puppet she had full control of, and she'd ruined everything with Dad. Audrey had to wonder what sort of doubts her mum had put in his mind, what she had said to convince him she no longer had a place in his new family?

Audrey bit her cheek hard enough that it hurt and scared away a tear threatening to escape. She sneaked a look at Alex walking alongside her, his mop of dark hair almost in his eyes, a slight dimple on his cheek that seemed to let him get away with a lot at school. Mrs Masters in English the other day had been ready to tear shreds from him for handing in some homework late until he'd flashed her a smile, with an excuse that his mum hadn't been well, and she'd let him off with a warning.

They followed a track into the woods, unease mounting for Audrey. It was dark, not a single lamppost, not a shop in sight, and the only sounds were of the wind and cracking of the branches around them.

'Was your mum really sick?' she asked, more because she was nervous than the need to know.

'What? Oh, you mean my excuse for Mrs Masters. All true – Mum hasn't been well for a while.'

'I'm sorry.'

'Don't be, it is what it is.' He didn't seem to want to talk about it so, given how she was on the topic of mothers, she let it be.

They came to a clearing and he set down his bag on an overturned log, then took out some beers. He handed one to her after he'd unscrewed the top and then, after doing the same to his, clinked his bottle against hers.

'Cheers, Merry Christmas, Audrey.'

'Merry Christmas,' she just about managed. Although she wasn't sure about beer. She'd had a sip once but never a full bottle.

They sat next to each other on the log, sipping at their beers, Alex laughing every time there was a noise and Audrey almost leapt out of her skin. She didn't know what she was imagining, they were totally alone – even dog walkers weren't going to come out here at this time.

They got talking about camping, being out in the middle of nowhere. Alex had been as a kid plenty of times; he couldn't believe Audrey never had.

'Mum was never keen,' she admitted. 'Dad would be, though.'

'Yeah? What's he like?'

Audrey told Alex all about her dad, his new life, the photographs he sent and the stories he told from the other side of the world. 'His whole life is like one big adventure.' An adventure she'd no longer be a part of, it seemed.

Alex cracked open another beer but Audrey was still working on her first. She took another gulp, not wanting to seem boring.

They talked more about school, laughing at some of their teachers' efforts to make their lessons interesting. 'It's as though they think if they dress it up enough,' said Alex, 'chemistry will become this really interesting subject all of a sudden. Do you think they're waiting for us to have a light bulb moment and suddenly declare we love it?'

Audrey laughed. He was good company, as she'd known he would be, but when she glanced at her watch, she realised they'd been talking away for so long that her time was nearly up. It was marching on towards eleven o'clock, but before she could mention it, Alex pulled her to her feet.

'Look up.' He smiled.

She tipped her head back and, sure enough, a sliver of moon had crept out from its hiding place and, in a sky peppered with stars in the gap right above them, it was as though it were their own private display, a slice of magic nobody else could see.

'Wow,' she breathed, not feeling the cold at all.

When she turned to look at him she almost stumbled back because his face drew close and all of a sudden he was kissing her.

Audrey didn't think it was possible for another person to feel this good. The only boy she'd ever kissed was at a Halloween party when she was ten. And that had only been a peck on the lips, nothing on this level. Alex had the softest lips, even with a hint of stubble grazing her chin every now and then as their mouths explored and grasped at something new. His hand that wasn't holding the beer made her shiver when it sneaked beneath her hair and pulled her closer. She wanted to put her arms around him but didn't know what to do with her own bottle.

And then he was kissing her with an urgency she wasn't sure about. His mouth left her lips, moved down her neck and across just below her ear lobe, and he was making noises of pleasure that gave off a warning sign she couldn't ignore. She thought she might have said his name, she wasn't sure, but in the next moment she heard a smash and realised she'd dropped her beer. It had hit a piece of rock and shattered everywhere, the broken fragments glinting in the light of the moon.

'What's wrong?' he asked, grabbing her arm, and she pulled away angrily. He held up his hands. 'I just didn't want you to stand on the glass.'

'I . . . I . . .' This was embarrassing. She'd reacted as though he was pushing her around when he was only trying to help. What could she say now? She'd made a total idiot of herself. He was popular; she was new to the school. Was he expecting something to happen, something more than a kiss?

He kept saying her name but every time he got closer she pulled away. 'I have to go home.' She started to run.

'Audrey, wait!' His voice came after her. 'Audrey . . .'

But his voice faded because she was moving fast, weaving in and out of trees, getting as far away from trouble as she could.

But whatever way she turned, she couldn't find her way out. She came up to one thicket after another, faced with a maze of woodland that would pose a challenge in the day, never mind at night.

Audrey would've given anything right now to be home at Gran's house, tucked up in her nice, warm bed.

Instead, here she was, out in the elements and she didn't know what to do.

Chapter Nineteen

Veronica

After Audrey went out, Veronica had shut the front door to her home and for the first time in a long while, the walls held a peculiar silence she wasn't used to anymore. She'd soon put the radio on for some company and revelled in some Christmas carols – something else she'd missed experiencing but had slowly begun to enjoy again with Layla playing so many on the piano.

Veronica was glad Sam was spending the night away. It might give both her and Audrey a chance to get a bit of perspective after their confrontation earlier. Sam could let her hair down at the wedding, Audrey could have a good time with her friends, and perhaps when Sam came back to Mapleberry tomorrow afternoon they could both be rational. And it was time Audrey learned a few home truths about her own father. Veronica would've told her some earlier if she'd thought it would help. But she hadn't wanted to interfere. She'd got most of her family back and this time she'd do anything not to let it go.

She added another log to the fire. It was really getting cold and although she couldn't wait for the snow, despite the few flakes earlier, she was thankful it wasn't forecast just yet. Sam had to drive home tomorrow, Audrey was out for the evening – she only wanted snow when she knew everyone was safe.

The fire crackled away and although Claude didn't quite understand boundaries when she tried to knit, he was getting the hang of it. Every time he swiped for the wool she removed him from the arm of the chair and gave him a stray piece to play with. She made good progress with Layla's hat, making the pompom to go on top. But when there was a knock at the door and Layla's little face peeked in at the window, she had to hide the hat and the wool away in her bag.

'Don't even think about it,' she warned Claude, who had a crafty eye on the bag.

'This is a lovely surprise.' She hadn't expected her little visitor today. Although Charlie didn't look too relaxed. 'You all right?'

'Stressed. Here's the thing: Bea has the flu and she can't have Layla this evening. I'm on a half night shift, last one before my Christmas break, and I can't find anyone to swap with me.'

'Say no more – in you come, Layla.'

'I didn't want to ask. I can collect her in the early hours if needs be.'

'Don't be ridiculous, all night is fine by me. Layla can have Sam's bed – she's staying over at the wedding venue and won't be back until lunchtime tomorrow.'

Charlie smiled. 'So she is, she did mention it, but in my panic I totally forgot. But even so, are you totally sure?'

'You ask me that every time, and every time I tell you the answer is "yes".'

'I don't really know how to repay you. You're a life-saver.

It was either this or I volunteer to swap tonight for Christmas.'

'No, you're not doing that. Now go and get Layla's things and drop them over. Everyone's out anyway and I'm already lonely. Claude doesn't say much.' Layla sniggered.

His face relaxed into a smile again. 'You're used to having company.'

'It didn't take long to change my ways,' she agreed.

Charlie was there and back in no time; all the child really needed were some pyjamas, a toothbrush and the teddy bear she slept with every night and she'd be fine.

'Well, this is an adventure, Layla.' Veronica took out a portion of frozen bolognese. 'I'll boil up some pasta and we'll have this for tea. I was only going to have a sandwich but a growing child like you needs more than that. Now, what pasta do you like? We have spaghetti, rigatoni, tagliatelle or penne.'

'Spaghetti!' Layla said excitedly. 'That one's the most fun.'

'And the messiest.'

'Can I practise my piano?'

'Off you go, this will take twenty minutes or so.' She switched off the radio and the silence that had made her uncomfortable a short while ago was gone, and Veronica couldn't be sorry. Layla was going to impress her dad with these carols come Christmas Eve, she was sure of it. They'd kept it a secret for so long, quite how they'd managed she'd never know, but they had and it was going to be the best gift for Charlie.

Veronica and Layla shared dinner and conversation before settling in front of a Christmas movie with nothing but each other and the Christmas lights for company. And Claude, of course.

When Layla yawned yet again, Veronica suggested she get ready for bed. 'Come on, do your teeth and get into those pyjamas while I get your bed ready for you,' she said, leading the way.

'Do you think my daddy will ask your Sam on a date?' Layla suddenly asked.

Veronica laughed at the direct question as they reached the top of the stairs. 'Would you mind if he did?'

'Of course not, I want it to happen.' She gasped and covered her mouth. 'Do you think it won't come true now? I wasn't supposed to say it out loud.'

'I wouldn't worry about that. The wish made its way up to the North Pole plenty of time ago – I'm sure it's being dealt with by Father Christmas and all his helpers.'

'Do you really think so?'

'I know so.'

While Layla did her teeth, Veronica tugged the sheets from Sam's bed and, as she did so, something colourful dropped out from beneath them. It took her a moment to realise what it was: the teddy bear she'd given her years ago, the bear Audrey had mentioned being on Sam's wardrobe. Veronica had known she had it after Audrey told her, but she hadn't figured on Sam keeping it with her for sleeping. And something tugged at her, the childhood Sam had missed because of her, the girl who'd been happy-go-lucky at one time but not after Veronica became really bad. She bit back a sob when she heard Layla coming in. She only hoped Sam got some comfort from the bear; it's what she'd always intended when she gave it to her.

'Check?' Layla asked, opening her mouth for inspection.

'I believe you.' Veronica smiled. 'I don't need to check.'

'Daddy sometimes gets me to use those funny red tablets that leave marks on your teeth.'

'I remember Sam bringing some of those home from school too. She thought they were a lot of fun – she'd chew them without cleaning her teeth just to shock me.' It was funny the little things you remembered. They seemed insignificant at the time but it was those fragments of the past that made up the life you once knew. And when you no longer had that life, you'd give anything to piece together those seemingly unimportant occurrences that could give you back a sense of identity.

Veronica put Sam's teddy on the shelf against one wall and once Layla had arranged her favourite teddy to one side of the bed so she could climb in, she offered to read to Layla.

Layla smiled. Perfectly capable of reading on her own, she said, 'You can read ten pages. Then I'll take it from there.'

Trying not to smirk, Veronica perched next to her and opened Jacqueline Wilson's *Dancing the Charleston*. And when she'd read her quota – probably three times what Layla suggested, but she wouldn't let her stop – she left Layla to enjoy more of the story.

'Lights out by nine,' she called behind her. 'I'll come up again to tuck you in.'

Veronica made a cup of tea and logged onto Facebook to see if any of her new friends were around. She'd grown accustomed to their banter; there was never big news, but it was good to talk, and in a way much easier than on the telephone or in person. It was as though you were able to show a little more of yourself through your words. She couldn't remember having this kind of kinship since her nursing days, and the connections were blossoming more every day.

There was already a message waiting for her from Morris, thanking her for the Christmas wreath. 'It's been a long time since anyone gave me anything quite so thoughtful,' he told her. 'You get to my age and you feel invisible.' Veronica told him he was being melodramatic and he liked that she'd called him out on it; he said she challenged him. It wasn't long before their banter turned a little more personal.

Morris: I need you to help me understand something, Veronica.

Veronica: I'll do my best.

Morris: I've lived in this house for four and a half years. I go to the village high street, I've drunk in the pub on occasion when my son comes to visit, I've taken my grandson to the play park, which I understand (from my conversation with your beautiful granddaughter when she delivered the wreath) is opposite your home. So why, then, have I never seen you? I recognised June from her photograph, Bridget too, but as much as I look at your picture I just can't place you. I know I've never met you before.

On the computer she could be anybody she liked, she could pretend, she didn't have to be the crazy lady from number nine. Except she wouldn't lie, not to Morris; already she thought too much of him to do that. They had a lovely group with June and Bridget, but already she felt a special connection with Morris, who took their chats into the messages section rather than in the group. Veronica felt like a modern woman with these talks. Was she online dating? It certainly felt like it, especially when she felt this uncomfortable with the conversation.

Veronica: How do you know we've never met before? You could've passed me in the street any number of times.

Morris: I know I haven't, I'd remember you . . .

Veronica: Flattery will get you nowhere, Morris.

Morris: Neither will avoiding my question.

Veronica shut the laptop. Enough for tonight. Her heart was thumping and it reminded her of the times she'd launched into a full-scale panic attack, and that certainly wasn't on tonight's agenda.

She left the laptop closed for a good thirty minutes, enough time to go and tell Layla she should pop her light off now. She tucked her in, promised she could play the piano in the morning, although not too early if Audrey needed a lie-in.

She looked at her watch. Audrey should be home soon, so she didn't have too much longer to wait up. Sam probably didn't remember but she'd always waited up for her too. Sometimes Sam had stayed out until three or four in the morning and Veronica had never got a wink of sleep until she heard the key in the lock, the footsteps on the stairs and seen the strip of light from the bathroom run under the door to her bedroom. Only then had she turned over in bed and gone to sleep.

Veronica looked at her laptop, sitting innocently on the table as though teasing her to open it and answer Morris's question. He'd probably given up and was watching television instead by now, so she braved typing a response. She could send it now, let him mull over what he thought, and she'd face his response in the morning.

She took a deep breath. Morris, June and Bridget had told her things in confidence, a trust had developed between them all, and yet Veronica still hadn't managed to bring her problem out into the open.

But perhaps she could now tackle this hurdle with the help of Morris's kindness, which she felt even through a screen, running through wires or however it was the internet connected these days.

She stretched her fingers the way she did before playing the piano, and typed . . .

Veronica: You won't have seen me since you moved to Mapleberry because I don't leave my house. I haven't left my house in five years.

There, she'd told him. Hands rested in her lap after she pressed the return key. She felt good now it was out there. Another person knew. Audrey talking about agoraphobia, giving it a name when she first realised her Gran had a problem, had been like a slap in the face, but a much-needed one. And telling Morris now, it was another step she'd taken. Quite in what direction she wasn't sure yet.

She was about to close the laptop for the night when the funny sound came as he sent a reply . . .

Morris: I knew it . . . if we'd have bumped into one another we'd both remember . . . we'd have ended up in the café or the pub, talking nineteen to the dozen, we'd have gone for a walk for hours, getting home long after dark . . .

Veronica: You've been reading too many romance novels . . .

Morris: I can't deny it, they're my guilty pleasure. Tell me this, Veronica from number nine, why don't you venture out? Mapleberry is a beautiful village, especially in the winter, the big tree on the field all lit up and waiting for people like us to mark another Christmas. You're missing out . . .

Veronica: I know I am. And the reasons for my agoraphobia are lengthy. I won't bore you with them all this late at night.

Morris: Bore away, happy to listen/read. But pause a second, I'm going to need a nightcap first . . . nice strong whiskey should do it. Get yourself one, I've a feeling we'll need it . . .

Was this what online flirting was like? Veronica decided she quite liked it! With a giggle that belied her age, she popped the kettle on to make a camomile tea. Anything too strong would have her awake until all hours.

She settled back down with her cup, and when he told her to 'fire away' – she could imagine him sipping his whiskey as he took everything in – she poured out the whole story.

When she'd finally finished and her wrists ached from all the typing, she discarded the remains of her tea that had gone cold. But she caught sight of the clock as she did so. Audrey was ten minutes past her curfew now, and she was starting to worry. She almost sent her a message but held back. Ten minutes wasn't a big deal, was it? She'd probably got carried away chatting to her friends, but her concern had her peeking out of the shutters in the lounge all the same, to see if there was any sign of Audrey. She'd assured her gran she wouldn't walk home on her own so Veronica had visions of this Alex escorting her home and, if she was lucky, she'd catch a glimpse of him.

Veronica did her best to relax and it helped that Morris had already sent another message by the time she got back to her laptop. He told her everyone had their issues, this was hers, and he added in one of those funny GIF moving pictures Audrey had shown her on here, of a teddy bear doing a dance with the words 'We got this' above.

Veronica felt tears welling up. She'd kept herself isolated, cooped up for such a long time, missing out on so much. And all it had taken was a bit of time with a laptop to realise even if she never left this house again, she didn't have to go through life alone – there were people out there willing to go above and beyond to have the friendships she wanted and needed.

She'd told Morris more in these conversations than she'd ever told anyone over the years, but Morris didn't seem to have given up on her. And even better, he was having a laugh with it all; she was giggling away like a schoolgirl at his witticisms and it was a long time since she'd laughed so hard. How could a friend on the other end of a computer become someone who felt so real, so alive?

She was just beginning to wonder whether he'd ask her to meet in person, when Layla came downstairs, rubbing her eyes.

'Why aren't you asleep, young lady?' Veronica was straight up, ushering her back up the stairs.

'I can't get to sleep and when I heard you laughing I felt like I was missing out. What were you laughing at?'

'Just the television.'

'The television wasn't on.'

'I just switched it off a moment ago,' she fibbed. 'Now, enough of the questions, you get yourself to sleep or your daddy is not going to be very happy with me when he comes to collect a worn-out little girl.'

'I know,' she said excitedly and not at all sleepily. 'We could do a shift like Daddy, stay up now and then go to bed when he does.'

'Nice try.' Veronica pulled the duvet up and gave Layla a kiss on the forehead. 'Goodnight, again.'

'Goodnight, again.'

Veronica was about to get back to her messaging when her phone rang. Audrey's number flashed up on the screen. She hoped this didn't mean Audrey would be asking to stay out later; she was exhausted and she knew she wouldn't be able to sleep until Audrey was tucked up in her own bed.

She answered the call but she couldn't make out what Audrey was saying. 'Audrey, calm down.' Her heart skipped a beat, panic beginning to set in. 'Audrey, please, calm down, I can't understand a word.'

'Gran, I can't get home.'

'What do you mean, you can't get home? Where are you?'

'I don't know.'

'What do you mean, you don't know?'

She babbled out some more details and from what Veronica could pick up, she'd gone for a walk in the woods with Alex, the boy she was keen on. And then he'd kissed her and she'd run away. He hadn't hurt her but she was going on about not being sure, not feeling ready, and something about having some beer too.

Veronica did her best to keep calm. 'Is Alex there now?'

'I don't know where he is,' she shrieked. 'I don't know where I am, Gran.'

Veronica hadn't been in those woods for many years but she knew one thing: they were enormous. Getting lost would be easy. 'Audrey, can you use the map function on your phone, find your way out somehow?' She did her best not to think of her granddaughter all alone, frightened, lost.

She waited for Audrey to answer, but the response didn't come. And when she realised she'd lost the phone signal and couldn't get an answer again, Veronica felt a familiar warmth rise up in her body. Her breathing was increasing rapidly and the room began to spin. She did her best to take the deep breaths she'd been taught about when she'd tried to manage a panic attack before. But it wasn't working. She stumbled into the kitchen and, almost too dizzy to do so, steadied herself enough to bend down to the bottom drawer. She took out a brown paper bag, pulled the top apart, pushed her face into the opening and shut her eyes and breathed. And she counted in her head, allowing her breath to calm as she did so.

'Veronica . . .' A timid voice came from behind her, where she'd slumped against the wall oven, the bag still over her chin, mouth and nose.

It was Layla. How long had she been there? Judging by the worry on her face, long enough.

She kept the bag in place. A few more breaths, just a few, to get her equilibrium.

Layla's eyes filled with tears. 'You're scaring me.' She clutched her teddy bear to her chest, her little face creeping further and further behind it.

Veronica at last took the bag away. Layla had already sat at the table. She wouldn't be going to bed again, not like this. 'I didn't mean to scare you, I'm fine, honestly.'

She had to focus on Audrey now. She tried her number again, a second time, a third.

Should she call the police?

'Veronica, what's happening?' Layla's voice brought her back out of her trance.

The laptop on the table made its peculiar incoming message sound and Veronica thought about how happy and relaxed she'd been conversing with Morris, how easy it was to escape the feelings of panic that were usually triggered by far less than what was going on now.

Veronica didn't answer Layla's question, instead she brought up Sam's number on her phone. She was about to hit the green button to make the call when she clicked away from it. Panicking Audrey's mother when she didn't have much to tell her was pointless.

And then Veronica's phone rang again. It was Audrey.

'Gran, my phone keeps dropping out,' she panicked. 'I'm cold, I'm really scared.'

'Can you hear traffic?' If she could find her way back to the main road, she'd get her bearings, but if she didn't, she could end up miles away from Mapleberry.

'No, I can't hear . . .' She broke off. 'I thought I heard someone coming.'

Veronica shut her eyes, breathed slowly and calmly. 'Can you see anything at all? Audrey, you need to calm down,' she said when she heard sobbing. 'We need a land-mark, anything that may help.' She put as much authority into her voice as she could and stayed on the line until Audrey could name anything that might pinpoint the area of the woods where she was.

'There's some water,' Audrey said all of a sudden. 'I've found a pond, I think, not very big.'

Veronica remembered there were a few ponds in the woods, some that had walking trails around them and were accessed from parking areas closer to the roads.

'Good. Anything else?'

'Nothing,' she sighed, although at least she wasn't crying anymore; she seemed to find having Veronica on the end of the phone a lifeline. 'Wait, hang on, there's something on the other side. A stile!'

Veronica knew there were a few of those too. 'Anything else?' She tried to quell her panic at the radio silence until finally Audrey came back on the line.

'I can see a field with a row of barns, or they could be stables, I'm not sure. It's too dark to tell.'

There was only one farm on the other side of those woods, so Audrey had to have stumbled all the way to the boundary. Veronica felt they were getting somewhere. Or at least they had been until the call dropped out again. And this time, Veronica couldn't get her granddaughter back no matter how many times she redialled her number.

Veronica sat with her head in her hands and Layla softly rubbed the space between her shoulders. 'It'll be all right.'

'I wish your daddy was here,' she said out loud. He'd go there to get Audrey for her, she knew he would. He'd scour those woods until he brought her home.

'He's good in a crisis,' Layla agreed, tears dried up for now.

The practicality of Layla's summation made Veronica realise the only person here who could help Audrey now was her.

But how on earth was she going to do that?

'What's that funny sound?' Layla flipped up the top of the laptop, easily distracted, but when she saw Veronica clutching the paper bag still in her hands, her eyes shut as she tried to think of how she could possibly fix this. Her voice wobbled. 'Is Audrey going to be OK?'

Veronica couldn't share her fears. 'Yes, of course she is.' She had to be.

She put the bag down and picked up her phone again, and this time dialled the number of a local taxi firm. She rarely swore but she almost did when the wretched engaged tone blasted in her ear. It was a Saturday night near Christmas and she suspected this was going to be harder than she'd thought. She tried another two firms after that, then retried the original one again. But no success. She wanted to cry, she wanted to curl up in a ball and wish for this all to go away, but most of all she wanted Audrey here with her, she wanted to see her head off to her room with an absent goodnight and a smile Veronica treasured more than the teen knew.

'I don't want Audrey to get hurt.' Layla sniffed, the tears back again. This wasn't what Charlie would've wanted for his daughter. He'd trusted Veronica and here she was letting Layla down, Audrey, Sam too.

Veronica hugged Layla. 'She won't get hurt. I'll get to her – the taxi drivers will fit us in soon, I promise.'

She tried each of the taxi numbers again and again. Finally, she got through. 'Taxi please. Name is Veronica Bentley. House is number nine, Mapleberry Lane, Mapleberry. I need the taxi fast. Ten minutes? Great.' She said it as though she booked these all the time. As though she went out every Saturday night on the town and it was no big deal.

She hung up and the second she did, it hit her. She knew what this meant. And Layla did too.

'Veronica, you have to do it,' Layla urged. 'You have to leave the house. For Audrey, she needs you.' And as Veronica tried to focus on the small task of putting on her coat and shoes in the hallway, Layla got herself ready, found the house key and Veronica's bag. She even passed Veronica the brown paper bag she'd already been using in case she needed it again.

Veronica suspected she'd need a lot more than a flimsy little bag to save the day.

The taxi was going to be here in ten minutes. And after five years of failing to venture beyond the end of the garden path, Veronica had ten minutes to psych herself up and do this.

It was time to go and rescue her granddaughter.

PART FOUR
A Christmas Gift

Chapter Twenty

Veronica

Veronica's thoughts flipped between Audrey's tearful account of what had happened and the rage Sam would surely feel if she knew how Veronica's legs didn't want to move right now.

Six minutes until the taxi was due.

Layla was perched at the lounge window, arms resting on the sill, looking between the wooden shutters out onto the street.

Veronica was on the sofa, coat on, shoes on, brown paper bag clutched on her lap, her phone too in case, by some miracle, Audrey was able to call again. She'd a good mind to wring this Alex's neck, this boy who'd got Audrey into trouble when she should've been enjoying a pizza and a movie. She tried to focus on what she'd do to him to teach him a lesson, not on how heavy her limbs felt, how much her heart was beating as though outside of her chest.

These four walls had become her safe place; for the last five years she'd known little else. Her mouth went dry when there was a knock at the door.

'Come on,' Layla urged. 'Veronica, get up.' The little voice went on at her but she was frozen on the cushion of the sofa, the cushion only hours ago she'd relaxed into.

And then Layla went to the door. In a minute the taxi driver would ask her to come out, and when she didn't, he'd drive off. Audrey would be left, still in trouble, scared and alone, the way Sam must have been when Veronica hadn't been there for her over the years. Maybe the situation wouldn't have been quite so dramatic, but there would've been times Sam needed her to step up and she'd failed miserably. All the big milestones in Sam's life – leaving home, getting married, having a baby, going through a divorce – had been negotiated on her own because her mother didn't have enough oomph to pull herself out of her pit of misery. And the only person Veronica could blame for all of this was herself.

A man bobbed down beside the sofa. Veronica couldn't look at him. She wasn't even sure Layla should let a taxi driver come in like that; he could be casing the joint to come back another time and ransack the place.

A soft voice said her name. It was a velvety, smooth voice that calmed her in an instant. She shut her eyes as he talked. Saying all the right things: 'Let's go and get your granddaughter', 'Audrey needs you', 'There's no time to waste', and lastly, 'You can do this'.

'I can't.' She daren't open her eyes.

The man's hands, cool but reassuring, clasped her own. 'We've got this.'

Her eyes popped open and she gasped with surprise. Because this wasn't a taxi driver. This was her friend.

'Morris, it's you. What are you doing here?'

He didn't take his gaze from hers. 'A little birdie replied to my Facebook message.' He winked over at Layla.

'Good job she did as I was about to have another night-cap and go to bed.'

Veronica looked at Layla, who still had hold of her teddy bear. She couldn't thank her enough, because having Morris here was, she knew now, exactly what she needed. And she never would've asked him herself.

'She wrote with nice big capital letters to say you were in trouble, then she gave your address and told me to come quick,' Morris went on. 'I didn't hesitate. A friend in need takes precedent over my hot cocoa.'

'I thought it was whiskey.'

'Oops,' he said, grinning. 'I confess, I was trying to be cool, pretending I had a whiskey, but to be honest a milky drink before bed is much better for me. I think it keeps me looking young.'

More giggles from Layla, but she shot up when she heard the taxi's horn beep outside.

'Your granddaughter needs you,' Morris urged, 'and you can fill me in on the story in the taxi – how does that sound?'

She found herself nodding as she stood up, her hand looped through the crook of his elbow. She had to go to Audrey, be the one to put things right rather than the one who was responsible for every damn thing that went wrong.

They filed out to the taxi and she breathed steadily, as though that same paper bag from earlier was over her mouth and nose. She focused on the vast expanse of sky above, the endless space that had always felt less fearful than it should when she looked out at it from the back garden or the kitchen window. And now, it was a comfort blanket, the delicate stars peppering the dark, one of them winking as Veronica reached the end of the path.

She managed to give the name of the farm to the taxi driver and tell him she wanted the car park at the edge of the woods, the closest point she suspected they could park up to reach Audrey if she was where Veronica believed her to be. Hopefully the girl had had the sense to stay put, by the stream, near the stile with a view of the stables.

Layla shuffled all the way up and along the back seat. 'I should go in the middle as I'm short,' she said, as though this were just another outing, rather than not only a ridiculous time for a girl her age to be going out but also Veronica's first time beyond the safety of her house in years. 'But you need to sit there. Then you're next to Morris,' she instructed as Veronica took the middle seat, 'and he can hold onto you like I'm going to.'

Veronica shut her eyes and stretched her hands to each side, finding Layla's small warm hand on one side and Morris's much larger hand wrapped around hers, giving it a squeeze, from the other. And then, as the car pulled away, Morris asked what Audrey had told her about the area of the woods she was in. He believed it was exactly where Veronica thought, the perimeter of the farm, and assured her they'd have no trouble finding her.

Veronica didn't dare let doubt creep in, her only focus his soft voice and positivity until the taxi pulled into the car parking area she remembered from years ago when she'd taken herself off on long walks, enjoying the shade of the woodland in the summer, the crisp leaves in the autumn and the bite of cold in the winter.

The bite of cold. She felt panic rise, thinking of Audrey

freezing to death out here, but now that Morris had paid the taxi drive extra to hang around and wait, she didn't have time to think about anything other than finding her granddaughter.

They took the path down into the woods, the steps that led all the way to the perimeter of farmland. Layla walked between them. Veronica felt sure she saw her skip part of the way, as though she couldn't help herself, but the action kept her spirits lifted.

They trudged on, Veronica's heart pounding. They were getting close. They were almost there, and if Audrey wasn't, what would they do then? They should've called the police, they should've got sniffer dogs out, a search and rescue team, called on all the neighbours so the whole village turned out, they should've had radio announcements, television, anything to put out an alert.

'Gran!' The shriek almost scared the living daylights out of Veronica as they drew closer to the stile and the pond Audrey had earmarked.

'Audrey?' She couldn't see her but the crunching of twigs had her granddaughter flinging herself at her so hard she almost lost her balance.

And for once it was Veronica doing the comforting, the holding, the reassuring. She stroked her granddaughter's hair, shushed her, held onto her all the way back to the taxi and then all the way home as Morris talked away to the driver the entire time, as though this hadn't been a crazy mercy mission a few nights before Christmas.

It was three o'clock in the morning when Audrey came into the lounge and found Veronica sitting in her favourite chair. 'Can't sleep?' she asked her gran.

'I'm having trouble.' Veronica smiled. 'You can't sleep either?'

'I slept for a while, but my eyes are so puffy from crying I think that woke me up. I feel like they're stuck together. I looked in on Layla – she's sleeping like a baby.'

'I'm not surprised, it was a bit of excitement for her.' Veronica had already texted Charlie all of the details – she'd apologised profusely, understood why he'd never trust her with Layla again, but he'd written back to tell her not to be ridiculous. He suspected Layla would want him to up his game if this was what a night in with Veronica was like.

'I'm really sorry, Gran.'

'You've said that, many times, and no harm done.' Thank goodness the charge on Audrey's phone had lasted long enough for her granddaughter to call her and give her an inkling as to where she was. Otherwise, with the cold, tonight might have played out very differently. 'But I could wring that boy's neck for taking you into the woods and giving you beer.' She suddenly gasped.

'What's up, Gran?'

'What if he's still in the woods, lost? Oh Audrey, he could freeze to death.'

'Don't panic. He sent me a text – several, in fact.'

'And what did he have to say for himself?'

'He looked for me when I ran off, he kept looking until just after midnight when he found his way out of the woods and went home. He woke his mum, they were about to call the police to report a missing girl when I finally answered his texts to say I was home.'

'What happened in those woods, Audrey?' She wasn't sure she was ready for the answer.

'He kissed me.'

'And . . . ?'

'That was it. I panicked, I thought he'd want more and I didn't know if I was ready.' She began to cry and Veronica put an arm around her, relieved Alex was home, glad he hadn't tried to force Audrey into anything. They were just teenagers, having a little fun, but unfortunately for them it had gone wrong. 'Are you going to tell Mum?' She looked up from beneath those beautiful eyelashes of hers.

Veronica gave her a look that didn't need anything extra to be added. She had no choice but to be completely honest with Sam, because if she knew one thing about her daughter, it was that keeping her in the dark would be far worse than anything else you could do. Sam was practical, she faced up to things, she needed everything laid out in front of her to make her own decisions.

Veronica watched Audrey fiddle with the thread of cotton hanging from the bottom of her pyjama top. She looked five years younger when she was ready for bed, no make-up, no attitude, just Audrey.

And then a big smile passed across Audrey's face. 'Gran . . . you left the house.'

She matched her granddaughter's smile and then managed to repeat, 'I left the house.'

'You did that for me.'

'I had to.'

'I didn't do it on purpose, you know, but if I'd known that's what it took to get you out of here, I might have tried it sooner.'

'Don't even think about joking, Audrey.' This is what she should've had with Sam. She should've told her off and grounded her for things she did wrong, made up and talked and smiled and made jokes when the tension lifted. She'd missed out on all of that. And with Eddie too. The son she'd let down worse than Sam. What she'd done to him had been unforgiveable and she'd lost him for good. Something that would be with her until the day she died.

'Does this mean you'll go out again?' Audrey asked.

'I want to . . .' Her voice came out timid, because really, she had no idea. Going out because she'd had to, summoning the courage with others holding her up, knowing the stakes were high, was one thing. But moving past her agoraphobia in a way that would put her back to normal was going to be a long haul.

'Then maybe we'll take it slow, eh?'

'I like the sound of that.' She loved this girl; having her back in her life was a blessing she never wanted to take for granted. And when Sam came home, she'd tell her everything, not just about Audrey tonight, but about Eddie and the truth of what happened all those years ago. She'd left it too long already. No more secrets – it was time. 'Now, it may be three o'clock in the morning, but how about some cocoa?'

'Cocoa? Don't you mean hot chocolate?'

'Same thing.'

Audrey followed her into the kitchen, and when she took the cocoa out of the cupboard she asked, 'Didn't Morris mention he needed a cocoa when he got home?'

Veronica shrugged and measured milk into a jug before pouring it into a pan. 'I don't remember.'

'I think he was hinting at coming in.'

He had been, but it had been quite a night already, and

Veronica wanted to get Layla to bed. And so she'd decided that another day she'd invite Morris over to thank him for what he did tonight. Without him she wasn't sure even Layla's persuasion would've worked. And that would've meant Audrey could still be in the woods, freezing cold and scared. And Veronica would've let Sam down all over again.

As Veronica stirred the cocoa mixture, she told Audrey, 'I'm pleased Alex sent you those messages.'

'You are? You're not demanding I delete him from my contacts?'

'That's not my choice to make. It'll be Sam's.' She turned off the heat and poured the cocoa into the waiting mugs before taking them over to the table. 'So,' she began once she was sitting down, 'apart from tonight's debacle, how are you enjoying life in Mapleberry?'

'I assume this question is because you now know about my plans to move to New Zealand.'

'I'm that obvious?' Veronica clutched her cocoa mug between her palms. 'We'll come to that later, but for now I'm only asking about Mapleberry and being here, with me.'

'I like Mapleberry, and living with you has been one of the best things to happen in a long while.'

Veronica was momentarily flummoxed at how to respond. She'd expected a shrug, a nonchalant response that Mapleberry was OK. 'I never thought I'd hear you say anything like that,' she told Audrey. 'Not when you came here all stroppy, messy, attitude firing off all around these walls like little missiles I had to dodge.'

Audrey couldn't help but laugh and covered her mouth so she didn't wake Layla. 'That's quite an image and

I wasn't that bad. OK, maybe I was,' she added when Veronica cast her a look.

'Why did it get so unbearable with your mum, Audrey?'

Audrey sipped her cocoa quietly. 'I blamed her for Dad leaving.' She didn't meet Veronica's gaze now, instead looking into the milky depths of the mug. 'After he went, she was always on at me about everything, or at least that's how it felt. She asked questions all the time, rarely let up. I felt I couldn't start to have my own life or make any decisions. We'd have our moments where everything was fine, we'd actually be able to have a conversation, and then she'd do something and I'd go back to being angry.'

'But was it always Sam's fault?'

The look on Audrey's face told Veronica the teen hadn't tried to think of it that way before; it was a revelation that probably came from having space from her mum and stepping back to see the bigger picture.

'No, it wasn't. Sometimes I'd be rude, upset, annoyed, and I wouldn't even know why I was doing it. It was like I was someone else and one version of myself was telling me to pull myself together, the other part of me refused to stop. The worst was if we ever talked about school. Not just the trouble I got in before the summer, but whenever we talked about studies, exams, my future. And I hated the school I was at up there. I didn't have many friends apart from Sid.'

'Sometimes it's a case of quality over quantity.'

'I know, I learned that the hard way. There were some mean girls in our year, and they riled me all the time. You'd think if we just ignored each other it would all be fine, but they were like hens, peck peck pecking to get you to react, to create drama. But Sid says they've laid off him a bit – one of them told him he was cool for the prank we pulled. And I know it wasn't cool, it was stupid, but anything that makes his life easier is good as far as I'm concerned. I don't know how he sticks it – I desperately needed a change of school.'

'I think it may have worked.'

'Don't tell Mum, but I'm almost enjoying it.' She gave a small smile.

'I won't tell her, don't worry.'

'All my life I felt like I'd fallen between the cracks, that I couldn't get out. I felt helpless, no matter how much I wanted things to be different.'

Veronica understood where Audrey was coming from. She'd fallen into a crack too and had only just had the opportunity to peek up from down there and see that, actually, there could be a life worth joining if she was brave enough to take one rung of the ladder at a time.

'I want to prove myself to Mum,' Audrey admitted. 'I want to pass my exams and go on to a college to learn make-up artistry; it's what I've wanted for a long time.'

'You have direction – a lot of kids don't have that.'

'So why can't Mum see it?'

'She does; she just wants what's best for you, but it sounds as though you're well on your way to achieving that.' She sipped her cocoa. 'Was the New Zealand plan another opportunity for you to start over and make life changes?'

Audrey nodded. 'I miss my dad.'

'That's allowed.' Veronica gave Audrey's forearm a pat. 'It's natural, but take it from me, I know what it's like to have a child who worships their father and doesn't see the other person half the time.' She hadn't meant to sound so passionate, but it was frustrating knowing exactly how Sam felt, seeing Audrey push her away.

'Mum favoured Granddad over you?' The girl's eyes swam with tears and Veronica could see how hard this was for Audrey, how much she must have bottled up. She saw where the anger had come from when Audrey yelled at Sam after she found out Simon had already said he didn't want her going to New Zealand; it came from a place of fear, of fear that you couldn't control what was going on around you, that it was happening regardless of your input. You could flail around for ever and never make a difference. Audrey and Sam weren't so different, and neither was she. Because all of them seemed to be scared of losing control in one way or another.

'Your mum had a difficult childhood,' Veronica explained. 'There are things that went on that you wouldn't know about, but it's probably why she's so hard on you. She wants to be the perfect mum, she doesn't want to make the mistakes I made, and that means sometimes she makes the wrong decisions or seems a bit full-on, as though she's trying to control you rather than let you have the freedom to make your own choices.'

'Why didn't she tell me Dad had said he didn't want me to go?'

It seemed Audrey's overnight separation from her mum had finally made her realise this hadn't been Sam's doing, but Simon's all along. Perhaps being stranded in those woods had given Audrey a chance to really think about the mess her and Sam had found themselves in, her father's rejection, the family problems that had reached their boiling point a long time ago.

'Your mum and dad were in love once,' Veronica began,

'and I'm sure your dad will always love you. But by God he has his faults, and I'm sorry if this shocks you, but he's selfish.' She held her breath, waiting for her remark to backfire, and when it didn't, carried on. 'I don't think he means to be. But he is. He puts himself first, always. I could see it for myself, but Sam and I weren't close enough for me to talk about it with her. My marriage wasn't perfect either; your mum chose a man very much like her own father, I'm afraid. And in a marriage you have to put both parties at the forefront of your decisions, your actions. Simon left your mum and you, not the other way around. He went off with another woman and broke Sam's heart.'

Audrey, mouth agape, set down her mug. 'Dad met Heather after he and Mum broke up.'

Veronica shook her head. 'No, Audrey. And your mum never told you because she never wanted to hurt you. She's always protected you and I did the same for her over the years. Because Herman, your granddad, was lovely in many ways and we had a good marriage right up until I met a wall I couldn't climb over. He wasn't there helping me over, he was cowering on the other side hoping I wouldn't embarrass him. But I never told Sam any of that, I never shared my point of view with her, I backed away. I could see how happy she was, a real daddy's girl.'

'I never realised . . .'

'We talked about it recently,' said Veronica. 'And I need to talk to her some more. But for now, all you need to know is that Sam's overprotectiveness comes from a place of love, not one of interference and wanting you to do exactly what she wants. She longs for you and her to have what we never did. A relationship.'

'I want that too.' For almost four o'clock in the morning, they were doing well at such a deep conversation, but maybe waiting for the perfect time had always been Veronica's mistake. The perfect time wasn't always handed to you on a plate; sometimes you had to look out for the opportunity to move forward even before you felt ready. And at seventy-one she was at last grabbing that chance.

'Gran, you and Mum will get there.' Audrey must have read her thoughts. 'Don't give up on each other.'

She wanted so much to believe that what Audrey was saying was true. 'I'll do my best and I'm sure she will too. But I need you to talk to your mum, about your dad, your future, about last night. I'll give her the gist of what happened but then you'll need to sit down and work things through.' Audrey nodded. 'Now, if we don't go to bed we'll never wake up to answer the door to poor Charlie when he comes to rescue his daughter from the mad woman at number nine.'

When they'd rinsed their cups, Audrey wrapped her arms around her gran, and in the darkness of the kitchen Veronica tried to imagine Sam doing the same, holding the hug to let the meaning seep through, to let them both know they had a place in each other's hearts for ever.

Chapter Twenty-One

Sam

Charlie had come to collect Layla this morning and Sam had been sad to miss seeing him. All the while at the wedding yesterday, when she wasn't thinking about the wrath of Audrey since finding out about Simon's decision, Sam had been wondering what it would've been like to have Charlie at her side. Watching other couples dance, she'd realised despite Audrey's protestations at her having a relationship following Simon, she'd never been that sorry not to follow through with any of the men she'd become involved with over the years because none of them had ever come close to being right. Until now. Until Charlie.

'Layla enjoyed the sleepover?' Sam asked after she'd unpacked and went into the kitchen. Her mum seemed on edge. Audrey was hiding out upstairs, which was to be expected after finding out about Simon. Maybe they'd had words about Audrey's behaviour; the atmosphere was certainly tense, no doubt about it.

'She did. Sam, come, sit down.'

Sam didn't like the expression on her mum's face and she was right not to when the truth came flooding out about Audrey and everything that had gone on last night.

'She must've been terrified in those woods,' said Sam. 'I

can't believe she went there, and she was drinking!'

'Keep your voice down, keep calm – she did the right thing and called me.'

Sam exhaled hard and long. 'The right thing would've been not to go off with that boy in the first place. The right thing would've been to come home and meet her curfew. The right thing would've been not to drink beer!'

'She knows she made a mistake. She also knows I'll be telling you, and after this you can both discuss it rationally. You had a row before you left – don't make it into another one today. I want you to know that any punishment to be dished out will come from you, not me. I didn't want to interfere.'

Sam went over to the kitchen sink, rested her hands against it and looked out of the window. This had always been a good place to think about your troubles; she'd done it enough when she was younger, and she'd seen her mum do it too. A few pathetic flakes of snow made an effort to fall but disintegrated the second they hit the grass. How could Audrey put herself in such a vulnerable position? And why do it when she was out of town?

But there was another focus now, which wasn't all about Audrey. Sam turned to look at her mum, twisting the sleeve of her cardigan between her fingers, the way she did when she wasn't sure what to say or do. The habit had annoyed Sam growing up, she'd wanted to yank the material from her mother's hands, yell at her that she needed to be the mum who was there for her, not the person in need. But now, she saw the vulnerability. And what her mum had done last night had been nothing short of miraculous. She'd stepped up, she'd saved the day, she'd been a mother when Sam wasn't there to do it herself.

Sam went over to her mum's side. 'You went to get Audrey.'

'I had no choice.'

'You left the house.' She threw her arms around her mum. 'You did that for me, you did it for us.' But then the smiles quickly faded. And she felt the tears come. The tears that had built up since the confrontation with Audrey, the upset she'd felt since coming home today, the crying she'd not done enough of when her mum was present physically but not emotionally.

And she couldn't stop. Big, jerky sobs wracked her entire body.

She felt her mum's hand on her back, circular motions forming, the comforting feeling she'd only ever got from one parent in years gone by. Until now.

Slowly Sam felt herself calm, getting perspective ready for the next step.

Audrey ventured downstairs an hour or so later. Sam had passed through a gamut of emotions, from anger to sadness and now a balance she hadn't felt in a long time. Because today she felt hope for the future, for all of them. She gave her mum a grateful look as she took her laptop and disappeared upstairs to let Sam and Audrey have some time together.

'I'm not going to yell at you.' Sam watched Audrey sitting opposite as though she was facing a firing squad. 'But we are going to have a little talk about boys, sex, drinking alcohol and all the other things we usually both avoid.'

Audrey cringed. 'As long as it's not a conversation about you and sex, I think I can handle it.'

Over a cup of tea each they began to talk, not that Audrey didn't know the facts of life, of course, but what she needed to hear about was responsibility, being ready, emotions that could so easily become confused. And she needed to hear it all from Sam and nobody else. They talked about friendships as much as boyfriends, boundaries on both sides. They discussed underage drinking, and Audrey declared her first taste of beer 'revolting'.

'A boy taking you into the woods is something that should ring alarm bells.'

'But I know him.'

'You might know him, but do you trust him?'

Audrey shrugged. 'I'm not sure. I think that's why I ran.'

'Then that tells me you didn't know him well enough. Going for a hot chocolate in the café might have been a smarter thing to do.' Audrey nodded and Sam wondered, if they'd been doing this all along – communicating – it wouldn't be so overwhelming. But Audrey had never been ready to listen and absorb before, and neither had Sam, who knew she'd been prescriptive in everything she said. She was having to learn how to not only talk to her daughter but listen too. Sam got the impression Audrey's latest experience had been eye-opening enough to tell her you couldn't always trust a boy, or a man, for that matter. People lied, told half-truths; judgement played a huge part in your decisions, whatever age you were.

'I'm going to need his first name, his last name, and I'll take it from there,' said Sam, watching her daughter's fear set in.

Audrey recoiled. 'What are you going to do?'

'I need to speak with his parents. No arguments, Audrey.' And for once she didn't give any. There was no yelling back at her, no defence already prepared, no barking that she was overreacting.

Once Sam had the information stored in her phone, ready to try to find out who the parents were and make contact that way, Sam moved onto another order of business. 'Why didn't you talk to me about New Zealand?'

'Would you have listened?'

'Probably not at the start. What mother wants to hear that their daughter wants to get as far away from her as possible?'

'That wasn't why I was doing it.' Audrey looked up sheepishly. 'OK, maybe it was partly that at the start when I was feeling angry with you. But it was more than that. I wanted to be with Dad. I miss him.' Her voice wobbled. 'He doesn't bother calling me very often.'

'I'm sure he's busy with work, and then there's the time difference.'

'He doesn't come and see me either.'

'It's expensive.'

'Mum, stop making excuses!' The fiery Audrey Sam had come up against countless times over the years reared her head. 'And I know he left you for Heather – you never told me that.' Her voice simmered to a firm line of argument.

It looked like her mum had filled Audrey in, and it was something of a relief. 'You didn't need to know.'

'Maybe I did; perhaps it would've stopped me painting you as the baddie in all of this. You know I did, right?'

Sam fiddled with the edge of the pile of placemats in the centre of the table. If she twiddled enough, the wicker would come unravelled, so she left it alone, patted it gently.

'I know you did. I didn't want to turn you against your

dad. I didn't want you against me either, but I thought that with me here, I got the best of you anyway. I got to see you every day, I got to see you grow up, he didn't.'

'I don't think he's too bothered.'

Sam's stomach lurched. 'Please don't ever think that. Dad has made mistakes, he isn't the most forthcoming with contact, but he loves you. If he didn't, he wouldn't make contact at all. He doesn't do it because he has to, he does it because he wants to. He's just not very good at it.' She raised a laugh from her daughter. 'I didn't need to rub it in that he's terrible at being a father across the miles. That's exactly what I think, by the way, but telling you wouldn't have made it any easier for you and it wouldn't have made me feel better either.'

'I thought if I went over to New Zealand, I could slot in and be part of a big family – siblings, two parents, a lifestyle that's completely different.' Sam's heart constricted. A family. She wanted more than what she was giving her. 'But over the last few months, since coming here, I see I've already got a pretty good family.'

Sam released the tension from her hands balled up in her lap as she heard the hurtful words change to a sentence that had her almost daring to hope they could move past this and come out the other side happy. 'You do?'

'Yes – you, Gran, Layla, even, she's been like a little sister to me. She annoyed me at first, but she's just like me. She has a dad, not a mum, she needs other people, she needs Gran, and me. She's worse off too because her mum died. I have two parents, both still alive, one a bit useless, but now that I know, I can deal with it.'

'You sound far too rational,' said Sam.

'True, the Audrey in the summer would've flipped out

324

and probably gone to New Zealand anyway, stuff whether her dad wanted her or not. But the Audrey now can see a bigger picture.'

'I'm liking this Audrey now.' Sam smiled. 'But please believe me when I say it's not that your dad doesn't want you. That's not why he said not to come, why he won't pursue the visa at the moment.'

'Don't defend him.'

'It's not defending, it's just expressing what he's so pathetic at communicating himself. He loves you but he's settled in a new life. Reading between the lines, I'd say he's scared that you joining them will make him solely responsible for you and he isn't sure whether he can do it or whether he'll mess it up. I know he feels guilty for leaving us both.'

'How can you be so sure you know what he thinks?'

Sam smiled gently. 'I was married to him – I know him. He was a good dad in many ways but responsibility was never his forte. He showed that when he walked out. He tries to shut the door on anything that's too hard, to only go through a door that's familiar with no surprises, one he knows he won't fail with. Part of his learning curve needs to be to tackle things he's uncomfortable with, like getting to know his teenage daughter, but that's not for me to tell him and it's not for me to guide him through. I don't want you to fall out with him over this.'

'I won't – I still love him.'

'I'm glad.' She didn't want Simon to disappear from Audrey's life. Quite the opposite: she hoped he'd stay in it, despite the distance. 'Write to him or call him to say hello. You might have to be the one to make the first move every time, but once you've got hold of him, you'll know he loves you. And why don't you suggest going on holiday there? I know he sends money every year. Perhaps get to know one another at the stage in life you're at now. It'll be very different to when he left. I think when you're with him, he'll realise what an amazing daughter you are and perhaps he'll stop being such a jerk and panicking. Sorry.' She shouldn't call him names, not to Audrey.

'He is a jerk, Mum, for what he did to you. To us. But he'll always be my dad.'

Sam understood that more than most. She'd been so absorbed by her own father she hadn't given her mum a look-in most of the time because it was all too difficult. And wasn't it a basic human tendency to avoid a challenge when you could bask in something that already made you happy?

'I never mentioned a holiday to him,' Audrey pondered. 'Maybe it's a good idea.'

'I'd say so.'

'Would you come? To New Zealand with me?'

'You want me to go on holiday with you? To stay with Heather and Simon?' She almost laughed until she realised Audrey was serious. 'Maybe. Talk about it with your dad, we'll discuss it too, perhaps make some plans. I'm sure there's plenty you and I could do together, and also lots I could do on my own while you spend time with the other part of your family.'

Audrey didn't ask straight away, and when she did, she looked worried, as if she wasn't sure of the answer. 'Would you have been sad if I'd emigrated?'

'You don't need to ask, surely. I'd have been heartbroken, but I also know you're growing up and at some point you'll do what you want to do. That's OK. All I hope is that you'll come and see me now and then.' She wished she'd done the same with her own mother, but it was no use trying to turn back the clock, the hands only ever ticked in one direction.

'I like it here, but I won't be a burden to Gran for ever,' said Audrey.

'Something tells me she wouldn't mind if you were.'

'Do you think she'll start going out of the house more now she's done it once?'

'I think she's got a long road ahead of her. We've got you, and I suppose Alex, to thank for getting her to go out last night. It was a huge thing – I still can't quite believe she did it.'

'Me neither. And Morris stepped in too.'

Sam leaned forward and, just like that, she got her wish: she and Audrey were gossiping like two girlfriends about the new man in her mum's life. Before, an almighty row would've played out for days, maybe weeks, and they would never have reached a mutual understanding. Audrey would probably have been up in her room, looking at her books on New Zealand, still dreaming of an escape; Sam would've been sitting on her own in the lounge of their big house in Cheshire, wondering where it had all gone so wrong. Now they'd had the parent–daughter showdown, the advice had been doled out, and they'd managed to move on.

'I think we need to look at getting Gran some professional help,' said Sam when they'd finished talking about the silver fox from around the corner and what his intentions were towards Audrey's grandmother. 'I did a bit of research online – there may be medication or therapies that can help her. But I'm no expert and I think it's time I supported her and got her the help she needs.'

'She's lucky to have you.'

'I don't know about that.' Sam knew she'd neglected her mother and the serious problems she had. She'd hidden from them over the years and hadn't spent any more time in this house than was necessary. But when she'd needed her the most, her mum had finally been there, and now it was Sam's turn to do the same.

Audrey put her finger to her lips when Sam's mum came downstairs.

'Safe to come in?' her voice timidly called around the door jamb.

'Very safe.' Audrey smiled.

She brought her laptop in with her and set it down on the table where Sam and Audrey were talking.

'You're up to something,' Sam said.

Her mum looked about to deny it but must've known it was hopeless. 'I've been thinking what we can do to Alex – a punishment, if you like.'

'Gran, I don't think—'

Sam put up a hand to stop her daughter. 'I want to hear this.'

'I took the liberty of finding his parents' names – well, Morris asked around and it appears my new friend June had heard of the family and Bridget managed to find an email address for them. Goodness knows how she did it so quickly.'

'If you guys were in charge of the country!' Sam shook her head. 'God help us all . . .'

'Sam, I don't want to overstep . . .'

'But?' When her mum hesitated she urged her on.

'Well, I was trying to take away part of the stress for you, Sam.'

'Mum, would you just tell me what you're up to.'

'I thought rather than take this through official channels, perhaps Alex could do a few things to help out and show he's a good person underneath.'

'What did you do, Gran?'

'I've been looking at the kindness calendar for some inspiration, and between me and my new friends we've drawn up a little January calendar for young Alex.'

Her mum seemed to be waiting for approval. 'I'm happy with that.' She winked at her daughter. 'This will tell us more about Alex as a person – it might help you to know whether you can trust him.'

Her mum continued to unveil her plans. 'His parents were relieved to hear Audrey was fine. They'd known all about the woods, of course, but not about the beers. When I told them, they were falling over themselves to apologise on his behalf, and when I asked whether they'd mind if I got him involved with some community service acts, they sounded relieved that I wasn't going to the police or the school about their son. I've heard Alex's mum has been unwell for a while so I think we should all be glad things worked out in the end.'

Sam agreed, and she and Audrey went around to the laptop so they could see what the oldies had been planning between them. The conversation thread in their closed group was long, all of them putting their opinions forward. They'd drawn up a draft plan that allocated Alex three tasks a week – he would be in GCSE studies, so they didn't want to go over the top, just enough to let him know the seriousness of underage drinking and taking a girl into the woods late at night. Tasks were wide-ranging: round up a couple of mates to come and put away all of June's garden furniture that was sitting out in all weathers, waiting for someone strong to come to the rescue; put Morris's Christmas decorations back in the loft for him after his son got them down the last time he was here; fill a bird feeder every Sunday for a month, to hang on Veronica's bird table; and lastly, their absolute favourite, do Bridget's weekly shop for her for four weeks. She'd already made up her list and topped it with incontinence pads – a couple of varieties he'd be sure to have to search for and maybe even ask behind the counter.

'She doesn't need them yet,' said Sam's mum, as though they were talking about headache tablets, 'but Bridget says young lads baulk at the idea of buying sanitary towels, and because at her age he'd see through that in an instant, she's chosen the next best thing.'

'Hey, what does it say there?' Sam peered closer. 'Morris!'

'What's he written?' Audrey quickly looked before her gran could shut the laptop. 'Condoms!' She was laughing as hard as Sam. 'Gran, it could be your lucky night!'

'Stop it, the both of you,' she scolded, but her voice shook and gave away her amusement. 'I think the idea is to make Alex uncomfortable, but maybe it's Morris's way of telling him to practise safe sex when he's old enough to have it.'

'He's sixteen,' said Audrey.

'Still too young,' Sam and her mum said at exactly the same time.

With her mum going back to make more plans via her online friendship group, Sam warmed a couple of mince pies in the microwave. 'Cream?' she offered Audrey. 'I've done one for Gran too,' she said when the microwave pinged.

'I'll run it up to her.'

When Audrey came back, she was laughing. 'Gran's really into this Alex project – she's set up a Zoom meeting with Morris, Bridget and June, and they're having a right old laugh.'

'Zoom? Your gran knows how to use Zoom?'

'I taught her.'

'You've been good for her.'

'Even though I made her leave the house last night?'

'*Especially* because you made her leave the house.'

Audrey caught a morsel of mince pie that dropped from her spoon and settled it on top of the cream. 'So are you ever going to tell me who Eddie is?' She put a spoonful into her mouth.

Sam hadn't expected the question, but this time she didn't avoid it. 'I suppose it's time I did.' She finished the last of her mince pie, brushed the stray crumb from the tablecloth onto the plate, and then began to tell her daughter all about Eddie, the brother she hadn't seen since he was thirteen years old and her mother made an unimaginable decision.

Audrey took a while to digest what she was told, but when Sam had finished, she picked up her phone. 'I think you and Gran could do with some space this time. If neither of you talk about Eddie, it's probably time you did.'

'I know.'

'I'll head out, if I'm allowed.' Seeing Sam's confusion, she added, 'I thought I might be grounded, you know, after last night.'

'To be honest, there's so much going on in my head

that punishing you is the last thing on my mind. I think you've learnt a valuable lesson.'

'In that case, I'll go and see Layla. Charlie's lent us his wheelbarrow and we've got front paths to grit with salt. He's helping us.' She smiled. 'Otherwise I don't think we'd manage. I've taken a spade from Gran's shed.'

'I wondered what that was doing by the front door.'

'It's freezing out there so make the most of sitting this act of kindness out,' said Audrey. 'I'll tell Gran to come downstairs.' She didn't wait for Sam's assent; she called up the stairs to say Sam needed her in the kitchen.

Her mum probably thought it was a cooking-related emergency. Unfortunately it was anything but.

Chapter Twenty-Two

Veronica

S he looked around the kitchen, sniffed the air, but there was nothing in the oven or on the cooktop. 'Audrey said you needed me.' She couldn't even see any ingredients lined up.

'Sit down, Mum.'

'This doesn't sound good. I thought you were happy with the Alex plan?'

'I am – this isn't about that.'

'Then what is it?'

Sam took a deep breath. 'I think we've all put it off far too long, left too many things unsaid in this family. That's certainly the case with Audrey, and I know it is with you and me as well.'

'Right then. Tea?'

'No, Mum, no tea. Not yet, just talking.'

No tea? Not even as a distraction? But the usual panic didn't rise up; perhaps she'd been having too much fun with Operation Punish Alex upstairs, laughing too hard at some outrageous suggestions she was glad Sam and Audrey hadn't seen. Condoms were the least of their worries.

'I want to talk about Eddie, Mum.'

Veronica had known this was coming. How could it

not? She grappled with where to start, but thought back to the way she'd told Morris. It had been in the written word, not the spoken, but she'd managed it. Now she had to find strength; she was learning to do that a lot these days, to prove herself worthy of a happiness she'd never thought she'd be able to find again.

'You were a daddy's girl through and through,' Veronica began, Claude leaping up onto her lap so he didn't miss out on anything. Having him there helped, her hand rhythmically stroking him from between his ears, down along his back. 'When I got bad, you clung to him all the more, the normal parent rather than one who was starting to become an outcast.'

'I never thought about it that way. But I'm starting to understand.'

Veronica knew she had to be thinking of Simon's relationship with Audrey. 'All you could see, and I don't blame you, was that your mother wasn't doing the job she should be doing. I wasn't a very good parent in that kind of state. I'd let you down. What you didn't see was that your dad actually made it worse for me. In our wedding vows we said the words: "in sickness and in health", and I've no doubt we both meant them. But I don't think Herman even considered that a sickness could take the form of something he didn't recognise. If I'd had heart problems or cancer or anything else he could see with his own eyes, I think it would've been easier, he might have supported me more. But an anxiety disorder? Not a chance. Remember all those arguments we had?'

Sam hung her head. 'I used to turn my music up loud – I hated listening to them.'

'They happened all the time and whenever I got worse,

the arguments escalated. They chipped away at me. Herman didn't understand, I retreated even more and he reacted worse each time. The rowing began to overshadow everything else, including what was best for our children. We were both guilty of not seeing that. And Herman was a proud man.' She paused. 'He was embarrassed by me.'

'Mum, I don't think—'

'No, Sam. He was. And you were blinkered – you never saw it.' Where this confidence had come from, Veronica had no idea, but the words were flooding out now as though whatever dam had been blocking them had been removed. 'It's the same with Audrey and Simon. She loves her dad; you never told her the truth about him and so in her eyes he's still the golden boy.' She didn't let herself react to Sam's watery eyes and the realisation that her dad may not have been quite the perfect man she'd always considered him to be. 'You hated me when Herman died, you resented me, I know you did. I used to think you wished I'd died instead.'

Sam gasped. 'I never, ever wished for that. I promise you.' She sniffed and chose her next words carefully. 'You're right to think I resented you – I did for a long time and I'm not sure I ever stopped. It became easier to do that than face my own grief half the time. And not just grief when Dad died, but after losing Eddie too. Meeting Simon was my ticket away from here, out of Mapleberry, a chance to leave it all behind. I got caught up enough to think it was what I wanted. I won't say I didn't love Simon, but over the years I have sometimes wondered whether I would've even married him in the first place if things had been different at home, if I'd been happier here. But please believe me when I say I never hated you.

335

I just wanted my mum back. I wanted the woman who made butterfly cupcakes with me for my sixth birthday, the mum who dressed up as a caterpillar for my animal-theme party one year, the mum who held my hand when I lay in a hospital bed with suspected appendicitis and they shoved needles into me to test my blood. That was the mum I wanted, and I didn't know how to reach her.'

Veronica wished she could've brought the woman Sam was talking about back a long time ago, but no matter how much she'd wanted to, she'd never been able to turn a corner. 'I'm sorry, Sam, I'm sorry for everything.'

Sam's voice softened. 'Do you have any idea when it all started? When you began to not want to go out. Something must've happened to trigger it, but I don't think you ever told me.'

'I didn't tell you, but I do know.' Veronica pulled a tissue from her pocket and blew her nose, sending a perturbed Claude leaping off her lap and into the lounge. 'One day at the hospital I was working a regular shift. You were ten at the time, it was the day after your birthday, and the evening before I'd taken you and a bunch of friends to ice-skate—'

'And we had the giant hot chocolates afterwards to warm up.' Sam beamed. 'I remember. They came served with a side bowl of smarties. That was a good birthday.'

Veronica let the moment settle. 'The next day at the hospital there was nothing out of ordinary until towards the end of my shift. It was dark outside; the ward had gone into that lull after dinner, before visiting hours began. I was heading back to the nurses' station and all of a sudden someone shoved me from behind. I fell to the floor and whoever it was kept hitting me around the head, scratching my face as I turned to try to get away. They kicked me hard and I couldn't fight them off.' Sam was shell-shocked, but Veronica couldn't stop now. 'I'd seen worse enough times; nurses suffer such dreadful abuse, both physical and verbal, but this incident really shook me. There was blood everywhere from my nose and my lip, and I couldn't stop shaking as my colleagues picked me up off the floor. I hadn't seen it coming, that was the worst thing. The other nurses and doctors were wonderful, cleaned me up, but I didn't want to go home. It was a woman who'd attacked me and her family came to apologise on her behalf. She had mental health problems and I doubt she was in the best environment. I thought I was fine, no harm done. And I wasn't taking it any further. I just wanted to carry on as normal.

'A week or so later, as I left the hospital following a late shift, I crossed the car park and I swear I heard someone behind me. When I turned, there was nobody, but I kept hearing footsteps. I turned around again and again, in circles, unable to see anyone, waiting for someone to beat the living daylights out of me. I was dizzy, I couldn't breathe, I sank down onto the concrete and all I remember is one of the nurses I'd been on shift with hoisting me up and taking me inside. I'd had a panic attack over nothing, just because I thought I'd heard something. And that was what scared me the most. It wouldn't have been so bad if it was justified, but it was my mind playing tricks on me.'

Veronica watched her daughter and wondered; would Sam have sat as patiently as this if she'd told her everything years ago? Probably not. It was a lot to take in, unpleasant information to wade your way through and attempt to understand.

'The second time I had a panic attack was when I was in the park with you. A jogger ran past my shoulder, giving me no space, and I was terrified. I couldn't get you out of the swing – it had a funny hook across the middle to stop you falling out and my fingers couldn't work it. A few of the other mums were staring – I was convinced they thought I was mad. I thought I was going to be sick.

'The next time it happened was in the supermarket and I can't remember why that one was, only that all I wanted to do was get home to the safety of my house. I had a few more attacks after that and gradually the boundaries of my world diminished. I gave up the job I'd always loved, I stopped seeing friends and eventually they stopped calling. I wouldn't go outside unless it was absolutely necessary, and even then I couldn't wait to get back home again. Your father dragged me out a handful of times, to school, mainly, when our presence was required. I tried to tell him I wasn't up to it but he never listened. This house –' she looked around the walls that had hugged her safely for so long – became my safe harbour. Going out anywhere in public became my biggest fear; I was constantly fretting that I'd have another panic attack and not be able to breathe, that nobody would help, that I'd die, that everyone would see how useless I really was.'

'Mum, I wish I'd known.'

'Would it have made any difference?' She swished her hand. The answer didn't matter now. 'I used to be good at problem-solving, but that was for other people. I worked as part of a team when I was a nurse, I frequently faced issue after issue in my working day, but when it came to my own troubles, they were impossible to deal with. I had no idea how to join the real world again, and then I lost you. And I lost Eddie.'

'I wish I'd known Dad wasn't supporting you, that you were basically alone in all of this.'

Not only had he not supported her, he hadn't even tried to understand. But who knows what he'd been thinking and they couldn't ask him now, so Veronica had learned to let go of some of her anger over the years. She knew it wasn't going to change anything to blame anyone else. And Herman was still Sam's father, she still loved and missed him, and Veronica had her moments when she wished he was by her side. She wondered, had he lived decades on, if he would have eventually tried to help her or would it have been the thing that broke them in two?

'Mum, what happened with Eddie?'

'When you left, I got much worse. My world was crumbling. It felt like an avalanche coming for me, the weight of it about to engulf me no matter what I did. Eddie was thirteen.' Her voice caught. 'He needed his father but he'd gone, I couldn't bring him back, and I couldn't do the job of one parent, let alone two.'

'I should've stayed for him,' Sam said, shaking her head guiltily. 'He's my brother.'

'No, Sam, you're not going to take any of the blame. It was my doing, nobody else's.' Veronica needed to gather herself for this part. Nobody, least of all Sam, who needed to hear this the most, had ever got her to talk so much. Not even the counsellors, who'd tried their best in the early days, their forlorn looks when she refused to come around to their way of thinking, who still appeared in her thoughts every now and then when she wondered where Eddie was now, whether he was happy.

'Eddie was a late baby,' she began. 'I was forty when he came along and you were a teen.' She let herself indulge in the happier memories of that time, bringing home a new bundle of joy, watching his first smiles, savouring the feel of his heavy head against her chest as she rocked him to sleep after feeding. 'Eddie came as a total surprise. I'd struggled to get pregnant a second time after I had you and in the end we just accepted we wouldn't add to our family. Life carried on and then, when we least expected it, Eddie came along. He was only a baby when the attack at the hospital happened, and at first he was a comfort. Going home and hugging you and cradling Eddie in my arms, it helped me hold onto things that mattered the most. I could see that my children, my precious family, was still intact and hadn't been broken.

'It got harder after that. I tried to act as though I was back to normal rather than constantly on edge, but it wasn't so easy. As Eddie went through the terrible twos, the challenging threes and then before primary school, he was far more of a handful than you ever were. I guess it's the difference between boys and girls. He had so much energy. Herman taught him to play football outside in the street to give me a break, especially if I'd worked nights, and I kept my worries and my anxiety largely to myself in return. I knew Herman didn't want to talk about it. If I ever tried, he'd give me a hug, tell me I'd be fine and I was safe now, and then he'd move on. I don't think he could ever see how deep-rooted my issues had become. How could he when I didn't even see it myself? It went on for years, slowly building, slowly wearing me down bit by bit.

'Having you and Eddie see and hear all the fighting between me and your dad was difficult. I wanted to be able to soothe you both but I couldn't. And when Herman died, the fragile pieces of me that were just about clinging on fell away. He'd been holding our family together when everything that went wrong was my fault. I felt guilty, ashamed of how little I could do for my own children; I couldn't even cope with their grief.'

When Veronica began to cry, Sam passed her a fresh tissue and made them both a cup of camomile tea. The break in the tension allowed Veronica to gather her thoughts before she carried on, tea in front of her. She clasped her hands around the mug, although not for warmth, the open fire did that job well enough, but more as a way of tethering herself to the moment to let it all sink in.

'Was it you or Dad who asked Auntie Dotty to help out?' Sam asked.

Veronica grunted. 'Your auntie Dotty always thought I wasn't good enough for your dad, and when I started to have problems, she leapt in with gusto. I saw it as almost an I-told-you-so. I don't doubt she loved you and Eddie, especially you. She'd never had children of her own and I could tell she enjoyed having the company, someone to spoil with trips to the zoo, cafés at the weekends, visits to the cinema and the shopping centre, places I couldn't cope with anymore.'

'I loved Auntie Dotty,' Sam admitted before she looked at her mum. 'We were in touch a lot over the years. But I always wanted to do those things with you. Auntie Dotty was wonderfully kind, fun sometimes, but nobody could've ever taken your place.'

Dotty was dead now but it still gave Veronica a certain level of satisfaction to hear Sam's words. 'Perhaps I should've been more grateful to her, but we'd never got on and so I left it to Herman to thank her for her help. She was there for you until you moved away, and I'm glad you kept in touch. I don't resent her the way I once did.'

'She had her moments but I think she was really lonely,' said Sam, 'and I think it's what made me bond with her. I was lonely too.'

Just when Veronica thought she couldn't feel any more sadness, Sam's words struck her down again. 'I never thought of you as lonely – you had so many friends, boy-friends, and your dad for a time.'

'I guess loneliness isn't always about the number of people. Perhaps sometimes it's the inability to connect with the one person you want to see you the most.' She sipped her tea and Veronica did the same because it felt right. 'Why didn't you reach out to Auntie Dotty when it came to Eddie?'

'You and Eddie had always got on, but not after your dad died.' She knew by Sam's look that she wasn't wrong there. 'You were different children. You turned to your auntie, to your friends, you busied yourself with your exams and focused on going to university. Eddie, on the other hand, retreated into himself. He was like Herman in that way: he didn't wear his heart on his sleeve, he kept a stiff upper lip when he thought he should do. I think that's why he never tried to turn to your auntie Dotty. That or the fact he couldn't stand that god-awful perfume she wore that infiltrated the entire house whenever she came over.'

Sam began to laugh. 'Don't speak ill of the dead.' When Veronica covered her mouth, she laughed again. 'It was revolting, I agree. I even tried to buy her a different bottle one Christmas.'

'How did that go down?'

'Quite well, although I'm not sure she ever wore it.'

They shared a moment, one that should've happened long before now but hadn't since before Sam reached her teens.

'Mum, I should've done more to help you.'

'I've told you, Sam, none of this is your fault. You couldn't have helped when I was uncommunicative, keeping things to myself because I felt as though I was slowly going more and more crazy. And after you left, I couldn't cope with anything, especially with Eddie. I didn't want to ruin his life like I'd ruined yours.'

She never let herself think about the dreadful day she'd made the call to social services. The day she had blocked out. It was as though she'd had a mini breakdown and pushed away all the feelings that made it terrible. But now she had to share.

'The day I called social services, it was following another panic attack, the worst yet. I was out buying a gift for Eddie's thirteenth birthday. I was determined to get him something special because I knew I wasn't fulfilling much of a parent role, particularly after Herman died. Eddie had become a shell of the boy I'd brought into the world. He'd stopped smiling the way he once had, he didn't laugh like he used to, especially after you and he drifted apart, and Auntie Dotty was never going to relate to a teenage boy the way she did to you. I didn't deserve Eddie's love and he definitely didn't deserve what a sorry excuse for a mother I'd become.'

'What happened that day?' Sam's voice broke into the

memories, the horrible pain of that time.

'You know how good he was at drawing?'

Sam smiled. 'I remember. He put me to shame; even at ten he was drawing things an artist would have difficulty with. Remember that elephant he drew after a school trip to the safari park? And the magpies he did for a school project? Those looked like they'd been taken from the pages of a printed book.'

'His favourite thing to draw were birds, do you remember? He'd always complain they didn't stay still long enough.' Eddie had loved to talk about animals and wildlife; it was a passion as much as his art. He'd longed for a pet of his own, but his dad said a firm no and Veronica didn't have the gumption to argue, and when Herman had gone she didn't have the strength to try anything new. The familiar became the only thing she could cling onto. 'For his thirteenth birthday I wanted to buy him some art supplies and a robin redbreast. I'd seen a figurine in the toy shop, a model on a stand with all the intricate details, but I couldn't even manage to buy it for him – my panic attack in the shop ruined it, and I'd failed him yet again. When I got home that day I shut myself in my bedroom. I didn't even answer the door to the woman from the art shop who dropped around the things I'd chosen without a request to pay her. She was incredibly kind to do that. I'd been at the counter, my credit card hadn't worked, the man behind me in the queue started to get agitated and I don't know why it sent me into a state but it did.

'For days after that incident I didn't eat, I didn't wash, I didn't cook Eddie meals or do anything for him. I didn't know how to pull myself together and I couldn't even look him in the eye when I was such a mess. In the end I called the number of a social worker recommended to me by a friend at work who'd tried to help me. It was one of the last times people bothered to call in and try to coax me out of whatever it was I was trapped by. I'd put up such resistance nobody knew what to do anymore. I called the number and I told them I couldn't look after my son. Full stop. They came to the house, they saw the state it was in, that a thirteen-year-old was trying to look after himself and hold things together. By then the bills had mounted up, the electricity had been cut off, the house was freezing. They took him to a safer place.'

'Just like that?'

'It happened over time.' Veronica was so ashamed, she hadn't ever wanted to share those details. 'I had a counsellor come and talk to me more than once, but I'd made my mind up. In my head I had nothing to offer. I couldn't love or respect myself, let alone a child. You'd left, and your brother deserved so much more than I could give. I refused all contact, he was fostered by a family with other children and I thought he was better off. He came to the house once; I knew it was him because he called through the letterbox. I covered my ears, so I couldn't hear his voice, the pain, the anguish. I'd lost him.

'I had more counselling over the years. Auntie Dotty knew what had happened and, to give her credit, she tried to talk me around in her own unique way, but by making me feel guilty for letting Herman down,' she explained to Sam. 'The irony that he'd let me down in more ways than she'd ever know wasn't lost on me and I told her to please leave me alone. She didn't come back after that.

'The counsellor made some progress with me, I began to see glimmers of hope, so I wrote to Eddie a few times but he never wrote back. I couldn't blame him. I stopped when I suspected he was far better off without me. I functioned day to day, just about, but I'd stopped seeing friends and when I went out it was quick – I talked to nobody unless I had to.

'One day, around the time Eddie turned twenty-three, a former nursing friend reached out to me and told me she'd heard Eddie was married with children of his own. This friend knew the family he'd married into and he'd moved out to Canada.'

'Eddie's in Canada?'

Veronica's breathing didn't feel right. Her palms clammy, her mouth dry, she felt dizzy, but then Sam's hands were on her shoulders, pressing them down, telling her she was all right, she was here at home, she was OK.

'Slow, even breaths, Mum. Come on, I'm here, I'm not going anywhere. You're OK.'

Sam's voice sounded in her mother's head, over and over. And when her breathing steadied and the nausea subsided, Sam filled her a glass of water from the tap.

She took a few sips, closed her eyes and Claude, sensing he was needed, jumped onto her lap, making her smile as he purred in reaction to her attention.

'I should've told you Eddie emigrated,' said Veronica. 'But I didn't want you to hate me any more than you already did.'

'To be honest I don't think I'd have felt anything. I'd numbed myself to a lot of it; I felt I lost my brother a long time ago. I tried to get in touch with him when I first left but he was angry I'd walked away and gradually I stopped trying.'

'I never gave you and Eddie a chance to have a proper

relationship. Never blame yourself for any of the trouble between you and Eddie – that responsibility rests solely on my shoulders, and I'm sure he knows it too.' Veronica's love for her children had never died; it was her mental state that had put up a roadblock and not let anything past. 'I found out Eddie has two sons.'

'I'm pleased.' Sam smiled through watery eyes.

'Eddie came back to England five years ago,' Veronica admitted before she lost her nerve.

'Back to Mapleberry?'

'Close by, yes. But I messed it all up again.' She had to lay everything out for Sam to see now, and whatever way Sam reacted, any judgement she passed, Veronica would take every single hit. 'I managed to get contact details and I arranged to meet him. He refused to come anywhere near the house so we agreed to meet in the park in the next village. It was snowing heavily that day, the roads were quiet, but I still got in the car and drove over there. I parked up and it was chaos.' Her smile faded when she remembered the effect that had had on her. 'People swarmed the place, families having snow play, others bundling into the café. A snowball hit my windscreen and scared the living daylights out of me. I had my hand on the door to step out and go meet Eddie in the café on the other side of the park, where we'd arranged, but after that I couldn't do it. I froze.'

'You didn't get out of the car.'

Veronica's eyes filled with tears. 'I went home, locked myself inside, and I called him. I begged him to come to the house but he wouldn't. And that was the last time I heard from him. That day was the last time I left the house. Five years ago.'

Sam went around to her mum and, careful not to upset Claude, she wrapped her arms around her, hugging her tight, and Veronica let herself be comforted. For everything she'd done, all the lives impacted by her actions, she had a small sliver of peace with Sam now.

Chapter Twenty-Three

Sam

When Sam woke up on Christmas Eve morning, she felt like a big kid pulling back the curtains of her childhood bedroom. But it was different now. Not only because she was older but because the walls of this house were finally filled once again with a happiness that was continuing to build, a love that had always been there but wasn't easy to see. Until now Sam had kept herself one step removed from her old life and her mother, but not anymore. Veronica had taken some enormous steps in the right direction and Sam was determined to do the same.

Looking out onto the back garden, Sam smiled. The sun was shining brightly this morning, making the light dusting of frost shimmer with magical delight. She realised she must have slept in for the first time in a long while because she couldn't remember the last time she woke and didn't have to put the light on.

With the house quiet, she crept downstairs to put the kettle on. Tonight was the carol concert and not only was she excited to hear the culmination of all Layla's intense piano practice, she couldn't wait to see Charlie's reaction. After he'd told her all about his wife in the café that day, she hoped it would be a gift like no other to hear his daughter play the instrument her mum had loved so much. He so deserved it because somehow he'd managed to teach Layla to remember the very best things about her mum rather than just the sadness of losing her. And that can't have been an easy thing for a single dad who had to deal with his own grief too.

Charlie had told Sam that Layla had really come out of her shell since coming to Mapleberry, and Sam knew that the little girl and this incredible man had been a blessing that brought joy to Veronica's life. She hated to think what her mum might have been like without the pair of them moving into the area. Sam may never have got the chance to talk to her mother the way they'd done in recent days; Veronica might have passed away as a woman Sam had barely known . . . And so tonight, both Layla and Charlie deserved the concert of a lifetime.

The kettle rumbled to its crescendo and brought Sam out of her thoughts. She was working a four-hour shift, from late morning to mid-afternoon, and then it would be on to Christmas Eve for real. She usually enjoyed this day the most over the festive season, but she already had a feeling this year would top any other.

Audrey was next downstairs as Sam finished making her tea. Yesterday Audrey and Layla had worked hard again to grit more people's front paths, then Audrey had soaked in the bath for quite a while when she came home, and after than she, Sam and Veronica had gathered in the lounge like any other family, talking about the likelihood of a white Christmas, what time they needed to start preparing the big Christmas lunch, who was going to bring the fold-up table out of the study and into the kitchen so they could attach it to the round table and make some kind of big spread.

'What are your plans for today?' Sam asked her daughter.

'I'm meeting up with Vicky.'

'Don't forget the concert tonight.'

'I won't. And I have to get back to make mince pies too, remember? Layla and I will be standing outside the front gate handing them out and wishing anyone who passes by a Merry Christmas.'

'You'll need plenty,' said Sam. 'Mapleberry Lane is the main route into the village and on to the shops, or to see the big tree.'

'Noted.' Audrey smiled. 'So I'll be back just after lunch. Vicky and I want a quick Christmas meet-up – we'll grab a coffee at the Mapleberry Mug.'

Sam turned. 'I won't be done until three o'clock.' She felt it only fair to warn her daughter.

'Doesn't matter; maybe we could get a discount?'

Sam ruffled her hair, which made her pull away and groan, but she was smiling as she pushed bread into the toaster.

Sam tried to stop her grin as she took her tea upstairs to drink while she got ready. Finally, a daughter who wasn't embarrassed to see her mum out in public. Long may it last. It probably wouldn't, but for now she'd appreciate it.

Audrey tried again for a discount in the café when they came in an hour after Sam's shift started. Sam had tried not to watch the door constantly to see if they'd turn up but Clare had been onto her. When she overheard Audrey joking, Clare threw in a Christmas gingerbread man on the house for both girls.

The girls didn't stay long. They made a point of saying

goodbye when they were done, and as they left, the door swung open, bringing in Charlie.

A smile beamed Sam's way. 'You all ready for the Christmas Eve party tonight?' That's what he'd been told was happening, a party, he just didn't know yet that Layla was the star performance.

'Apart from going home to change after work, I'm ready. Audrey's making mince pies to hand out at the garden gate – it's on the kindness calendar, make mince pies for someone you don't know – so they thought they'd go the whole hog and make them for as many people they don't know as possible.'

'As long as there are some leftover for the party.' Charlie smiled, the little scar she'd got so used to seeing moving as he spoke. 'Veronica seems to have quite the collection of recipes and her pastry is better than I've had anywhere else.'

'Don't let Clare hear you say that.' Sam ushered him over to his usual table by the window the second it was vacated. She took away the empty cups and plates and returned with a cloth to wipe down the top. 'What can I get for you today?'

'What I'm after isn't on the menu.'

'Isn't it?'

Palms rested on the thighs of his jeans, he said, 'I'm making a mess of this. Flirting was never my strong point; I've always been useless at it. Here goes . . . What I'd really like . . . is a date.'

He looked so worried her heart went out to him. A man who seemed so capable, who faced life and death decisions in his job every day, was struggling with something relatively simple in comparison.

'You want a date, with me?'

He laughed and looked around the café. 'Unless you can think of anyone else who'd subject themselves to dating a single dad, a paramedic with erratic hours and someone who really should know how to put on a clean top,' he added as, unbuttoning his coat, he immediately noticed the mark on the front of his jumper. 'That'll be Layla. I hugged her earlier – she'd had a hot chocolate before I sent her over to your house and she's always one for getting a moustache from the chocolate powder I sprinkle on the top.'

Clare hollered over to Sam as a queue began to form.

'I'd better go, Charlie.'

'Right, sure. It's fine. When you get a minute, I'll have a coffee.' He'd already taken out his phone and was scrolling through something as though he hadn't asked her out at all.

'I finish at three o'clock, the party starts at six,' she told him, 'so how about I come and knock on your door around four?'

He looked up and smiled. 'It's a date.'

Clare's voice beckoned again.

'I'll see you at four o'clock.' And as she turned, she tried to act as though she hadn't just lined up meeting a man she really wanted to get to know a lot better, the first man in a long time who made her feel wobbly on her feet.

She made his coffee and took it over to him before getting back to deal with the still-forming queue. The rest of today's shift was going to pass excruciatingly slowly.

'Mum, you look amazing.' Audrey gaped at Sam when she came downstairs at ten minutes to four. 'Is this all for the party tonight?'

'I wanted to make an effort.' She shrugged. She'd washed her hair and put in big rollers she'd borrowed from Audrey so that the ends flicked up and bounced in a way that suggested she'd been to the salon. She had on a dark charcoal cable knit dress that flared out from her hips and made the skirt lift up if you turned around fast enough.

Sam didn't miss her mum looking over as if she may have already put two and two together.

'You're ready early,' said Layla, most put out. 'I've got a party dress upstairs but Veronica won't let me put it on yet in case I spill something on it.'

'I think that's very wise.' Sam picked up her house key and dropped it into her handbag.

'Are you off out?' her mum asked.

'You smell nice.' Layla came closer, saving her from her mum's questioning for a moment as she lifted Sam's wrist. 'What is it?'

'It's Miss Dior, Blooming Bouquet.'

Layla's eyes widened. 'It smells like one of those perfumes Daddy sometimes lets me try in the store but then tells me I can only have some when I'm old enough to buy it myself.'

'It is expensive,' Audrey added and her brow furrowed. 'You don't wear it very often.'

'I thought I would tonight. It's a special night.' She crouched down to Layla's level. 'I tell you what, seeing as it's so special, how about when I get back for the concert and you're all dressed up too, I let you put on some of the perfume?'

'Really? Yes please!' She went back into the kitchen to carry on with her position at the cooker, cutting the pastry rounds for Sam's mum to fill with the homemade sweet mincemeat.

Audrey was still staring at her – she knew this wasn't all in aid of the party – but when Layla demanded her attention she let Sam off the hook and happily went back to the kitchen.

But Sam's mum was still looking at her suspiciously. 'Going somewhere?'

'Mum, you can see that I am.' And because she couldn't keep it to herself any longer, she confessed, 'I'm meeting Charlie.'

Her mum clasped her hands together. 'I hoped you were.'

'Do you think Audrey minds?'

'Does she look like she minds?' They peered into the kitchen, where Audrey and Layla were using pastry offcuts to make a weird-looking dinosaur shape, with mincemeat for his eyes. Audrey was making it roar past Layla's ear while she made another. 'You're entitled to be happy, Sam, and Audrey knows it.'

Sam reached out and took her mum's hand. 'We're all entitled to happiness – *all* of us.'

'That we are.' Her mum smiled. 'Now, before we get too sentimental, can I ask that you and Charlie knock before you come in tonight?'

'Of course. Layla can take it from there. I can't wait to see his face – this will be the best gift and the biggest surprise.'

'She's worked very hard.' Her mum walked her to the door. 'Have a good time, Sam, and see you in a couple of hours.'

Sam left what had become the beating heart of

Mapleberry Lane, wrapped in the glow of the laughter coming from the kitchen and the warmth in her mother's eyes. She headed down the path, along the pavement and to number twenty-five.

Charlie opened the door the second she knocked. He was all ready to come outside in his jacket, the collar turned up and grazing the stubble on his jaw. And as the winter's night settled around them, she realised she hadn't wrapped up enough. She'd thought they'd hang around at his house rather than venturing out, but she didn't mind what they did as long as she got to spend time with him.

'I should've brought a scarf – mind if I head back and grab one?'

He leaned behind the front door and plucked a knitted navy scarf from the hook behind. 'Take this one, it's my spare and I thought I'd lost it but I found it in my car earlier. I usually get through three or four scarves every season – I'm forever leaving them places.' He pulled the door shut. 'Layla usually buys me one for Christmas because she knows me so well. And we're not going into my place because it's a bit of a mess. I could blame Layla and all her paraphernalia, or I could man up and say that I left all my gift wrapping until the last minute and the lounge floor is covered in scraps of paper, Sellotape and empty bags. I need to get all the Father Christmas presents done when she's out at your place. And I'm babbling, sorry – nerves.'

'No need to apologise, I'm a bit nervous too.'

'Yeah?' He held the little gate at the end of the path open for her.

'I don't mind helping you with the wrapping later.' She smiled.

His eyes sparkled in a way that suggested he wouldn't mind either. 'You're on. But first we need a walk. There's a snow symbol on the forecast right now – I wanted to get out and about and hope that it started to fall.'

She looked up at the sky. 'I don't think we're going to see snow for a while yet.' She wound the scarf around her neck, unprepared for it to smell quite so familiar. He must've worn it recently – it had a hint of the hair product or soap he used and that she caught an occasional waft of if he passed by closely enough. 'But it's a beautiful evening and I could use the walk. I've been eating too many mince pies, I know there's more to come tonight, and let's not even think about the amount of food we have to get through tomorrow.'

'Your fault entirely, I was restrained in the supermarket.'

'You liar! You were worse than me!'

'Guilty.' He grinned as they started walking towards the other end of Mapleberry Lane.

Sam began to laugh when she saw the path of a house a few doors down from Charlie. 'Don't tell me, the girls gritted there.'

He shook his head at the scattered salt and the big clump by the gate they'd left in a pile. 'Hey, I was in charge of the wheelbarrow, they were supposed to spread it evenly.'

'The kindness calendar has been really good for Audrey and Mum. I'm glad Layla got them involved.'

'I don't think they had any choice.'

'No, I don't suppose they did. Your daughter is somewhat persuasive.'

'Yeah, and I kind of love that about her too. Her mum was the same, never took no for an answer.' He puffed out his cheeks as though he'd misspoken. 'I apologise. Here we are on what I'm hoping is our first date and already I'm talking about another woman.'

'Charlie, she'll always be a part of your life and it's important you do talk about her – Layla needs that. I never talked about Simon with Audrey, but if I had I could've saved us both a lot of pain and confusion.'

'You're telling me I should learn from your mistakes?'

She smiled up at him and then, because the way his gaze dropped to her lips had her uncomfortable, she looked back the way they were going. They turned the corner and the big tree was in view.

'It looks even better from a distance.'

'Village life for Layla is everything I hoped it would be.'

'Village life is a lot better than I remembered.' Sam chuckled. 'It felt stifling before, but I realise now that it wasn't to do with the village and the small number of people here, it was to do with me and my family and the way things were at home. Mum's made progress lately, but after Christmas I'll book her in with a doctor to see if we can go one step further.'

'You're a good daughter.'

'I haven't always been.' She bit her bottom lip, the guilt something she was ashamed of, no matter how much her mum had said none of it was her fault. Maybe it was human nature to look back and wish you'd done more or tackled things differently. The power of hindsight.

'I think Veronica knows she had her failings too. But you're both together again now, it's a start.'

'How do you always know how to say the right things?' She smiled up at him.

'It's in the job description,' he confessed. 'Calming people down, persuading them to do one thing, not another; it takes a lot of work to be able to do it. Talking of jobs, how are you enjoying the café?'

'My feet don't always thank me for it when I have a long shift.' Glad of the flat knee-high boots she had on now with thick tights, her feet were coping just fine after a short stint at the Mapleberry Mug earlier. 'It gets crazy busy sometimes, like today. It's not for me but Clare loves it.'

'You sound ready to move on elsewhere.'

'Clare and I have talked about it, she knows I'm looking at full-time work doing a completely different job, and she's happy to keep me on until I'm ready. I'll work extra hours for Christmas and New Year, and then I think once I've moved into my flat, I need to start making some hard and fast moves towards the career I always wanted.'

'You're decisive, I like that.'

'How's this for decisive?' She pointed in the direction of a cart at the side of the field that had appeared especially for Christmas Eve. 'That looks like a mulled wine cart – how about we grab one? It'll warm us up, you know, with all this snow.'

His breath came out in little puffs when he laughed. 'Come on, I'll shout you. But if it does snow tonight, you owe me a second date. I think it's only fair.'

She didn't disagree.

Sam rubbed her gloved hands together as the man at the cart, who was whistling Christmas carols, ladled a ruby mixture into polystyrene cups and added orange slices to each.

'He could do with a tuning fork.' Charlie winced as they walked away, over to the far side of the field where they could drink their mulled wine and enjoy the view of the tree and the lights without too many people crowding them. The cart was like a magnet on a cold Christmas Eve night, drawing people over with the scent of spices hanging in the air.

'This flat you're buying,' Charlie began, pausing for a sip of mulled wine. 'It's for you, not Audrey?'

'That's right. But Audrey knows she can come over and stay whenever she likes. We've talked and all three of us think she's best at Mum's, and I think Mum is best with her for company too. I also know distance for Audrey and I might work at mending some of the issues we've had over the years. She's my daughter, which means I want her with me, but I had to listen to what she wanted too.'

'It'll be difficult to let Audrey go, even though she's not going anywhere and you won't be far away.'

'It always has been, whenever she'd wanted to do things I disagreed with or talked about paths in life I thought were completely wrong. I was scared I was losing her, petrified we'd go the same way as Mum and I. But I can see now that I'm more likely to keep Audrey in my life if I let her move forward the way she wants to. I need to sway between control and giving advice. Maybe that's part of parenting as your kids get older.'

'Are you any happier about Audrey wanting to pursue a career in make-up artistry?'

'I'm getting there. The more I talk to her, the more I can see that not only is it what she wants, but she's thought about it properly. It's not just something she's picked on a whim.' The mulled wine warmed her throat and the spices gave her a jolt. She was on a date and Charlie was so easy to be with she'd almost forgotten. 'I'm sorry, now

I'm ruining the date by running on and on about my personal life.'

'Hey, it's part of who you are. And I like hearing about your plans. I can't remember the job title you told me ages ago, I know it had something to do with education and psychology. Am I close?' His features concertinaed into a hopeful expression.

'An educational psychologist,' she explained. Saying the title out loud reinforced how much she wanted to follow the career she'd set her heart on years ago. Over time she'd put it down to life taking unexpected twists and turns; some things just weren't meant to be. But since losing her job in customer services, she realised she was ready to pursue her passion at last. 'Quite how I'll get to that new career title is anyone's guess.'

'Hey, if anyone can do it, Sam, I'm sure you can.'

His words fell welcomingly on her. 'Once I'm in the new flat, I'm going to look into doing some work experience. That'll give me an idea of what I need to do, whether it's go back to college to do a short course or getting a job at the bottom of the ladder.' And she wouldn't mind that one bit. She was looking forward to climbing up the ladder again and discovering what was on every rung, maybe even towards the top.

'I'm glad you're buying the flat. It'll be good to have a place of your own.'

'I won't be a few doors away anymore.' She shrugged. 'You want to see less of me?'

'I'll confess that wasn't the way my mind was going. I was thinking that once you have your own place and Layla is back at school, I could come over when I'm not on shift. We'd have the entire flat to ourselves.'

361

She hid a smile behind another sip of mulled wine and, as she drew the cup away from her mouth, she felt something decidedly cold on her eyelash.

Charlie turned around and around on the spot, his mulled wine in one hand, neck craned to watch the snow fall from the sky. 'Ha! Told you! Snowing!'

'Hardly,' she laughed, remembering back to the moment outside the house when a snowflake had spun its way down from the sky, landed on his cheek and he'd looked utterly gorgeous as he gazed up in much the same way as he was doing now, trying to see the snow for himself.

Charlie took their empty cups over to the bin and dumped them. Warmed through, Sam was watching the tree, the families gathered at its base, the magic of Christmas Eve in the air. And when she least expected it, she felt Charlie's hand wrap around her own, and even through the material of her gloves she could feel the warmth of his skin as he turned her to face him.

She started to laugh. Because the lonely flakes of earlier were replaced all of a sudden by snowfall that got a whoop from the crowd, had kids twirling in excitement, that sent her heart soaring as he dipped his head to kiss her.

And the kiss was worth the thousands of days she'd waited to move on, to find someone else. Charlie was exactly what she'd been waiting for and she never wanted to come up for air.

They arrived back at Charlie's house to get the Father Christmas presents finished so Layla would be none the wiser, and like a pair of teenagers, it was next to impossible to keep their hands off one another. Sam would wrap a present and feel Charlie's hand on the back of her neck, tugging her hair and sending a tantalising thrill down her spine. He wrote the labels 'From Father Christmas' and, as he concentrated on disguising his writing, she'd wrap her arms around his torso, kissing his neck, his groans not something he wanted his daughter to hear. They paused enough times to give in to the thrill of the kiss again, each time dragging themselves away, knowing they had to get this finished and over to the house by six o'clock.

'Surely it won't matter if we're a little late to the party,' Charlie complained as he trailed kisses from her mouth to her cheeks, to her neck when he moved her hair out of the way and down to her collarbone.

'I'm afraid it will.' She kissed him full on the mouth, the temptation to stay there almost too great. 'Come on, clear away this mess or you'll ruin Christmas for Layla for ever.'

'The guilt trip? Works every time.' He gathered up the detritus and by the time he'd hidden all the presents away, ready to put out later that night by the tree, and cleared up all the evidence that any wrapping had happened here at all, they headed to Veronica's.

'Why are you knocking on the door?' Charlie asked when Sam didn't take out her key.

But Layla opened the door the second he asked and in a loud, clear voice told them, 'I formally invite you to the Christmas Eve carol concert.'

'I thought this was a party,' Charlie whispered into Sam's ear. 'I didn't realise I'd have to sing.'

She almost wanted to push him back out of the door and down to his place where they'd be alone. But he'd have to wait. They both would.

Layla wore a sparkly emerald green dress that just

reached her knees, cream tights and red glittery Mary Janes. Audrey had dressed up in a black cotton dress with a Christmas motif on the front, Sam's mum had on her favourite plum cardigan, and Audrey had obviously done her make-up and hair for her. If Morris really was interested in more than friendship, then Sam hoped he realised how lucky he was to find her mum.

'If you'll all follow me through to the concert hall, please.' Layla led the way down the hall and to the study.

'Wait!' Sam said and leaned in to whisper to Layla, who kept them all standing there while Sam ran upstairs to get the bottle of perfume. 'Shut your eyes.' She sprayed the mist into the air to fall onto Layla and then sprayed it onto a wrist and instructed her to rub them together.

Layla sniffed her wrist and then it was back to business. 'Follow me, please.'

'There's a concert hall?' Charlie didn't let go of Sam's waist as they moved along, as though she wouldn't know where to go if he didn't guide her.

When they reached the study, there were kitchen chairs, as well as spares from the shed that unfolded outside in the warmer months, lined up along the wall so they could see the piano. Charlie had clocked the upright instrument but still didn't seem to have any idea what was going on.

'Daddy, I'm afraid I've been lying to you,' Layla began in earnest. Charlie didn't look too sure where this was going. 'I haven't only been coming to see Veronica and work with the Kindness Club.'

'Right . . . Where have you been?'

With an eye roll she said, 'I've always been here, well, apart from the other night on our adventure.' Sam noticed Audrey cringe, but Charlie wasn't angry, just bewildered.

'One item on the kindness calendar was to learn a musical instrument. And I wanted to learn the piano, like Mummy.'

Sam didn't miss Charlie gulp or the sheen of tears in his eyes. Layla had had a long time to prepare for this moment, but Charlie hadn't.

Sam wanted to put a hand on his arm, reassure him, but she didn't want to interfere with Layla's moment.

'You've been learning piano?' He was talking in a way that suggested he was doing his best to cover up any wobble in his voice by asking questions to deflect the attention away from him, at least for a moment.

'Veronica taught me.'

He looked across at her. 'You play? I had no idea.'

'I hadn't played in a very long time,' she admitted, lifting Claude from the piano stool he'd been keeping warm. 'It was Layla who showed me the simple joy of music all over again. I taught her some carols that we're going to enjoy now. Take it away, Layla.'

Sam shared a smile with Charlie and he nodded her way, as if to say he was coping, he was holding himself together from something so emotionally charged and unexpected. It was a look that told Sam all she needed to know about this man. He was special, he made those around him feel special, he was someone she wanted to keep in her life. And the way he was with Layla? She'd never known a better father figure to bring into Audrey's life.

Layla began with 'Jingle Bells', followed by 'Silent Night' and 'Joy to the World'. And when she'd played a few others, Sam's mum joining in with the left hand on some of the more complicated pieces, and they'd applauded her, she wanted to do them all again, with singing.

Charlie's voice must have been the loudest in the little study at number nine as they all sang along. He'd passed through the emotion of the surprise and was now enjoying every single second. Sam looked from him to Layla, noticing how the connection never broke between father and daughter. She hoped Audrey and Simon could find a way to nurture their relationship in whatever way it evolved. She smiled at her mum, knowing that a house filled with music was what she'd likely needed all along. Her dad hadn't supported her, had never allowed that simple antidote Veronica needed, and although Sam knew she'd never stop loving the man she'd worshipped her entire life, she knew there was room to move her mum into a bigger place in her heart.

'And now,' said Layla after the last line of the last carol had been sung, 'if you'd like to make your way out of the concert hall to the kitchen, we will be serving mince pies.'

But Charlie didn't obey her instruction. He scooped her up in his arms, kissing her cheeks and making her squeal with laughter. 'I am so proud of you – tonight was the best surprise you could've ever given me. And your mummy would be very, very proud of you too.'

'I know.' Layla shrugged before escaping to run into the kitchen. 'Wait till you see our dinosaurs!'

'Dinosaurs?' he asked Sam, pulling her close while nobody else was watching.

She was about to tell him about the pastry shapes they'd made, when Layla's head poked around the doorway. 'If you want to kiss each other that's OK, but I can't guarantee there will be any mince pies left by the time you've finished.'

Charlie grinned and tapped Sam on the bottom as he followed her into the kitchen, murmuring into her ear, 'You'll keep.'

There were plenty of mince pies to go around, and once they'd eaten, the five of them, Sam's mum included, wrapped up in their coats and walked to the end of the path to fulfil another item on the kindness calendar. Mince pies were handed out to all and sundry: locals they knew, people who'd come to Mapleberry for the tree and the mulled wine alone, mothers, daughters, fathers, sons, grandparents, friends heading to the local pub, all out on this cold Christmas Eve.

And Sam's mum didn't waver in her time by the garden gate. She stayed there greeting person after person, a genuine smile for each and every one of them.

Sam woke up on Christmas Day grinning. She seemed to be doing that a lot lately. Last night she'd dreamed of Charlie. In her dream he was a snowman with five scarves dangling from his neck and a pipe that let him inhale coffee. Already she couldn't wait to see him again today, and judging by the way he kissed her goodnight after the party, he was probably thinking exactly the same by now.

Sam stretched her arms above her head and she knew, even before she peeked out of the curtains, that it was going to be one of those beautiful, clear crisp days as the sun shone fiercely. The house was quiet and a little on the chilly side, so the fire would be in full use again today. The frost in the back garden sparkled as she looked down on it from her bedroom. There was no proper snow yet so no white Christmas, but Sam didn't much care. Mapleberry was already pretty with just a sprinkling of white, the icing on top of a quaint village that had risen in her estimation.

The morning flew by in a sea of preparation. The three women who'd clashed so badly when they were first cooped up under one roof now peeled, chopped and prepared vegetables, clattering trays and utensils around as they pulled them from the cupboards. Veronica's recipe book moved from person to person as they weighed ingredients, double-checked timings, co-ordinated basting the turkey with putting the stuffing in to ensure it had enough time to turn a crisp golden colour, found enough serving dishes to set out on the table and host the meal that brought family and friends together the world over.

Sam made sure the champagne was chilling and, before Charlie and Layla were due to arrive, she went upstairs to put on her favourite jeans with the brand-new forest-green silk-velvet wraparound top she'd bought in readiness for today. And when Charlie came through the door twenty minutes later and laid eyes on her, it seemed he approved of her choice as much as she appreciated the dark denim jeans he had on with a sky-blue textured shirt that was soft to the touch when he hugged her and her hands draped around his shoulders.

Layla told them all about what Santa brought and Sam did her best not to let on that she'd wrapped enough of those gifts to already know the details. Charlie kept a hand on her knee under the table most of the way through Christmas lunch, and if anyone noticed, they were too polite to say anything. Sam checked every now and then for steam coming out of Audrey's ears, but nothing. She was laughing away with Layla most of the time or impressing her by detailing the professional make-up brush set Sam bought her for Christmas, complete with a gorgeous black and clear acrylic stand to put the brushes out on show like the professional she was sure to be one day.

'What's Morris up to today?' Sam asked as she passed the still half-full dish of pigs in blankets around the table to shakes of the head and moans about being too full.

'His son and his family are visiting today,' her mum told her, 'but he said maybe he'll stop by for drinks this evening. Bridget and June would like to come too. We could open up the Baileys. If that's all right with you all?'

'Mum,' Sam smiled, 'it's more than all right.' And she felt Charlie squeeze her knee in reassurance. He was doing a stellar job of eating one-handed and she liked that he didn't want to let go of her. She didn't want to be parted from him either.

Audrey drowned another serving of roast potatoes in gravy. Sam wondered where the svelte teen put it all. Charlie heaped more glazed carrots onto his plate and tried in vain to get Layla to eat a Brussels sprout. She'd gone so far as to lick the edge of one that still sat forlornly at the side of her plate. They pulled crackers between them, the snap making Sam jump every time. They cringed at the terrible jokes offered inside, tried to work out what half of the plastic prizes were, knowing that most would end up in the bin, and the laughter didn't stop when they took turns to act out the charades written below the jokes.

Dessert didn't happen for a good couple of hours after the main dinner, and after that, when they all headed for a walk, Sam's mum going to the end of the path and no further, Sam had a chance to talk to Audrey again as Charlie and Layla took the lead.

'Do you think Mum's getting herself ready for Morris?'

Sam asked her daughter after she closed the gate behind them.

'Huh?'

'Audrey, what's going on with you?' She eyed the phone in Audrey's hand. 'You keep checking that thing. It's not Alex again, is it?'

Audrey reacted in true teen mode: a roll of the eyes, a tut for good measure. 'It's not Alex.'

'Is it your dad? How's his Christmas?'

'He's had a good one; he called this morning, remember?'

'I'd forgotten. Then who are you messaging or texting or whatever it is you're doing?'

'Promise you won't be mad.'

Sam lifted her face from where it was buried in Charlie's scarf. She'd kept it from yesterday and she liked having a piece of him close when he wasn't by her side. He and Layla were well ahead now and he'd already hoisted Layla up onto his shoulders.

'I can't promise unless I know what it is.'

'I've done something.'

'Audrey, why do I get the feeling I won't like this? Is it New Zealand again? Have you made plans?'

'No, nothing like that. Honest.' Audrey took a deep breath. And then she told Sam everything, what she'd been up to without letting on to her or her gran.

By the time she'd finished, Sam didn't know whether it was a good thing or not, whether the result of her actions would be devastating or a success. Whether it could make her mum's life better if it worked, or worse if it didn't.

She guessed only time would tell.

Chapter Twenty-Four

Veronica

Veronica hadn't woken up with a foggy head on New Year's Day for as long as she could remember. After the Christmas Eve concert, Layla had been so pleased with its success that she'd requested a New Year's Eve concert with just as much piano-playing and food, as well as a very late night.

Last night the walls of Veronica's home had been filled with family and friends. Morris had come over on Christmas night and he and Veronica had started doing a puzzle together at the extra table. It was a scene of Mapleberry, a beautiful jigsaw he'd bought her for Christmas knowing her heart lay here in the village. He'd been more eagle-eyed than her, slotting in far more pieces, and every day since then he'd been back to her house and they'd worked on it some more. Last night had been the big reveal to everyone: Sam, Audrey, Charlie and Layla, June and Bridget.

There was no time to feel sorry for herself and be lazy when Claude jumped onto her bed, reminding her it was time to feed him. 'Come on you, downstairs we go.'

Veronica was grateful when she noticed that either Audrey or Sam had laid a new fire in the grate. It wasn't lit yet but it was all set for her, and so she had her breakfast before heading upstairs to get ready. She even put some make-up on. Only basic colours, nothing over the top, but she was getting used to seeing a new and improved Veronica, and she liked it. She liked the confidence that made her feel as though this year might be the start of a rather different life.

'Just you and I today, Claude,' said Veronica when she came back down. He'd assumed his position on the arm of her favourite chair in the lounge. Sam and Audrey were having something posh, known as brunch, at Charlie's this morning – Veronica had been invited but she was happy to be in her house without anyone else. For the first time in years, she didn't feel lonely; in her head she was in a far better place than she'd been in a long while and she no longer felt the need to add anything in, like the radio, the television or anyone else. It was a strange conversion from the person she'd been before to the happier one she was now.

Veronica smiled as she saw the collection of empty bottles on the bench beside the sink – Baileys, wine, brandy Morris had brought over, and Babycham, which Bridget had been ecstatic to find and drink to relive her younger years. She'd have to take the bottles outside, but first, a cup of tea. Sam had gifted her with a beautiful ornate teapot with a matching set of four cups, the design delicate pink roses that Veronica hoped to see come up around the door this summer after her gardener suggested the idea to make her home even prettier. Maybe this year she'd even be able to smell their sweet scent as she made her way down the garden path on her way out for the day.

With Earl Grey brewing in the pot, Veronica looked

out at her little back garden. The ground looked packed down and hard, covered in an effort of snow that wasn't anywhere near the amount they'd been promised.

The day after Boxing Day, Sam had gone with her to the doctor. Leaving the house hadn't been without drama. Veronica had refused at first, not because she was scared of the doctor but because she was anxious about what she'd have to do. She didn't want to be dosed up to the eyeballs or be sitting on some shrink's couch every week for the foreseeable future. She had people around her now and she was already making progress.

'Mum, come on, we don't want to miss the appointment,' Sam had urged that day. Hovering in the doorway with Veronica refusing to step out of the hall, she was doing her best to hold in any frustration, Veronica could tell.

Veronica had her coat on already but the next step was proving difficult.

'Come on, Mum. Getting a doctor's appointment is like winning the lottery, remember.'

Veronica managed to laugh. 'You're not wrong there.' And yet her legs still wouldn't move.

'It's less than twenty steps to the car, Gran.' Audrey's voice came from behind her as she emerged from the kitchen, along with the tempting homely smell of warmed bread. Munching on a slice of toast, her midriff bare in her pyjamas with the cropped top, Audrey was talking as though all Veronica had to do was go twenty steps and get a pint of milk and she'd be done.

Veronica looked at Sam, infuriated that she couldn't pull herself together for her daughter. She was standing there encouraging, coaxing, with not a single ounce of annoyance on display.

'Count to twenty,' she said, 'shut your eyes if you need to and I'll lead you to the car. Then we'll take the next step. You did it for Audrey, remember.'

'She's right, Gran.' Audrey touched her gently on the arm. 'Can't waste the hair and make-up now.' It was the fourth day in a row she'd taken such care with her appearance, a ritual that she thought might prepare her for this.

Veronica took one step outside the house and stopped. And then she shut her eyes. She felt Sam's arm link through hers, then she took twenty steps and stopped. Without opening her eyes she called back to Audrey, 'It's more than twenty steps.'

'I never was good at estimating,' came Audrey's voice from behind her, and then she heard the front door shut and a car door open. And as the warmth of the car enveloped her, she somehow managed to get in.

The doctor had been kind. They were fifteen minutes late for their appointment but he saw them anyway. Veronica wondered how much Sam had played the agoraphobia card, the problems of actually getting there, but in front of him Veronica didn't mind talking. He put her at ease; he reminded her of an older version of Charlie, the type of man she met in her work as a nurse, the type of man who fitted the job to a tee. He told her about other cases he'd treated and passed her several articles she read in the car on the way home. One woman had talked in a magazine about how she had therapy and medication, and described how agoraphobia had been like a prison for her. She'd worked through it, joined telephone recovery groups and said never again would she take for granted stepping outside of her own front door without being fearful. It felt insurmountable to Veronica to ever reach that stage, but maybe now she could with people on her side.

By the time Veronica got home from the appointment, she didn't feel the need to go to bed as she'd expected. She thought she might have been worn down by the events, but she and the doctor had put a plan in place. They were going to combine medication with some therapy, the doctor seeing it as her best chance of success. Sam seemed happy with it, Morris was too when they shared it with him, and her life was now filled with enough family and friends that she was ready to take this step. She wondered how she'd be this time next year. Maybe she'd make it to the village tree-lighting ceremony in person rather than have to watch a video of it on a tiny screen.

Now, with her first appointment behind her and both Sam and Audrey at the Mapleberry Mug, Veronica filled one of her rose-embellished cups with tea and took it into the lounge. She set it down and unrolled the kindness calendar. December had been a frantic month. It was like being a schoolgirl again, tasked with a subject from each teacher when none of them had thought about how much work it would mean in total. Layla's teacher was more than a little enthusiastic. And in less than a week Layla would be back at school. Veronica dreaded to think how much would be on January's kindness calendar; she might have to suggest having a word with this Mrs Haines to reduce the amount they were responsible for. Then again, it was all part of the fun, and even better now Veronica knew she had things going on in her life. Maybe she'd try to get some of her new friends involved. They'd all been kind when she shared her personal story, and maybe soon she'd be brave enough to go over to their homes and visit.

They invited her enough times. One of these days she'd surprise them all by saying yes.

Veronica was just finishing her tea when she saw, in her peripheral vision, the snow beginning to fall. Audrey would be happy; she'd been going on about making snow angels or whatever they were called. Veronica hadn't ever made one, but she understood you lay on the ground on your back in a starfish shape and then swished your arms up and down, your legs back and forth. If she was to join in with that, she really would earn her reputation as the crazy lady from number nine.

About to pour a second cup of tea before the others came back and take it into the study to play the piano, Veronica was interrupted by a knock at the door. Spotting Audrey's and Sam's keys on the little table in the hallway, she tutted. 'You girls, memories like sieves.'

But when she flung open the door, it wasn't Sam. And it wasn't Audrey.

'Hello, Mum.'

Chapter Twenty-Five

Veronica

Veronica's hands shook as she made more tea; she was surprised the china pot didn't smash into a thousand pieces. Eddie was here, waiting in the lounge. She'd kept him at the door as she froze, the shock almost too much. She'd wondered if someone had put something in her Baileys last night – was she hallucinating? But Eddie had stepped over the threshold of what had been his first-ever home and taken the lead by removing his shoes and sitting on the sofa. She could still see the thirteen-year-old boy she'd hurt badly, the boy who'd never understood her or the reasons he was sent away, but also the man he'd become, strong and resilient enough to come and try.

Veronica had offered tea much in the same way you would to a neighbour coming over for a chat, or to Sam after she finished a shift at the café, or the way you offered tea to a grieving relative at the hospital when there were no words to convey how you felt and how sorry you were.

She didn't manage to take the cups to the lounge as instead Eddie appeared beside her. It was he who took the cups. He who led the way when it should've been the other way around. She thought she might burst into tears if this moment ever came, back when she used to dream about it, but now she was numb. How did you even start to apologise to the son you'd wronged in the worst way possible?

He took something from his pocket and passed it to her. A photograph. 'This is my family; I thought you might like to see it. That's Rosa, my wife,' he said, leaning forward to point out the order, 'then Lottie and Ariana, my daughters.'

'They're beautiful, really beautiful.' She couldn't stop staring at them. The girls with angelic blonde hair Eddie had had himself, just like Sam. His hair was darker now, a natural change to the colour he'd been born with. She'd been the same as a young girl, blonde to dark, to the grey that it was now.

'Lottie is six, Ariana seven. They're quite a handful.'

'I'll bet they are.' She couldn't stop staring at the picture. This life she knew nothing of.

'You're looking well,' he told her, snatching her attention from the picture. She tried to hand it back to him but he put up a hand. 'Keep it, it's for you.'

She pressed her lips together in an effort not to let them wobble and give away the emotion that was threatening to overcome her. She focused on her breathing the way she'd read about in an article Morris found for her. He was quite resourceful, looking into every facet of her condition that he could. He'd even found a Facebook support group, but she hadn't joined up. She didn't know whether she would either; maybe one online group was quite enough.

She put the photograph up on the mantelpiece next to the one of Sam so it would stand upright. 'I'll have to find a frame and put it inside.'

But he'd come over to her, and his presence, so close, had her holding her breath this time. 'Is that Sam?'

She mumbled a yes.

He was smiling as he looked closer. 'My hair was that blonde once. She must dye it, surely.'

The teasing brother comment relaxed her a little. 'Don't say that to her – I think it's supposed to look very natural.'

'It does, but that's what brothers do, isn't it? They rile their sisters.'

She smiled and pointed to the next picture. 'This is Sam's daughter, Audrey.'

He nodded. 'I've met her.' He sat down on the sofa again and Veronica took her favourite chair. 'She's the reason I'm here today.'

When his voice caught, Veronica ducked out of the room and into the downstairs bathroom. She needed a minute. This was overwhelming and she didn't want to fall apart; she didn't want to ruin any of it.

She splashed cold water onto her cheeks, looked at herself in the mirror and said out loud that she could do this. She couldn't let him down again. All of a sudden she was back in the car that Christmas he'd come over from Canada, she was in the car park near the café where they were supposed to meet, a snowball hurtling towards her, shaking her enough to send her home.

But she wasn't there now. She was safe.

She went back to Eddie. 'I needed a minute,' she said. 'How did Audrey manage to get in touch?' Best to move the conversation on so she could hold it together, and he seemed to appreciate it too. Better than them staring at one another and crying at how unfair it had all been.

'She's calling herself a supersleuth.' He grinned, looking

so much like Herman it took her by surprise. 'She's quite proud that she found me. She said Sam told her my in-laws lived near Mapleberry and somehow Audrey then managed to join a few residents' groups and, after digging, found the family who had a son-in-law called Eddie. She got a message to me and I got in touch. We moved back to the UK last month and have settled in Shropshire, but we're here for Christmas to be with Rosa's family.' He cleared his throat. Just when Veronica thought he oozed confidence, he showed how difficult this was for him too. 'Audrey and I have met up twice in the pub – don't worry, I only bought her colas, nothing stronger,' he joked, as though humour might make this easier. 'We talked a lot. I wasn't sure about meeting her at first, but because it wasn't you and it wasn't Sam, because I'd never met this girl before, it somehow made it easier.'

He toyed with the cuff of his jumper sleeve. 'Audrey told me she's been going through a hard time at home and ended up coming here to live with you.'

'You must've been surprised to hear that, I'm sure.'

'I get that things change; I'm not so screwed up I can't see it.' He let his comment settle. 'She also passed on some things Sam might have told her and some information you gave her too, about Dad and the way he was.'

He took a while to look at her. 'I can't say I'll ever truly understand why you gave me away, why you couldn't keep me and find a way through it, but talking to Audrey has helped my anger subside. And I don't blame Sam, she shouldn't have had to pick up the pieces, and she tried with me, but I didn't want to know.'

'You must be furious, hate me, even.' Veronica couldn't let herself off the hook. 'What I did was unforgiveable.'

'Life's too short to hate anybody, Mum, even the man who lives next door to us and insists on using his leaf blower every evening at dinnertime to clean leaves off his pretty pristine drive.'

She appreciated his ability to make his point and still leave her hopeful they weren't done for ever. 'I am sorry. I am really sorry, Eddie, for everything.'

'Audrey says you've been seeing a doctor and have a plan to move forward.' Maybe the apologies could only go so far and Eddie was confronting this the only way he could, gradually.

'I'm hopeful. I was in a very bad place back then, Eddie. I'm sorry for what I did, but I honestly think if I hadn't let someone else take you, I would've ruined your life. I'd already damaged Sam, she didn't come back until recently; it seemed the kinder thing to do was to let you go.' He hadn't touched his tea and Veronica suspected neither of them would.

'Audrey also told me you stepped up when she was in trouble. You left the house for the first time since . . . since you were supposed to meet me.' She nodded. 'That was very brave. And if Ariana or Lottie ever pull a stunt like that, I might have to send you to the rescue. I'd kill them otherwise.'

Veronica smiled. 'I'll bet you're a good dad.'

'I like to think I'm not bad. I have my faults, I don't always have the patience, but I love my kids to bits.'

'So do I.' She looked over at the photograph of his family. 'I'm pleased for you, you seem to have a good life.' One she didn't know she could ever be a part of.

'Tell me about Sam, Mum.'

Veronica told him all about Sam as a teen, Sam when

she ran off and got married and never came back, and the Sam who'd finally met a man worthy of her, the Sam who worked in the café as a stop-gap, and the daughter who baked with Veronica in the kitchen as though history was just that – in the past.

'Charlie sounds the sort of bloke I'd like to see my sister with.'

'Maybe you could meet him one day?'

'I'll be going to see Sam after this. Audrey texted me to say they're at the Mapleberry Mug. She knew I was coming here now, so I have to see Sam while I'm still feeling brave enough.'

'Are you excited about seeing her?' The siblings hadn't done anything wrong, it was all her, but she knew Sam felt responsible for Eddie. 'She feels guilty for not being there for you.'

'She shouldn't.'

'I know. But make sure you tell her, won't you?'

'Of course.' Hands on his thighs, he pushed himself to standing.

'Thank you for coming, Eddie.' She had no idea whether this was it as she followed him to the door. 'I know it must've been very hard for you.'

At the front door he pulled it open but stopped, his back still to her.

And then he spun around and pulled her into a hug, the body of an almost thirty-year-old man tormented with the pain of a thirteen-year-old boy who must've felt unloved and forgotten when he'd never been those things at all.

When he eventually let her go, she asked him to wait. She went to the kitchen and returned with the robin she'd bought for his birthday. 'I got you this when you turned thirteen and I never got the chance to give it to you. You know, you used to like drawing the birds and always—'

'—complained the robins never stood still long enough,' he finished for her.

'You probably don't draw anymore, but I want you to have it.'

He took out his phone, searched for something and handed it to her.

In front of her were sketches of all sorts of things, from an owl, a bird of prey, a deserted barn in the middle of a field, to a scene of a summer fete and a winter village filled with locals soaking up a Christmas atmosphere.

'Are these yours? These pictures?'

'All mine – I display them in a garden centre and the restaurant there, up in Shropshire. I went in there on the off-chance they'd be interested and they were. They've even sold a few. So by day I'm an electrician and by night and weekend, when I get a spare minute, I'm a wannabe artist.'

'Nothing wannabe about these.' Veronica couldn't stop admiring the skill, the perfection, the way he brought things to life in both colour and black and white. 'There's so much I don't know about you.' She handed him his phone.

'I'd better come back then.'

Her heart clenched. 'Would you? Really?'

He nodded, and with his quiet contemplation he looked even more like his father. Perhaps in a modern world Herman might have understood her condition more and been alongside her while she dealt with it. She liked to think so.

'Your tree is impressive,' he said, as though he didn't want to leave just yet. 'Big, too.'

'Sam and Audrey, as well as Charlie and Layla, persuaded me this year.'

'You mean you don't usually have a tree?'

'How could I?' She didn't look away. 'How could I celebrate Christmas when I'd ruined so many lives?' Her voice shook. 'It wasn't right.'

He'd been fiddling with his keys, looped around his fingers, but looked up. 'One day at a time, eh?'

'One day at a time.'

Eddie stepped outside as the snow began to fall harder, making the likelihood of snow angels even stronger. 'I've got a sister to go and find,' he called back brightly. 'I'll see what I can tease her about. What are her weaknesses?'

'You're getting no hints from me.' Veronica smiled. And when he went off down the path, laughing and with a spring in his step, she watched him until he was out of sight.

And if they hadn't finished all the booze on New Year's Eve, right now she'd be pouring a big glass of fizz, toasting the magic of Christmas wishes that had come true and brought her the best gift of all.

She still wasn't sure whether she deserved it, but she was learning, slowly, to give herself a chance to be happy.

The snow fell every day from New Year until the tenth of January, when Veronica finally had a chance to sneak a look at the kindness calendar for the month. There were some interesting items on there and she was glad to see the pursuit of another teddy bear drive. She loved knitting those things, she could easily do one a week, and she made good use of any offcuts too.

Audrey passed down the hallway and spotted Veronica with the calendar. 'We've all been far too busy, Gran, but today's the day.'

'Today's the day for what?'

'Check out the tenth.'

She must've skimmed over it as she tried to take in all the information at once. Layla hadn't dropped the calendar in until today, but there in the tenth square was, 'Make an angel'. Veronica assumed it was to be a decoration for next year's tree.

Audrey thrust her coat at her. 'Why do I need this?' Making angels was an indoor activity, surely.

'We're going out to the garden.' She rolled her eyes heavenwards. 'We're making snow angels.'

Since her visit from Eddie, Veronica's life had felt a bit like a life raft sent out to a stormy sea, rocking and unsure of itself. But she'd talked at length with Sam, who seemed to be on the phone to her brother every day, Morris had comforted her when she cried over all the missed time with her only son, and her friends had been there when she got the call from Eddie to say he was bringing Rosa and the kids to meet her in a couple of weeks' time. Veronica had spoken to him on the phone several times since; she'd even had a meeting with him on Zoom, with Audrey in the background waiting impatiently to show her cousins the set of make-up her friend Sid sent her for Christmas. Veronica had a feeling there'd be plenty of makeovers going on when these girls met, and Audrey was already telling Ariana and Lottie about Layla, as though she were another member of the family.

'We'll all catch a cold rolling on the ground,' Veronica insisted, but already Sam and Charlie were knocking on the window, beckoning them outside. Charlie dumped a snowball into Sam's hair and her retaliation was one right in his face, smearing it in for good measure.

'Gran.' Audrey handed over her coat.

'Oh, very well.' She'd been too busy watching how happy Sam was. The guilt must have eased since meeting up with Eddie, and she hoped the pair would have a good relationship from now on, whether it involved her or not.

Bundled up and shutting the front door behind her, Veronica watched as they all lay on their backs. Her square patch of lawn out front was just about the right size for all five of them to fit in together. Veronica wasn't sure she'd be able to get up again, but she got down on the ground to join them anyway.

Looking up at the sky, black except for a few stars winking back at them, the cold on Veronica's face had her smiling. She swished her legs back and forth in the way the girls had told her, she moved her arms at the same time, and when she heard a passerby laugh, she couldn't care less. This was her, this was her life, and nobody could take it away from her.

The Kindness Club had brought her new friends, given her her life back, brought her granddaughter and daughter back into her life. Somehow, by trying to make other people happy, they'd allowed themselves to find happiness. The Kindness Club had lifted a layer away and enabled them to start unravelling what had gone wrong over the years. And Audrey's kind heart, as well as some meddling from locals, had given Veronica the best Christmas gift ever, fulfilling the winter wish she'd made.

'So, Gran, any New Year's resolutions?' Audrey asked when she helped Veronica to her feet.

'Yes, never to roll in the snow again.'

'Oh, come on, Mum, you had fun, I can see it on your face,' Sam teased, before Charlie grabbed her from behind and swung her around to kiss him.

And when Veronica saw Morris at the gate, she wondered whether their date tonight – a walk over to the Mapleberry Mug for a late-night hot chocolate – would finish with a kiss just like that.

He looked her way with a glance that suggested she may well be right.

Veronica might be seventy-one, but happy ever afters could happen at any age, she thought. And she was well on her way to hers.

Acknowledgements

The year 2020 has been unlike any other I've known and something good to come from these challenging times has been seeing the little acts of kindness we can all do, whether it's helping out a neighbour living on their own by doing their shopping, supporting local charities or simply doing the right thing by staying home and abiding by all the rules we've all had to face. This seemed such a fitting book to write under the circumstances and I absolutely loved introducing a kindness calendar as part of my story.

Intergenerational friendships and family relationships are among the topics I love to explore when I write a new book and I adored writing Veronica's character, especially when she started to make her own friendships with the group she met online. I hope that readers resonate with her and understand that with kindness and friendship we might just find away through any hardships we face.

A big thanks always goes to my family for giving me the time to write, the encouragement and letting me vent or bounce ideas around when I need to.

An enormous thank you to everyone on the Orion Publishing team too, in particular Olivia Barber, whose support and encouragement from the ideas stage right through to the final book that ends up in the hands of my readers, is something I'm very grateful to have.

Thank you to every single reader who has taken a chance on my books, I hope you enjoyed your visit to Mapleberry. And I'd love to hear from you if you have a kindness calendar in your area!

Credits

Helen Rolfe and Orion Fiction would like to thank everyone at Orion who worked on the publication of *The Kindness Club on Mapleberry Lane* in the UK.

Editorial
Olivia Barber

Copy editor
Clare Wallis

Proof reader
Natalie Braine

Contracts
Anne Goddard
Paul Bulos
Jake Alderson

Design
Rabab Adams
Tomas Almeida
Joanna Ridley

Audio
Paul Stark
Amber Bates

Editorial Management
Charlie Panayiotou
Jane Hughes
Alice Davis

Rights
Susan Howe
Krystyna Kujawinska
Jessica Purdue
Richard King
Louise Henderson

Production
Ruth Sharvell

Marketing
Tanjiah Islam

Finance
Jasdip Nandra
Afeera Ahmed
Elizabeth Beaumont
Sue Baker

Operations
Jo Jacobs
Sharon Willis
Lisa Pryde
Lucy Brem

Sales
Jen Wilson
Esther Waters
Victoria Laws
Rachael Hum
Ellie Kyrke-Smith
Frances Doyle
Georgina Cutler

Publicity
Patricia Deveer

If you enjoyed *The Kindness Club on Mapleberry Lane*, you'll love Helen Rolfe's heartwarming story of romance and second chances.

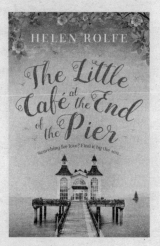

Searching for love? You'll find it at the little café at the end of the pier . . .

When Jo's beloved grandparents ask for her help in running their little café at the end of the pier in Salthaven-on-Sea, she jumps at the chance.

The café is a hub for many people: the single dad who brings his little boy in on a Saturday morning; the lady who sits alone and stares out to sea; the woman who pops in after her morning run.

Jo soon realises that each of her customers is looking for love – and she knows just the way to find it for them. She goes about setting each of them up on blind dates – each date is held in the café, with a special menu she has designed for the occasion.

But Jo has never found love herself. She always held her grandparents' marriage up as her ideal and she hasn't found anything close to that. But could it be that love is right under her nose . . . ?

Welcome to Cloverdale, the home of kindness and new beginnings . . .

Sometimes it takes a village to mend a broken heart . . .

Cloverdale is known for its winding roads, undulating hills and colourful cottages, and now for its Library of Shared Things: a place where locals can borrow anything they might need, from badminton sets to waffle makers. A place where the community can come together.

Jennifer has devoted all her energy into launching the Library. When her sister Isla moves home, and single dad Adam agrees to run a mending workshop at the Library, new friendships start to blossom. But what is Isla hiding, and can Adam ever mind his broken past?

Then Adam's daughter makes a startling discovery, and the people at the Library of Shared Things must pull together to help one family overcome its biggest challenge of all . . .

Step into the enchanting world of Lantern Square . . .

Looking for a fresh start? Welcome to Butterbury . . .

Hannah went from high-flyer in the city to small business owner and has never looked back. She's found a fresh start in the cosy Cotswold village of Butterbury, where she runs her care package company, Tied Up with String.

Her hand-picked gifts are the perfect way to show someone you care, and while her brown paper packages bring a smile to customers across the miles, Hannah also makes sure to deliver a special something to the people closer to home.

But when her ex-best friend Georgia arrives back in her life, can Hannah forgive and forget? With her new business in jeopardy, Hannah needs to let the community she cares for give a little help back . . .

Meanwhile, mystery acts of kindness keep springing up around Butterbury, including a care package on Hannah's own doorstep. Who is trying to win her heart – and will she ever give it away?